"Just the right dose of delicious steam. Amy Lea has crafted an ode to all of us who struggle with self-acceptance while remaining determined to love ourselves."

—Ali Hazelwood, *New York Times* bestselling author of
The Love Hypothesis

"F̶ h, fun, and extremely sexy. *Set on You* is a romance of unex-pe̶ d depth."

—Helen Hoang, *New York Times* bestselling author of
The Heart Principle

"S̶ *on You* is energetic, steamy, bubbly, and so, so fun. But more th̶ 1 that, it's also a hugely important book that celebrates body p̶ itivity in the most joyous way possible."

—Jesse Q. Sutanto, author of *Dial A for Aunties*

" ̶ *on You* is an incredibly fun and sexy slow-burn, enemies-to-̶rs rom-com that had me invested from the first page. And in b̶ ween all the steamy and swoony scenes, there's also a thoughtful e̶ loration of body positivity and the true meaning of loving your-se̶ "

—Kerry Winfrey, author of *Very Sincerely Yours*

"S̶ *on You* is the best kind of workout: one that ups your heart rate wi̶ its swoony hero, makes you sweat with its slow-burn tension, and̶ eaves you satisfied with its themes of empowerment and self-acc̶ptance. With a fresh, hilarious voice and a deeply relatable pro-tagonist, this romantic comedy is enemies-to-lovers gold."

—Rachel Lynn Solomon, national bestselling author of *The Ex Talk*

TITLES BY AMY LEA

Exes and O's

AMY LEA

PENGUIN BOOKS

PENGUIN BOOKS

UK | USA | Canada | Ireland | Australia
India | New Zealand | South Africa

Penguin Books is part of the Penguin Random House group of companies
whose addresses can be found at global.penguinrandomhouse.com.

First published in the United States of America by Berkley,
an imprint of Penguin Random House LLC 2023
First published in Great Britain by Penguin Books 2023
001

Printed and bound in Great Britain by Clays Ltd, Elcograf S.p.A.

The authorized representative in the EEA is Penguin Random House Ireland,
Morrison Chambers, 32 Nassau Street, Dublin D02 YH68

A CIP catalogue record for this book is available from the British Library

ISBN: 978–0–241–99754–3

www.greenpenguin.co.uk

MIX
Paper from
responsible sources
FSC
www.fsc.org   FSC® C018179

Penguin Random House is committed to a
sustainable future for our business, our readers
and our planet. This book is made from Forest
Stewardship Council® certified paper.

To all the "crazy" ex-girlfriends

author's note

Dear Reader,

Thank you so much for choosing my romantic comedy *Exes and O's* as your next read. While this story is generally light and humorous, I would be remiss if I did not include the following content warnings: emotionally abusive ex, on-page gaslighting, portrayal of child with illness, mentions of deaths of loved ones, and deliberate use of the word *crazy* throughout.

Note: this last one is vehemently condemned by me and the main characters. Please take care while reading.

With love,
Amy Lea

Exes
and O's

❤ chapter one

YOU KNOW YOUR day is going swimmingly when you've been projectile vomited on and someone stole your Greek yogurt from the staff room refrigerator. And it's only seven in the morning.

Eager to leave the memory of my hellish night shift behind, I'm in formation at the edge of the platform, stance wide, pointy elbows out, among hundreds of tired morning commuters primed to battle for a rare open seat on the subway.

I've learned a thing or two about navigating a crowd from witnessing five-foot-tall Grandma Flo barrel her way through the grocery store, whacking innocents with her faux-crocodile purse with no apologies.

Boston subway commuters may not be as ferocious as grocery store grannies, but they'll trample you for an open seat all the same. I have a grotesque scar on my left shin to prove it.

Thankfully, no blood is drawn in today's war. In a rare turn of events, I have my choice of three seats: one beside a man three-too-many edibles deep, passionately air drumming; another next to a woman with bubble-gum-pink hair open-mouth smiling; and one across from an adorable elderly couple bundled in matching red parkas thick enough for a perilous Arctic expedition.

I nab the seat across from the elderly couple and set my purse at my feet, eager to avoid all reality with my trusty worn paperback. This book has all my vices: a ball-busting heroine with a sharp tongue and a kind-eyed yet emotionally constipated ex-boyfriend.

A few paragraphs into a juicy yacht scene, my phone dings with a text. It's from my sister.

CRYSTAL: Hope you had a good shift. We'll meet you at the apartment soon. Just loaded all your boxes in the car! Cheers to new beginnings. 🎉

Crystal is two years younger than me, though everyone assumes she's the older one because I've been overstaying my welcome in her one-bedroom condo for the past eight months.

"New beginnings," I mutter to no one in particular, trying to psych myself up for a morning of manual labor.

I've only recently peeled myself from rock bottom after my happily ever after plot twisted into a Nicholas Sparks tragedy. Truthfully, the prospect of more change triggers my gag reflex, but I'm trying to stay optimistic. Moving out means I'll be free to read on the couch for six straight hours without anyone throwing shade, and Crystal gets privacy with her new fiancé, Scott—who I'm swapping apartments with.

The subway veers around a sharp curve with an earsplitting squeal, causing the entire length of my thigh to press against a complete stranger's. The luxury of public transit. When I brave a glance at my cozy neighbor, a pair of hooded, azure eyes ensnares mine from behind tortoiseshell-framed glasses. The striking sky-blue shade of his eyes offsets a full head of lusciously thick ginger hair.

As a lifelong connoisseur of romance novels, I'm keenly aware that eye contact lasting longer than three seconds is ripe with romantic potential.

"Good book?" His voice is thick, almost sleepy.

Stunned, I scrutinize his face for any sign of sarcasm. That's the thing about reading romance. Book covers depicting unfairly attractive, half-nude models embracing in a passionate lip-lock are perennial targets of mocking and snobbery. Welcome to the patriarchy.

Sweat pools into the underwire of my bra when he smiles, revealing teeth so white, they appear artificial under seizure-inducing subway lighting. His question takes me off guard, and he can tell, because he bashfully follows it up with, "I read a little romantic suspense, if you're wondering."

My toes curl inside my nursing shoes. Has fate gifted me an emotionally adept, romance-reading Prince Harry look-alike? Because I'm eternally void of all chill, I spew questions at rapid-fire speed. "You read romance? Who have you read? Which titles?"

I refrain from sudden movements as he tilts his head, dithering. "Okay, you got me. I lied. I just wanted an excuse to talk to you. I do read, though," he adds, his gaze falling to my purse at my feet.

"What's your genre of choice? And please don't say poetry," I beg. For the record, I hold no ill will toward poetry, but I was ghosted in college by a dude who did slam poetry and the wound still cuts deep.

"Horror. I have a sick addiction to it, actually," he admits, pushing his glasses up the bridge of his nose.

The seams of my proverbial corset threaten to burst with suppressed delight. I'm not a horror reader, but men south of sixty who regularly read fiction are an endangered species that must be protected at all costs.

"Malevolent spirits or blood and guts?"

He grimaces, struggling under the weight of his choices. "Can I say both? Is that creepy?"

"It is borderline morbid. But I'm okay with it." *More than okay with it.*

"I'm Nate." His introduction is followed by an enchanting Disney prince–like smile.

"I'm Tara." Our gazes lock again, kicking my heart into overdrive. It's hammering fast and furious. Either I'm going into cardiac arrest, or I'm having a meet-cute with the blueprint of square-jawed perfection. It's hard to say.

If I weren't wearing my most unflattering, shapeless nursing scrubs, I'd probably twirl around the subway aisle, arms outstretched, like a blissful middle-aged person in an allergy medication commercial who's finally experiencing life's joy without watery eyes and nasal congestion.

In the span of ten minutes, I've learned all there is to know about Nate. He's twenty-five (five years my junior, but I'm willing to embrace the Cougar Life), works at an investment firm, owns his very own condo, would choose mustard over ketchup if stranded on a remote island, and is secure enough in his manhood to admit his fondness for Taylor Swift's latest album. Creatures like him are a romance reader's wet dream. The man just oozes soul mate potential, and I'm eagerly absorbing it like a ShamWow.

In fact, peak soul mate status is reached when he waves enthusiastically at a cherub-faced toddler waddling up and down the aisle. Hello, dad material.

Cue the violins. I've just fallen in insta-love.

If this were a romance book, the clouds would part as we exit the subway at any given stop, lockstep, hand in hand. We'd spend the cool October day doing the usual things soul mates do: ignoring all responsibilities, discovering random dives around the city, drinking liquor wrapped in a brown paper bag, and revealing all our emotional baggage as the sun sets. At the end of the night, he'd fold me into a passionate embrace under the starry sky and bless me with a foot-popping kiss, preferably with a little tongue.

Turns out, this is no romance book. I don't even have the chance to name our golden retriever and four unborn children. In the nonfiction life of Tara Li Chen, the following events unfold in chronological order:

1) The subway comes to an abrupt halt. Hordes of people funnel to the exit.

2) A new group of commuters push and shove their way in. A lanky dude wearing a *May the Gains Be with You* T-shirt over a full Lycra getup beelines it for the only remaining seat, to the quiet dismay of a very pregnant woman.

3) By the time the crowd settles, Soulmate Nate is no longer next to me. In fact, he's vanished entirely.

4) And so has my purse.

LIVE WITH TARAROMANCEQUEEN—THE DEATH OF THE MEET-CUTE

EXCERPT FROM TRANSCRIPT

[Tara appears on-screen at an upward chin angle, seemingly out of breath, hair slicked back in an unflattering founding fathers' ponytail. She power walks down a bustling city sidewalk in a seedy neighborhood.]

TARA: *Hello, romance book lovers, welcome back to my channel, where I talk all things romance. First, I'd like to apologize for my hiatus the past few days. I've been super busy with work and packing for my move, which happens to be today. Yay!*

Since I'll be spending the better part of my day schlepping boxes, this episode is going to be super brief. I want to talk about meet-cutes.

You all know I'm a sucker for a good meet-cute. I mean, they're a beloved staple in romance. The best ones involve the spilling of a scalding-hot beverage, or a near-death experience. Sometimes it even verges into meet-ugly territory, where they dawdle in mutual loathing and delightfully petty prejudice for half the book. That is . . . until they discover each other's emotional sides and fall head over heels in love.

[Tara waits impatiently at an intersection and stares into the camera of her brand-new phone, brow cocked.]

Thanks to the internet—don't even get me started on online dating— real-life meet-cutes are DEAD and I'm in mourning. In today's harsh world, any stranger, no matter how beautiful, who makes eye contact for longer than a few consecutive seconds most definitely has nefarious intentions and will mug you in broad daylight. I speak from experience.

Is all hope lost once you hit thirty? I'm beginning to think so. If anyone would like to prove me wrong with some adorable, real-life meet-cute stories, I'm all ears.

COMMENTS:

I met my husband online. We've been happily married for ten ♡
years. Meet-cutes are overrated.

Tara, I completely agree with you. I'm waiting for my in- ♡
person meet-cute too. Preferably in between rows of dusty
mahogany shelves in a public library. 😍

• • •

EVERYTHING IS FINE. EVERYTHING IS FINE.

I mentally repeat that phrase as I haul myself up the stairwell to my new apartment. To my new life.

It's fine that I got mugged. It's fine that I'll need to cancel all my credit cards. It's fine that I had to buy a new phone. It's fine that I'm moving into a new apartment, sight unseen. It's fine that it boasts a chronically broken elevator, even though I'm a staunch proponent of a sedentary lifestyle. IT'S ALL FINE.

When I reach the third flight, I take a momentary lean against the wobbly handrail, balancing my heart-shaped throw pillows. In between wheezes, I force my mouth into a smile, a trick I use to reset when I'm spiraling into a negativity vortex.

There's no reason to hate on my brand-new digs. It may not be the Ritz, but from what I've seen of the run-down, orange-tiled entryway and probably haunted concrete stairwell, it's the nicest place I can afford on the direct subway line to the hospital that isn't a roach-infested basement apartment. And Scott was charitable enough to leave me his gently used bedroom furniture, free of charge.

As I press on and upward, I remind myself change is good. This move is more than just the apartment. It's a new chapter of my life. A chance to start anew, after eight months of wallowing, mourning the life I was supposed to have with my ex-fiancé, Seth.

This time last year, I was blissfully engaged, planning an elaborate Cinderella-inspired dream wedding from the comfort of our Beacon Hill condo. Then, six months before the wedding, Seth decided the season finale of *Survivor* was as good a time as any to pick a dramatic fight, concluding he "couldn't tolerate me anymore."

The tribe had spoken.

Seth Reinhart would be the tenth man to break my heart.

Starting my life over was a trip, to say the least. But after months of therapy and star-fishing on Crystal's floor, I've finally come into my own.

I've embraced a morsel of change, starting with a bold haircut (a long blunt bob). My bookstagram and BookTok accounts—niche corners of the internet where literature-obsessed folks bond over books—are thriving. I've secured my trusted inner social circle of exactly two—my sister and Mel—the respective Carrie and Samantha to my Charlotte (even though we're all probably Miranda).

Maybe this year I'll surprise everyone and take up a new hobby, like looming, archery, or mountain biking. Seth always resented my lack of hobbies, aside from reading. Maybe I'll purchase a succulent, or seven, and name them after the von Trapp children from *The Sound of Music*.

I'm reinvigorated with endless possibilities by the time I reach unit 404. So much so, I open the unlocked apartment door with triple the force necessary, like a pro dancer taking center stage, making an impassioned entrance into my shiny new life.

The moment I enter, it's clear that this new chapter is no improvement from the last. In fact, it's worse.

Before me is a magnificently muscled, entirely naked, tattooed man bending an auburn-haired woman over the kitchen island.

Welcome home, Tara.

♥ chapter two

THINGS GO TITS up from there. Literally.

I let out a bloodcurdling screech from the depths of my gut, tossing my throw pillows in the air. The auburn-haired woman yelps, endeavoring to cover at least half her enviably ample bosom. The tattooed man curses and dives for cover behind the butcher block island, like a World War I soldier under siege in the muddy trenches.

But it's too late for me. I saw *it*.

The penis belonging to my new roommate, Trevor Metcalfe.

It's not like I expected to cross the threshold into a *Sex and the City*–worthy life of fabulous riches, cosmos, whirlwind romance, and girlfriends who are readily available to drop their lives at a moment's notice whenever disaster strikes. But I was not expecting *this*.

Normally, I wouldn't entertain the prospect of moving in with a stranger. But the rent was cheap, I have student debt, and any-where was preferable to my parents' place, where I'd be forced to compete for attention with Hillary, Mom's ankle-biting, narcissis-tic Chihuahua. Besides, Trevor is Scott's best friend and coworker at the firehouse. I figured it was safe to trust my soon-to-be brother-in-law, but apparently you can't trust family.

You'll never see each other with your shift work. It'll be the same as living alone, Scott had assured me.

The illusion of living alone seemed plausible, given that my and Trevor's conflicting shift schedules prevented us from meeting prior to today. I rotate between day and night shift every two weeks, and apparently, so does he. So far, we've only exchanged a couple of texts, which consist of my request for the dimensions of my new room for my bookshelf. No small talk.

The topless woman gapes at me, justifiably peeved I interrupted her Big O. Aside from disappearing into the void, I do the next best, highly logical thing: mumble a vague yet sincere apology, cover my eyes, and sprint away in the only direction possible—down a short hallway.

"This is fine. It's all fine," I mutter, taking refuge through the first door on the right. I slam it shut, savoring the relative coolness of the door against my searing skin.

As a nurse, I see genitals aplenty, particularly during my stint in the ER before I transferred to the neonatal ward. But making eye contact with a live human (a mega-ripped human, to be pre-cise) in the throes of passion a mere ten feet away is a first.

When slowing my breath becomes a herculean task, I try a technique my therapist taught me. *Take in your surroundings. Note everything logically, with no judgment.*

I'm in a tiny, outdated bathroom. It's white from floor to ceiling, save for a plush navy-blue towel hanging behind the door and the matching hand towel next to the sink, both probably belonging to a man with a nice, sizable— Nope. We're not going there. Focus, Tara.

Cracked yet clean ceramic subway tiles adorn the wall in the gleaming glass shower. For a bathroom formerly shared by Scott and Trevor, two thirtysomething men, it's impossibly clean. I run my index finger along the rim of the smooth porcelain sink. It's spotless. Not a stray man hair or glob of dried toothpaste to be found.

Weak and weary, I park myself on the porcelain throne. I should probably commence a new search for another place to live, but the very prospect of probing the bowels of Craigslist prompts a heaving gag. Instead, I self–eye bleach to videos of baby farm animals until my feet lose all circulation.

I know I have to go out and face the music at some point. But like a coward, I delay the inevitable by FaceTiming Mel.

She answers immediately, preening her ultra-lush lash extensions. She's a curvy influencer, like Crystal, except instead of fitness, Mel's specialty is fashion and beauty and all things aesthetically pleasing. Today, a shimmery purple shadow sweeps across her eyelids, accentuating her dark eyes. Her contour is also on point, showcasing her bone structure. She's so stunning, it's frankly offensive.

Based on the floor-to-ceiling window behind her, she's at home in her bougie apartment in the theater district. "Where the hell are you?" she asks.

"I'm hiding in my new bathroom," I whisper.

"Why are we whispering?" She lowers her voice conspiratorially.

"Because. I just walked in on my new roommate. Naked."

She lets out a strangled gasp and slaps a hand over her violet-painted lips. "Naked? As in, ass out?"

"Penis out," I correct. "Actually, he was more than naked. He was boning a girl in the kitchen," I explain, taking it upon myself to snoop in the shower.

The moment I open the hefty glass door, I'm hit with a zesty, far-too-sexy spiciness that's surely a biohazard. I sniff the body wash to confirm the origins of the scent, and it immediately clears my airways. *Cinnamon and cedarwood*, according to the bottle. Next to the body wash is a basic two-in-one shampoo-and-conditioner combo.

Poking around a virtual stranger's shower feels illicit, but technically this is *my* shower now. I've already seen this man's nether regions, so does it really matter if I know his preferred brand of toothpaste (Colgate—Max White Expert Complete)?

"Jesus, take me." Mel clasps a hand over her chest and pretends to faint on her chaise. She quickly rights herself, fully alert and ready to sip the proverbial tea, which she likes piping hot. "Okay, tell me everything. On a scale of Danny DeVito to Henry Cavill, how attractive is he? Spare no detail."

"I wasn't looking at his face." His face was but a blur on account of his naked body, which definitely leans in favor of the Cavill side of Mel's scale. The memory will live on forever, seared onto my retinas.

"I take it you're gonna hide in there until the end of time?"

"Yes. I think I'll just rot in here." I examine the glittery soap dispenser next to the sink, which doesn't belong among the rest of the practical, low-maintenance products. It's labeled *Toasted Vanilla Chai*. This is a woman's touch if I ever saw one. Maybe it belongs to the big-breasted, auburn-haired woman.

As Mel tells me about a time she accidently walked in on her brother doing the dirty, I swiftly move on to the medicine cabinet. Before opening it, I catch my hopeful reflection in the mirror and cringe. What was previously a perky ponytail this morning has sagged. I try tightening it to add volume, inadvertently making it worse. There's zero volume to be had here. Each strand is dead slick to my scalp and severely pulled back, accentuating my shiny forehead. I really need to blot.

Giving up on myself entirely, I explore the cabinet. Inside is an opened packet of assorted color toothbrushes, a shaving set, a single razor, a bottle of shaving cream, Listerine mouthwash (Cool Mint) and a jumbo bottle of Tylenol.

As I pluck the bottle from the shelf to examine the expiration date (expired in July 2021), a floorboard creaks in the hallway, right outside the door. Panicked, I fling the Tylenol back where I found it and side-shuffle away from the sink. A few beats of silence tick by before there's a knock.

"Tara?" Trevor's voice is gravelly and baritone. Very audiobook worthy.

"Mel, I gotta go," I whisper, frantically ending the call before she can respond.

"You okay in there?" he asks.

"Totally fine. More than fine. Why wouldn't I be?" Yikes. I sound like Minnie Mouse on uppers. I make a point to lower my voice. "Was she your girlfriend?"

There's a beat of silence. "No. She's not my girlfriend. She just left, by the way."

"Oh," I say, mildly disappointed. It would have been nice to have another woman around, like an unofficial roommate of sorts, especially since the majority of Crystal's and Mel's time is devoted to their respective long-term, committed relationships and full-time thriving social media careers—both of which I lack. While I love being a book influencer on Instagram and TikTok, it's a hobby, not a career.

There's another extended silence before Trevor says, "Listen, I'm sorry we had to meet like that. I didn't think you were moving in until later today. I feel like an asshole."

I sink to the floor behind the door, noodle legs pulled to my chest. "It's fine. I mean, it's your apartment, technically."

"It's half yours now."

"Do you regularly have sex in communal living areas?"

"Well, not anymore." Based on his half chuckle, I picture a charming, tilted grin that could melt the panties off any given straight woman. "I swear I'll disinfect the whole kitchen. Thoroughly."

"Much appreciated," I say genuinely. It's nice knowing the surface I eat my Pop-Tarts over will be void of bodily fluids.

A few beats go by. "So, uh, are you ever gonna come out of the bathroom?"

"That depends. Are you still naked?"

"I'm fully decent, I swear."

I press my cheek closer to the door, craving the vibrations of his voice. "I might stay in here a little longer. It's comfortable." This tiny space is actually kind of soothing, reminiscent of a Scandinavian spa.

His footsteps disappear down the hall, only to return a few seconds later. "I have Cheetos. And don't worry, I washed my hands."

My mouth waters instantly at the tried-and-true sound of a crunching bag. Be still my heart. I reach to turn the knob, opening the door wide enough to make a grabby-hands motion through the crack. He's still not visible, with the exception of his hand as he passes the bag like a dicey drug deal. There's a light dusting of ashy-brown hair on his wrist and knuckles. His palm is massive, almost twice the size of mine. I catch the tail end of a detailed, dark-gray tattoo in the area below his thumb, but before I can make out the design, his hand disappears behind the door.

Starved, I descend on the bag, ripping it open like an ape. In the span of under three minutes, I've demolished at least a quarter. Ashamed of my blatant gluttony, I slide it back through the crack. "Sorry, I've had a traumatic day."

The bag crunches. "Shit. Because of me?"

"No. My day was already a wash before you."

"Why?" he asks, passing the bag back.

"Today was supposed to mark a brand-new start. A turning point in my life. But I got mugged on the subway," I admit through a crunch, "by a guy with some serious soul mate potential. The meet-cute was going so well until he stole my purse."

"Wait, you got mugged? And what's a meet-cute?" He repeats *meet-cute* slowly, like it's a foreign concept. I watch his large hand reach through the crack for the Cheetos. There's a Roman numeral tattoo on his wrist, partially obscured by his sleeve. I take a mental photo so I can decipher it later.

"A meet-cute is when two love interests meet for the first time,"

I rattle off impatiently. "But yes. I got mugged. I was reading on the subway when this guy next to me started chatting me up. You should have seen this guy, Metcalfe. He was a snack. Definitely didn't look like a mugger. Not that muggers have a particular look, but you know what I mean . . ."

We pass the bag back and forth as I rehash the story of Nate, from that initial moment of eye contact to when he jacked my purse (and all my hopes and dreams).

"Well, that's shit luck either way," he says, sympathetic to my plight.

"Right? I'm starting to lose hope. Every time I meet a potential man, something goes horribly wrong. The last guy I met through a friend seemed normal, until he requested photos of my feet."

"Foot fetish?"

"Apparently. I don't want to fetish-shame, but I think I'm cursed. Today it's a mugging. Tomorrow, probably a kidnapping. Some guy will lure me to his car with candy. I'll go because I like free food. And he'll toss me in the trunk and set my body on fire." I grimace at the missed opportunity of flaunting my latest favorite number, a high-neck pink dress, in an open-casket funeral. I've already advised Crystal of my wish to be buried in it, and she's assured me she'll make it happen.

"Okay, that got dark real fast. This is why you should never trust strangers with candy," Trevor warns.

"Technically you're a stranger, with Cheetos," I remind him, fishing a rogue Cheeto from the floor. I toss it in the trash can next to the sink.

"You're a stranger too. In my bathroom. Who knows what you've done to my toothbrush."

I have the sudden urge to change our stranger status. The hinges squeak as I pull the door open, poking my head out like a meerkat emerging from the protection of its sandy burrow.

Trevor is, indeed, fully clothed, back resting against the wall, long legs extended in front of him.

The top of his effortlessly tousled mop of dark hair juxtaposes with the short, neatly trimmed sides. Even through his Boston Fire Department hoodie, his biceps are mature, unyielding tree trunks. In comparison, mine are flimsier than a rice noodle.

His Adam's apple bobs as he takes in my disheveled ponytail riddled with dry shampoo, scanning downward over my oversize maroon sweatshirt, which reads *Nonfictional feelings for fictional men* in Times New Roman font.

Now that he isn't nude and his tattoos are adequately covered, I'm able to assess his eyes. They're the color of honey, like an inferno of crackling firewood resisting merciless golden flames. They probably take on a mossy hue when the light hits them just right. Under the protective swoop of dense lashes, they're foreboding, guarded. And when his gaze meets mine, my stomach betrays me with an uncalled-for barrel roll.

In an effort to maintain an iota of normalcy, I squint to blur his face out of focus, distracting myself with a humungous Cheeto. "Should I trust you, deliriously handsome stranger?"

His mouth shapes into a crooked smile as he stands, towering over me on the bathroom floor. "Nah. Probably not."

❤ chapter three

One month later

ACCORDING TO GRANDMA Flo, the first moment you open your eyes sets the tone for the rest of the day. I liken it to an ill-advised opening scene of a novel, or a rom-com where the main character wakes up in full makeup; unstained, crisp pajamas; and perfectly intact barrel locks.

Though in reality, I routinely wake up looking like a cadaver from a grisly crime scene. Sickly, pale, and disheveled.

A blue, pre-sunrise glow peeks through the blinds, which tells me it's one hour too early for consciousness and definitely far too late for the rhythmic squeak of the mattress and the steady drum of the headboard slamming against the wall across the hall.

It's been one month since I moved in, and this is the third woman Trevor has brought home (not including the redhead from move-in day). One look at Trevor and it's easy to understand his success with the ladies. Not only is he a heroic firefighter, but I've deduced he resembles a mildly less tortured, darker-haired version of the lead *Sons of Anarchy* outlaw biker, ready to whisk you away for a life of crime on his Harley-Davidson. In reality, Trevor doesn't actually own a motorcycle. He owns a plum-colored used Toyota Corolla with like-new, spotless interior. But he does have the foreboding, tattooed-badass look going for him.

I certainly don't resent Trevor for having a healthy sex life. In fact, after over a year of celibacy, I'm seething with jealousy. But cobwebs on my downstairs aside, sleep is a precious commodity as a shift worker. After back-to-back night shifts, I was looking forward to sleeping in today before transitioning to day shifts.

I fold my pillow over my head in a sad attempt to muffle the cries of pleasure. But somehow, they just grow louder. There's only so much *Yes, Oh God,* and *Fuck* I can withstand before morbid curiosity sets in.

Is Trevor Metcalfe really that good in bed? Or is this woman faking it for the sake of his fragile male ego?

Must be faking it, I decide.

Without notice, my traitorous imagination gifts me a visual to accompany the audio. Trevor's tattooed, sinewy forearms cage me in as his lustful gaze sweeps over the contours of my body. His thumb makes languished strokes on the underside of my wrist as he pins my hands above my head. The weight of his solid, muscled body puts pressure exactly where I want it. He presses the softest bite into my neck, sending a trill of electricity to the forgotten corners of my body before he—

I snap my eyes open, loosening my death grip around my blanket I didn't know I was clutching. Where the hell did that come from? Am I that hard done by?

I refuse to be remotely turned on by the sounds of my room-mate and a random woman going at it. Not today, Satan.

Despite being objectively hot, tattooed bad boys like Trevor are not normally my type. It's the white-collar sort with front-pleated chinos, cross-country runner bods, and boy-next-door-turned-respectable-plant-daddy energy that usually make me feel some type of way. And while Trevor is an exception to this, I have no intention of crossing that line with him. After the year I've had, platonic, drama-free cohabitation is just what I need. Besides, given the gorgeous women he brings home, he's certainly categorized me as nothing more than an obnoxious, sexless human.

Bleary-eyed and frustrated with the uninvited tension between my thighs, I throw on my favorite cable-knit sweaterdress from the floor and snap a cute bow over yesterday's French braid. I even apply an extra layer of mascara, full foundation, and bronzer in prepar-ation for my Live video session this morning with Grandma Flo.

By the time I drift into the kitchen for my morning Pop-Tart, the screaming coming from Trevor's bedroom has thankfully dis-sipated, replaced by a relative calm. As I toss the singed pastry onto my plate, I catch Trevor's hookup tiptoeing toward the front door. Aside from the wildly matted hair and general fatigue from physi-cal exertion, her professional-grade winged eyeliner is smudge-free. The beam of light from the tiny kitchen window above the sink gives her tanned skin a luminous, postorgasmic glow.

When our eyes meet, she stops in her tracks. "Morning," she whispers, promptly averting her gaze to her bare feet, as if bracing for judgment.

Because I'm an emotional beacon with far too many feelings, I won't touch a man's penis if I don't know his middle name. But I don't judge others for partaking in casual sex. In fact, I envy their ability to take what they need while avoiding emotional damage.

"Hi. I'm Trevor's roommate." I'm about to wish her well and continue on about my day, but for reasons beyond me, I thrust my plate in her direction. "Want a Pop-Tart? It's raspberry."

She eyes it like it's a rare delicacy. "You are doing the lord's work. I'm starving." She plucks the Pop-Tart from the plate, basking in the underrated glory of that first sugary bite.

The familiar creak of the pipes and sputtering water down the hall tells me Trevor's taking a shower, so I don't bother using a hushed voice. "Not surprised, from what I heard. You need to replenish your calories."

She half chokes on her bite. "Sorry." She pauses. "I'm Gabby, by the way."

I don't bother to hide my eager smile. "Tara."

Two Pop-Tarts later, Gabby and I are besties. Turns out, she's a badass. At the ripe age of twenty-four, she already runs an Etsy business selling handmade jewelry (I've ordered a dainty gold necklace). She's also a member at the same fancy gym as Crystal. And despite my initial protest against physical activity, she's convinced me to join her for an aerial yoga class later this week.

The moment Gabby leaves to catch her Uber, Trevor sneaks down the hallway, freshly showered. His ashy hair is damp, unsure which way it wants to fall. A pair of gray sweatpants hangs low on his hips, and of course he's shirtless.

When he spots me parked on the stool at the island, I zero in on the intricate bird wing sweeping from his robust right shoulder and over part of his sculpted chest. He has a smattering of other tattoos on his arms and back, as well as another set of Roman numerals on his left rib. And while he makes a regular habit of waltzing around shirtless, identifying the particulars of each design is like solving a jigsaw puzzle, slowly but surely, piece by piece.

Today, I follow the sweeping wing leading to the bird's expressive eyes. Even colorless, there's a ferocity that screams to be noticed.

"Is she gone?" he whispers before so much as setting a toe into the open-concept kitchen and living area.

"No. I asked her to be our third roommate." My tone is far too sarcastic for early morning, but I don't know how else to act after hearing *that* (and accidently visualizing it). As he enters the kitchen, my chest erupts in ugly red blotches, heat dotting the crests of my cheeks. I think I need to lie down. "Didn't we talk about nudity in common areas?"

"I'll throw on a shirt if you clean up your books." He waves a vague hand toward the stack of paperbacks in the corner under the living room window. I used them for a book-stack-challenge photo shoot two days ago and have yet to move them back to my room, despite his numerous requests. In the meantime, he's piled them alphabetically.

Trevor has a phobia of clutter, which I'm discreetly desensitizing him to by adding a few personal touches one by one, so as not to spook him. My first add was my heart-shaped throw pillows, then the succulents, and, most recently, an admittedly revolting starry-sky canvas painted by yours truly at a wine-and-paint night. Trevor says it hurts his eyes.

"I told you the other day, I have no more room on my bookshelf. And you should be thanking me for adding character to the place. Your apartment was a cliché barren wasteland of nothingness before I moved in," I rightly point out.

If I had to describe my new apartment in one word, it would be *minimalist*, and even that's being too kind. Before I moved in, every wall and surface was bare, void of any clutter, color, or décor. To be fair, it wasn't always this way. Apparently, Scott took lots of stuff with him when he moved in with Crystal, leaving only a limited amount of basic furniture in the form of exactly one worn leather couch and matching armchair, a flat-screen television, and a small maple dining table tucked in the corner of the equally bland off-white kitchen.

I continue on. "And if you're going to keep having loud sex while I'm across the hall, the least you could do is let me decorate." My expression is pointed. The man disturbed my much-needed tranquility, after all.

He smirks as he opens the fridge. "Hey, I can't control other people's volumes."

"Sounded like Gabby had a good time, at least."

He tosses a ziplock bag of frozen kale on the counter, narrowing a suspicious gaze at the crumb-filled plates on the island. "Did you give her a Pop-Tart?"

I lift a shoulder, watching as he dumps a handful of kale into the blender. "She was hungry, and you didn't feed her."

His eyes bulge, like I've just suggested he take her hand in marriage, which I'm half-tempted to do. "Why would I feed her afterward?"

I make a sour face, pinning my stare at the swirly design on my plate and definitely not the swirly design on his immaculate bod.

"To thank her for the sex? You could have at least walked her out. She's so cool. Did you know she has a scuba diving certification?"

There's a break in the conversation as he blends his smoothie to a puree. "That's not how a one-night stand works."

"Do you mind if I invite her over this weekend? We're best friends now," I gloat, mesmerized as he pours his healthy concoction into a tall glass. "I think you'd like her, if you got to know her. She's wifey material." I give him what I already know is a nauseating wink, mostly to get a reaction out of him.

He maintains his death glare as he tips his head back, guzzling. "I'm not looking for *wifey* material, Chen." He sets the empty glass on the counter and marches down the hall, but not before casting one last glower at the Pop-Tart crumbs on the plates.

I follow him to his room, leaning on the doorframe like a swoony romance hero. A glimpse into Trevor's room is a rare opportunity, given that he usually keeps his door closed. The moment my big toe crosses the threshold, I'm giddy, tempted to snort that spicy signature scent like Leo, *Wolf of Wall Street*—style.

With an effortless tug, he pulls the fitted steel-gray sheet from his mattress, tossing it into the laundry basket nestled in his intensely organized, color-coded closet.

Meanwhile, I've declared a state of emergency in my room. Books are strewn haphazardly on my nightstand and every available surface. At least seven throw pillows have taken up permanent real estate on the floor. Trevor must think I'm a disaster.

I fold my arms over my chest, unable to take him seriously. "Can I ask you a question?"

"No," he grumbles, his eyes fixed on his phone. I catch a brief half smile as he scans a text and quickly fires off a response. I idly wonder if he's texting Gabby, or someone new already.

"Please."

He rolls his eyes. "Fine. But don't ask me if you can ask questions."

"I feel like I have to ask, because you don't seem to like questions."

"Sorry. I'm not a morning person." He definitely is not. Over the past month, I've discovered he's practically mute until midday. If I strike up a conversation before nine in the morning, it usually doesn't go much further than a few garbled mumbles. He gestures toward me, sighing, like he's given up. "What's your question?"

"What's it like to be the *dumper*?" I ask point-blank.

"What's a *dumper*?"

"In every relationship, there's the dumper and the dumpee—the one who gets their heart broken. Take me, for example. I'm always the dumpee. Never the dumper," I explain, omitting the detail that I've had the unfortunate pleasure of being dumped ten separate times, by ten separate men. "But I assume you're most often the *dumper*."

He grunts, fussing over his pillow. "You can only be a dumper if there's a relationship to dump. I don't do relationships."

"Let me guess: you don't believe in happily ever afters because of your mysterious, turbulent past?"

Based on my extensive knowledge of rakes and playboys in romance novels, I'd say it's a fair deduction. Though truthfully, even after rooming together for a month, I don't know much about him, aside from the fact that he's a firefighter, he drinks green smoothies, he has a lot of sex, and he's averse to clutter and mess.

His jaw flexes as he chucks the pillow onto the bed. It lands crooked, and he doesn't even bother to fix it. I've definitely hit a nerve.

I bite my lip, suppressing my morbid curiosity. "Sorry. That was too far. Crystal says I have an annoying tendency to box people into romance tropes and stereotypes."

He sits on the edge of the bed and watches me curiously. "And which romance stereotype are you?"

I stroke my chin, pretending to contemplate, even though I already know the answer. "I'm too broke to be a divorcée starting over with an inherited fixer-upper in the European countryside. I'm probably the clumsy sidekick who cracks blunt jokes at all the wrong times. The disheveled one who provides emotional support to the more desirable and levelheaded heroine." When I say it out loud to Trevor, my life does fit perfectly into a rom-com trope (hold the rom).

He slow-blinks. "You really think *you're* a sidekick?"

I drop my shoulders, resigned to my fate. "We can't all be main characters, Metcalfe. Some of us are nameless background people who are just . . . there."

"I'll take your word for it."

"I would like to get out of sidekick territory, though. Try something new. Actually, I just made a Tinder. Wanna judge my profile?" I toss my phone toward him. It lands with a soft *thud* on the mattress.

Since my meet-cute-turned-mugging on move-in day, my DMs have been flooded with people serving up the cold, hard truth: online dating is my only option. In a moment of weakness, I caved and downloaded all the apps.

"Would you swipe right on me if I were a stranger?" I ask.

Trevor huffs a one-syllable laugh, which I interpret as a definite *no*. Ouch. "'Seeking husband potential only. No test drives'? Is that actually your bio?"

I fold my arms over my chest. "When you've had your heart crushed to smithereens as many times as I have, you don't mess around. This bio weeds out the duds who just want to assault me with dick pics."

Mel spent a solid hour brainstorming prospective bios for me, the majority of which I turned down immediately, including:

I'll share my Netflix account;
Cooks Kraft dinner without consulting directions on box;
Looking for more than one type of happy ending; and
Early-onset dad bods welcome.

"Damn, who's the girl in the photo with you?" Trevor ogles my profile photo, a candid shot of Mel and me cheesing for the camera at a lush, sunlit vineyard last summer. He zooms in on Mel, interest piqued.

A tired growl escapes me. "Mel. She's my fashion influencer friend. The one you met the other day," I remind him. They met briefly when she came to pick me up for a mall outing. He gave her his best flirty eyes, practically impregnating her on the spot, turning her cheeks to Red Delicious apples.

Trevor continues to dissect the photo, zooming in and out like an FBI agent. "I'm not sure this is *your* best photo. Besides, no one will know which one you are."

"Excuse you." I yank my phone out of his grip. "This is my one good photo. I use it for everything."

Unlike Mel, who is Insta-famous for her flawless makeup and lusciously thick black hair I want to transplant onto my own scalp, I'm chronically unphotogenic. Even if I look bomb in person, I look like a serial killer in any given still photo. In fact, in high school, a webcam picture of me with vacant, Night Stalker eyes became a viral meme called *Crazy Ex-Girlfriend*. Yes, that is my one claim to fame. And yes, people have recognized me in public on exactly three occasions. This is why I exclusively take photos of books.

This Tinder photo of Mel and me just so happens to be the one photo of a thousand where I don't look like I dabble in random acts of cannibalism. Dare I say, I resemble an even-keeled individual with average emotional range and sufficient social skills.

"Any luck on Tinder?" Trevor asks, changing the subject from my apparently unideal profile photo. He stands to grab a T-shirt from his closet, slipping it over his head.

"No. It's kind of depressing, actually."

For proof, I show him the first profile that comes up. It's a thirty-four-year-old named Ted with a teardrop tattoo. I reckon he's killed before. Next is a guy in a corduroy newsboy cap, which could be acceptable if I were into the gaunt-faced, troubled, and egotistical academic types.

"You're being picky. Look at this one." He points to the third guy, Dax, who is rocking a skinny polka-dot tie. He's above average in looks, with tired yet gentle eyes, a little nerdy, innocent. And will probably shatter my brittle heart to pieces all the same. "His bio says he likes chicken nuggets and quantum physics. You practically live off chicken nuggets. This could be your soul mate."

"I don't think my soul mate is on Tinder. And he looks like his mom still cuts his nuggets for him into tiny bite-size pieces."

"If you say so."

I show him the next guy. "And then there's this one. With the dog."

"What's wrong with the dog?"

"He doesn't look like a dog guy to me, which tells me he's a manipulative sociopath who stole someone's dog to masquerade as his own."

Trevor lets out a soft sigh and heads into the hallway. "Well, I'd love to stand here and make sweeping, very specific judgments about internet strangers, but I'm heading out for errands. Need anything at the grocery store? Fruits or vegetables, perhaps?" he asks teasingly.

I follow him to the entryway. "Hey, I eat a perfectly balanced, healthy diet. And you certainly haven't been complaining about my cupcakes." I've gotten into the habit of baking Betty Crocker cupcakes from the box every weekend out of pure boredom (and gluttony). Each batch has been devoured quickly, thanks to Trevor.

He levels me with a knowing look. "Name one fruit or vegetable you like."

I rack my brain. My entire life, I've been a notoriously picky eater. Dad used to make me sit at the table for hours until I finished my dinner. I'd hold out until he'd cave and make me something I liked, like nuggets. Even two weeks ago, Crystal and Scott tried to make me eat a piece of cooked asparagus and I almost cried because of the texture.

"I like pickles," I announce.

"Pickles?" A smile flirts at the corner of his lips for a fraction of a second as he slips his arm into his jacket. "Fine. I'll buy you a jar."

"Oh, okay, but make sure they're dill pickles. I don't like sweet—"

A knock at the door interrupts me. Trevor pulls it open to reveal Grandma Flo.

❤ chapter four

GRANDMA FLO IS here for our Live video session a solid forty-five minutes early to "prepare."

As she slips off her extra-grip orthopedic winter boots, I take one of her grocery bags. This one is full of yarn and a box of digestive biscuits. "Grandma, this is my roommate, Trevor."

Grandma Flo tosses her coat at me and scrutinizes him with her sharp hazel eyes for an uncomfortable amount of time. "Roommate? Your new roommate is a man?" she asks, aghast.

"He's a colleague of Scott's. At the firehouse," I emphasize, in an attempt to lessen the shock, lest she assume he's some unvetted Craigslist stranger who's angling to roast my bones to make a ceremonial broth.

Her expression softens, as I knew it would. "You're a firefighter? My husband, Marty, is a career firefighter. Retired now, of course."

"I've worked at the BFD with Scotty for about ten years now," Trevor says.

His overt hide-your-wife-kids-and-extended-family vibes aside, Flo seems satisfied by Trevor's public service career. She shakes his hand and even gives him the afghan she knit me as a housewarming gift. It's a vibrant green, white, and orange, to remind me of my half-Irish heritage. When I make a show of draping it over the entire length of the couch, Trevor pretends to stroke it lovingly while subtly eyeing it like an evil object.

Grandma admires Trevor as she makes herself comfortable on the couch. "You know, you could be one of those shirtless male models on a book cover. Tara, do you have any connections? Maybe you can get this man some modeling work."

Unsure how to respond to that, Trevor flashes me a funny, closed-mouth grin.

"Grandma, I told you I don't have real publishing connections. I'm a book reviewer," I remind her. Ever since I managed to get her an early copy of a new Danielle Steel book, she's under the false impression that I have some sort of clout in the publishing industry at large.

She waves me off. "Trevor, would you like to join us for our Live video? We're talking about romance books." She bounces her thin penciled brows to entice him.

"I'd love to, ma'am," he says, all kind-eyed and gentlemanlike, "but I'm going grocery shopping. I've gotta pick up some fruits and vegetables for Tara before she dies of malnutrition."

I meet his smart-ass smile with a glower, because I know exactly how Grandma Flo is going to react: with another lecture about how I'll never find a husband if I don't cook.

As expected, she's severely disappointed in me, shaking her head as though she's failed as a grandmother. "Tara has never been one for domestic life. Certainly doesn't take after me. You know, at age ten, I could whip up a gourmet meal. Any meal. From memory," she brags, tapping her head. "I take it you still haven't made use of the cookbook I gave you?" she asks me. For my thirtieth birthday, she gifted me a cookbook she found at a yard sale titled *Easy-Peasy Recipes for One*.

"Um, yeah. I've used it," I lie, dodging eye contact entirely.

Ignoring me, she begins to indulge Trevor with some tales of my personal failings in the kitchen, including the time I microwaved tinfoil. Trevor finds this all too amusing.

"Dear, did you find a dress for your big Valentine's Day gala yet?" Grandma asks me eagerly.

My stomach fills with dread at the mere mention of the gala, despite the fact that Valentine's Day is my favorite holiday. The gala is an annual Boston Children's Hospital fundraiser for medical research. This year, it happens to fall on Valentine's Day. In keeping with the theme, the money will go toward the Children's Heart Center.

The hospital staff treat this event like it's senior prom. I'm talking formal wear, makeup, updos, and limo rentals. Last year was the first time I elected to work instead (due to life implosion). And while I toyed with the idea of skipping it again this year in favor of self-loathing on the couch in a haze of Cheeto dust, spending Valentine's Day alone feels a little too depressing.

I give her a wary look. "How did you even know about it?"

"I saw you clicked *Attending* on the Facebook," she says flippantly. "I could crochet you a dress if you'd like."

I pretend not to be horrified at the prospect of a hand-knit evening gown. "I was thinking of buying something, Grandma. But thank you."

Luckily, she doesn't appear too put out by my decline of her crochet services. She quickly gets sidetracked with a story about how she once crocheted an outfit for my mom and how Mom didn't appreciate the craftsmanship because she isn't a "domestic goddess," either. At some point during the rant, Trevor manages to make his quiet escape.

Once he's gone, Grandma Flo tells me about her new Instagram account, LoopsWithFlo. It seems Crystal and I are no longer the only social media influencers in the family.

"I already have fifty friends," she gloats, shoving her iPad an inch from my face to prove it.

I pace the living room, scrolling through her feed. She's documented all her latest creations: hats, blankets, scarves, mittens. She's even gotten the hang of filters and hashtags (#knittersofinstagram, #wool, #makersgonnamake). "They're called *followers* on Instagram, Grandma."

She takes a tiny bird bite of her digestive biscuit. "I want to learn how to get more friends."

"Crystal would know more than me, but it looks like you're only posting once every few days," I say, passing the iPad back to her. "You have to post consistently, daily even, to get maximum exposure."

She one-finger types *ask crystal about friends* in her Notes app while I set up my tripod and phone in front of the couch. Once Grandma Flo is satisfied the angle doesn't accentuate her neck wrinkles, it's showtime.

LIVE WITH TARAROMANCEQUEEN—SECOND-CHANCE ROMANCE

EXCERPT FROM TRANSCRIPT

[Tara and Grandma Flo sit side by side on a leather couch, knit afghan draped over their laps. Flo sips tea and scrutinizes her own image. Tara smiles happily into the camera.]

TARA: *Hello, romance book lovers, welcome back to my channel. I am stoked about today's episode for two reasons. First, you all know I'm trash for a second-chance reunion trope. Second, my lovely Grandma Flo is here as a special guest to share her story of a real-life second-chance romance with her childhood sweetheart.*

Before I get too carried away with Flo's story, let me explain the ins and outs of a second-chance romance for those newbie romance readers out there. Usually, second chances go a little something like this: Person A and Person B are destined soul mates, but something goes horribly wrong and they're separated.

FLO: *Sometimes for many years. Decades, even.*

TARA: *Yup. Fast-forward. The heroine is living a fabulous life in the city, probably New York, and must return to her backwoods small town to take care of unfinished business. She's usually engaged to a fancy architect who has zero time for her, leaving her vulnerable to the ruggedly sexy ex-boyfriend who's never left town and still pines for her.*

[Tara flaps her hands excitedly and turns to Flo.]

Tara: *Tell us a little bit about your and Martin's story.*

FLO: *Marty and I met in kindergarten. He was taken with me immediately, of course. I was quite the cutie-pie back then. His way of showing his affection was to torment me. Chased me around with bugs and frogs he caught in the creek. In the third grade, he jumped from the roof of a schoolyard shed just to impress me. Poor dear broke his arm. I signed his cast with a little heart, and the rest is history.*

TARA: *To clarify, you fell in love as kids?*

FLO: *Things ended when I caught him smooching another girl in the schoolyard. After high school, we both married other people. Lived right down the street from each other for most of our adult lives.*

TARA: *Did you always know you and Marty were meant to be?*

FLO: *Heavens no. You know, Marty wasn't the first man I dated after your grandfather died.*

TARA: *You dated other men before Marty?*

FLO: *Of course I did. A lady has to keep her options open. You can't just run into the arms of the first man who gives you a second look. That would be desperate.*

• • •

GRANDMA FLO GIVES me a knowing, wise-owl look. Did my own grandmother just insinuate that I'm desperate on Live video, in front of my thousands of followers?

I clear my throat, plowing forward. "Tell us a bit about your dating experience. Did you have lots of suitors after Grandpa died?"

"First I set my sights on the men at church, but they turned out to be a bunch of sticks in the mud," she says with a sassy eye roll. "I certainly wasn't interested in the rigmarole of courting someone new. One day I happened to be at the seniors waffle brunch, and guess who I ran into?" She jabs her sharp elbow into my rib for emphasis.

"Who?"

"Silas Reeves," she says dreamily, playing it up for the camera. "I dated Sil right after Marty. He took me to my first high school dance. He was a sensitive creature. And let me tell you, he was a looker. Picture George Clooney in his *ER* days, but with a larger nose and weaker chin."

"Sounds like a catch. What happened with him?"

She waves my words away like an irksome housefly. "His wife is still alive. Very inconvenient."

She starts rooting around in her massive purse, which is at maximum capacity with random receipts, lipstick tubes, and ancient packets of gum, until she finds what she's looking for.

It's a crumpled, stained piece of paper. She unfolds it to reveal a cluster of handwritten words and numbers in varying sizes, written in different-color pen. It's unhinged. It's madness. Phone numbers, addresses, occupations are scribbled in every open space. I lean in close enough to make out the name *Curtis Bell—Croaked in 2003*.

"Since Sil aged so well, it inspired me to record a list of all the men I've dated. I was quite the flirt back in the day." She chuckles to herself as she scans her list, scandalized by her past. "Tracked most of them down. But none really wowed me like Marty."

I scan her list in awe. What first appeared to be the scribbles of a person who lost their marbles suddenly looks like the work of a genius. A mastermind. "This ex-boyfriend list led you to your second-chance reunion with Marty?"

"Indeed. We hadn't talked in a long while after Sheila passed. So I rang him up and asked him to help me with some yard work." She does a double wink for the camera.

My wistful expression is quickly replaced by a frown. "Stories like yours don't happen to millennials. I'm still aggressively single with zero romantic prospects, swimming in debt, getting mugged on public transit. I've even resorted to online dating."

Grandma Flo shrivels at the horror. She doesn't know where to start. My mugging? My lonely future? The fact that I've just confessed my private life to the entirety of the internet?

Either way, the comments are coming in hot.

Omg, I so relate. Online dating is the worst! ♡

Yikes. That sucks. You should get a cat. ♡

Grandma Flo makes a tsk sound, severely disappointed with the youth of today. "The Facebook is no way to meet someone."

I don't bother to explain that Facebook is not synonymous with the internet writ large. "Tell me about it. But this is how it is now. This is modern dating."

"So, what you're saying is, you're looking for love and you're finally open to my help?" Grandma Flo's eyes light up like a Christmas tree. For years, I've warded off her offers to set me up with random suitors (including her church friend's eighteen-year-old grandson).

"So long as they're in my age category," I warn.

When she strokes her chin, I expect her to rattle off a laundry list of potentials. But she just shrugs and says, "I don't know of anyone suitable right now, aside from Ethel's grandson, Hank. The one who just got out of prison. I'll survey my girlfriends and get back to you."

I cringe. You know the dating world is bleak when Grandma Flo can't even muster up one measly option aside from a convicted felon. "I wish I could just meet the One in a laundromat like Mom and Dad. Or by crashing into each other on bikes like Grandma and Grandpa Chen. Or by reuniting with my childhood sweetheart like you and Martin." I let out a disgruntled sigh at all the romantic love stories in my family. "Romances like those don't happen in real life anymore."

She leans forward to the edge of the couch. "They don't *just happen*, Tara. You have to make them happen. Why don't you do what I did?"

"Try to date my exes?" I clarify.

"Why not? What better pool to choose from than already vetted men? Of course, leave out the duds," she advises. "But I remember you dated some fine fellows."

She's not wrong. Some of my exes are total catches. They're all somewhat similar. Generally kind, soft-spoken, good-natured, and trustworthy. The men most women friend-zone, ignoring their potential and understated sex appeal until it's too late. "You know what, Grandma? This could be a good place to start my search."

She leans in with yet another slightly disturbing double wink. "I'll tell you one thing. Men only get better with age. Trust me, second time's a charm. Maybe you can even find one on time for that Valentine's Day gala of yours."

By the time we end our Live Session, there's an avalanche of comments on our video, most of which are encouraging me to pursue my exes and get a date for Valentine's Day. In fact, it's garnered twice as many views as my usual videos.

Maybe Grandma Flo has a point. All the romance books and movies insist true love happens passively. Love, as we're told, is not something you actively seek out. The best love stories just magically fall into the laps of those who don't expect or want them.

But what if I don't want to sit around and wait for potential suitors like a demure flower who's just come of age? What if I want to take matters into my own hands? To prove romance-book-worthy love still exists?

Inspired, I grab my phone. It's time to do what I do best.

Internet stalk.

♥ chapter five

WHICH EX SHOULD I reach out to first? My high school sweetheart? My college boyfriends? Don't forget to let me know in the comments. You can also vote in the poll—"

My video is interrupted by a figure taking up nearly the entire width of my bedroom doorway behind me on camera.

"It's only six in the morning and you're already plotting something sinister," Trevor remarks in a hoarse, early-morning voice. He's in a plain white T-shirt, which has no business contouring his every muscle the way it does.

I swiftly turn my attention back to the camera, but not before shooting him a stern look over my shoulder. "Sorry. That was my roommate. Anyway, as I was saying, you can vote in the poll in my stories. Bye, everyone!" I wave, hitting *End*.

Trevor is appalled by the state of my room, horror-movie eyes darting from the half-emptied box in my doorway to my bed, where the remainder of its contents are scattered. He gulps when he spots the item behind me. "What the . . ."

"Behold. My hit list." I gesture to my masterpiece like it's a sparkling Cadillac on *The Price Is Right*.

Rescuing my old college corkboard from the depths of my storage space, I created an FBI-style link chart of my ex-boyfriends.

TARA'S EX-BOYFRIENDS

1. Daniel (childhood love)
2. ~~Tommy (ninth-grade boyfriend)~~
3. ~~Jacques (Student Senate boy)~~
4. Cody (high school sweetheart)
5. Jeff (frosh week fling)
6. Zion (campus bookstore cutie)
7. Brandon (world traveler—the one who got away)
8. Linus (Brandon rebound)
9. Mark (book club intellectual)
10. ~~Seth (ex-fiancé)~~

Not to brag, but I'm basically Carrie Mathison from *Homeland*, uncovering treasure troves of pertinent information on each of my targets, including but not limited to: high school athletic and academic achievements, grandparents' obituaries, etc. Next to each name is an accompanying photo from social media, as well as contact details, including handles, email addresses, phone numbers, workplaces.

The only ex I wasn't able to find anything on is ex number one, Daniel Nakamura (humanity's shining example of all that is good in the world), who is a ghost online.

"Should I be scared?" Trevor asks, perusing my list.

"Not unless you're my ex."

He doesn't look so sure. "So these are all your lucky ex-boyfriends?"

"During our Live Session yesterday, Grandma Flo inspired me to embark on a second-chance romance quest." I follow up with a detailed explanation of what a second-chance romance entails, as well as Grandma Flo's love story and how it relates to my new plan. "And bonus, if my ex-boyfriend search goes as planned, maybe I won't have to be alone on Valentine's Day or at the gala. Maybe I'll have a plus-one."

Trevor rewards me with a dead-eyed stare. He's probably regretting wasting the last five minutes of his life. "You want to date your exes because you don't want to resort to Tinder? And because your grandma married her childhood boyfriend?"

"That's a gross oversimplification." I pause, biting my thumbnail. "But basically, yes. Grandma Flo says men only get better with age. Sure, some of these guys were boneheads years ago, but what if they've turned into amazing people?"

Even more than that, this quest for a second-chance-romance hero fills me with something I haven't felt since the early days with Seth: butterflies. Ridiculous as it may be, thinking about my exes is nostalgic. It's that innocent, childlike anticipation of seeing your crush in the morning at school. That delicious flutter in the base of your stomach when they give you a passing glance in the hallway.

Both Crystal and Mel were hesitant about this plan, righteously reminding me that career fulfillment alone should be enough to make me happy. But unlike their respective influencer careers, I'm not die-hard passionate about nursing, even though I enjoy it. I've always been a bit of an anomaly, finding purpose not through what I do but through my relationships with friends and family. But when everyone is absorbed with their own lives, where does that leave me at the end of the day? Alone in my twin bed, listening to my roommate's sex-capades?

If I'm being honest with myself, I'm sick of being single. And if my time as a singleton has taught me anything, it's that just because I don't *need* someone in my life doesn't mean I don't *want* one.

Realistically, I should be lauded for my willingness to take on a whole separate human's personal traumas in addition to my own. That's strength.

Trevor turns his attention back to the box at his feet. "What does all this junk have to do with your exes?"

While poking around in my storage space last night, I found a large box appropriately labeled *The Ex-Files*.

I explain to Trevor how this box has been with me since middle school. To be fair, it started as a shoe box (decorated with magazine cutouts of my celebrity crushes). Over the years, it got bigger, with physical artifacts from each successive relationship. Love notes, movie ticket stubs from first dates, articles of clothing, you name it.

Trevor bends over and fishes out a true-to-size royal-purple penis wax candle, appropriately named the Pecker Flame. He examines with caution, and I note how it fills his large, callused palm with commendable girth. *He can most definitely handle a hose*, I think to myself before blinking that errant thought to the abandoned cellar of my mind.

His brows pinch together, completing his confused face. "Please tell me this isn't a mold of your ex's . . ."

I wince when he tosses it back into the box as if it's a used dildo. "God, no! It's just a candle. I got it as a gag gift from my college roommate on the night I met ex number six, Zion."

Trevor manages to find an ancient Fruit by the Foot wrapper. He holds it between pinched fingers, quietly disturbed. "And this?"

"From the night ex number one and I had our first kiss," I say, taken by the memory.

Trevor officially thinks I'm a loon.

I turn his attention to the mementos of boyfriends past scattered atop my bed and hold up a boldly patterned body-con dress. He watches leerily as I hold it in front of my body, willing it to magically fit again. "I wore this the first night I had sex with ex number seven, Brandon."

"Where's the rest of it?"

"Okay, *Dad*." I roll my eyes, moving on to my next find. Will I wear this cobalt-blue, zip-up, backless peplum top again? Probably not. Do I want to keep it indefinitely because I wore it on my first date with Seth? Absolutely.

Trevor shakes his head, overwhelmed when I brandish my shoe box full of old Valentine's Day cards and love letters. In fact, he even starts ordering the books on my shelf, probably to escape my chaos. "What is it with women and Valentine's Day?" he mutters.

"Let me guess: you're part of the ninety-five percent of people who like to moan and complain about Valentine's Day being nothing but a tacky commercial holiday, blah blah blah. Am I right?

And before you go on to slander it, I feel the obligation to tell you it's my favorite holiday of all time. I take it very seriously."

His lips tighten in amusement. "I never said it was tacky. I just mean—"

"You think love should be celebrated every day, not just one day," I finish for him.

Based on his miffed expression, that's exactly what he was going to say.

"Everyone says that," I note. "And yes, it's true. But life gets busy. Why not use it as an excuse to take stock of all the people you love in your life and go the extra mile to make them feel special? Even something as small as leaving a cute note. I don't get why celebrating love openly has to be considered tacky. If anything, the world needs more excuses to eat chocolate and celebrate love for the sake of it, don't you think?"

He studies me for a moment before shrugging. "Sure, if you say so. But you need to throw this stuff out. You have no room for it."

"But what if I get back together with one of them? I can't just toss out tokens of our past. How cute would it be if I still had the menu from the very first restaurant we went to?"

He ignores this, still alphabetizing my books. "Didn't you say you're always the dumpee? If all these guys broke up with you, why would you want to get back with them?"

"Because they were all great people. And I can only assume time and maturity have made them even better. They all have soul mate potential. Most of them, anyway." At least I think so, if my memory serves me correctly.

"Even the guy with the shark face?" Trevor jabs a thumb toward

Seth's photo. It's his LinkedIn photo, and I chose it specifically because he looks like a smarmy, country-club arsehole named Tripp who pops his collars and paid someone to take his SATs. His face is crossed out with ominous, double-thick marker the color of blood.

"Shark face?" I repeat.

Trevor leaves my now organized shelf and steps around the box, officially entering my room to examine the photo closer. "Don't you think he kinda looks like that shark from *Finding Nemo*? With the teeth?"

I clutch my stomach in a burst of evil laughter. Where has Trevor Metcalfe been all my life when I needed someone to trash-talk my exes? "You have a point."

He points to numbers two and three, who are crossed out. "What happened with these guys?"

"Jacques is married, which is fine because he broke up with me via chain email in ninth grade," I say, conveniently leaving out the fact that when I reached out last night, he immediately unfriended and blocked me. "And Tommy . . . you can see for yourself."

I show him Tommy's Facebook profile, which is full of politically frightening memes. Trevor does a brief scan of his timeline, searching for any redeemable qualities. Based on his frown, he's failed. "Okay, I understand why he got the ax," he says, passing my phone back.

"Yup. I'm single. Not desperate. Besides, he probably still hates me after I keyed his car."

Trevor takes a startled step away from me. "You keyed his car?"

"I'm not proud of it. But I was fifteen years old," I point out. "I went full Carrie Underwood. It was a nice car too. Red with a sunroof. Dad nearly flipped his lid when the cops showed up at our doorstep. I felt awful. Spent my whole summer working to pay for the damage."

His mouth shapes into a full grimace. "Poor Tommy."

"Lest we forget what *Tommy* did to deserve it." Spikes of heat pierce my neck. "He kissed another girl at the semiformal. The night we planned to lose our virginities to each other. Then he called me crazy when I got mad at him over it. The gaslighter. So I felt compelled to show him what *crazy* really is." I'm about to rant about the stigma of calling people "crazy" willy-nilly, but Trevor is still grimacing, tilting his head back and forth, seemingly unconvinced my actions were justifiable.

"Anyways, I gotta get to work. I'm meeting Jeff, number five, on my lunch break." I slid into his DMs this morning after he posted a twenty-part, eloquently written tweet about ocean pollution.

Trevor peers at Jeff's photo on my ex list. He's sipping a Corona on a beach in white sunglasses and a Hawaiian shirt. "White sunglasses straight from the Douchebag 101 starter kit. If that's not a red flag, I dunno what is," he remarks, pausing to check his phone, which just dinged in his pocket.

He smiles again as he reads the message, only it's a wider smile than the one I caught when he was texting yesterday. People don't casually text and smile for no reason. Maybe there's hope for his black heart after all. I'm tempted to ask for the identity of the woman who wields the power to make Trevor Metcalfe smile like a little boy, but I refrain.

While I wait for him to finish his text, I pull out that exact pair of white Oakleys from the depths of the box like a magician. Trevor barks a laugh when he lifts his eyes. I put the glasses on for dramatic flair. "Oh, come on. It's early-2000s chic. You don't think they suit me?"

He shields me from view with his hand. "No. Very disturbing."

"You're really killing my vibe, Metcalfe." I head past him toward the doorway.

I wait in the hallway as he follows me out of my room. We're face-to-face. My forehead technically only reaches his chin, reminding me I'm vertically challenged thanks to the Chens, my dad's side of the family. I study the rise and fall of his chest for a long beat before meeting his gaze.

The orange tint of Jeff's sunglasses sets Trevor's eyes alight, like tiny flecks of gold. My breath hitches when he gently pulls the glasses off my face, warm fingertips grazing my cheekbones. Even without the protective shield of the lenses, his eyes still sparkle like a pot of riches.

He clears his throat and takes half a step back. "It's just . . . They're exes for a reason. Aren't they?"

I think about Trevor's words for the first half of my day shift. People love to say exes are exes for a reason, so they don't have to dwell on the past. But personally, I've always thought second-chance love stories were the most satisfying of them all.

♥ chapter six

"JEFF IS OFFICIALLY twenty minutes late," I announce to my followers. "Will keep you all updated." I let out a forlorn sigh and wave goodbye to the camera.

To make matters worse, my jasmine tea is no longer hot. At least the café is cute. Floor-to-ceiling bookshelves span the wall, complete with a dinky yet charming sliding ladder straight out of *Beauty and the Beast*. Recalling Jeff's vegan diet, I selected it purposely for its free-trade, non-GMO, and organic menu, printed on beige paper allegedly made from wheat straw.

While I wait, Harmon, the barista, tells me about some literary fiction written by a deceased white dude that "changed her life." My eyes gloss over at the description, but I maintain an eager smile, assuring her that it's HIGH on my TBR (to-be-read) pile.

When Harmon goes back to serving customers, I check my

phone. Comments have flooded in on my video from early this morning.

Who is WHITE T SHIRT GUY and where can I find him? ♡

Is that your new roommate??? ♡

Screw the exes. Date the roommate!! ♡

ROOM-ANCE ♡

I wheeze at the thought of dating Trevor I-don't-subscribe-to-love Metcalfe, of all people. But before I can properly entertain the ridiculous idea, a flash of neon out the window catches my eye. The neon turns out to be a helmet, worn by a lanky man in a baggy T-shirt, sleeveless fleece vest, and khakis whizzing down the side-walk on a Segway. Without notice, he halts his Segway directly in front of the shop, peering at the sign above.

The moment his helmet comes off, the recognition sets in. The vibrant, sunny sky-blue eyes. The long, curly, surfer-dude hair I used to love running my fingers through. The dimpled chin. And his strong nose, which always seemed a little too large for his face.

When he spots me gawking at him like a zoo animal through the window, he gives me a small wave. I work down a swallow of my tea when he wrenches the glass door open with the force of a man who gives zero fucks.

The café patrons turn to stare when the bell smashes against the glass door. He swaggers toward me, long arms outstretched for an embrace. "Tara. You look rad."

The helmet tucked under his arms crushes my ribs as he goes for a full-body hug. His body is an iceberg, probably because he's been cruising around the frigid streets of Boston bare-armed. It crosses my mind that maybe he can't afford a warm coat, or maybe he was ill prepared for the cold weather. He holds our hug for a beat too long before I duck out of his arms.

"Long time no see." I force a smile, taking my seat. "Thanks for meeting on such short notice."

"No prob," he says.

I delay my response, expecting him to acknowledge that he's over half an hour late. But he doesn't say anything. Instead, he tugs the chair back, allowing the legs to scrape across the tiled floor, garnering a wince from me and everyone within our vicinity. He drums his knuckles on the wooden tabletop and just smiles at me, closed-mouthed, like he's expecting me to speak.

"You didn't wear a coat? Aren't you cold?" I gesture out the window. "It's November."

As he plunks the helmet onto the floor at his feet, I note the layer of hair covering his arms is literally white from frost. "Nah, bro," he says, like old-school Justin Bieber casually appropriating Black culture. "My body is a furnace."

I cringe, casting a distressed glance at the time on my phone.

"So, you're a nurse now, right? Thought I read that on Facebook," he says as I chug the rest of my now room-temperature tea.

"Yep. I work in the NICU at the children's hospital," I explain. "I love it. It's nice to work with patients who don't complain."

My attempt at humor falls flat. Instead, Jeff's expression turns grave. "I had a buddy whose cousin's friend's baby died after a nurse gave it the wrong dose of medication."

I sit back in my chair, quietly disturbed. "Oh, wow. That's terrible—"

"That's why I refuse to go to hospitals," he cuts in. "I only practice holistic wellness."

I start stress-tearing my napkin into thin strips, unable to muster the strength to defend the scientific advantages of modern medicine. The memory of dating this man is like a delayed, distorted film. While I recall snippets of being with him lazing in the courtyard, the memories fail to bring me any sense of longing or comfort.

His Hollister-model looks, pot addiction, bare-minimum personality, and staunch hatred for anything mainstream may have charmed my eighteen-year-old self, but at thirty, I just feel a bizarre maternal urge to give him my coat and some life advice.

"So, Jeff, last time we saw each other you were taking Environmental Science. What did you end up doing?" I ask.

"Dropped out junior year. Got a sick inheritance after my granddad passed. Gave me some time to figure things out."

"Oh? Where are you currently working?"

"Nowhere. I'm really not cut out for the nine-to-five. Thinking of starting a nonprofit. Or getting into the beekeeping business." *No health insurance* is my only takeaway from that statement.

"Beekeeping?" I'm not confident in my ability to feign interest in bugs, however crucial they are to sustaining the ecosystem. The universe officially has it out for me. This is just swell.

He nods. "Yup."

Now that he's sitting in front of me, giving me one-word answers, I do recall complaining about his poor conversation skills. He's basically a human boomerang, bringing every topic back to himself sooner or later, which I blamed for the demise of our relationship. I began to suspect he was losing interest when he started responding to my multi-paragraph texts with *Kk*. I never knew whether he wanted to keep talking or if he wanted me to disappear from his life entirely. And based on the fact that he eventually stopped texting me altogether, I'd say it was the latter.

When Jeff stares longingly out the window at his Segway, like it's his long-lost love or firstborn child, I start crushing the strips of napkin into tight balls, fantasizing about tossing myself into the nearest ditch.

We attempt some stilted conversation about the science of composting, a topic I know absolutely nothing about. When that trails off, I reach for my coat, explaining that I have to get back to work for the bimonthly all-staff meeting.

"So, I'm curious. Before we go, why did you reach out, anyway? For closure?" he asks.

"Closure?" My laughter comes out shaky as I reach for my coat. "Why would you think that?"

"You were pretty into me in college," he declares with no shortage of confidence.

My cheeks flush. "I mean, I guess it would be nice to know why we stopped talking."

"Listen, I'm gonna be honest." A grave pause. "You were great. We had a lot of fun together. But you were . . . a little . . ."

"A little what?"

He bites his lip, hesitant. "Clingy. A bit of a stage-five clinger."

"Stage-five clinger?" I lean back in my chair, clasping a weak hand over my chest like I'm in grade school, obediently pledging allegiance to the flag. Did this man really just call me clingy? The gall. The gumption.

"You texted and called me. Nonstop," he says matter-of-factly.

"Okay, that's an exaggeration. It's not like I sat by my phone waiting with bated breath for you to text me," I lie. I might have. But it seems like poor timing to come clean. And it doesn't make me *crazy*. I was in love, damnit. "In my defense, you told me you wanted to get married."

He gapes at me. "No. I definitely never said that."

"You did. The night we danced in my dorm room to that Toploader song. You said it would be our wedding song."

"You thought that meant—" Red-faced, he runs his hands down his cheeks. "Obviously I didn't mean it. I was eighteen years old. I didn't even know how to do my own laundry back then. And I was probably just trying to get into your pants."

"So you told me you wanted to marry me for fun? You can't say shit like that, Jeff," I warn.

"Yeah, I learned my lesson." He snickers, almost to himself. "You know what they say. The hotter the girl, the crazier she is." He goes on to mansplain this awful *Crazy Hot Matrix* YouTube video he swears by. When he catches my blatant eye roll, he adds, "No disrespect. I mean that as a compliment. You're a really good-looking girl." His flattery misses the mark.

"But also really crazy?" I venture.

He shrugs. "I'm just one of those guys who needs more freedom, ya know?"

I want to poke a pin in his inflated head with a hundred-point list of all the reasons he's in the wrong here, all the instances when he led me astray, but I refrain for the sole purpose of preserving my dwindling dignity. Instead, I nod in mock understanding as Harmon collects my empty teacup.

The moment I stand, Jeff practically launches out of his seat, dragging his chair legs across the floor yet again.

"Well, I better get going. Catch you later, Tara."

Or not.

1. Daniel (childhood love)
2. ~~Tommy (ninth-grade boyfriend)~~
3. ~~Jacques (Student Senate boy)~~
4. Cody (high school sweetheart)
5. ~~Jeff (frosh week fling)~~
6. Zion (campus bookstore cutie)
7. Brandon (world traveler—the one that got away)
8. Linus (Brandon rebound)
9. Mark (book club intellectual)
10. ~~Seth (ex-fiancé)~~

MANAGE TO MAKE it back to my day shift just in time for the all-staff meeting. It starts off like any other. The doctors and nurses hash out their pent-up grievances against each other, blaming the other party for all that is wrong in the NICU. Tensions are particularly heightened ever since last week, when someone broke the $5,000 coffee machine in the exclusive doctors' lounge. The perpetrator remains at large, and now us nurses are stuck sharing our basic-bitch Keurig with the doctors, who have been hoarding all the best pod flavors.

Another fifteen minutes go by as people pose miscellaneous questions they should be asking their direct supervisors in a one-on-one meeting.

"Don't forget, the charity gala is coming up on Valentine's Day," Jordan, the head nurse, reminds us. "Tickets are on sale starting Friday for those who can make it. We're actively accepting items for the auction."

Mention of the gala in three months fills me with dread. After my date with Segway Jeff, I'm no closer to a plus-one. In fact, I feel further away from that prospect than ever. Him calling me *clingy* and *crazy* doesn't sit right with my spirit, especially considering he never communicated how he felt about me until now. Years later.

The only positive takeaway was the closure. Come to think of it, a postmortem analysis on where it went sideways for all my exes would be nice before attempting to rekindle the flame.

Lucky or unlucky for me (not quite sure which), the one ex I don't have to social-media-stalk is right here in the room. Seth, my ex-fiancé, happens to be a doctor in the NICU. Perhaps he'll have some extra insight I could use to my advantage with the remaining prospects.

"Hey, Seth?" I call out, poking him in the back as everyone filters out of the meeting room.

He spins on his heel as if in slow motion, delaying his fate. This is how it's been since our breakup. In the rare event that I have to interact with him, he regards me like a chore, like that one drawer in your house piled with junk that you'd rather not deal with.

"What's up, T?" he asks impatiently, hands on hips, chest puffed out like God can't touch him.

"Can we talk?" I whisper. "In your office," I add, eyeing our coworkers, who are huddled behind the nurses' station, buttered popcorn at the ready, pretending not to eavesdrop. That's the thing about workplace romances. The initial dating makes for juicy gossip. But the breakups, no matter how civil, are gold mines of scandal.

Admittedly, the immediate aftermath of Seth's and my breakup wasn't without drama. I took things hard after he canceled our wedding. I was in denial, on the verge of tears whenever I saw him, jumping at any opportunity to talk to him. Begging for scraps. Any little tidbit of information that could explain why he changed his mind after our three-year relationship. Why he gave up on the future we'd dreamed of. Even my shift supervisor took me aside and told me in the nicest way possible to "get my shit together."

On the other hand, Seth's reputation was completely untarnished. He wields power, as a doctor, as a man. He acted smug, like he was the "bigger person" for handling our breakup so seamlessly, with zero emotion, of course. After all, overt feelings are for unhinged women. And in a professional setting, surrounded by practitioners of the medical sciences—people of logic—there is little place for emotions.

Seth's eyes dart to the onlookers, then back to me, hovering around my forehead. "Uh, I really don't think—"

"It's not about us. At least, not really," I assure him, my cheeks turning pink. "I'm doing some self-reflection, and I need some advice." If I know Seth like I think I do, fluffing his ego always works.

It does. He gives me a curious brow raise and ushers me into his office, as if he's scared I'll make some sort of scene.

His windowless office is canary yellow, which is hilarious, given that he's anything but a sunshine-and-rainbows person. In fact, he's requested for it to be painted gray multiple times because he says yellow undermines his professionalism.

Filling the majority of the space is a bulky glass desk, which no longer houses the framed photo of our engagement photo shoot session at the apple orchard. There's a small bookshelf to the right, stocked with wartime nonfiction and medical journals. Only the most serious of literature for Seth.

Sitting in this orange chair with the rickety, loose arm gives me flashbacks to that time, just days after our breakup, when I cried in his office. I'd used up all his Kleenex while spit-firing ways in which we could "fix" our relationship. In response, he shooed me out of his office, telling me I needed to get over it and "move on."

"How can I help you?" His tone is irritatingly calm, almost condescending, like I'm a patient and not his ex-fiancée. He's leaned back in his chair, legs crossed, resting his arms behind his head, unapologetic about taking up space.

I suck in a deep breath, bracing for judgment. "I'm looking to reunite with my exes. To get a second-chance romance, kind of like my grandma's. The one who took over our wedding," I remind him.

His eyes go round like dinner plates. "Umm, you're aware I'm with Ingrid now, right?"

How could I not know? Ingrid is another doctor, who works in Oncology. They started dating two months after our breakup. Watching Seth fall into another relationship so quickly, as if the years we spent together were simply an unfortunate blip, was a whole new level of gut-wrenching. Seeing them together in those early days, stealing kisses in darkened corridors or cuddling in the cafeteria in the booth that used to be ours, was torture. It doesn't help that Seth is boisterous when he likes something. He made it known to the entire floor how "chill" Ingrid is compared to other women, how she loves beer and sports, and how she's basically a "hot dude" (aka the perfect woman).

"Obviously. Every happiness to you both," I force out. "You can rest assured, you are not a contender," I clarify, mortified he'd even get that impression.

Seth pretends to wipe the nonexistent sweat off his forehead as he pours coffee from his travel thermos into his Harvard Medical School mug, crest pointed toward me. "That's a relief. Though I kind of feel like I have an obligation to warn the rest of these men."

I give him a pointed look, ass half out of the chair. I should probably get out of here before this turns south. "Really, Seth?"

"Relax, Tara. I'm just messing with you." He plays off his belittlement like it was nothing, reaching for his smiley-face stress ball. He tosses it upward like a child. "Anyways, I have an appointment soon. What's your question?"

"I wanted to know, for research purposes, why exactly you broke up with me. You never really gave me a proper explanation, other than telling me you couldn't handle me. And I thought it might be nice to know what I could do better going forward."

The tension is as visible as a panty line under Crystal's workout leggings. Neither of us breathes, blanketing the office in complete silence, save for the dull beeps of various machines and faraway chatter echoing from the hallway. I tug at the collar of my scrubs, body erupting with a sickening, prickly heat from Seth's piercing stare. "I didn't give you a fulsome explanation because, frankly, I didn't know if you were in the proper mental space to handle it."

I flatten my spine against the back of the chair and meet his hard gaze. "I'm ready to handle it now. Why did you end things?"

He clears his throat, still tossing the stress ball back and forth between both hands, refusing to give me the decency of his full attention. "That's a loaded question. But for one, we never had any shared interests. You hate sports, and you never wanted to hang out with my friends."

My eye twitches. Seth knows full well he never invited me around his friends, all of whom are doctors or trust-fund kids I have nothing in common with. Crystal thinks he was embarrassed I was a lowly nurse. That I wasn't as educated as they were. On one occasion, I overheard him telling his boss at the staff holiday party that I was planning to go back to school to get my master's degree—which was a complete lie.

He continues on. "But besides that, the biggest thing was your distrust of me. You were really cling—"

I cut him off, unable to stomach the c-word again. "Okay, let's not forget how sketchy you were in the lead-up—"

"Well, actually." He holds up his finger, commanding the floor. I almost burst out laughing. It's a running joke between myself and the other nurses that Seth is NICU's resident *Well Actually Guy*, intruding on completely private conversations with technical corrections and irrelevant facts he found on Reddit. "Multiple studies show that trust is foundational to any relationship. If you don't have trust, you have nothing. That's something you'll need to learn if you want to maintain a long-term, healthy relationship," he tells me, feigning concern.

"Trust isn't something you have to learn. It's something you earn," I say, my tone firm, fists clenched in my lap. "And I think we both know your behavior at the end didn't exactly scream *devoted fiancé*."

"That's what happens when you pull the leash too tight." He tosses the stress ball onto the desk, clearly done with this conversation.

I stand, letting out a jaded sigh. Why did I ever expect to have a productive conversation with Seth? "I think our versions of the truth are two very different things, Seth."

He lifts his mug high for a slurpy sip and shrugs, like he can't be bothered. "Guess so. Good luck with the witch-hunt either way."

♥ chapter eight

MCDONALD'S IS PACKED tonight, full of loitering teenagers and distressed moms screaming at their children to *sit down* and eat their damned Happy Meals. I take in the familiar comfort of greasy fast food that permeates the air, eliciting a loud rumble from my empty stomach.

Trevor brought me straight here after discovering my lifeless body star-fishing on the living room floor. When I denied his offer of an ultra-healthy homecooked meal, he practically dragged me to his car.

"You need to eat. I need you alive to cover half the rent. Come on, I'll bring you wherever you want to go," he'd promised. As an unapologetic glutton, I wasn't about to deny the prospect of being chauffeured to eat wherever I wanted. Admittedly, his spicy scent was also an energy booster. Two hits and I was up on my own two feet.

Trevor stands in line for our orders while I secure a table near the window. As I wait, I come up with so many things I wish I'd said to Seth. He railroaded me in that conversation at work today, like he always manages to do. Meanwhile, I'm left to come up with sick burns and vicious insults long after the fact, when no one cares anymore except me. Story of my life.

I'm also disappointed in my college self for completely misreading my entire relationship with Jeff. My stomach turns when I think about how I skipped around campus, fancy-free like the human version of a heart-eyes emoji, ignoring the signals entirely. Had I known he considered me to be a total nutjob, I never would have wasted my time on him.

For the first time in my life, I'm starting to understand why romance heroines dramatically swear off men. Maybe I should do the same. Love would surely fall into my lap the moment I did so.

Trevor arrives with our food stacked on one tray. The moment he spots the sprinkled salt and a dab of ketchup smeared across the table, he backs away, shaking his head. It might as well be fresh blood from an open, oozing wound. "No."

I haphazardly wipe the mess away with my napkin. "Come on. Sit. It's perfectly clean now," I assure him, gesturing to the open seat across from me.

He looks into the dirty booth and shakes his head, his eyes flickering to the comparatively clean booth on my side.

I pat the space next to me and scoot over.

With zero enthusiasm, he slides in beside me like the diva he is, knee bouncing under the table. The warmth of his thigh grazing mine sends a zing down my spine. I'm now hyperaware we look like one of those cute couples who sit on the same side of the table at restaurants because they can't keep their hands off each other.

"Is it the screaming kids?" I ask, tearing the wrapping off my Quarter Pounder like a frenzied child on Christmas morning.

"No. I don't mind kids, actually." As I chew that first, glorious bite, he waves a hand around at the floor, full of slushy, brown napkins. "It's a postapocalyptic nightmare in here." He zeroes in on a glob of hardened sweet-and-sour dipping sauce I missed at the corner of the table. I promptly scrub it away before he has a breakdown.

"My parents had their first date in a McDonald's," I tell him. When he squints at me in suspicion, I make sure to add, "Don't worry. I'm not trying to date you." It feels necessary to point that out. When I got home from work today, I noticed a basket of expensive-looking candies sitting on Trevor's bed, visible from the hallway. Trust, I tried to bury my curiosity and go on with my day, but I'm not known for exercising self-control. I tiptoed my nosy ass into his room to peek at the card, which read *To Angie, from Trevor*, with a smiley face.

The romantic gift struck me as odd at first, considering he's never mentioned anyone named Angie before and he's averse to relationships. It was only a couple days ago that he bristled at the idea of a wifey. Then again, maybe he doesn't want to settle for just anyone. Maybe he's already in love with a special someone.

Every good playboy hero carries a secret torch for one woman his entire life but refuses to do anything about it until the eleventh hour (probably when she's halfway down the aisle at her wedding to another man). Trevor certainly fits the mold. Dangerous, sulky, always brooding in the corner. This makes so much sense.

Unfortunately, I'll have to wait for him to bring it up unless I reveal I snooped through his personal belongings like a complete stalker.

Trevor doesn't respond to my assurance that I'm not trying to date him. He's too busy assessing the inside contents of his Big Mac, probably daydreaming about Angie. With the precision of a heart surgeon, he removes the pickles and sets them in the lid of his burger container. When he notices me ogling them like a starved hyena, he asks, "Want them?"

"Um, hell yes." Without hesitation, I pluck them from the container and pop them in my mouth, one after the other.

"So, did you give Jeff his Oakleys back today?" he prods, reconstructing his burger.

"Nope. It was too much of a shitshow. I completely forgot by the time it was all said and done." I squeeze my eyes shut, trying to gather my thoughts, which seem to fall back into place the more food I gracefully shovel down my throat. "He drove a Segway, if that tells you anything."

Trevor's lips twist in amusement. "It tells me more than it should. Go on . . ."

"Okay, first, he was late. I sat in the café alone for half an hour like a pathetic loser." I immediately self-soothe with a handful of fries.

"You're not a loser. People eat alone all the time."

"I would never eat alone in public."

"Why not?"

I plunge my fry into my ketchup. "There used to be this old couple who came to my grandparents' Asian fusion restaurant every Friday night for years. Zhang and Wen. My grandma Chen even reserved a special table for them. Knew their orders and everything. One Friday, they didn't show up. Then, over a year later, Zhang showed up alone. Wen had died of pneumonia. He told my grandma how hard it was to come back, but that he knew Wen would want him to. To this day, he still comes for dinner alone, every Friday. He still orders her meal, even though he doesn't eat it."

Trevor's face contorts and he sets down his burger, which he was eating methodically, edges first. "Jesus. That's terrible."

"And now you see why I don't like the idea of eating alone."

"Point taken. So, what happened with your date? Obviously he showed up. On his Segway," he adds gleefully, sipping his chocolate milkshake.

Trevor's face turns an increasingly vibrant shade of red as I rattle off the entire story, including how Jeff didn't wear a coat and how he wants to be a beekeeper. "That sounds made-up. I don't get it—you said all your exes were great guys worth reconciling with. Was this dude not weird in college too?"

I'm momentarily sidetracked by a man ambitiously carrying three ice cream cones through the parking lot, one of which is about to topple over at any second. "I don't know. I keep telling myself I was too homesick and drunk to make sound decisions. It's the only explanation." Had this not been my first introduction back to the dating scene, I have a feeling I wouldn't be taking this so hard. But being vulnerable and putting myself out there for the first time in forever, only to have a date crash and burn, does little to renew my hope for the future. "He assumed I asked him out for 'closure.'" I put air quotes around *closure*, half-mauled burger in my right hand, two fries in my left.

"Did you?"

69

"Well, yes. But he was just so . . . presumptuous. When I asked why he stopped talking to me, he said it was because I was too 'clingy' and 'crazy.' Can you believe he called me *crazy*?" I demand. "In fact, he said, and I quote, 'The hotter the girl, the crazier she is.' He even tweeted about it. Hashtagged #CrazyExGirlfriend." I slide my phone over with the screenshots of Jeff's tweets for Trevor's perusal.

He roots through them quickly, unimpressed. "You can rest easy knowing he only got three likes, one of which was him liking his own tweet."

"I kind of want to respond, give him a piece of my mind," I mutter darkly, drumming my fingers together as I consider scorching comebacks and accompanying threatening GIFs.

Trevor tentatively clears his throat after a slurp of his milkshake. "I don't think responding is a good idea. It'll only reinforce his opinion of you."

"That I'm crazy?"

"Exactly."

I wait a couple of beats and narrow my gaze at him. "Do *you* think I'm crazy?"

"I wouldn't use the term 'crazy.' But . . ."

"But what?" I snap. Do I care whether Trevor thinks I'm hot and/or crazy? *Certainly not.*

"You made a hit list of exes to pursue. And you made friends with my one-night stand and called her *marriage material*." He safely sticks to the *crazy* side of things, and I'm a little relieved.

"Gabby *is* marriage material."

He ignores that statement. "I mean, let's look at the facts. You also keyed one ex's car."

"I can't bear that cross my whole life, Metcalfe. I was fifteen. Give me a break. You sound like Segway Jeff." I roll my eyes dismissively. "Also, it's offensive and demeaning to be written off as crazy. Especially given the stigma of mental health. And maybe the real issue here is that some men can't confront their emotions. Instead of taking responsibility for your own behavior, it's easier to screw us, write us off as loons, and forget about us." I huff at the injustice, stuffing another handful of fries into my mouth like a goblin.

He considers that for a moment and frowns. "Point taken. You're right. But can you not admit that *people*, not just women, can act a little"—he looks to the ceiling, searching for the proper term—"intense sometimes?"

I toss my burger onto the tray and lean in. "If you're not *intense* and passionate once in a while, can you even call it love?"

"Sure can. It's called a mature, stable, adult relationship," he says, elongating each syllable like I'm a small child.

"And you would know from personal experience?" My tone drips with sarcasm as I wait for him to tell me about Angie, the love of his life.

Instead, he fires laser beams at me as he carefully folds his empty fry container. "I've had two serious relationships, thank you."

I hold out my hand, making a grabby-hands motion for his phone. "Let's see them."

He makes me wait a few blinks before begrudgingly relinquishing his phone. His first ex, Natalie Lowry, is stunning. She looks like a literal angel with her belly-button-length coffee-colored beach waves. "She was my high school girlfriend," he tells me, promptly moving on to the next profile before I have the chance to press for backstory.

The second ex, Kyla Sheppard, is leggy, raven-haired, and reminds me a little of a younger Olivia Wilde. She's mid-laugh in every one of her Instagram photos, which tells me she likes to have a good time—or at least wants to give that illusion.

"You should reach out to them." I light up at the mere thought. "Maybe you and I could go on ex searches together."

"No. I don't want a girlfriend. Too much work." He turns his phone facedown on the table, abruptly putting an end to that suggestion; stacks our trays; and dumps our trash in the bin.

What about Angie? I want to ask. But I refrain, instead grabbing my jacket to follow him outside, into the parking lot. "Is that a Jane Austen quote? You're basically a walking example of romance."

Trevor flashes me a flirty smile as he unlocks his car with his key fob. "Please don't put me and romance in the same sentence."

I pretend to laugh, when in reality, I'm more confused about him than ever.

♥ chapter nine

I'S BEEN A week, and Angie's identity still remains an unsolved mystery. Then again, I haven't dared to come out and ask. Trevor and I haven't seen much of each other due to our shift schedules, aside from the odd run-in while one is coming home and the other is leaving. Besides, poking around his love life like a thirsty Hollywood tabloid reporter feels needlessly cruel.

In the meantime, I've developed a theory: Angie is a woman Trevor is in love with but can't have because she's already married or engaged, which would explain the secrecy. Maybe they're desperately in love but she's been forced into a marriage of convenience she can't escape.

After multiple back-to-back overtime shifts covering for all my colleagues who take time off for Thanksgiving, I'm off for the day, all by my lonesome, as Trevor is on day shift. Normally being alone for extended periods of time depresses me, but today I'm taking Mel's advice to soak up the quiet and partake in some self-care. This includes a bag of chips, a stack of my favorite books, my rom-com soundtrack playlist, my weighted blanket, and maybe a little quality time with my vibrator.

Because life likes to give me a kick in the ass when I get too smug, I'm in the midst of the latter when Trevor returns home, whistling.

Shit.

Here's the thing. I've made two grave errors. First, I've bought a louder-than-average vibrator (its volume is on par with a Dyson vacuum) with far too many fancy settings. Second, I failed to close my bedroom door, because Trevor wasn't supposed to be home for another hour and a half. Damn him.

Panicked and sweaty, I attempt to hit the *Off* button on my device, but of course I end up increasing the intensity instead.

Trevor is already in my doorway by the time I've managed to locate the *Off* button. "Is it just me, or are you in the exact same position I left you in this morning?" His question is completely casual. But in my hot, bothered, and frustrated state, my brain can't help but turn it sexual.

It doesn't help that he's in one of his tight-fitted navy-blue fire department T-shirts. It's one of ten identical ones he keeps folded Marie Kondo–style in his dresser. I lurch upward when he leans his weight against my doorframe, his hair flopped over like it's done with the day, one arm behind his back.

"You're home!" I squeak.

"Yeah. One of the guys came in for his shift early." He pauses, assessing me. "You feeling okay?"

I abandon my vibrator under the covers and run the back of my wrist over my forehead, which is definitely clammy. "Thriving. Never better!"

His brows raise in suspicion. "You sure? You look a little red and fevery. There's a flu going around, you know."

"I'd know if I had a fever. I'm a nurse." I make a show of testing my temperature again with my wrist. "No fever. Just a little warm with the weighted blanket."

"Right. Apologies, Nurse Chen." When he grins at me, none the wiser, all the tension and frustration from being interrupted dissipates. Lately we've been bantering back and forth about who is the more qualified health professional. Trevor, who is technically also a certified medic, is very sure of himself. "Looks like you had a relaxing day."

I shrug. "It was average. Kinda lonely, though, aside from my book boyfriends." *And my vibrator.*

"These will keep you company." He pulls his right arm from behind his back to reveal two Halloween-size bags of Cheetos in his right hand.

"Really? . . . For me?" I ask in awe.

He smirks, tossing the bags onto the end of my bed. "Who else? One of the guys at work brought in extras from his kid's Halloween stash. Grabbed them for you before the others swarmed."

"Oh my God. I love you," I blurt out, already ripping one of the bags open. When the crests of his cheeks turn a dark shade of red, I walk back my overt enthusiasm. "Um . . . you look tired."

His lips curve into a small smile. "Gee, thanks. You know how to make a guy blush."

"Save a lot of lives today?" I ask through a crunch.

He frowns again. "No. Lost a few, actually."

I cover my mouth, as if trying to stuff the words back in. "I'm so sorry. I didn't mean to joke about that—"

"It's all good, Tara," he assures me, waving my words away.

"No. I should know better, being in health care. It was a shitty thing to say."

"Seriously, it's fine. Did you hit your reading goals for the day?" I can tell by his abrupt change in subject and tone that he's not really interested in talking about his day, as usual. Even when he's in a decent mood, he gets uncomfortable whenever I ask him questions about himself.

"Sure did," I say proudly, gesturing to my book pile animatedly, trying to sound extra upbeat in an effort to lighten his mood, even just a little. Whenever I had rough days at work where we'd lose patients, Seth wouldn't offer much support, instead telling me to *suck it up* because that was just the job. I always wished he'd make more of an effort to take my mind off things. "I got through two and a half books today, and it's been therapeutic."

"Whatcha reading now? Still on the Mafia romance?" he asks, leaning forward to get a glimpse of my book cover.

"Nope. Done with that series. This is one of my favorites," I say, lighting up at the prospect of sharing. "A country singer who's forced to go on tour with her ex, a sexy, broody guitarist."

"Second-chance romance?" he guesses. It's a game we started playing, where he guesses the trope based on a one-line description.

I mock surprise. "You're getting good at this. This one is also a forced proximity. They have to travel together on a tour bus. It's pretty hot."

He raises a curious brow as he takes a couple of steps into my room to rearrange my bookshelf again. "Yeah?"

I flip a few chapters back to a particularly steamy scene involving the kitchen counter and hand it to him. "You may relate to this one."

He sits on the end of my bed to read, the mattress sinking underneath his weight. His nostrils flare as he scans the page. "Basically it's written porn? But with no visuals."

I pluck the book from his hands and bop him on the shoulder with it. "You don't need visuals when you have your imagination. Besides, porn usually caters to the male gaze. Doesn't really do much for a lot of women."

"Of course. The emotional connection is key," he says sarcastically, reaching into my lap to open the second Cheetos bag.

I suck in a sharp breath when his hand paws dangerously close to my vibrator hidden under my covers. Before he accidently touches it, I shift it over with my leg and it falls with a clatter down the crack between the wall and my bed.

"What was that?" Trevor asks.

"Oh, nothing. Just a book. No big deal." I shrug it off, while internally I'm screaming and praying it hasn't skidded out from under my bed. I even peer over the edge to confirm.

His eyes flicker with something that looks like suspicion, so I ramble on as a distractive measure.

"Feel free to borrow my books anytime, by the way. Maybe you could learn a thing or two. Pick up a few tips and tricks to use in your relationships going forward," I offer teasingly.

He snorts. "What relationships?"

"Come on, you can't really want to spend your life alone."

"Being alone is my favorite," he says ultraseriously, crunching a Cheeto. "Days off when you're at work are the fucking best. I get the couch and the TV all to myself without you chatting my ear off in the background."

I launch a weak punch in his side. "Wow, shots fired. I'll try to make myself scarcer."

He cracks a small smile. "I'm just kidding, Chen. You're not too bad to be around . . ." Our eyes snag for a beat too long before he adds, "when you're not all frazzled, hunting down your exes."

I straighten my shoulders, ignoring the heat gathering in my neck, getting hotter and hotter the longer he smiles at me like that. From the edge of my bed where I was just . . .

"How goes the search, anyways?" Trevor asks.

Truthfully, I've been too busy with work the past week to put emotional effort into the ex search. Until today. "I'm now focusing on Brandon Wang. Sent him a message this morning, though he hasn't responded . . . yet," I note with a grimace. "He's one of my college boyfriends."

"All right. What's the story with Brandon?"

"We were just friends at the beginning of college," I say, finding myself smiling at the memory of him. "I always had a little crush on him, but I didn't act on it because he had a long-term girlfriend from high school. He broke up with her going into junior year, and a week later, we made out at a campus pub trivia night. After being in such a long-term relationship, he was really against putting a label on things, which drove me nuts. I mean, not knowing whether I was his *girlfriend* or not was so stressful. Do I list him as my emergency contact? Do I put him in my will? These are things any sane, responsible human needs to know."

Trevor covers his unapologetic laugh with his fist.

I reach over to give him a swift smack on the biceps, which frankly feels like hitting a metal pole. "Then things ended on a . . . dramatic note."

"Dramatic?"

"He wanted to travel the globe after college before settling down. He wanted me to go with him, and I didn't."

"Really? Why?"

"I'm not great with unfamiliar places. Plane crash movies traumatized me," I explain. "Airports freak me out too. The last time I was in one, I got arrested by airport police," I admit, raising a bitter brow.

Inspired by *Love Actually* and *Crazy Rich Asians*, I tried my hand at an airport grand gesture. Turns out, one can only evade airport security in the movies, lest you pay $850 for a ticket just to confess your love in front of hundreds of sleep-deprived travelers.

This juicy tidbit of my past thrills Trevor. He descends into a fit of deep laughter as I explain how my ill-fated adventure resulted in hours of interrogation in a tiny, dimly lit room until the border officers finally believed I was an innocent, hopelessly-in-love girl and not some crazed terrorist. To this day, Brandon remains blissfully unaware of my airport arrest on his behalf.

"Okay, this is worse than I thought."

"Look, if you attempted an airport grand gesture, everyone would say it was so romantic. But it's *crazy* when *I* do it."

He regards me like I'm a walking *Caution* sign. "Maybe you should approach dating more casually."

"I can't just hook up with someone casually."

"Why not? It's just sex."

When he says *sex*, my face flushes like I'm a prepubescent teen in health class, all giddy over some anatomy word like *labia*. I'm not sure if it's the fact that he's sitting an arm's length away from me, on my bed, but looking him in the eyes feels dangerous, vulnerable, like I'm staring into a solar eclipse, a second away from burning my retinas.

"You've never had casual sex?" His question comes out gruff.

My silence reveals me.

"Seriously? Never?" When I don't respond, he points at me. "I have a theory about you."

"Please enlighten me."

"You're obsessed with the idea of pursuing your exes because you're scared to meet someone new."

I scoff. "I'm not scared to meet someone new."

"Why do you only read books you've already read?" he challenges, gesturing to my bookshelf, filled with the worn and cracked spines of well-loved books.

"Slander. I read new books sometimes. But if you must know why I reread, it's because I already know I like them. I know how they end."

His eyes glitter with satisfaction. "See? You don't like new things. Same with food and traveling. You also hold on to things, like literal garbage from your exes, for example."

I ignore his weirdly accurate assessment. "It's not garbage. They're priceless, sentimental relics. And I can't just have sex with randoms, okay? Not everyone can turn their feelings off at the drop of a hat."

"It's really not *that* intimate. Just don't allow your mind to go there." He says it so casually, like it's second nature.

I lean forward, mattress creaking. "Can I ask you a serious question?"

He grumbles, and I mentally scold myself for the reflex. I keep forgetting how much he hates that question.

"Is a happily ever after really so terrifying to you?"

He holds eye contact for a couple of moments before standing, putting space between us. "Yes."

When I boldly ask, "Have you ever considered therapy?" his jaw tics.

Before I can discern whether he's pissed, amused, or soul searching, my phone vibrates on my bedside table.

BRANDON WANG: Hey, Tara. Thanks for the message. How are you doing?

My heart thuds against my chest wall. When I gasp for dramatic effect, Trevor leans in, shoulder brushing against mine as he reads my text. He watches as my fingers fly over my keyboard.

"Why are you typing your response in your Notes app?" he whispers in my ear, as though Brandon is in earshot.

"Because if I type in the text window, he'll see I'm typing. Ellipses are a sign of weakness," I whisper back conspiratorially. "And what if my thumb slips and I accidently send an unfinished message? Or an unedited message filled with typos?" When I'm done drafting my response, I pass my phone to him for peer review.

Hi Brandon!! Wow it's so nice to hear from you. I've been thinking a lot about you lately, wondering how you've been and if you're traveling anywhere. I miss you and was wondering if you want to go for a drink, or lunch, or dinner, or brunch? I'd be down for any of the aforementioned. If you can't, or if you're out of the country, that's totally cool too. But it would be great to catch up!! 🙂 🙂

Trevor's eyes incinerate the block of text. "No. No. No."

"What's wrong with that?" Before I can take my phone back, he tightens his grip and stands, holding it out of reach.

"You've lost custody of your phone. And the fact that you don't know what's wrong with that text scares me a little," he says, his tone clipped. "He will run far, far away if you send this."

"He won't. He's the definition of a nice guy."

"Nice guy?"

"Like . . . he's the kind of guy who answers telemarketing calls and ends up trapped on the phone for an hour because he feels too guilty hanging up."

"Sounds like a man with no backbone."

"Anyway, I don't subscribe to these manipulative *play it cool* bullshit games. Besides, Brandon knows me. He knows I have feelings, and lots of them."

Trevor runs his hand over his steel-cut jaw. "Look, all I'm saying is sometimes you can be . . . a little forward."

"Being forward isn't a bad thing. Am I supposed to pretend to be mysterious? Like the cool chick who acts like a bro, goes with the flow, and has no emotional needs?"

"I didn't say that. But you need to ease into it a little before you send him full-screen-length texts." He hands my phone back.

"I don't ease into things, Trevor. I go balls to the wall. With everything I do," I say, standing to match his height.

"Look, do you want to score a second chance or not?" he asks, making his way to my doorway.

"Obviously."

"Then trust me. Just wait a bit and think out your response properly," he instructs.

"Wait for how long? You know I have no patience."

"Just an hour."

"That might as well be an eternity."

"Come on. We'll clean the kitchen while we wait." When I give him scary eyes, he adds, "We can make cupcakes. I'll show you how to make them from scratch so you don't have to waste money buying that boxed crap."

I raise a brow. "You know how to bake from scratch?"

"Let's find out," he says, and I swear there's a twinkle in his eye.

• • •

AND FOR THAT hour, I forget all about messaging Brandon back.

Turns out, Trevor decided we're making lemon cupcakes with raspberry icing. He's not a Parisian pastry chef by any means, and he notes we put too much flour in the batter, but he knows his way around a kitchen. It's unexpected, and frankly a little unfair.

"These are life-changing," I say through a mouthful, placing the remainder neatly in a Tupperware container.

"You should send your grandma a picture and tell her they're from scratch. She'll be proud."

I shrug. "I dunno. She thinks the reason I'm still single is because I can't cook or bake. Do you think that's true?"

As he loads the dirty dishes into the dishwasher, he chuckles softly. "Tara, this isn't 1950. And for the record, you can bake. You followed all the directions. I think you just have it in your head that you can't do it."

He's not wrong. When I first started dating Seth, I'd started getting more adventurous in the kitchen, trying different recipes I found on Pinterest just to impress him, even though they included ingredients I didn't like. But no matter how hard I tried to stretch myself out of my comfort zone, he was unsatisfied with everything I made, claiming the food was too simple. *It has no flavor* was his favorite thing to say to me when I'd try a new recipe. Eventually, I just stopped trying altogether. I want to explain that to Trevor, but frankly, I'm embarrassed I put up with Seth's crap for so long.

"Who taught you how to bake?" I ask.

His jaw tightens as he bends down to close the dishwasher. "My grandma."

"That's really adorable. Were you close with her?" A grin spreads over my face as I picture a seven-year-old Trevor in a frilly apron, icing cupcakes next to a sweet little white-haired lady.

"I guess so." I stare at him hopefully, waiting for him to elaborate on his childhood, but he doesn't. Instead, he says, "We do a lot of cooking and baking at the firehouse too. Learned a lot there."

"Oh yeah? Like group meals?"

"Yup. We make most meals together every day. One of the guys on my shift used to be a chef in the military, so he takes food pretty seriously. The other day he made homemade ricotta gnocchi with pancetta, and crème brûlée for dessert."

"Damn. That's fine dining. Are you guys hiring?" I ask half-jokingly, leaning a hip against the island.

The corner of his mouth tugs upward into a half smile. "We're always accepting applications. Think you have what it takes? You'd have to be able to lift and carry about two hundred pounds."

I make a *pfft* sound. "Easy enough. I'm stronger than I look from hauling around books my whole life," I lie.

He gestures to himself. "Okay, let's see. Try lifting me."

"Like, actually pick you up from the ground?" I squeak.

"Yup. If you're as strong as you say, it should be no problem."

It's an impossible feat for my weakling body. I know this. Surely he knows it too. But something about Trevor brings out my playful side. Putting a smile on his usually stone-serious face has become one of my favorite tasks. And I'm always up for the challenge. Being the cause of those crinkle lines around his eyes and that deep, bellowing laugh gives me a high like no other.

To his amusement, I make a show of cracking my knuckles and bending my knees to loosen my joints, like a senior citizen warming up for tai chi in the park. He sucks in a sharp breath, bracing himself when I wrap my arms around his torso. While his spicy scent is an energy booster, he's a solid mass of muscle that's virtually unmovable. I attempt multiple times, even restrategizing the angle, squatting to lift him from under the bum, to no avail.

On the fifth try, he sets his hands over my shoulders and squeezes gently to stop me. I don't blame him. I've made this awkward. My forearms are folded snug under his ass and my entire front is pressed into his. "All right, Chen. You're gonna throw your back out."

"Yup. This isn't happening," I say, wincing as I straighten my spine. "In my defense, you're a giant, probably much larger than the average person who needs rescuing. And what I lack in strength, I'd make up for in bravery on the job."

He smiles. "I bet you would. Oh, and you have—uh—some flour—" He points in the vague direction of my face before reaching to brush it from my cheek. The gentleness of the swipe and the warmth of his thumb catch me off guard. My breath hitches when his eyes snag mine. They're a whirl of darkness pierced by flashes of gold, reflecting from the dim light above us, swirling with all the many things he keeps locked away.

Our eye contact breaks when my phone vibrates against the counter, pulling me back to reality, stopping my overactive mind in its tracks. Trevor steps back a few paces, his shoulders dropping in what looks like relief as he pops the container of cupcakes in the microwave for safekeeping (his grandma's trick to keep them fresh).

Before I have the chance to scold myself for making things weird with my prolonged eye contact, I see Brandon has texted again, preemptively, even without my planned response.

BRANDON: Want to catch up? There's a cool new mini putt
bar downtown I want to try out.

Trevor's smug-ass smile has me regretting showing him Brandon's follow-up text in the first place.

"This was a one-off, by the way," I point out, still in shock over Brandon's response as we head down the hallway to our respective bedrooms.

"You just can't handle the fact that I knew something about dating that you didn't," he says, pausing in my doorway.

I catch myself staring at the swoop of the bird's wing partially visible under his collar. I promptly snap my focus back to my phone. Back to Brandon. "Okay, dating guru, what do I say now?"

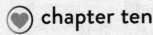 **chapter ten**

LIVE WITH TARAROMANCEQUEEN—THE ONE THAT
GOT AWAY

EXCERPT FROM TRANSCRIPT

[Tara sits crisscross applesauce on her bed, cradling a worn mass-market paperback like a newborn baby. The ex-boyfriend link chart is out of focus in the background.]

TARA: *Hello, romance book lovers, welcome back to my channel. Today we're talking about the One That Got Away.*

The One That Got Away is potentially one of the most tragic of all tropes. I'm hesitant to call it a romance trope, because more often than not, it ends in death and tears. It's related to second-chance romance and comes in many forms. It could be two lovers who get split up during war and famine, unable to find each other. Maybe one party disappears behind magical stones, two hundred years into the future, where they belong.

If you close your eyes right now, I bet a face comes to mind. It's someone you wonder about every so often. Someone you have to stop yourself from drunk texting, perhaps? You often wonder what could have been? Maybe you're already fully aware that you're missing this long-lost someone, which prevents you from moving forward in your life.

This is Brandon Wang for me.

Anyway, I've gotta finish getting ready. I'm about to meet him for drinks in an hour. If anyone has any advice or favorite One That Got Away books, let me know in the comments!

COMMENTS:

OMG he is HOT. Doesn't he look like Daniel Dae Kim?   ♡

My date advice is to ditch Brandon and date your roommate.   ♡
This is what we deserve!!

• • •

"CAN I ASK you a question?" I ask.

Trevor shoots me a one-eyed warning glare, evidently and understandably peeved that I've barged into his room without notice. When I flick the light switch, he covers his eyes like a vampire who's deathly allergic to the sun. "Have you ever heard of knocking?"

"I did you a favor. You're gonna mess up your schedule if you sleep any longer." He's been sleeping off his night shift, and I've been impatiently waiting for him to wake up for hours.

I'm due to meet Brandon in T-minus forty-five minutes, and I need a pep talk.

"What the hell are you wearing?" he asks through splayed fingers.

Miffed, I run my finger over the high waistband of my wrinkled, wide-leg linen pants. "My date outfit, thank you very much."

While plotting my ensemble on the subway ride home from work, I had a momentary freak-out and made a pit stop at Gabby's, Trevor's hookup and my new friend, to pillage her closet. As it turns out, she owns tons of handmade pieces collected from all over the globe, all of which have some elaborate story. These pants were hand-sewn by a ninety-year-old woman in the Tibetan mountains who has nearly lost her sight.

Trevor rests against the headboard and tilts his head, studying me from every angle like I'm an abstract museum painting. "No."

I scoff, my hands on my hips. "This is traveler chic. They're Gabby's, actually."

"Why are you wearing Gabby's clothes for your date?"

"Because . . . she's a world traveler, just like Brandon." As the son of diplomat parents, Brandon is well traveled. He speaks five languages. He's spent winters skiing in the Swiss Alps, summers riding camels through deserts in Morocco. You name it, he's done it all, three times.

Even though I take after Dad with my "gift of gab," as Mom likes to call it, what if Brandon dubs me an uncultured swine? What if things take a turn for the horribly awkward, like they did with Segway Jeff? What if he's nothing like I remember? What if I panic and ask for his hand in marriage?

As the horrifying possibilities besiege me, so does a potential solution. "Metcalfe?"

"Yes?" Trevor asks, slow and tentative, as if dreading my response.

"I really do need to ask you a question."

• • •

GRANDMA FLO WAS absolutely right. Men get better with age. At least, Brandon Wang certainly has.

His face was etched by the gods. How else can you explain his perfectly proportioned features? The enchanting dark-chocolate eyes I want to stare into longer than appropriate? Or the naturally blemish- and pore-free skin that looks airbrushed in person? If that wasn't unfair enough, he also has the sun-kissed tan of someone who's spent many a day experiencing the world. He certainly hasn't been rotting on the couch scrolling through Netflix's romance section, pretending he hasn't already watched every film five times (not that I'd know from personal experience).

We're seated in a turquoise booth, struggling to hear each other over the fifties tunes blasting over the sound system. He's practically glowing like in his current profile photo (a flattering shot of his sunburned self, grinning in front of an ornate temple in Thailand).

Brandon leans in like he's going to tell me a secret. "Can you believe it's been over ten years since we first met?"

My insides blossom with nostalgia. "God, no. It feels like just yesterday we were pulling all-nighters, hitting up the twenty-four-hour grocery store for those giant tubs of Neapolitan ice cream."

He mocks a retch. "That stuff was revolting. Especially the strawberry. I can't believe we ate like that. Nowadays, my body can't take it."

"It's all downhill after thirty, Bran. Or so I've heard," I say. I roll up the sleeves of my cardigan as the waiter with a Mr. Monopoly mustache drops a heaping plate of loaded nachos in front of us.

Polite as ever, Brandon waits for me to pull my first cheesy nacho from the top of the pile before methodically selecting his. As expected, he chooses a relatively plain one, which he smothers in sour cream. "Oh, definitely. I used to be able to fall asleep anywhere. I can't get a lick of shut-eye on planes anymore. Or any old pullout cot at a hostel. I'm a princess now," he says through a crunchy bite, massaging his neck for emphasis.

A grin spreads across my face upon recollection of the many instances when he fell asleep in the library, mid–study session. "You're basically a geriatric. Are you sure you can handle a round of mini putt without throwing out your back?" I joke.

"Oh, don't worry about me. I can hack it. Hope you practiced your swing." He cracks his knuckles, making a show of competitive spirit before peering at the nearest putting hole to our right. It's a *Star Wars*–themed hole with rotating lightsabers ready to block incoming balls.

Putters bar is admittedly an appropriate date spot, with the retro black-and-white-checkered floor and charming neon signage. It's located in a huge warehouse consisting of three massive mini-golf courses alongside two designated food and drink areas. Unlike a typical Astroturf course, each hole is a callback to a famous movie or television show. Behind the *Star Wars* hole, there's a partially obscured Dorothy from the *Wizard of Oz* at the end of a yellow brick road.

As I strain to see the other holes from my vantage point, I catch Trevor's eye. After much groveling and empty promises to be his personal chef for a week, he agreed to leave the supreme comfort of his bed to accompany me. Of course, he's subtly seated one booth down. To Brandon and any other patron, he's just a random dude. Little does anyone know, he's my moral support, at the ready to ensure I don't say anything I regret.

But the longer I talk to Brandon, the more I realize I didn't require backup after all. Turns out, my memory isn't totally unreliable. Brandon is as delightful and outgoing as he always was—practically a walking eharmony ad. He asks all the right questions, makes just the perfect amount of eye contact, nods at all the appropriate times. And every time he smiles, my heart does ten consecutive somersaults. I want a custom-embroidered pillow with his face on it. That got admittedly creepy, real fast. Why am I like this?

Like the precious creature he is, he's letting me scrounge all the cheesiest nachos for myself. It's reminiscent of long nights in the campus library studying for finals. Brandon and I would combine snacks. He'd bring sweet, and I'd bring salty. Candy bags from the corner store were his go-to, and he always saved the fruity ones for me, knowing I didn't like the other kinds.

As we plow through the nachos, Brandon tells me he's still traveling the world, all while doing freelance website design remotely. Despite the success of his business, he still craves the "authentic" travel experience, preferring to stay in hostels. He obliges me with some hostel horror stories, including mentions of cock-roaches and bedbug infestations. His dream is to live in a tiny hut over the water in a tropical paradise, without a cell phone or foot-wear. I try to envision that life for myself, to no avail.

"So where'd you get those pants?" he asks, leaning sideways to peek at them under the table. "They're so unique. My friend has a similar pair from Nepal."

My lips part, but zero sound comes out. Behind Brandon's shoulder, Trevor gives me a self-satisfied *I told you so* smirk while merrily sipping his beer. He promptly goes back to flirting with the cute blond waitress who's been chatting him up since we arrived.

Thankfully, the mustached waiter saves me before I dig myself a deep grave and blurt out a lie. He hands us our putters and golf balls and rattles off a brief description of each course. Brandon thanks him and remarks how he himself can't grow a mustache to save his life, quickly winning the waiter over with his natural, self-deprecating charm.

When the waiter leaves, there's a moment of film-worthy per-fection when Brandon and I just stare at each other, grinning, high off the memories of our younger selves. I almost wish someone would snap a photo of us in this moment. It would be the perfect movie or book cover.

We decide to start on the course labeled *Intermediate*. I'm not sure if it's the alcohol or a fairy godmother above, but I sink the first *Jaws*-themed hole in one go.

"We have a pro over here!" Brandon announces, chuckling at my mini happy dance.

We spend our time between holes reminiscing about college. He fills me in on what some of our old friends are up to, and I do the same. Cheat sheet: They're all married and having children. Except for us. Despite that depressing fact, Brandon's presence puts me at ease, so much so that I don't even know why I dragged poor Trevor along in the first place.

Halfway through, I loosen up and order a Bellini. Three drinks later, we're at the last hole, doubled over, belly-laughing as we recount a particularly messy night in residence that resulted in one of our friends sleeping in an orphaned grocery store cart in the parking lot (he's now a father and a tech millionaire). Brandon offers a celebratory high five as we return our putters. No wonder I got myself arrested by airport police for this guy.

I flash Trevor a stealth thumbs-up on our way back to the booth, silently giving him permission to leave if he so chooses. But he doesn't. He continues nursing his beer.

"Have you done any traveling since college?" Brandon asks, sipping his new drink.

His question is like an abrupt scratch on a record player. I mumble a low "No, not yet." This elicits a frown. "I've been super busy with work," I clarify, like that's the sole reason.

Brandon's face lights up with renewed curiosity. "There's always tons of jobs open for nurses at the Red Cross. You should totally look into it. It would give you so many opportunities to see the world, all while making bank."

"Really?" The very idea is disturbing, and yet my desire to please him compels me to keep going. "I'd love to do something like that. Or just take a couple of months off, pack my life into a suitcase, and hop on the first flight I can find," I say with the casual, dismissive air of a socialite who globe-trots via private jet at her whimsy, monogrammed Louis Vuitton luggage in tow.

He drums the table with his knuckles enthusiastically. "Why not? I mean, what's stopping you?"

Besides my extreme fear of flying? My aversion to the unfamiliar? My mountain of debt?

"Nothing, I suppose." I mentally slap myself as the words roll off my tongue with far too much ease. My gaze drifts from Brandon's face, catching Trevor behind him. He's wide-eyed, frantically making a cross with his arms, mouthing, *No*.

I ignore him, refocusing on Brandon, who's passionately describing his upcoming three-month trip to Indonesia to spend some time in Borneo. Deep in the rain forest at Sepilok.

"What's Sepilok?" I ask, my jaw tensing.

"An orangutan sanctuary where they teach young orphans how to live in the wild. I was there a couple of years ago, and it changed my life. Orangutans are so humanlike. So sentient. It's incredible. I think you'd absolutely love it."

What would ever give him the impression I would love that? Does he actually know me at all? "I mean, it sounds . . . cool." I pretend to nod with interest, while plagued by graphic images of the woman who made international news after a monkey tore off her face.

"We could even go to Bali, check out some of the smaller, underrated islands. They don't get enough credit."

While the thought of lying on a warm beach with Brandon sounds like heaven, I still can't get past the flying. And the monkeys. But for some ridiculous reason, I say, "Let's do it."

Behind Brandon, Trevor buries his face in both hands.

"You're really in?" Brandon beams with affection. "You're so different than you were in college."

I perch my elbows on the table and smile. Now that I've started this persona, I can't seem to stop. "Yeah. I mean, it sounds like the trip of a lifetime."

"I gotta say, I was shocked when you reached out. What made you think of me?"

A series of unfortunate events in my love life, obviously. And I'm about to tell him so, until my phone lights up with a text.

TREVOR: Don't tell him about the ex search unless he already knows.

I had no intention of hiding the search from Brandon, considering it's broadcasted all over my public social media account. But Trevor's warning throws me off my game. Will Brandon think I'm nuts? Just like the others?

"Oh, uh, just thinking about college," I stammer, groping for the nearest napkin to shred.

Brandon smiles, delving into a long-winded monologue about all our prospective adventures, including jetting over to Thailand to spend a week at an elephant sanctuary.

"So, after all the excitement of traveling, what's next for you?" I ask at the first opportunity, convincing myself that I could stomach traveling if it means the two of us settling into a detached home with a sprawling lawn near my parents, or maybe across the street from Crystal and Scott's future home. Brandon and Scott would get along swimmingly.

The crease between his brows deepens. "Do you mean where to after Indonesia? Probably Peru, or—"

My heart sinks like an anchor. "Oh? Are you not planning to settle back down in Boston?"

"Why would I stay in Boston?" He's genuinely confused.

"Well, you're thirty. Don't you want to settle down soon? Have kids?"

Trevor is giving me his urgent horror-movie eyes again, as if I've just asked Brandon to divulge his Social Security number.

Brandon notices my pointed glare at Trevor and glances over his shoulder. Trevor abruptly averts his eyes, suddenly taking a supreme interest in the salt and pepper shakers.

Brandon swings back to me, confused and probably questioning his own sanity. "Uh . . . Probably not. You?"

"I mean, yeah. That's always been the goal. Marriage and kids in my early thirties."

I barely have time to register Brandon's indifferent shrug, because Trevor coughs, half choking on his drink.

Brandon turns, concerned. "That guy is choking."

"Nah, he's fine," I say, waving his worry away with my mangled napkin, which resembles a worn flag that's been shredded in a gruesome medieval battle.

Brandon isn't convinced, and I'm not shocked. He's always had a Good Samaritan complex, which attracted me to him in the first place. One time, we missed our dinner reservation because he insisted on helping a stranded woman on the side of the freeway change her tire, despite not knowing how.

He peers over his shoulder once again. "You okay, buddy? We have a nurse over here." He points at me, preemptively offering my services.

Trevor hits his chest with his fist like a macho marine. "All good, man. Thanks."

Satisfied that the stranger in the booth behind us is not having a medical emergency, Brandon turns his attention back to me. "Sorry, what were we talking about?"

Before I can offer a response, a new text comes through.

TREVOR: Meet me in the bathroom NOW.

I let out a tortured sigh, scooting out of the booth. "Be right back. Just going to the restroom."

"No worries. Take your time," Brandon says cheerfully, clearly relieved that the topic of children has come to an abrupt end.

Trevor is pacing in the dingy narrow hallway outside the bathrooms, his fingers linked behind his head. "What the hell are you doing?"

"I'm just having a casual conversation. Why are you freaking out?"

He huffs. "You brought up children."

I scoff, as if I haven't already named our three unborn daughters. "Look, I hate small talk. It's not my vibe. And it's not like he's a stranger. He's an ex. When we broke up, he said maybe things could work out in the future. I'm trying to find out where he's at."

Trevor eyes me sideways. "No. It's way too soon for that conversation. He's about to hurl himself off the nearest ledge."

"He invited me on a three-month trip. How is it too soon?" I frown. "I don't want to just hook up or casually see each other. I'm putting it all out on the table."

"And then some," he grumbles, partially distracted by the waitress he's been seducing all evening. She gives him a flirty smile, thick high ponytail swaying, expertly balancing a tray of pizza. He returns her smile briefly before turning back to me with a scowl. "You're not seriously going to follow him on that rain forest excursion, are you? I thought you said you hate traveling. And what about work?"

I immediately shut down Trevor's pessimism. "You know what? You should just go hang with that waitress. You're distracting me, and I don't need your unsolicited two cents."

"My two cents was solicited, actually. Do you not remember begging me to come with you? To make sure you don't mess this up? To save you from yourself?"

"I appreciate it, but I need to do this my way. I need to know if I'm wasting my time." Before he can protest, I spin on my heel and march back to the booth.

The glimmer in Brandon's eyes when he spoke about travel has now dulled. In fact, his expression is generally serious, like it used to be five minutes before exam time. He smiles when I settle across from him, but the joy doesn't quite reach his eyes. This date has officially taken a turn for the worse.

"I just don't know if I see myself settling down and having kids, to be honest. I don't want to waste your time," he finally confesses.

My stomach bottoms out. While I respect his decision, I've always clung to the eventuality of having children. Visions of Brandon and me living a fabulous life in the suburbs all but evaporate. "Really? I mean, I guess I just thought when we broke up the first time that you'd be ready, sometime in the future."

His face looks pained. A heavy silence fills the space between us as we sip the rest of our respective drinks. In fact, Brandon is chugging his like he's dying of thirst. Then he twirls his glass, dragging the puddle of condensation around the table in a figure eight. "Sorry, Tara. You're a great girl. Honestly, the best. I love spending time together. I just . . . I'm not looking to settle down in one place with a family and white picket fence. And if you're still remotely the same girl you were in college, it wouldn't be fair of me to give you false hope and lead you on."

The chaos of mini putters and bar patrons blurs around me as I struggle to recover from his truth bomb. There's nothing I can do but let out a strained laugh, which sounds reminiscent of an injured whale stranded on the beach.

Another one bites the dust.

1. *Daniel (childhood love)*
2. ~~*Tommy (ninth-grade boyfriend)*~~
3. ~~*Jacques (Student Senate boy)*~~
4. *Cody (high school sweetheart)*
5. ~~*Jeff (frosh week fling)*~~
6. *Zion (campus bookstore cutie)*
7. ~~*Brandon (world traveler—the one that got away)*~~
8. *Linus (Brandon rebound)*
9. *Mark (book club intellectual)*
10. ~~*Seth (ex-fiancé)*~~

♥ chapter eleven

T WAS SO close. He was so close to being perfect." I pace frantically in the empty space between the living room and the kitchen, replaying the night with Brandon. In the end, we parted ways amicably. He forcefully insisted on paying the bill out of pure pity before leaving me with a lackluster kiss to the forehead.

Trevor cringes at me from the stool at the island. "Stop pacing. You're making me dizzy. And I think the best course of action here is to put the teddy bear away and go to bed." Why is he so responsible?

My pacing quickens, as well as my grip on the stuffed teddy bear Brandon bought for me so many Valentine's Days ago. "Nah. I'd prefer to overanalyze and pinpoint the moment it all went up in flames. For future reference. So I don't keep messing things up."

A hint of a smile plays across his lips. "I have been known to put out a flame or two. Anything I can do to help?"

I'm touched by the offer, but at this point, I've already dug my own grave halfway to the earth's core. "Not unless you can turn back time."

He stands from the stool. "I may have something."

"Do you have some sort of secret time-traveling wardrobe?" I ask hopefully, following him into the hallway.

"Obviously. Doesn't everyone?"

I'm puzzled when he stops outside my bedroom door and points to the mess of clothes on the floor. "If you're about to try to convince me that cleaning is therapeutic, I might punch—"

"Be quiet and put your bathing suit on," he orders before disappearing into his bedroom, closing the door behind him.

"My bathing suit?" I call.

"Yup."

I blink, dumbfounded. "Is this some weird sexual ploy? Are you trying to hook up with me right now?"

He makes a *tsk* sound, like the idea is absurd. "God, no."

I'm too busy freaking the hell out about wearing a swimsuit in front of another human being, let alone a ridiculously attractive human being with the body of a god. Insecurities aside, my curiosity has spiked, so I swallow my pride and throw on my trusty floral one-piece and fluffy bathrobe.

Trevor is waiting at the front door when I emerge, clad in navy-blue swim trunks, a black T-shirt, and . . . army-green Crocs.

It takes all my willpower to resist laughing and pointing like a child, and he can tell, based on his death glare. He's silently daring me to comment, and of course, I do.

"I didn't take you for a puttering-around-in-Crocs kinda guy," I say, following him out the door.

He grunts, leading me up the stairwell. "They're practical."

"I would advise you not to wear those in public. Especially in front of women, if you want to get laid," I say, failing to muffle my snort-laughter.

"Does it look like I need help getting laid?" he asks over his shoulder.

I swallow. *Definitely not.*

Not three minutes later, Trevor and I are wrapped in flimsy towels, teeth chattering, freezing our asses off on the roof. This rooftop is nothing like one of those fancy high-rises with a lush garden and pergola draped with twinkle lights. It's sparse, with an ancient covered barbecue and some rickety, cobweb-infested lawn chairs. Luckily, the building is too low to take the brunt of the harsh wind.

I'm shivering so violently, I don't even stop to admire the picturesque view of the dilapidated four-story directly to our left. Confused and wildly annoyed, I'm about to flee back inside when Trevor nudges me to the right. Behind a massive rusted square structure housing an exhaust fan is something unexpected.

A hot tub.

It's randomly placed. Kind of like the hot tubs that magically appear at opportune moments on *The Bachelor*. Surrounded by a plastic deck area and a bench, the hot tub itself is tiny. I'd guess it seats a maximum capacity of four people, and even that's pushing it. I lean over to inspect. It's ancient, but void of gross hairs and questionable debris. And if neurotic Trevor seems to think it's appropriate for use, it must be so.

"Hot tub time machine. It's a great place to overanalyze," Trevor announces, tossing his towel on the bench before pulling the cover off the hot tub. With every twist and stride, he emits a certain brand of dangerous energy in his wide, dominating, UFC-like stance. I imagine a toxic rock anthem partially drowned out by thunderous applause from a bloodthirsty live audience.

"Har-har, you are so clever," I say, holding my robe closed.

Trevor lowers himself chest-deep in the water, his eyes closed as the misty vapor coils upward, disappearing into the brisk air around him.

I hesitate to follow. Sure, I'm desperate to escape the frigid winter air in favor of the comfort of a warm bath, but the idea of sharing a pint-size hot tub with Trevor feels . . . intimate. Then again, we're merely platonic, opposite-sex roommates, right?

My lustful gaze traces the lines of his broad shoulders above the surface of the frothy water, roped with the dense, effortless muscle of a man who spends his days busting doors down. The uncalled-for image of him in full fire gear, emerging from a collapsing building engulfed in flame, hurtles through my mind. A young woman's limp body is draped across his arms like it's no big deal. Just a normal day in the life of Trevor Metcalfe.

"Get in before you freeze." His order snaps me back to reality.

Reflexively, my fingers clamp over the lapel of my robe, pulling it tighter, just teetering on the balls of my feet. He's surely judging me like I'm a socially inept weirdo who doesn't understand the mechanics of using a hot tub.

The very act of dropping my robe in front of him feels dangerous, a little illicit. I don't know if it's the mixture of trauma and alcohol from earlier, but it's kind of thrilling. Some forgotten, seductive side of me—my alter ego, if you will—takes over entirely. I'm basically a Miss USA contestant during the bikini round, strutting my hot bod down the runway in five-inch heels. The moment the lights hit me, I wow the judges with a sassy yet classy pose before removing my sarong (robe) with an expert flick of the wrist.

Unfortunately for Trevor, he missed the entire thing. By the time I dramatically drape my robe over the back of the chair, he's already closed his eyes, confirming that I'm a nonsexual being to him. I could be entirely nude, nipples out and about, and he probably couldn't be bothered to steal a glance. Or maybe he's so in love with Angie, he can't bear to set his eyes upon another woman's body.

Marginally comforted by this conclusion, I submerge myself as the jets start in a rumble of foamy bubbles. The heat envelops my body, contrasting the harsh chill.

Aside from the hum of the jets and the faint sound of traffic horns in the distance, it's surprisingly tranquil. It reminds me of that time I went to a high-class spa with Mom and Crystal on Mother's Day. I was nearly kicked out twice by an employee whose sole job was to walk around and shush people. Silence and I have never been more than distant acquaintances.

"I can't believe you didn't tell me about this top secret hot tub," I say.

Trevor squints at me through the mist, as though abruptly reminded of my presence. "Figured Scotty told you. And you never asked me about the amenities."

"Because I didn't think there were any. The building doesn't even have a working elevator."

"Well, now you know." When he closes his eyes again, I'm transfixed by the little bubbles of vapor on his unfairly thick lashes.

"This sucks balls," I whine, unable to stop dwelling on the night. I sink neck-deep in the tub, cozying against a jet. "Brandon was eighty percent there. I didn't have a ton of expectations for Jeff. But I had a good feeling about Brandon. I kind of expected things to fall into place."

"Hate to break it to you, but Brandon wasn't eighty percent," he tells me gruffly.

"He was." I stare upward to the inky black sky. "He and I get along so well. Always did. Back in college we spent hours together and never ran out of things to talk about. We're aligned on everything when it comes to morals and—"

"Fifty. Maximum," Trevor cuts in. "He didn't want the same things as you, period. What were you gonna do? Travel with him for months, hating your life, only to realize he doesn't want to settle down? It woulda been a big waste of time. You could be compatible as chocolate and peanut butter, but what does it matter if you don't want the same things?"

I do like chocolate and peanut butter. But that's neither here nor there. Why must Trevor make me confront harsh truths? Brandon and I didn't want the same things. Sure, he and I could have been happy together in a snapshot in time. But a full life with him would mean giving up everything I value and leaving my family and friends behind. I'm always willing to compromise for love, but uprooting my entire life for travel and zero commitment doesn't seem worth it.

Troubled by the realization, I elect to change the subject entirely. "Do you bring all your ladies up here?"

Trevor appears preoccupied with his mountain of bubbles, pushing them left to right. I take his lack of verbal response as a yes.

"I've heard hot tub sex sucks," I say, mostly to rattle him.

This gets his attention. "I beg to differ." His voice comes out low and strained, which does something to my insides.

I dry-swallow the lump in my throat. Am I turned on right now? I readjust myself in my seat, away from the blast of the jet. It's the jets. It must be the jets. It means nothing. Anyone who shares a tiny apartment with a dangerously attractive man is going to get hot and bothered every so often. It's basic science.

"It's like the shower," I say. "It's a hot fantasy, but in reality, it's too much friction. And there's a high risk of urinary tract infection. Especially in here. Who knows how many weirdos from this building have used it."

A slight smile plays across his lips, but he doesn't respond. I've officially made it awkward. Perhaps it's too early to talk about sex with Trevor. We've only known each other for two months.

"Did you know my social media followers are obsessed with you?"

He freezes. "What?"

"You haven't followed me yet?" I sigh, disappointed. "That time you came into my room, I was still on Live. You were in the video for a split second, and my followers liked what they saw."

"I see. I don't know whether to be flattered or weirded out," he says, unimpressed with himself. It strikes me that Trevor exudes a unique brand of confidence. He carries himself with a self-assured gait, yet he doesn't seem to know how to take a compliment. His humor is a little self-deprecating, just like mine.

Before I can respond, the rooftop door creaks open. A short, stubby man with a wispy white comb-over comes sauntering around the corner, impossibly tiny towel curled around his neck.

Trevor gives me a classic Jim from *The Office* look. The wide-eyed one he does into the camera when Michael Scott says or does something obscene.

"Evening." The man nods politely as he swings a ghostly white leg into the water, testing the temperature.

I retract my original statement. This hot tub is not suitable for more than two.

When the man's toenail inadvertently brushes my leg under the water, I stealthily shift closer to Trevor. The man doesn't appear bothered by the close quarters. He comfortably rests both arms behind him on the edge of the hot tub, taking up more than his fair share of space.

"Gerald, from fifth," he announces, his eyes half-closed.

"Tara and Trevor from fourth," I respond, actively avoiding Trevor's tight-lipped smile, because I'll burst out laughing if I do.

It isn't long before Gerald is barely even lucid, his head tipped back, seemingly in a state of bliss. I have no choice but to pick up where I left off, as if he's not here. I flick water in Trevor's direction. "Trev, tell me your life story."

He screws up his face. It appears he'd rather do anything else. "I'm really not that interesting."

I let out an audible growl and drag my fingertips over the water, flicking it in his direction again. "You're so mysterious. I'm beginning to think you're a 007 secret sleeper agent."

He cuts me a sly grin, amused by my conspiracy theories. He gears up to splash me back, but refrains. Gerald has perked up and appears keen to listen in. "If I were a spy, I wouldn't be living in our shitty apartment. And I most definitely wouldn't live with a roommate who never stops talking. You'd blow my cover for sure."

"You're deflecting. Steering the subject away from you. That's classic spy shit. Why are you so mysterious over the most basic things?" I urge, circling back to my original question. "You even get cagey when I ask what you ate for dinner."

"Because I'm not that interesting. I doubt you care what I ate for dinner last night."

"I care," I assure him.

He shrugs lazily. "All right. You'll regret saying that when I text you every single thing I eat and drink." My fingers tingle at the prospect of exclusive access to his daily life, however insignificant. "Anyway, what else do you want to know? My favorite color?"

"Nah. Something I don't know." *Like Angie's identity.*

"I never told you my favorite color."

"It's dark green. You have multiple dark-green T-shirts."

He doesn't argue that point. Instead, he plays with the bubbles for a few moments, shaking his head in amused disbelief. "What else do you know about me?"

"You're really making me do all the work here, aren't you?" I sigh. "Okay, fine. I know you're good at finding deals at the grocery store." When I first moved in, he insisted I accompany him on a Costco trip, where he examined the flyer for deals for a solid ten minutes before so much as pushing the cart down the first aisle. When I grabbed a bag of prewashed and prechopped lettuce, he nearly had a heart attack and went on a tangent about how much more "yield" I get for my money if I buy a full romaine head. His penny-pinching ways remind me of Dad, who wears his clothes until they're so worn with holes that Mom has to purge them in secret.

"You're a good cook too. Somehow you make vegetables look marginally less nauseating. You have a very particular way you like the dishwasher filled. And I can tell when you've had a good or bad day at work."

"How?"

"When it's a bad day, you stomp around a little and raid my snack stash before showering. When it's a good day, you still raid my snacks, but when you shower, you hum a tune that sounds suspiciously like 'I Knew You Were Trouble' by Taylor Swift."

He appears semi-amused (and doesn't deny his shower song), so I push a little further. "Now that I've proven myself, I reserve the right to ask you something important."

He swallows nervously, bracing for it.

"Who was your first celebrity crush?" I ask, lifting my top half out of the water to get some relief from the heat.

I can't confirm, but I think Trevor's eyes drifted to my chest for a fraction of a second.

"He looks like a Pamela Anderson type to me," Gerald chimes in, jabbing a thumb in Trevor's direction.

Trevor gives him a look of solidarity. "I liked Pam. Britney Spears too."

I smirk. "That's very . . . typical."

Trevor angles toward Gerald. "Gerald, who was your first celebrity crush?"

"Miss Dolly Parton," he responds proudly. He waves a hand toward me, signaling it's my turn.

"I have many. The kid from *Casper* was probably my very first. But I'd say my first sexual awakening was Zac Efron in his *High School Musical* days."

"What got you? The sweeping bangs? The piercing blue eyes?" Trevor asks.

"Definitely his angry dance in *High School Musical 2*."

"I won't even pretend to know what you're talking about," he says with a headshake.

"Nowadays, I'm pretty into Dwight Schrute," I inform.

Trevor chokes. "From *The Office*?"

"Yup."

"Do you mean Jim?"

"Nope. Dwight."

He shoots me a disturbed look. "Are we thinking of the same Dwight? Glasses? Owns a beet farm?"

"The only Dwight on the show," I confirm. "Okay, hear me out—"

He lobs his head back with his deep laugh. "Are you really going to try to convince me Dwight Schrute gets your motor running?"

"He does. You wouldn't understand," I shoot back, drawing my shoulders up in defense.

"What gets you hot? The puke-mustard short-sleeved dress shirts? His affinity for *Battlestar Galactica*?"

"His pure dedication to Angela, of course. Anyway, you're distracting me." I clear my throat, eager to keep this going. "Next question. Why did you become a firefighter?"

Trevor's face hardens to stone. "It's not an interesting story."

"You're the worst." When I reach to retighten my bun, I note my fingers are prunes and my hair is starting to frost. It's time to get out of here. I stand to exit the tub. The moment the frigid air hits my skin, gooseflesh erupts. I make a mad dash for my towel on the lounge chair.

Trevor nods his chin toward Gerald as he steps out of the gurgling water, swim trunks dripping. "Have a good night."

Fifteen minutes later, I'm warm and dry, star-fishing with a book in my usual spot on the living room floor. I'm bundled in my flannel pajamas, partway through my chapter, when Trevor emerges in respectable sweatpants and a T-shirt. I expect him to walk over me and head for the television, or simply judge me from above, but surprisingly, he stretches out on the floor next to me.

"This is weirdly comfortable," he admits, lining his shoulders up with mine.

"See? It's amazing. Life-changing," I say, keeping my eyes on the page.

"I wouldn't go that far."

"I have some of my most genius thoughts down here."

"I'm sure you do," he says, reading over my shoulder. "What's this book about? Looks like a cowboy romance."

"You'd be correct."

"Second-chance?"

"Indeed. And a secret baby too. My favorite." He chuckles softly, and there's a beat of silence before I turn onto my side, facing him. "You're a good friend for coming with me tonight," I say, staring at his dense lash line with envy. My fatigue is causing me to see two Trevors, which is less disturbing than it should be.

A tiny grin forms. "I'm sure any one of your other friends would have done the same."

"I don't know. I don't have all that many friends. Aside from Crystal and Mel, and realistically, Crystal has to be my friend by default. Sometimes I feel like they're a bit dismissive of me. When I told them about the ex thing, they laughed it off like it was a joke." It's not that I don't love Crystal and Mel. They're my best friends. But sometimes I can't help but feel like a third wheel.

He watches me thoughtfully. "I don't believe you have a hard time making friends."

"It's harder than you'd think, especially at thirty. I have lots of acquaintances. But close friends I could call up last minute and snuggle with? Not so much."

"Hm. That surprises me. They're missing out."

"You think so?"

"I know so."

One glance at his tiny, stubborn smile and my stomach flutters. My body tenses with new awareness of the press of his shoulder against mine.

My thoughts are spinning, aching to unpack my body's reaction to his touch, but my mind is pulled elsewhere—to his eyes. The kitchen light illuminates the rich ring of dense forest green, surrounded by another loop of gold in his irises.

Our shared gaze holds for a beat longer than casual before his eyes fall to my mouth. His throat bobs with a slow, almost hesitant swallow, and his jaw goes soft.

Based on my extensive catalog of romance knowledge from books and film, these are signs of an impending kiss.

Trevor Metcalfe wants to kiss me.

♥ chapter twelve

MY MIND IS fuzzy static.

I can neither do nor think of anything but the quickened pace of my breath and the dizzying way Trevor has pinned me in place with just one look.

Instinctively, I sweep my tongue over my bottom lip. Electricity courses between us in wavy cartoon lines. The mental barrier I've placed to convince myself he is not my type has vanished into a poof of swirling black and purple smoke.

I don't know if it's the liquid courage, the fact that my date with Brandon went sideways, or the steam from the hot tub, but I do the unthinkable. I inch closer, pressing my arm flat against his. Close enough that his face blurs entirely. He doesn't move, allowing the radiating heat of our labored breath to collide and pass through each other, in and out.

My heart thrashes wildly, and I'm convinced I can hear his too, syncing with mine in a tangled, pulsing rhythm. Encouraged by the comfort of our proximity, I position my head just so, for the perfect alignment of our lips. He holds himself there, tentative, the tip of his nose grazing mine like a whisper.

I ache for him to put me out of my misery, close that millimeter of desperate air, and brush his soft lips against mine.

But instead, his eyes snap open, wide with fear as I approach. He's on his feet faster than the Flash, dodging me like I'm a toothless sex predator.

He rakes his hair haphazardly, wobbly in his footing. "Uh, I should get to bed. Early shift tomorrow." His gaze is glued to the floor as he careens down the hallway, bolting for his bedroom.

If I were a normal person, I'd shake the whole thing off and yell a casual "Goodnight," like absolutely nothing happened. But when I move my lips, nothing comes out. My body is like my college PC laptop I never shut down. Loud. Disruptive fan. Overheating when more than two tabs are open simultaneously. Powering down at the most inconvenient of times.

I'm rigor mortis as the stranglehold of humiliation prevents me from doing anything but wish for a swift, painless death.

LIVE WITH TARAROMANCEQUEEN—AWKWARD KISSES

[Tara wears an ill-fitted fluorescent workout top and messy bun. She lies on a red mat at the gym. Unlike the patrons in the background, she is not doing physical activity.]

TARA: *Hello, romance book lovers, welcome back to my channel. Today we're talking about kissing. Now, there are a lot of awkward kisses in books and film. Usually, I'm here for them either way. But one thing I'll never get on board with? Kissing in the rain. Sure, the allure of a passionate, wet lip-lock may be what some consider spontaneous. Marginally sexy, even. Nature makes people do weird shit. But is the short-lived thrill worth resembling a drowned sewer rat and getting pneumonia? Unlikely.*

And even worse than rain kisses are upside-down, Spiderman-style kisses. Who does this? Are the mechanics of a normal, upright kiss not stressful enough? I have a hard enough time deciding if I'm going right or left or if I'm top- or bottom-lip heavy.

Have you ever experienced an awkward kiss that made you want to dissolve into dust and nothingness? Tell me about it in the comments below!

• • •

FROM THE SWEAT raining down my face, one would presume I've been waterboarded by a hostile government or murderous terrorist group.

Nope. I'm just here in my own special little ring of hell, sweating out my regret in Crystal's Muscle Fit class with twenty other red-faced patrons. In the last few months, she started teaching in-person classes at the gym, which are in such high demand, people book weeks in advance.

Crystal observes my poor biceps curl form like a drill sergeant.

"Keep engaging your core. Just ten more seconds and we're done," she instructs in her encouraging-trainer voice.

Beside me, Mel is holding strong in those last few curls, barely breaking a sweat.

Beads of salty, alcohol-infused sweat seep past my lash line, stinging my eyeballs. I'm now half-blind, and the pop tune blasting over the sound system certainly isn't doing much for my stamina. When my sweaty fingers lose their grip on the barbell, I know it's game over. It lands with a thud at my feet, turning the heads of the other ladies in class.

Mel hands me my water bottle, and I refrain from dousing myself like a heroic Olympic decathlete crossing the finish line to victory. I've never sweat so much in my life. This can't be normal, or healthy.

I'd do unspeakable things for a shower right now—preferably the type where I'd do nothing but stand there in the steam, critically evaluating my life decisions, letting the water wash away the glaring memory of the dumpster fire that was last night.

Being turned down by two separate men in the span of two hours is a first—with the exception of New Year's Eve circa ninth grade, when, drunk off two wine coolers, I valiantly confessed my love for not one but two crushes while rocking a distressed-denim vest.

But at least teenaged me wasn't stuck in a tiny, eight-hundred-fifty-square-foot apartment with them. Avoiding Trevor Metcalfe, my off-limits roommate whose bedroom is a mere five feet from mine, is not so simple.

I haven't seen him since last night, after he lurched away from me like I was an ailing troll. Immediately, I hauled ass to bed before I could make matters worse. By the time I woke up this morning, Trevor was long gone for his early shift.

In the light of day, the weight of last night's error in judgment is staggering. To the point of indigestion. Sure, our shoulders and noses touched for a hot second. We may have even flirted a little. He may have gazed longingly at my lips. But flirting is Trevor's default mode. He can't help himself. And for all I know, maybe he was simply staring at a zit on my face.

The blunt truth remains—none of it meant a thing. We don't want the same things, a crucial consideration, as he pointed out himself. Besides, there's still this mysterious Angie person in the picture.

Why did my traitorous brain venture into the forbidden and unavailable? Why did I let my followers coerce me into thinking Trevor would be a good idea? Why must I be so overeager in every aspect of life?

I contemplate my options as Crystal confidently leads the class through a series of cooldown stretches on the mats, which are more on my level. I'm grateful for the chance to be horizontal.

Once the class is over, Mel and I stick around on the mats, watching Crystal do a quick ab workout on her own.

"I have something to tell you guys," Crystal announces, mid-crunch. "But before I say it, you have to promise not to freak out."

"I make no promises," I declare.

"You're pregnant, aren't you?" Mel asks, retying her ponytail. She quickly adds, "Not that you look pregnant or anything. But I've been getting a maternal vibe from you. And you've been pinning house décor ideas on Pinterest."

Crystal claps her palms together. "Scott and I . . ." Her voice trails off, and she stares at me like she's about to drop some bad news. "We decided to elope in March. In St. Lucia."

"*Elope?*" I repeat, stunned. "As in not even immediate family?" There goes my fantasy of being a no-nonsense, ball-busting maid of honor.

"Yup. Just us." She keeps her eyes on her running shoes, which tells me she's anticipating protest. "I know you guys were hoping for a normal wedding, but I'm just not feeling it. Neither of us are really interested in the planning and the drama."

I don't entirely blame her. When I was planning my wedding to Seth, dealing with the Chen side of the family was no joke. First, Grandma and Grandpa Chen insisted on inviting at least twenty "close friends" they play mah-jongg with. This includes one woman who insisted on a plus-one for her deceased husband's urn, which she brings with her wherever she goes. Then there are Dad's three siblings and ten adult cousins, many of whom are feuding and refuse to be seated at the same table.

Crystal and Mel eye me expectantly, noticing I'm staying tight-lipped. Truthfully, I'm picturing Dad's face, which will be one of cutting disappointment. He's been waiting ages to host one of our weddings. Fatherly pride aside, he lives for a good party, particularly if he gets an excuse to be in the limelight.

Belatedly, I shrug. "I completely support whatever you guys want to do, so long as you livestream your ceremony. I want to live vicariously," I add.

"Did Scotty want to elope too?" Mel inquires, deep in a downward-dog stretch.

Crystal shakes her head. "He was up for whatever I wanted to do, as long as we get married as soon as possible. He's mostly excited to go on a honeymoon."

Mel sits upright and gives her a subdued *aww*. After a string of short flings in the past year, she's in a phase where the sheer mention of commitment makes her full-body shudder. Her commitment phobia aside, I understand her decision. I'd be off men too if my last boyfriend rocked an exclusive wardrobe of turtlenecks.

Aware of Mel's less-than-enthusiastic outlook on love, Crystal tries to backtrack with an unromantic ramble about the merits of saving for a down payment on a home instead of "frivolously" spending it all on one day.

"Do you think you'll ever be interested in something long-term?" I ask Mel. The last few guys she brought home, she tasked with labor around her apartment (like fixing her leaky faucet) before sex. What a queen.

Mel avoids my eyes, struggling to pick at a hangnail on account of her sparkly acrylics. "Absolutely not. I like my life the way it is. I get to focus all my energy and attention on my business without having to feel guilty. I don't have to compromise what I want to watch on Netflix or what I want to eat for dinner."

"Do you ever feel . . . lonely?" I ask softly.

She studies her coral running shoes, obviously not eager to dwell much longer. "Nope. I have Doug to keep me warm at night."

"Her vibrator," Crystal whispers.

"We support you and your battery-operated relationship either way." I lean in to smother her with a sweaty hug.

She cracks a smile while not-so-discreetly worming out of my embrace. "Take it from me. Men are burdens to be abandoned at the first sign of trouble. Anyway, someone tell me something fun and scandalous. I just killed the mood."

I volunteer myself as tribute. She lives for gossip, and I'm willing to sacrifice my dignity for her temporary amusement. "Okay, fun story, I tried to kiss Trevor last night."

Crystal propels upward in a hard-hitting crunch, bewildered. "What fresh hell? You tried to kiss *Trevor*?"

Mel slaps the mat enthusiastically. "I saw that coming a mile away."

"How did this even happen? And what happened to your exes plan?"

The pinks in their cheeks darken to crimson with secondhand embarrassment as I rattle off the grisly details of last night.

"Wait, Trevor went on the date with you and Wanderlust Brandon?" Mel asks.

"I'm not sure why you're getting dating advice from *Trevor*. He's a great guy, don't get me wrong. But he wouldn't know a relationship from his ass," Crystal remarks, holier than thou.

I don't know why, but I feel an overwhelming urge to come to his defense. "Didn't he give you solid advice for grand-gesturing Scotty?" Last summer, Crystal broke up with Scott temporarily when a photo of the two of them went viral and a bunch of trolls fat-shamed her. Trevor helped her orchestrate a grand apology right here in the gym where they first met.

"Well, yeah, but—"

"Give him some credit. He's not a total nimrod." My tone is terse, raising their suspicions.

"But why would Trevor give up his night to supervise your date? Do you think he likes you?" Mel asks.

"No. It's not as weird as you make it sound." I pause for a moment as they both watch me, appalled on my behalf. "I mean . . . okay. I made things weird with the kiss. But I'm gonna apologize tonight. It'll be fine. I'll blame it on the alcohol. Things will go back to normal," I say assuredly, more to myself than them.

Mel's concern transitions into a knowing grin. "I think you should sleep with him. Just once. Get it out of your system."

I shudder at the thought of a one-night stand. With my roommate. Of all people. "God, no. Do you even read the romance books I loan you? Every time romance characters have sex to *get it out of their systems*, they end up hopelessly attached. And besides, Trevor doesn't like me that way." I look away, suddenly very interested in the woman near the window squatting what appears to be my body weight.

Since move-in day, I've lived with the truth that I am not Trevor's type. I held on to that fact with pride, like a lifeline. Without the unspoken sanctity of our strictly platonic relationship, my perfectly stable living situation goes straight down the tube.

"And he's definitely not *your* type," Crystal echoes, with a pinch more force than necessary.

"Well, my type is *trash*, apparently," I grumble, thinking of Jeff. "So it kind of leaves it open to interpretation."

"A die-hard, emotional romantic and a guy who only believes in one kind of happy ending? That's a recipe for disaster if I ever saw one." She resumes her butterfly crunches.

I frown. "Why are you looking at me like I need an intervention?"

Mid-crunch, Crystal levels me with a hard stare. "Because I know how you get. You get obsessed. *Dickmatized*, as the great Ali

Wong would say. You would fall in love with a tree branch if you spent enough time with it."

"Okay, rude. I have standards," I shoot back.

"I'm sorry. It's just, you have a tendency to fall hard and fast . . . I mean, you had a crush on the mailman at Mom and Dad's. The stock boy at Trader Joe's. The DJ at Grandma Flo's wedding." Crystal is anything but a sugarcoater.

My first instinct is to go on the defensive and remind her of her own crappy exes. But to be fair, she isn't saying anything that isn't true.

I've been this way my entire life, misinterpreting kindness for affection, ready to launch into fantasy mode at any given moment (*He looked in my general direction, so it must mean he wants me to be his wife. Right?*). I'm like an overenthusiastic dad on a trampoline who jumps a little too far to the left and lands crotch-first on the springs.

Perhaps the most pathetic part is that I've been in a staring contest with my phone all day, waiting for Trevor to text me. To say something. Anything. To acknowledge what happened. When my phone screen illuminates in my hand with a notification from Instagram, I check my texts for the seventy-fifth time, confirming I have exactly zero.

I desperately need to get my priorities in order, which do not include Trevor, who is so fundamentally wrong for me, it's almost laughable. I must keep my eye on the prize, securing my second-chance love story, definitely not getting my heart broken yet again.

"Trust me, if I was thirsting over Trevor, you'd know. I wouldn't stop talking about him. And besides, he's made it quite clear he's not interested in me. He's probably with another woman right now," I say, wincing at the thought. "And I'm pretty sure he's having a torrid affair with a married woman who's the love of his life."

Crystal readjusts her messy topknot. "Impossible. He's a straight-up man-whore. Not for you. You've come so far since Seth and the wedding. You're finally happy again, living on your own. I just don't want Trevor bludgeoning all your progress to death."

"Don't forget, men are a burden. Seriously," Mel adds.

They're right. They're both completely right, and I know it. The last thing I need is to pack up my life for the third time this year. I need stability, desperately.

"I know. You don't have to worry. I'm focusing entirely on my exes."

Crystal looks unconvinced. "Promise?"

"Promise," I say with conviction, despite the strange bubble in my throat as the words come out.

♥ chapter thirteen

TREVOR STILL ISN'T home. It's six, and according to his work schedule on the fridge, he was off at five. He's certainly avoiding me. He's probably spent the entire day plotting the least dramatic way to banish me from his apartment.

I've spent the afternoon cleaning like Cinderella. I even made a fresh batch of cupcakes *from scratch*, proudly displayed on the kitchen island for the taking. It's a flimsy apology for trying to assault him with my lips, but it's the best I could come up with on short notice.

Doing some book TikToks is the only thing that keeps my mind from twisting into a frenzy. I'm doing a fifteen-second book review video when Trevor's muffled voice filters in from the hallway outside the door.

I set down my phone immediately, willing myself to loosen up. Play it cool. I can do this. I can face him like a grown-ass woman.

I can bravely look him dead in the eyes after he blatantly rejected me. It's fine. THIS IS FINE.

His deep voice carries over the jingle of his keys. Has he brought home a new conquest? I strain to listen for a second voice like the massive creep I am.

"You're okay, though, right?" he asks.

Silence.

"Okay, good. I gotta go now, but—"

Silence.

"Yup. Love you, Angie."

Angie. The same Angie he sent a basket of candy to. The Angie he *loves*?

I think about how Crystal laughed hysterically at the idea of him in a romantic relationship, and my stomach pinches harder than it should. I'm a statue, holding my breath so I can eavesdrop on the rest of the conversation when the door finally opens. There's a dusting of snow on his beanie, which he shakes off while keeping his phone in between his ear and shoulder. He's not ready for eye contact, laser focusing on unlacing his boots.

I wither a little inside, secretly wishing to fall into a wormhole and never return.

"Yup, sleep tight," he says into the phone, giving me a vaguely dismissive chin nod as he ends the call.

Before he can even shrug off his coat, I'm hovering over him in the doorway, ready to launch into an already prepared speech.

"Hi," I say, not so casually leaning a wrist on the wall. It's a very awkward stance that I don't recommend.

"Hi," he says distractedly, meticulously rolling his hat into the sleeve of his coat. There's a small ashy smudge on his left cheek from what I imagine was an eventful shift, being a hero and whatnot.

I brandish a bogus smile. "I made cupcakes. Used the same recipe you showed me. I think they turned out lumpy, but feel free to try them."

He glances at them on the island and nods appreciatively.

We stand in a face-off for a torturous length of time before the word vomit pours out. "Trev, I'm really sorry about last night. I was such a mess after Brandon, and the hot tub made me loopy. I've read steam and alcohol can really—"

"It's fine." He holds up a hand to stop me but still doesn't meet my gaze. He's busy scrutinizing the heap of books in the middle of the living room floor.

"I'll pick those up," I promise, plowing forward. "I hate that I've made things weird by trying to kiss you. I swear I'm not harboring some weird obsession with you."

"Really? You mean you don't have a shrine to me in your closet?" he deadpans.

Did he just crack a joke? Surely this is a positive sign. I jump at the chance to play along. "Not a shrine, exactly. I have been collecting your hairs from the bathroom, though. I almost have a full lock now."

He appraises me. "A full lock? You could do a lot with that."

"Yeah. I'm thinking of splitting it half and half, a tuft for the voodoo doll and a sprinkle for the love potion I've been lacing your smoothies with," I explain, matching his stern expression.

He clears his throat. "I have been coughing up a lot of hair balls recently."

Neither of us wants to break character, but he relents, the corners of his lips unable to suppress his amusement. It's only when his chest vibrates with a disarming, hearty laugh that my posture eases, thankful for a grain of normalcy.

"I'm being serious, though. I'm not into you that way," I repeat for good measure. "But after last night, I consider you a good friend, and I don't want to lose that. I know you may not think of me as a friend yet. But—"

"Of course I consider you a friend." His tone is warm yet firm.

"Really?"

"Yup. I gotta keep you on my good side. You know too much about me and my secret spy identity. And now that I know you have a voodoo doll of me . . ." He gives me a small nudge with his elbow as he inches around me.

"Let's just forget last night ever happened. Please?" I stick my hand out for a handshake, desperate to seal the deal before he changes his mind.

I'm relieved when he takes my hand in his, holding it firmly for a beat longer than expected. "Already forgotten, Chen."

While he picks his choice of cupcake, I return to my spot on the couch. He settles next to me, apparently too exhausted to argue over my choice of entertainment: *The Bachelor*.

He squints at this season's latest mediocre white boy, Wyatt from Texas, as he takes a shirtless jog through a tranquil meadow to get his head in the game for his group date with twenty women. "What's so great about this show anyway? Isn't it all fake?"

"Definitely fake. I'm not sure how many people are really on there for true love anymore."

Trevor watches the group date with intense curiosity. This one involves the girls getting down and dirty at some random farm, shoveling manure and pretending to love every second. When this season's front-runner, Bethan, pops on-screen, Trevor deems her "hot."

I roll my eyes. "Meh. She's one of those types who thinks liking sports over girly things is a personality trait."

By the time the one-on-one with shy girl Piper comes around, Trevor is hooked. "Is Wyatt really gonna send her home because she didn't tell him her life story on the first date? They hardly know each other."

"On *The Bachelor*, unloading dark secrets and rehashing child-hood trauma is the key to getting the rose. You need to get personal, and fast." I dash to the kitchen to grab a fresh bag of BBQ chips from the pantry.

When I return to the couch, he absentmindedly reaches for a handful. "Oh, looks like he's kissing her anyway."

"You say that like you haven't kissed half the women in Boston."

He stops to look at me, mid-bite. "Well, not in front of a bunch of people, at least. Imagine making out with all the TV crew around. Knowing it'll be broadcast to the world."

"Why do you hate PDA so much? It's kind of cute, to declare your love for someone in front of others."

"Nope. Kissing and cuddling in public is weird. No one wants to see that."

"Maybe not full-on tongue make-outs. But pecks and cuddles in public are adorable."

He shudders. "No."

"Let me guess, you're not into affection in general." I side-eye him. "You hate cuddles, don't you?"

"I don't mind cuddling. But only with women I have serious feelings for."

I nearly swallow a potato chip whole, springboarding off the opportunity to pry about Angie. "Women you have serious feelings for, huh? Like your gorgeous exes, Natalie and Kyla? Or . . . someone else?"

He keeps his lips tight and shrugs, obviously enjoying my burning desire to know. "You're always asking questions about me, but I never get the chance to ask about you."

My brows knit together. "You already know everything about me."

"Not everything. You never actually told me what happened with you and Seth."

Damn. I didn't expect that. I examine my split ends, suddenly unnerved. "Seth is . . . just . . . I don't know. He sucks."

"Why were you engaged to him if he sucks?" His tone isn't judgmental. More curious.

"That's a long story."

"I have time."

I keep examining my hair, mustering up a logical explanation. "Okay. Fine. When I first met Seth, he was finishing his pediatric residency. He was still technically a student, getting his certifications at the same time. He was shy, sweet, almost timid. Wicked smart, at the top of his class but didn't brag. I was so attracted to him because of his passion for his job. He was the young doctor who cared a little more than the others. He took extra time to reassure his patients' parents. He was really well loved."

"What changed?" he asks, reaching for the chips.

I pass him the bag. "A few things. He was—technically, he

is—a great doctor. And that went to his head, fast. Status, as well as the money. Once he got that first paycheck, he just changed. Started buying lavish things. Showered me with gifts. He's one of those people who will make you feel like the center of the universe. But when he's not shining his light on you, you might as well be a frozen-tundra dwarf planet in the darkest, most inhospitable corner of the galaxy."

"Must have been tough seeing him change into a different person."

I stretch my arms over my head and yawn. "Yeah. We fought about it all the time. I was desperate for things to go back to how they were in the beginning . . . so I panicked and proposed."

Two years into our relationship, I planned an elaborate proposal (if Monica Geller could do it, why couldn't I?). With him as a man who'd just discovered power, I may as well have castrated him with a rusty spoon.

"And he said yes?"

"Yup. He said he felt pressured because his parents were pushing him to settle down since he was finally done with school. He was never involved in wedding planning. He got super cranky about anything to do with it."

The resentment had been a slow, demoralizing build. I buried myself deep in wedding planning while he decided to spend the remainder of his unmarried time like someone with just one month left to live. While he worked hard, he also played hard. On his days off, he gambled carelessly at the casino; went on random trips with his new, wealthy friends; and impulse-purchased a luxury sports car.

I handled this new side of him about as well as I handle all other change: like a jellyfish trying to do ballet. I accused him of having a quarter-life crisis. He accused me of being a twenty out of ten on the Richter scale of crazy. And then we were done. Just like that.

"Anyway, when he finally broke things off, he told me I was too much for him. Too needy. And that he didn't love me anymore. Wasn't sure if he ever had." I hang my head. The memory of those words still stings. "You think I'm pathetic, don't you?"

"No." Trevor shakes his head, his eyes locking to mine. "The opposite. I think most people who go through something like that would give up on love entirely. And you haven't."

"Believe me, I've wanted to. It's way easier to settle for a paperback prince than it is to put yourself out there. But I'm a glutton for punishment, I think." I huff a weary breath.

"You definitely are. But that's what makes you *you*," he says, catching me off guard with a disarmingly sincere smile.

I blink it away before I melt into a puddle. "Anyway, my turn to ask you something."

He sits up a little straighter, preparing himself. "All right, shoot."

"Who's Angie?"

♥ chapter fourteen

TREVOR HAS YET to admit Angie exists, aside from joking about her being his spy handler. I've long given up pestering him for the truth. Technically, it's his business. If he doesn't want me in it, who am I to push?

Either way, during our limited time together over the holidays, I've learned it's all about the small victories with Trevor Metcalfe. For example, he's now weirdly into *The Bachelor*. The other night when I was watching *Little House on the Prairie*, he asked why I wasn't watching *The Bachelor* and when did the next episode air? He's also started reading on the couch with me during the evenings, borrowing the thrillers I haven't had the heart to read because I don't take plot twists well.

Ever since I accused him of being secretive, he texts me photos of everything he eats when we're not together. Today, it's asparagus-stuffed chicken (because of his New Year's resolution to eat healthy). In response, I sent him a photo of my prized box of Rainbow Chips Ahoy! cookies, which I impulse-purchased after crossing ex-boyfriend number nine, Mark, off the list.

Mark and I had been members of a book club we both didn't like but didn't know how to politely leave. We only dated for a month, but it got serious fast. He even introduced me to his parents and his ailing grandfather, which is why I was shocked when he broke up with me after I casually made a comment about a friend's engagement ring.

When I messaged Mark randomly on the day after Christmas, he told me straight up he wasn't interested in meeting but that he wanted his old Beatles T-shirt back. I dutifully excavated it from the Ex-Files box and dropped it off in the mail this morning.

TREVOR: You better save me some of those cookies.

I snicker to myself as I duck into the hospital stairwell. Usually, I spend my breaks in the nurses' lounge, but after my colleagues caught wind of my ex-boyfriend search, I can't go a minute without one of them pestering me for details about my dates and the remaining exes. That's something Crystal warned me about: when you're open with your personal life online, people feel entitled to know everything about you. And if you dare prefer to keep some things private, you need a good excuse.

I snap a shot of two empty cookie container rows and send it to Trevor.

TARA: No can do. Someone stole my Greek yogurt again from the communal fridge. I need all the nutrients I can get. 🍪

TREVOR: I told you to write your name on the yogurt container.

TARA: I did! In double-thick Sharpie.

The ellipses signaling he's typing pop up and stop numerous times before he finally responds.

TREVOR: Tara, will you accept this link? 🌷🌷🌷🌷🌷

The text is followed by a link to the casting call for the new Bachelor season.

TARA: I'm not even going to ask how you came across that. 🫣

TREVOR: Yeah, best not to ask. So are you gonna apply??

TARA: No way! I didn't like Kurt in *The Bachelorette*. He's too much of a playboy for me. I don't think he's reformed his rakish ways. How would I know he's there for the right reasons?

TREVOR: Is anyone? Aside from thousands of new social media followers? It could be good for your bookstagram. 😉 And you'd make for some good TV.

TARA: I'd be the girl who loses her mind two weeks in because she's already fallen in love and can't handle the fact that he has 30 other girlfriends. 😅

TREVOR: Nvm. You may not actually qualify anyways.

TARA: I'm perfectly eligible! Not that I'm applying . . .

He sends a screenshot of the eligibility small print, which specifically states *Applicants must never have been convicted of a felony or ever had a restraining order entered against them.*

TREVOR: If the car vandalism doesn't count you out . . .

I send him a selfie of my demonic eyes.

Trevor responds with a shot of his faux-scared face, and it gives me life. He's in his Boston Fire Department T-shirt, and his hair is perfectly tousled as usual. He's at work, based on the partially obstructed body of another firefighter in the background.

TARA: FYI I was never charged. And I've never had a restraining order against me, thank you very much.
TREVOR: . . . Yet. 😬 Btw, I'm off at 6 today. Want me to pick you up from work? It's New Year's Eve and I wouldn't want you to get mugged on the subway again.
TARA: Yes please! Text me when you're here.

As soon as I hit *Send*, the stairwell door lurches open behind me.

"Cyber-stalking your exes?" Seth asks ever so casually as he passes by me. He's one of those people who take the stairs instead of the elevator on purpose and brags about it. Even when we were together, he never bothered to hide his disappointment that I'd take the elevator instead. It got to the point where I was thankful not to be on shift with him so I could take the damn elevator in peace without him shaming me.

I pull my phone to my chest protectively. "None of your business."

Based on the glint in Seth's eyes and the upward turn of his thin lips, he's definitely seen my social media. "You're making it everyone's business by blasting it online." He's not wrong. But before I can respond, he adds, "You're actually doing it, huh? The witch-hunt?"

The fact that he's keeping tabs on my search is an interesting development. In fact, he's consistently one of my first story viewers. Mel thinks it means he's still hung up on me, but I know Seth. It's purely a control thing. "Please don't call it a witch-hunt. And are you really that shocked I've moved on?"

Seth leans against the railing. "I mean, let's be honest. You don't let go of things easily."

I shoot him daggers. "Excuse me for being a little upset that you canceled our wedding."

Without eye contact, he arrogantly smooths his hand over his gelled hair. "Can I offer you a bit of advice?"

"Nah, I'm good, thanks." I nearly shove an entire cookie in my mouth and avert my focus to my phone.

"Whoa, attitude. You don't have to be so rude. I'm trying to be nice."

Knowing Seth, he'll argue with me all day, so I treat him to a painfully fake smile. "Sorry, but I'm good. Really. Though I appreciate the concern. Bye," I say primly, simply to make him disappear.

My tactic works. Without another word, he continues on down the stairs, out of sight.

• • •

WHEN TREVOR TEXTS at the end of my shift, I'm already in the lobby, itching to get the heck out of here. I'm eager to spend my quiet New Year's Eve plotting my strategy to reunite with the remaining exes. Daniel and Cody have been consistently leading in the polls as my most popular exes. My followers are suckers for a childhood love reunion romance.

TREVOR: Hey, come to the 6th floor.
TARA: What? Why?

There's no sign of his car idling in the front entrance, so I double back to the elevator and press the button for floor six. Despite working in this hospital for years, I've never ventured to the sixth floor before.

When the elevator doors swing open, Trevor is pacing to the left of the reception desk in front of a glass case holding framed photos of tiny, colorful handprints formed like butterflies. He's unknowingly turning the heads of everyone within a twenty-foot radius in his fitted fire department T-shirt. When he sees me, he gives me an upward chin nod. His tense stance tells me he's in one of his withdrawn moods.

Behind him is a massive, vibrant wall mural of lush jungle greenery and a sign that reads *Boston Children's Hospital Heart Center*.

Trevor watches me tepidly as I take it all in, stunned.

"What is—?" I start.

"Before you say anything, you should know—"

A tiny brunette figure zips out of a room to the right. It's a girl, no older than eight. A baggy purple hoodie and striped pajama pants hang off her waiflike figure, further emphasizing her delicate frame. Her face is gaunt and hollow, juxtaposed by an unexpected toothy smile that somehow reminds me of Trevor's. With a bountiful giggle, she launches herself into Trevor's arms.

When Trevor picks her up and spins her like a wholesome nineties sitcom dad, my ovaries threaten to erupt. "Jeez, Angie. You're getting heavier every week."

Angie.

This is *the* Angie. The mystery girl he loves.

My theory was so wrong, it's almost laughable. Angie is a child, not a woman trapped in a loveless marriage of convenience. The basket of candy makes so much more sense now. I fight to work down a massive lump in my throat as a group of chattering nurses pass by.

Playboy Trevor has a child . . . with a heart condition?

The moment my brain settles on that conclusion, Angie drops another bomb. "I gained a pound, Uncle Trev."

Uncle.

I'm rendered mute, frozen, my mouth hanging open as I digest the newest twist. Angie is his niece. Through my shock, my stomach flips, gutted that Angie is a patient in the heart center. Why would Trevor choose to reveal his niece to me like this? In such a heavy-handed manner? It strikes me as uncharacteristic.

Angie casts a skeptical glance at me. "She your flavor of the month?" she asks bluntly.

I let out an embarrassingly loud hoot. You know you're a playboy when your kid niece takes a jab at your lifestyle. This girl speaks her truth, and I'm here for it. "I'm not his flavor of anything."

"She's my roommate," Trevor explains, giving her a gentle pat on the head. "And don't listen to everything your mom says about me."

I give an awkward jazz-hand wave. "I'm Tara. It's really nice to meet you, Angie."

"My real name is Angela, but everyone calls me Angie." She extends her small hand in a surprisingly strong and purposeful shake.

"I'm Tara. Everyone calls me Tara." I realize my joke fell flat on its face when she side-eyes me to Trevor before turning around.

Trevor laughs at my expense as we follow her into her room. It's meant for two patients, although the bed nearest the door is vacant. Angie has a prime spot next to the window, though it has a rather unfortunate view of the parking lot.

Angie hops onto the bed with ease, pulling the hot-pink comforter back to reveal floral sheets tucked with military precision, like Trevor's bed at the apartment. Trevor gestures for me to take the chair by the window, while he parks himself on the edge of her bed.

He asks about her day, how she's feeling, whether her mom came by yet, and if they'll be doing anything special for New Year's Day tomorrow. He doesn't ask about her dad, who I'm assuming is his younger and only sibling, Logan. He's mentioned Logan just once, during a conversation about childhood TV shows, describing how he and his brother used to watch *Are You Afraid of the Dark?* religiously on Nickelodeon. I make a mental note to confirm the family dynamics later.

The drab wall across from the foot of Angie's bed is proudly covered with what appears to be her own artwork. Most of the paintings depict cozy houses, blue skies with bright-yellow suns, and big-petaled flowers.

Trevor extends his arms over his head in a labored stretch before standing. "I'm gonna go grab a coffee. Want something from the cafeteria, kid?"

"I'll take the usual," she responds with the confidence of a forty-year-old.

Before heading out, he glances at me over his shoulder. "Can I grab anything for you? More cookies?"

"If I eat another cookie, I might hurl," I admit, offering a weak smile.

I'm a jumble of nerves under the weight of Angie's Mafia-boss stare when Trevor peaces out, footsteps growing faint. It's like I'm back in middle school at the height of puberty. There's no logical reason to be anxious. Angie is a child. And I'm at work, in my own element, technically.

"You're a nurse?" Angie inquires, breaking the silence.

I nod, gesturing to my scrubs. "I am."

She gives me a comically skeptical squint. "Why haven't I seen you around? I know all the nurses." For a moment, her confidence shakes me, and I almost question my own identity.

"I don't work on this floor. I work with very sick newborns, actually, in the NICU a couple of floors down."

I anticipate a sass-filled response, but she gives me a silent nod, like she understands.

"What kind of stuff do you like to do, Angie?" I immediately cringe at my own question. What can she really do while in the hospital? "I mean, when you're not . . ." Oh God. I'm not prepared for this. No wonder I work with babies. They don't talk. I inwardly curse Trevor for springing this on me.

A coy smile tugs at her lips. "When I'm not in the hospital?"

I meet her smile and relax my posture ever so slightly. "Can I ask what you have?"

She reaches for the Disney coloring book atop the side table. "DORV." I'm only vaguely aware of the acronym. I know the D stands for Double and the V is Ventricle. But I can't recall the middle letters. At the risk of sounding like a fool and losing all credibility in front of Angie, I make a note to Google it.

She continues. "I got a new heart when I was a baby. But now Dr. Lam says I need a new one," she explains matter-of-factly.

"You're very brave" is all I can think to say without being patronizing. She's too mature for the bullshit.

She watches me for a beat before settling on a fresh page in the coloring book. It's Snow White's enchanted forest. "I watch a lot of princess movies."

I perk up. "Who's your favorite princess?"

"Rapunzel."

"She's my favorite too. I love *Tangled*. Do you have any others?"

"I like Moana too. And Anna. But not Elsa."

I laugh. "Why not Elsa?"

"She's kind of boring. She likes being alone. I don't like being alone." Isn't that the truth? Her honesty churns my stomach. With Trevor's demanding shift schedule, I wonder how often he's able to visit her.

I hang my head, picturing her sitting in her room all by herself. "I don't like being alone, either."

Trevor returns with a package of blue raspberry Jell-O in hand, along with a coffee and a vending machine–size bag of Cheetos, which he drops in my lap.

I thank him profusely. My diet is officially a smear on humanity.

A nurse I recognize from around the hospital over the years

follows close behind Trevor. She smiles at me and doesn't bother to question my random presence. "Time for your meds," she chirps to Angie.

While the nurse fusses with Angie, Trevor and I give them space, stepping into the hallway. From the way he keeps his head ducked, his hands in his pockets, I think he senses I'm a little shook.

"Why didn't you tell me Angie was your niece? Your niece who's a patient at the hospital where I work?" I fury-whisper. "I thought she was some woman you were hopelessly in love with."

"A woman I'm in love with? Really, Chen?" he repeats, sarcasm abundant. It's as if I thought Angie was his extraterrestrial friend who required immediate assistance returning to her home planet. I treat him to a frosty look until his expression softens. "I'm sorry. You just took me by surprise when you asked me about Angie. It wasn't meant to be a big secret. Besides, your theories were too amusing to come right out with the truth."

I gape at him. "This is how you decide to reveal her identity? And you say *I* have a flair for the dramatics. Of all people, I would have understood," I say, lowering my voice as a tiny pale child passes by with a nurse.

"I know, I know. It's just, Angie doesn't like when people treat her differently. I thought if you knew going into it, you'd have a warped perception of her. She's really strong for a kid of her age and in her circumstances."

I frown, bracing myself. "She said she had DORV?"

"Yeah. Double-outlet right ventricle. In a regular heart, the pulmonary artery connects to the right ventricle, whereas the aorta connects to the left. In Angie's heart, both the pulmonary artery and the aorta connect to the right ventricle, causing it to circulate oxygen-poor blood," he explains. "When Angie was born, she had her first heart surgery. But it was so complex, she needed a transplant. She's never been healthy like most kids, but last year, she started getting really sick and the doctors realized her body was rejecting the heart. It's rare for that to happen after so long. So she's on the transplant waiting list again."

"That's awful. I can't even imagine." I grimace. "But I'm still confused. Why would you want me to meet her?"

He shifts his weight, his gaze to the floor. "I was kind of hoping . . . you'd help me with something."

"With what?" I ask.

"Her tenth birthday party," he says earnestly. Angie certainly doesn't look like an almost ten-year-old, given her tiny frame. Although now her righteous sass makes a lot more sense. "Her mom, Payton, is way too busy with work, so I offered to do it." Pained, he lets out the remaining air in his cheeks. It's on the tip of my tongue to ask, *And what about your brother?* But I don't. "I know you're good with parties and events," he says. Over the past few days, I've been in full planning mode for Crystal's bridal shower in a few weeks. He's all too familiar with my Pinterest aesthetic board.

"I am . . ."

"I know it's a lot to ask, though, and I completely understand if you're too busy—"

"I'm in." Given that I cobbled together and revamped my former wedding into a brand-new wedding for Grandma Flo a couple months ago (while emotionally wounded), I'm certain a child's party will be a piece of cake. "When is it?"

"Not for a month and a half. February fifteenth."

Exactly seven weeks away. I drum my fingers, Mr. Burns–style. The gears are already turning with the possibilities.

His squared shoulders fall with relief. "Thank you. Seriously."

The nurse emerges, signaling we can head back in. We stay for a little under an hour, and I watch in amusement as Trevor lovingly teases her about anything and everything, like her latest crushes ("You still in love with the kid on your soccer team?"). She gets him back with some sizzling burns of her own ("Do you still eat dinner all alone every night?").

When it's finally time to leave, I promise to come back and visit on my breaks, if she wants me to. This pleases her. She even asks me to write down my schedule so she knows when to expect me, which I take as the highest compliment.

Trevor and I are silent as we wait for the elevator. The beeping and the high-pitched laughter of the women at the nurses' station echo behind us.

My thoughts are heavy with a whirl of questions and concerns as we step into the elevator. "What are her chances?"

"They're hopeful we can find a donor." He shoves his hands in his pockets. "But you never know. I want her to have a good birthday . . . just in case."

There's a long pause as I take in the expression on his face. After years of dealing with parents in the NICU, I'd recognize it anywhere. It's terror.

Naturally I want to fold him into a comforting hug, but I settle for a reaffirming pat on the forearm. His muscle flexes underneath my touch.

"Don't worry, Trev. She's gonna have a kick-ass party. I'll make sure of it."

LIVE WITH TARAROMANCEQUEEN—FIGHT CHILDHOOD HEART DISEASE STACK CHALLENGE

[Tara looks somberly into the camera, dressed in a red sweater with tiny white hearts.]

EXCERPT FROM TRANSCRIPT

Tara: Hello, romance book lovers, welcome back to my channel. Today we're talking about something non-bookish.

Did you know approximately one out of four children diagnosed with congenital heart defects will require surgery within the first year of life? And potentially more in the future?

In honor of all children diagnosed with congenital heart defects, @Emilybooklover, @MeganReadsRomance, @CurvyFitnessCrystal, and @Melanie_inthecity have teamed up. We will be donating one dollar for every red-and-white book stack any of our followers post throughout the month of January to support local Boston families of children with heart defects.

Further, my grandma (follow her at @LoopsWithFlo) is donating crochet dolls to the children's hospital for every fifth stack. Don't miss out! They're adorable!

COMMENTS:

Wow this is such an amazing cause! ♡

You are amazing Tara. ♡

This is a cause close to my heart. My son was diagnosed with ♡
CHD at two years old. He had surgery and he's perfectly
healthy now. I'm posting my stack tomorrow!

❤ chapter fifteen

IT'S A BLINDINGLY sunny mid-January afternoon, or so Trevor tells me. I wouldn't know, because I'm cloaked in shadow on the couch, curtains drawn like a comic book villain, Grandma Flo's afghan hiked to my neck. In addition to crafting scenarios in my head that will never come to fruition, I'm two hours deep in YouTube montages of shirtless Chris Hemsworth in a last-ditch effort to boost my morale.

"You're gonna make a permanent imprint in the couch," Trevor warns.

"Don't judge. I've never been better. In fact, I'm thriving here," I croak, peeking at him over the back of the couch. He's doing his biweekly kitchen deep clean, furiously scrubbing the stovetop. The chemical scent of the industrial-strength cleaner never fails to render me light-headed.

"Yup, you're the picture of wellness." He pauses his scrubbing, silently judging my staticky hair. "You need to get out of this apartment. Get some fresh air." He slants an ear toward the kitchen window. To the fickle, chaotic, unpredictable world.

It's been a rough start to the New Year, to say the least. After spending the holidays as the only singleton in my family, I decided to go hard on my ex search.

Since Daniel is still unsearchable, I tried my hand at Zion, the campus bookstore guy I went on a few dates with. We walked dogs together at the animal shelter and bonded over books. He'd play the guitar (terribly) for me while I awkwardly nodded and pretended to love it. Things ended when he decided he needed to stop dating and focus on his "studies."

I don't follow him on social media anymore, but a little light Google stalking revealed his consulting firm's phone number. When I called him, we ended up having a half-hour-long chat. He seemed happy to reconnect but made it clear he was "too busy" with his business for romance. I guess some things never change.

After Zion and a few glasses of wine at Mel's, we did some digging on Cody Venner, my high school sweetheart. Turns out he's now a big-shot real estate agent. Judging from his photos and short bio on the broker's website, he has his shit together, despite the fact that the trousers he's wearing in his professional full-body shot hug every crevice of his undercarriage. Thankfully, I had enough self-awareness to preserve him for a future, less intoxicated version of me.

Because I can't leave well enough alone, I scraped the bottom of the barrel and reached out to number eight, Linus Batton. Linus and I met through a college friend. He always mispronounced my name, calling me "Taw-rah" instead of "Tare-uh." I let it go initially—frankly because it made me sound more sophisticated—and by our third hangout, it was too far gone to correct him. Things fizzled out between us naturally when I started working full-time at the hospital while he pursued his master's in engineering. Since college, he's been designing bridges, as well as dabbling in triathlons.

Linus has since been a loyal Liker of my posts on my non-bookish Instagram account, which I interpreted as a surefire sign he would be down to father my children.

As per Trevor's advice, I invited him for a date at a board game café, despite the fact that I don't like board games. I even limited myself to generic conversation instead of gushing soliloquies full of intense feelings. Through a couple of rounds of Risk (probably my least favorite game of all time, but Linus's favorite), we bonded over songs we mutually despise (Maroon 5's latest), notable books we've read (all romance for me, all techno-thrillers for him), and the recent season of *Deadliest Catch* (his guilty pleasure).

I was flying high, so pleasantly surprised at how well things were going that I casually mentioned my failed engagement with Seth. I hit a wound—a fresh, gaping, infected one at that. He tearfully confided that he too canceled his wedding last year with his boyfriend, Zach. He then began wedging him into our conversation at every opportunity. *Zach always loved that movie. Oh, Zach and I were supposed to take a hot-air balloon ride for our anniversary.* Even when I segued into what I assumed was the safe topic of a YouTube video of a sheep stuck in a tire swing, his eyes welled up because it reminded him (somehow) of Zach.

While I understand the heartache all too well, the last thing I want to do is get tangled up in some sort of love triangle where I'm the evil new girlfriend, the roadblock between Linus and the person he's truly pining for. So we ended the night on friendly, platonic terms.

1. Daniel (childhood love)
2. ~~Tommy (ninth-grade boyfriend)~~
3. ~~Jacques (Student Senate boy)~~
4. Cody (high school sweetheart)
5. ~~Jeff (frosh week fling)~~
6. ~~Zion (campus bookstore cutie)~~
7. ~~Brandon (world traveler—the one that got away)~~
8. ~~Linus (Brandon rebound)~~
9. ~~Mark (book club intellectual)~~
10. ~~Seth (ex-fiancé)~~

"Since you're my life coach now, do you have any suggestions to turn my day around?" I avert my gaze from the swell of Trevor's rippling biceps as he attacks the island countertop with a steel sponge.

"Who says I'm your life coach?"

"Me. Obviously."

He huffs. "That title comes with too much power. Besides, you do not want me giving you life advice. And even if I were qualified, you wouldn't listen to me anyway."

I pout. "I listen! Most of the time."

"Sure you do." He snickers. "Why don't you declutter your room? Or better yet, burn the Ex-Files items of the dudes already crossed off the list?"

I perk up, perching my elbows on the back of the couch. It

might be therapeutic to get rid of some of it. "Like burning them in a cleansing ritual? Would you help me?"

"No. I'm just kidding. I can't support open fires. Why don't you go sit in a coffee shop and talk to people?" he suggests.

"That's a possibility. I do like coffee shop people. They're always willing to spill the tea." I drum my chin, considering. "What are you up to today? I tried texting Mel and Crystal, but they're both busy."

He cocks his thick brow. "Sounds like I'm your third choice."

"You'd be my first choice if you didn't give me so much attitude." I give him a pointed look. "Picture this: We people-watch on the Common. Maybe go to the plant store for a new succulent. I could even buy you a snack, as long as it's under five dollars. I'm broke."

"Whoa, you're really threatening me with outright fun," he says dryly.

"Oh, come on. You need fresh air too. You're going to poison us both with chemicals if you keep cleaning."

He finally lifts his gaze from the countertop. "I'd love to freeze my nuts off with you outside, with no snacks, but I have to get to work soon."

I point to our side-by-side schedules posted on the fridge. "You're not on the schedule tonight."

"I know. I have the food drive tonight."

"Food drive?"

"We do it every year at the firehouse. Go around in the fire trucks and pick up donations around the city."

That sounds heaps more appealing than lying on this couch,

staring into the void. Then again, just about anything trumps that. "Can I come?" I ask meekly.

"You really want to come to work with me?" He squints, confused.

I barrel-roll off the couch and shimmy onto the stool in front of the island. "I swear, I won't get in the way. Manual labor isn't my strength, but—"

"We leave in an hour."

• • •

MY TOES TAP in my boots as I endeavor to find a half-decent radio station. Trevor is laser focused on the snowy road. I'm tempted to prod him a little, ask what he's thinking about, but I refrain, recalling how annoyed Seth used to get when I asked him that same question.

Curiosity aside, I'm hesitant to disturb the peaceful ambience. Trevor's quiet brings me a sense of comfort. In the presence of anyone else, I usually feel an unspoken obligation to maintain lively conversation. But with Trevor, I don't feel the pressure to do anything but just exist.

The silence can no longer be sustained when Shania Twain's "Any Man of Mine" filters through the speakers. Without permission, I crank the volume and belt the intro with abundant soul, church choir–style.

Trevor casts me a concerned side eye. His mouth is fixed in a stern line, but his knee is bouncing along with his fingers drumming the steering wheel. Even a macho dude like Trevor isn't immune to the mood-boosting magic of a Shania Twain classic.

"You like this song," I conclude, pleased with my discovery. "You're tapping your knee to the beat."

He purposely stops tapping like a miserable curmudgeon. "Nope."

I reach over the console to shake his biceps. It's more like a pathetic attempt at a shove, because my palm doesn't come close to spanning that solid mass of muscle.

My head tilts like an eager puppy listening to the sound of kibble trickling into an empty dish. I expected him to defend this until the end times. "Can I ask—" I stop myself before he can cut in and say no. "Why do you hate when I ask if I can ask a question?"

"Because it freaks me out."

"Why?"

"There's no question more anxiety-inducing than *Can I ask you a question?* It could be anything. You could be asking me to divulge all my darkest secrets, or what I ate for lunch."

"Nine times out of ten, I'm asking what you ate for lunch. Anyways, I was going to ask, why don't you sing songs you like? You only hum your T. Swift shower song. Why not belt the lyrics too?"

He lets out a single laugh, checking over his shoulder before seamlessly merging into the lane. "Yeah, that's not my thing, sweetheart."

I ignore the way my stomach flips when he says *sweetheart* in that thick, sexy, I-just-woke-up voice. Logically, I know it's pure sarcasm. But that has no bearing on my physiological response. I'm very aware of the many layers I'm wearing underneath my peacoat. My cream-colored, chunky-knit sweater suddenly scratches against my skin like an itchy heated blanket. When I reach to close the vent, Trevor notices and promptly turns the heat down two notches. He also turns off my seat warmer.

The rest of the drive is silent, save for my singing. I think he's grateful to escape the car when we pull into the parking lot of the redbrick firehouse. It's wide with four massive garage doors, each housing a red truck. As I step out of Trevor's car, I'm hit with the scent combination of gasoline, rubber, and a faint hint of smoke.

Scott comes marching around the corner of the engine bay, fully suited in fire gear, his helmet tucked under his arm. He double-takes when he spots me, running a hand through his thick, overgrown hair, which he's very proud of. "Hey, what are you doing here?"

"She needed some sun. She was slowly turning into a vampire," Trevor tells him nonchalantly. "I'm just gonna go gear up. Be right back." He gives me a playful nudge to the back of the shoulder.

Scott waits for Trevor to be out of earshot before giving me a quizzical expression. "That was weird," he mutters under his breath.

"What was weird?"

"Oh, nothing." He drops his eyes to his boots, quickly changing the subject. "Hey, did you know Trevor got promoted before the holidays?"

I slow-blink. "What? A promotion?" Why wouldn't he tell me?

"He's the new lieutenant." Scott's expression softens. "Don't take it personally that he didn't tell you. He doesn't tell anyone anything." Before I can respond, he ushers me along. "Come on, I'll introduce you to the rest of the crew."

Meeting the team distracts me from angsting over Trevor's secrecy. Notably, there's Kevin, who is the first to tell me that under no circumstances will he lift a finger today, due to a back injury. Paula is one of three women at the station and is grateful for my presence. She even insists I need to ride in her truck to debrief about the latest season of *Euphoria*. Everyone is laid-back, boasting friendly demeanors that hit me like fresh ocean air, compared to the polluted smog that is the hospital, with its endless drama.

And then there's Cameron. He's built like a lumberjack, towering over even Scott, who's well over six feet.

Cameron introduces himself with a burly handshake. "How you doin'?" he asks in a Joey Tribbiani New York–style accent. "You're Scotty's sister-in-law, huh?"

"*Soon-to-be* sister-in-law," I correct, shooting Scott a look. "Although they're eloping to tropical paradise without me. Leaving me behind in the dead of winter."

Cameron gifts me with a Calvin Klein model smile. "Hey, it's not so bad. I'm here in Boston."

Before I can react to his blatant confidence, Trevor materializes behind me. "Ready to go?" he asks, eyeing Cameron.

I go to respond, but the visual of Trevor suiting up changes life as I know it. Men in uniform have never sparked the fanny flutters, until now. Even in a completely shapeless jacket, his sex appeal has skyrocketed to new heights. The whole thing plays out in my mind in slo-mo. Flexing tendons, strained forearms, all dipping and twisting like art in motion.

The corner of his mouth quirks up when he notices me blatantly ogling him like a tiger awaiting a hunk of raw, bloody meat to be tossed into its enclosure. I think I may have just ovulated.

"Why are you staring at me like that?"

My cheeks burn, and I do a one-eighty to beeline for the first available truck, which happens to be Cameron's.

As I take my first step, Trevor gives the collar of my peacoat a soft tug. "Nope. Not that one. You're my responsibility today." His tone is neutral, although I can't help but feel as if I'm burdening him. Like he's obliged to babysit me.

I shrug it off, following him into the correct truck. There are two face-to-face seats on either side in addition to a row along the back. He promptly points me toward a face-to-face seat, taking the backward one. Kevin is our driver. Sadly, I'm not in Paula's truck, or Scott's. But the other two guys, Ernie and Jesse, are supportive of my suggestion to crank the music.

Everyone but Trevor belts a Queen song as the truck barrels down the city streets toward the first pickup location. Ernie even offers me a red Twizzler. I thank him, peeling one out before passing the bag to Trevor. When he reaches for it, I catch the tail end of a tattoo that extends to his wrist.

"When did you get your first tattoo?" I ask through a sticky bite.

"When I graduated high school. I moved to Arizona for a while for college. I was missing home when I got this one." He pulls back the sleeve to reveal an artfully designed compass on the inside of his wrist.

"You were in college?"

"Yup. Had a scholarship for rugby."

More breaking news. Yet another major detail about Trevor Metcalfe I was unaware of. I try to ignore the press of our knees together as the truck slants downhill. Trevor doesn't seem to notice or care, because he doesn't shift away.

"I had no idea you played rugby at the college level."

"I dropped out after the second year." He catches my concerned-mother reaction and quickly adds, "Came home and joined the BFD."

"Why did you leave?"

He lifts a shoulder in a shrug. "Lots of reasons. I got injured after the second season. But mostly because I hated being away from home. And Angie was born during my second year. I knew my brother wasn't stepping up, so it didn't feel right to be so far away," he says. "My grandma passed away in that same year too."

"She must have been really proud of you for getting a scholarship."

His jaw tics, and he averts his stare to his lap, clearly done with the conversation.

One layer at a time with Trevor, I remind myself as we arrive at our first stop. It's a local grocery store. The owner and staff wait in the entrance as Trevor and the crew retrieve the food donations. A reporter in a vibrant emerald jacket hovers on the sidelines, snapping photos. Trevor blinks away the flash as he squats down to lift a box of canned soup.

"You don't like the paparazzi?" I prod.

He passes the box to Kevin, who grumpily agreed to take on the role of stacking the boxes in the truck. "Nah. I'd rather do it without all the fanfare—" He pauses when a stout, balding man approaches, his hand extended.

"I was told you're the man in charge here. I'm Yoni, the store owner," he says.

Trevor meets his handshake. "Good to meet you, Yoni. I'm Trevor."

"I just wanted to thank you guys before you head out. It means a lot."

"We couldn't do it without the donations. So thank *you*," Trevor tells him.

Yoni nods, casting a proud gaze at the stack of boxes in the truck. "The food bank is a cause close to my heart. As a young boy, my family relied on it. I do what I can to give back."

Trevor gives him a terse nod and a slap on the back. "Mine did too, man. Full circle, huh?"

I bow my head at the revelation as we return to the truck. I feel terrible for all the times I teased him for being cheap. An apology is necessary, though now doesn't seem to be an appropriate time.

We repeat the pickup at five more locations. One is another grocery store, while the other four are random neighborhood checkpoints. And by the time our route is over, the truck is stuffed to capacity with donations. With each pickup, Trevor's mood lightens. At one point, I even catch him mouthing the words to a Bon Jovi classic. It's not much, but I'll take it.

The last stop is to drop the boxes off at the food bank. Even I partake in the labor, taking mostly the boxes with pasta and other light goods.

By the time it's all over, Trevor and I are flat-out exhausted. In the car, I find myself lazily studying his profile. I never noticed before, but the man has a beautiful nose. Perfectly straight. Proportionate to his face. It's slightly pointed, almost pretty boy, contradicting the rest of his gruff exterior.

When he side-eyes me, I blink, stopping myself from staring at him.

"Hot tub when we get back?" he asks, moving a hand over his right shoulder. He winces slightly as he reaches for his seat belt.

"Yes. I need it. Is your shoulder okay?"

"Yeah, all good. It acts up once in a while. I dislocated it in rugby, and again a couple of years back during a fire call. It hasn't been the same since." He reaches over the console and nudges my arm. "Hey, thanks for coming today."

"Thanks for bringing me, even if I annoyed you."

He pins me with a small smile as we pull out of the parking lot. "Not at all. Everyone loves you. Especially Cam," he adds, his expression unreadable.

I snort at the memory of Cameron flirting with me when we reconvened at the food bank. He strategically positioned himself next to me while we unloaded the items. And while he's a little too bro-ish for my liking, the attention was kind of nice, especially after my shit dating luck. "You think?"

"You make everyone smile."

I beam like a child in a toy store. I shouldn't get such a soaring high from a simple statement of affirmation from a friend, but I do. Mel and Crystal compliment me on the regular. But praise from noncomplimentary Trevor feels hard-earned, like junk food after working out versus junk food after lazing about on the couch all day.

We drive a couple of miles in silence. The steady squeak of the wipers nearly soothes me to sleep. With every swipe, my lids grow heavier. When my eyes close completely, his voice snaps me back to full consciousness. "My mom died when I was thirteen. In a fire."

I pause for a moment, so as to ensure I've heard him correctly. "What?"

"You keep asking why I became a firefighter."

I sit up in my seat, pin straight, cracking the window for some much-needed fresh air.

His face flickers with annoyance when I open the window, so I savor the blast of cold air for a brief few seconds before closing it again. "Summer going into eighth grade. My mom was napping inside after a double shift. My brother and I were outside with some neighborhood kids. A woman who lived in our building came running out, screaming about smoke in the building. The fire had blocked all the exits. Two firemen had to go in through the window to get her. She passed away later that day from the smoke inhalation." His tone is emotionless, but his face is pained.

My gut clenches, unable to imagine. "I'm so sorry, Trevor."

"It's fine. It was a long time ago," he says, his eyes on the road. "Logan and I went to live with my grandma after that. The one who taught me how to bake."

"Were you close with your grandma?"

"Yeah. That woman was no bullshit. We always joke that Angie is her reincarnation," he says with a small smile. "When she took us in, she had to take on another job to support us. She was always worried about how we'd get through the month. I felt like shit about that. Sometimes I wonder if it's our fault she kicked the bucket early, you know? Like maybe all the extra stress caused it."

"I doubt it. And even if it did, I can guarantee she wouldn't have had it any other way." I pause, turning toward him. "That must have been really hard. Losing your mom and your grandma."

"It was," he admits. "Anyway, was that personal enough for you?"

"I don't want you to feel pressured to talk about things like

AMY LEA

that. Especially if it upsets you," I tell him. I let a few beats of silence go by before speaking again. "Congratulations, by the way, on your promotion. Scotty told me."

"Thank you."

"Why didn't you tell me?"

"Just didn't think it was that big a deal," he says.

"It is to me," I assure him. I rest my head back against the seat, cursing myself for the shit timing of my fatigue.

"You get one more question, and then no more talking, okay?"

This perks me up momentarily. I rack my brain for a juicy one. "Okay. If you could picture any woman to break your non-relationship spell, what would she be like? Hypothetically."

He goes stiff as a board. "I dunno, Tara. What do *you* think she'd be like?"

My lids close as I visualize. "Hmm . . . Beautiful. Probably the type who would watch sports with you. Eat a burger. Drink beer. One of the not-like-the-other-girls."

"What's that?"

"Exactly how it sounds. The girl who doesn't care what anyone thinks. Isn't needy or anything like a stereotypical girl. Like Seth's girlfriend, Ingrid."

He chuckles. "So . . . the opposite of you."

"Basically. You know how in *How to Lose a Guy in 10 Days*, super-cool Kate Hudson pretends to be a clingy, emotional, fern-obsessed girl to make Matt McConaughey dump her?"

He clears his throat. "No, but go on."

"I always hated that movie because that girl was me. I was the annoying one that no guy would ever want to date. Anyway, I think that's the kind of girl you'd be with. The cool one."

162

He watches me for a moment. "You're tired. You should take a nap. Save your voice before you talk my ear off," he instructs, giving me an unexpected yet gentle squeeze on the forearm.

I can barely even register the delicious scorch of his touch. His eyes ensnare mine unexpectedly, and for some reason, I can't look away. His small smile is the last thing I see before my lids flutter to a close.

• • •

ALL I SEE is beige. The fabric of the interior ceiling of Trevor's car. There's a hot sensation pooling in between my thighs, countering the coolness of the car window soothing the side of my head.

My skin is a live wire. Tingly, pulsing, and sensitive to the tiniest gust of air. Soft lips dance past my chest, making a trail down the valley of my stomach. I can't see his face, but I know it's Trevor. The tiniest scrape of his stubble sends a ripple through me. I'm counting my breaths, because if I don't, I'll surely pass out. And with each inhale, his spicy scent overpowers everything else. It's all around me and I want to bask in it like a load of warm, freshly dried laundry.

My breath quickens as his lips move past the curve of my belly button, over the groove of my hipbone, and down. One hand gently palms my breasts while smoothing over my thigh, parting my legs.

Somehow, I'm already undressed from the waist down, sweater bunched up around my stomach, and for some odd reason, I'm not surprised about it. There's pressure in my thighs as rough fingers dig into the softness of my flesh.

I angle myself upward to run my fingers through his hair, pulling in a light tug. He teases the patch of skin above where I desperately want him. Like the pain in the ass he is, he takes his lips off my skin and meets my eyes in a seductive challenge.

"Keep going," I whisper, arching my back to push against his compliant mouth.

My vision is a blur of stars as the pressure crescendos higher and higher and—

Click, click. Ding.

My eyes fly open. A harsh flood of fluorescent-yellow light hits me straight in the eyeballs, rendering me near blind. The sweet, chemical aroma of gasoline floods my senses as I force-blink my spotty vision away.

I let out a muffled cry. For the briefest of seconds, I think I've been kidnapped—until I take in the finger-drawn lopsided heart in the fog on the windshield I drew earlier in the firehouse parking lot. Past the window, there's a painted number *35* on the concrete wall that tells me I'm in the apartment parking garage.

Trevor grunts as he hauls himself out of the driver's seat.

A brief glance downward tells me I'm still in my clothes too, bundled in my coat. Layered leggings, wool socks, and boots laced tight.

Trevor is certainly *not* in between my legs. And his mouth certainly *isn't* down there, despite the warm, tingly sensation I feel, as if he really were.

Reality settles around me, like pixels slowly but surely filling a screen.

Hello, bleak reality.

It was a dream.

I should be grateful that I haven't been taken by some psycho who plans to hold me captive as one of three wives in his secret torture dungeon to birth an army of offspring, but I'm pissed. Frustrated. Like a kid reaching for a decadent piece of chocolate cake on the counter, only to have it snatched away by a health-conscious parent at the very last second.

I've received my fair share of oral sex, but no one has made me feel like *that*. Like he knew exactly what I wanted, without words. Sure, it was erotic and dangerous, but there was a comfort that's unexplainable. I didn't ask questions. I didn't fret about how I looked, or sounded, or tasted. Then again, it wasn't really *me*.

It was just a dream, I remind myself. It wasn't real. The feeling wasn't real. Trevor and I are platonic. Friends only. We do not see each other naked (except accidentally). And we are most certainly not together, despite how perfect it felt.

I clutch my throat, practically choking myself as I come to terms with the horror. I had a sex dream about Trevor. And I liked it. Really liked it.

This means nothing, I tell myself. Dreams are nothing but random compilations of subconscious thoughts, as logical Mel would say. Don't put too much stock in it. Who wouldn't have a naughty dream or two about a person they've heard having sex through very thin walls?

An impatient tap on the passenger window snaps me out of my spiraling thoughts. "You coming?" Trevor's deep voice is muffled from behind the glass.

Nope. Not anymore. Thanks for reminding me.

I need an intervention, and fast.

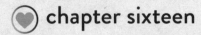 **chapter sixteen**

LIVE WITH TARAROMANCEQUEEN: THE HIGH SCHOOL SWEETHEART

[Tara is surrounded by green foliage. She looks at peace with nature, despite a pesky branch that keeps grazing her face.]

EXCERPT FROM TRANSCRIPT

Tara: *Hello, romance book lovers, welcome back to my channel. Today is the much-anticipated High School Sweetheart episode. I've gotten a ton of messages begging me to reach out to my very own high school sweetheart, Cody.*

High school sweethearts are my favorite book boyfriends. Ever since I was in middle school, I daydreamed about meeting my future husband in front of my locker. He'd be the popular, slightly dumb jock in a letterman jacket who discovers my secret, nerdy charm.

People scoff at misguided adolescent love, but I think there's something special about not having to navigate the minefield that is adult dating. First, you've probably known your high school sweetheart your entire life. You've witnessed each other's awkward braces stage, the acne, and the hacked bangs. There are no secrets. No surprises.

My personal favorite high school sweetheart of literature is Peter Kavinsky from To All the Boys I've Loved Before. Peter K is the ultimate, and you can't tell me otherwise. He's the adorable puppy-faced boy next door who's nice to everyone. Your parents. Your grandma. The loner kid in school. He's cute, innocent enough, although I do suspect he may crush Lara Jean's heart in college . . .

Anyways, backstory. I fell for Cody in tenth-grade science class when he enthusiastically offered to partner with a kid named Bruce, who no one wanted to sit within a three-seat radius of because he had BO. Cody and I had nearly every class together, which gave me ample opportunity to talk to him.

Things really ramped up during a science field trip in Vermont, where we spent hours walking through the woods learning the difference between coniferous and deciduous trees. We snuck away into the bushes and shared our first kiss. As karma would have it, we both got poison ivy rashes later that day.

I'm about to see him for the first time since our breakup before college. Wish me luck!

• • •

I'M STANDING IN a bush, and I'm not proud of it.

For the past half hour, Mel and I have been creeping across the street from an outrageously priced Victorian house for sale in the upscale neighborhood of Back Bay. Thanks to my daily social media stalk of Cody Venner's Realtor website, I discovered he's hosting an open house today for one of his listings.

After my R-rated dream about Trevor, and after coming to the stark realization that I only have two exes left and three more weeks until the gala, I doubled down on my second-chance-romance quest. Anything to distract myself from the fact that my attraction for Trevor may or may not be blooming into an all-out crush.

For the past week, we've been verging on dangerous territory. On evenings we're both off work, we sit side by side on the couch, binging TV or reading. Each night, we stay up a little later, knowing full well that breaking sleep patterns is a death wish for shift workers. His mere presence smooths all my swirling thoughts. Every time he smiles or laughs (or, God forbid, both), I lose all circulation in my limbs. With every accidental touch or brush of skin when we're on the couch or in our tiny kitchen, I'm spellbound to the point of doing just about anything he asks of me.

Two nights ago, I was on my tiptoes, trying to grab a bag of chips from the top of the fridge. Before I knew it, Trevor's entire chest was pressed against the width of my back as he reached over me to assist. When I spun around, startled, our eyes snagged for a few beats longer than normal before he handed me the chips, ruffling my hair like an annoying older brother—an act that harshly reminded me of our nonsexual-roommate status.

Finding Cody's open house listing was like discovering a single diamond in a steaming pile of horseshit. I launched out of bed this morning and put in some serious work painting my face using Mel's

Pink Peachy Glam makeup tutorial. Mel and I even prepared an elaborate backstory—that she mysteriously came into a large sum of money and is embarking on a new quest to flip houses with her own bare hands.

Is it desperate to randomly crash my ex's open house after not speaking to him for over a decade? One hundred percent. Am I shameless enough to risk the humiliation anyway? Beyond.

Just thinking about Cody Venner feels like slipping on a favorite tried-and-true sweater. Among a hundred other sweaters, you gravitate toward this one for every occasion, anticipating the bliss of that fuzzy, plush fabric against your skin. The freshly laundered yet familiar scent of home. Just the right amount of wear and tear for optimal comfort and movement.

"He was the perfect boyfriend," I'd explained to Trevor on my way out the door to meet Mel. "He was ambitious, great with my parents, involved in every club and sport. I didn't see it coming when he broke up with me before college. He was going to Penn State, and I was staying here in Boston. He didn't think we could do long-distance—"

Trevor shook his head. "Nah. Cody broke up with you because he wanted the freedom to fuck other girls."

"You don't even know Cody," I'd snapped, offended on Cody's behalf while simultaneously burdened by the memory of crying for multiple days straight in my bedroom after our breakup, combing through my box full of three years' worth of handwritten notes and drawings he'd sent me during class. There were moments I was convinced my lungs were collapsing, that my chest was caving in on me. That I quite literally couldn't live without him. Aside from Seth, Cody was by far my worst breakup.

Trevor doubled down. "I don't have to know him. I know the way men think."

Whether or not Cody intended to sow his wild oats in college is neither here nor there. Holding a decade-old mistake over his head would be shortsighted, particularly if our connection was as strong as I remember.

I've even perfected how I'll look when we lay eyes on each other. I'll do my brows-to-hairline shocked expression and whimper, "Cody Venner, is that really you?" in a transatlantic, old-school, black-and-white-movie accent.

But now that I'm here, I'm paralyzed with fear. What if Cody thinks I'm nuts for showing up? What if he laughs in my face? What if he full-out rejects me, like all my other exes? Or worse, what if he doesn't even remember me?

I'll stay in this bush forever, I think to myself as Mel tries to coax me out with the promise of snacks. It smells divine in here, like a Christmas tree farm. It's thick enough to shield me from the unforgiving wind. I'm finally convinced to emerge when she dangles the prospect of borrowing her shoes whenever I want.

After three steps, I think better of it and scamper back into the bushes like a skittish rodent. "Nope. Can't do it. This was a bad idea."

Mel yanks on my coat sleeve. "Look, I didn't spend hours perfecting my sexy prospective-house-flipper look for nothing. As long as you stick to the script, everything will be fine. Remember, you're just here for a second opinion on my house-flipping business. It's all but a strange coincidence that he just so happens to be the selling agent." She charges across the street at an alarmingly fast pace for someone in three-inch heel boots that she deems "house-flipper chic." She definitely watches too much HGTV.

Before I even take a step, I close my eyes and suck in a dramatic breath.

Relax. You've got this. This could be your second-chance romance. The very one you've been waiting for. He could be in that very house and you're wasting precious time, you nitwit!

My mental scolding works, because I strut forth like *Miss Congeniality* Sandra Bullock post-makeover, pre–twisted ankle. Hair blowing. Hips sashaying side to side to the beat of "She's a Lady." If only I had aviators to whip off with fierce attitude, revealing my soulful brown eyes. I imagine my gaze somehow ensnaring Cody from a distance, weakening him to his knees until he dissolves like an iceberg in the middle of the Sahara.

A foghorn pierces my ears, rudely interrupting my fantasy. A bright-yellow school bus lurches to a stop a few feet from me, brakes squealing. My sad little life flashes before my eyes. The elderly bus driver shakes his head, fury-motioning for me to get the hell out of the middle of the street.

Mel pulls me onto the sidewalk and brushes the nonexistent dirt off my coat, as if I've fallen on the ground or something. "Oh my God. You almost got crushed."

"See? It's an omen. A sign that this is a terrible idea," I whine.

She tugs me toward the decaying porch's peeling navy-blue stairs. "Come on. You're fine."

The porch steps sag under our weight. Our initial assessment was correct. This place is a serious project, but its original Victorian charm is still evident. The wood beams around the posts are carved into intricate curves and little swirls. The same swirls are embedded into the wood around the doors and windows, all of which look original.

When Mel opens the wooden double doors, a strong waft of

eucalyptus instantly clears my stuffed nose. The foyer is narrow, with an elaborate wooden staircase jutting from the middle, flanked by a winter garland. A heavily accented Bostonian voice booms from the back of the house.

And that's when I hear it. ". . . the previous owners knocked down the wall to create an open living area . . ." It's Cody. I'm sure of it. I haven't heard his voice in years, but there's a familiar cadence and rhythm to it that always reminded me of a TV news anchor.

Behind the staircase is an entranceway to the outdated kitchen. As Mel steps forward, a young couple and a man in a crisp gray suit pass the doorway. I instantly recognize the pronounced slope of his linebacker shoulders.

Mel points me to the kitchen to join the tour, but I hightail us upstairs to delay my fate.

For such a large house, the bedrooms are minuscule. Both bathrooms are severely outdated. I'm rambling about all the things I'd change about the house, momentarily under the grand delusion that I'm actually buying it myself, when Mel shushes me. "I think they're leaving."

"Thank you for the showing. We'll be in touch," a deep voice sounds from downstairs.

The door closes. Footsteps ascend the stairs. Panic ensues, and Mel tries to keep me in place, her hand over my mouth like a kidnapper. I'm like a mouse caught in a trap, just waiting to be discovered. It takes a solid moment, but I manage to wrench myself from her grip, ready to make a break for it. And I do just that. Heart pounding, I make it all of one step before slamming into Cody's chest.

"Whoa. Where are you going?" He places his large hands over

my shoulders, stabilizing me as he leans back, his eyes widening in recognition. "Tara?"

"Hi," I squeak like I've inhaled helium. It's a far cry from my rehearsed facial expression and script, but at this point, I'm just thankful he recognizes me.

A wide smile spreads across his face. "No freakin' way!" he says jovially, going in for a full-body hug. He used to smell like Dove soap and the laundry detergent his mom used. But now he's wearing a strong, musty cologne I don't hate.

From his Realtor photos, I knew he'd grown into his teeth. I knew he now boasted a wide, angular jawline that should probably be considered a crime. I knew his previously long, skater-boy blond hair was now coiffed to perfection.

But what wasn't evident from his professional headshots was his height. I'd forgotten how tall he was, nearly six feet, though not quite Trevor's height. I know this because Trevor hugged me exactly once, when I surprised him by cleaning the entire apartment a few days ago. When he pulled me into his hard chest, my cheek molded perfectly in between his pecs, the top of my head just skimming his neck. And yes, I was on the precipice of keeling over right then and there.

"I can't believe it's you," I manage, half-strangled in Cody's embrace.

He releases me, his eyes flickering over my chest. Thank God I wore my push-up bra today. "What are you doing here? In the market for a house?"

Just stalking you a little. Hope you don't mind. "Oh, no. I mean, yes. Kind of. My friend Melanie and I are just checking out—"

"I'm looking for an investment property to flip," Mel cuts in with sharp confidence, saving me from myself. "I've come into a large sum of money from my late great-aunt."

Cody buys her story. "Nice to meet you, Melanie. Tara and I actually went to high school together. Dated for, what? Two years?" He flashes me an enchanting, confident smile that reminds me of why I was so obsessed with him.

I'm about to point out that we dated for exactly three years and five months, but Mel makes a theatrical show of surprise. "No way! You dated? What a small world."

Cody turns to me. "Still in Boston, huh?"

"Yup. Stuck around. I'm a nurse at the children's hospital."

"And you're still an avid reader, I see?" He eyes the book jammed into my purse.

"Yup. That hasn't changed," I crow nervously. "I, uh, didn't know you got into real estate." *Lies.*

"Actually, you're the one who gave me the idea to do real estate."

"Really?"

"You said you could see me selling anything. That I'd make a good salesman."

I match his wide smile. "It certainly looks like it." My heart leaps. I'm the reason Cody found his dream career?

Cody refocuses on Mel. "You said you're looking for a property to flip? You're in the right place. This property is really special. So much history. The original owner was actually the granddaughter of one of the first Puritans who founded the city."

Mel pretends to rub her chin pensively, studying the ornate wrought iron light fixture hanging over the stairs. "I'm not sure this is the right one. I don't love history, and it's a little grand for what I need. I think my pet gerbils would get lost." She has taken this role-playing a little too seriously.

Cody isn't sure what to say to that. But lucky for him, an elderly gentleman and a woman who looks to be in her thirties in head-to-toe Chanel enter the foyer below. They're already examining the original crown molding, and they haven't even removed their shoes. I assume they're father and daughter, until the man gives her a playful smack on the ass. Cody glances down at them briefly with knowing recognition. "Oh, those are agency clients. I'm scheduled to give them a tour right now, but let's catch up, Tara," he suggests.

"I'd love that. Are you free this week?" I blurt, unable to keep my cool.

He tilts his head hesitantly. "It's a busy week for me, but give me your number and we can figure out a time to grab a drink."

"Great," I chirp, barely able to stop myself from jumping up and down like a fool. My insides explode with multicolor confetti.

He hands me his phone and flashes a charming smile at Mel. "If you change your mind about the house, give me a call." He smoothly slips her his card in between two extended fingers.

I'm still holding Cody's phone, blanking on my own number. When he anxiously peeks downstairs, I panic, typing it at warp speed, adding a little pink heart next to my name. The moment I type the heart, I regret it and go to delete it. But before I can, Cody snaps his phone back and shoves it into the depths of his pocket, clearly itching to get to his clients. "Looking forward to catching up, Tara."

♥ chapter seventeen

THE THING ABOUT being an avid romance reader is everyone assumes you're either a recluse with eleven cats, trying to escape your lonely, pathetic life, or a sex-crazed fiend. No in between.

After four days of texting back and forth with Cody Venner, he's assumed I'm the latter. Case in point:

CODY: What are you wearing right now?

TARA: My hospital scrubs! Just got off work.

CODY: I can work with that. Easy to take off.

CODY: I'm just about to hop in the shower. Wish you were here. 😌

I'm not entirely sure how we segued from a G-rated conversation about our old teachers to NSFW sexting. This is uncharted territory. Sweet teenage Cody certainly never sent texts of this nature in high school. This is the guy who timidly apologized over and over like a broken record during our first time. As a self-declared born-again virgin, I can say that sexting with Cody (however horribly) is the most action I've had in over a year.

Without notice, Trevor appears over my shoulder.

I gasp, red-faced, fumbling to lock my phone screen.

"You all right?" Trevor eyes me cautiously, peeking into my basket. He's joined me for a thrift shop visit to search for a rainbow leopard-print unitard I spotted here the other day. Its tackiness had made such an impact on me, I'd described it to Trevor in great detail and he concluded it was perfect for Scott's bachelor party in two weekends.

While Crystal has a tranquil spa day, Trevor and a few buddies plan to sneak into their apartment at the ass crack of dawn to pretend-kidnap Scott (with blindfold and rope). They're going to toss him in the trunk of Trevor's car and treat him to an artery-clogging breakfast, followed by an afternoon at the *Ninja Warrior* gym. I have no idea where the unitard fits into the equation, and it doesn't matter, because an employee sadly informed us that someone had the gumption to purchase it.

In order to shake off his disappointment, I challenged him to a friendly competition of *Find the weirdest shit* and he's accepted the task. So far, I've collected a hand-painted bust of E.T. (yes, the alien from the film), as well as a mint-condition ceramic piggy bank of two rabbits going at it with all they've got (because it reminds me of Trevor).

When I spin around, he turns away, shielding the discolored, half-disintegrated box under his arm.

"Show me," I say, popping onto my tiptoes.

"Your items aren't even close to beating this find," he goads, lowering the box. It looks like a box of Christmas ornaments, only instead of beautiful glass bulbs, petrifying decapitated doll heads sit snug in the holes. I envision them side by side, arranged in various straight lines, forming a pentagram as part of an elaborate satanic ritual.

I yelp and look away. "Those demented little faces are gonna haunt my dreams tonight."

He dangles a particularly distressed head by its patchy troll hair. "This one bears a striking resemblance to you, don't you think? Maybe I can haggle a good deal for you."

I whack him in the chest. "You are so mean to me. When I die, you'll regret it."

He shoves the box of doll heads onto a sparse shelf next to the nonfiction books. "Why? Will you come back and haunt me?"

"Yup. My Crazy Ex-Girlfriend face will be the first thing you see when you wake up in the morning." I bless him with a short-lived preview of my wide-eyed Joker smile.

The light from the window casts an orange glow off his amused face. "That wouldn't be so bad."

It wouldn't? He lets that statement linger for a fraction too long before my mind short-circuits and I'm compelled to fill the silence. "I'd also turn your pillows tags up, rearrange your spice rack, put the toilet paper roll upside down, and move your keys around. Maybe I'd even play Shania on the radio whenever you're in the car."

"I'm flattered you'd spend your afterlife taunting me."

Would I really waste my ghostly powers on Trevor? Come to

think of it, the ability to peep on him while he's in the shower wouldn't be too shabby— Oh dear. I'm officially a humungo perv.

I banish the sexual shower thoughts away, mentally securing them with a couple layers of duct tape, just to be safe.

My phone vibrates with a new text from Cody.

CODY: You should send me a photo.

"What are you and Cody texting about?" Trevor asks, pulling a random book on cupcake decorating off the shelf. He flips through with pretend interest.

"Well . . ." I turn my screen, revealing his texts.

His eyes flare as he reads. "Wow. He's really going for it, huh? I mean, I guess he's already seen"—he waves a lazy hand downward, toward my lower half—"it all before? Right?"

"He has. But he was never blatantly sexual like this. I don't know what to say back. I don't do nudes."

Trevor continues down the aisle in front of me, scrutinizing their book-filing system. The lack of alphabetical order in this thrift shop is troubling him. "Sorry, Chen. I got nothing."

"Really? I'm shocked you don't have a stockpile of nudes."

"I'll have you know I've never asked a woman for a nude in my life. And dirty texts aren't my style." He turns to face me again, his eyes smoldering.

"Hm. I thought you'd be the type who's into sexting and dirty talk and all that." My neck erupts with prickles at the memory of my illicit car dream.

He averts his stare entirely, deflecting. Yup. He's totally a dirty talker. "You're the one who reads hundreds of sex books a year.

Why don't you pull a line from one of those?" He gestures to the two worn bodice rippers in my basket.

"Dirty talk in romance novels doesn't translate to real life. I can't tell him I want to *ride his throbbing member* with a straight face," I point out.

An elderly woman pushing a full cart near us clutches her bosom and speeds off in the opposite direction.

I wait for Trevor to chide me for uttering the term *throbbing member* in a public place, but he doesn't. Instead, he lets out a distressed groan, his eyes closed. "That was a mental image I didn't need. This is so weird."

Something inside of me dies a little as he charges ahead of me. Splendid. I repulse him.

I spend some time regrouping before I follow him into the mystery/thriller section. "Sorry for disturbing you. But I have one last question. Is it appropriate to suggest an alternative location? I don't want to have virtual shower sex."

I nearly smash into his chest when he turns around. "I still don't understand your grudge against the shower."

"I told you, I don't do water sex. Talk to me about sex between the stacks in a library. Or anywhere with books." The moment the words come out of my mouth, I regret them.

He recognizes my slipup, because he clears his throat awkwardly and leans back against a book display, toppling multiple books onto their sides. "Books, huh?" He clumsily rights the books, not bothering to alphabetize them.

I'm very much aware of how small these aisles are. The books are closing in on me, pages threatening to swallow me whole. Trevor's sizzling stare manages to penetrate. I'm paranoid he can read my mind, which is a flurry of blatantly sexual thoughts. I'm contemplating peeling off my pink cable-knit for some air when Cody texts again.

CODY: Boo, don't forget to pick up the kids at my mom's
today on your way home.

I reread the text at least three times before I show it to Trevor, who stares at it, confused. "Who the hell is *Boo*? Is he trying to role-play with me or something?"

He opens and closes his mouth, pressing his lips together, like he's unsure whether to offer his opinion. "I . . . have a feeling that text wasn't meant for you."

Another text comes in.

CODY: Woops. Meant to send that to someone else.
TARA: Who? Your wife?

Little dots appear instantly, and then disappear. Proverbial crickets.

1. Daniel (childhood love)
2. ~~Tommy (ninth-grade boyfriend)~~
3. ~~Jacques (Student Senate boy)~~
4. ~~Cody (high school sweetheart)~~
5. ~~Jeff (frosh week fling)~~
6. ~~Zion (campus bookstore cutie)~~
7. ~~Brandon (world traveler—the one that got away)~~
8. ~~Linus (Brandon rebound)~~

9. ~~Mark (book club intellectual)~~
10. ~~Seth (ex-fiancé)~~

• • •

"DON'T BEAT YOURSELF up over him, Tara. He's a dog." Trevor's face is partially obstructed by the billow of steam.

After I struck Cody's name off the list, leaving me with only Daniel as my last hope two weeks before the gala, Trevor urged me to relax in the hot tub before making any rash decisions, like calling Cody's wife to tell him her husband is a cheater.

Unwinding from life stress in the hot tub has become somewhat of a ritual. I've come to look forward to these moments. I'm not sure whether it's the fresh air or the lack of distraction (aside from the times Gerald joins us), but Trevor tends to open up more than usual up here.

A few days ago, he confided in me about another rough day at work. He and the crew were the first on the scene of a fatal car accident that left the driver marred beyond recognition. Brutal as his description was, it's nice to have someone to talk to about even the worst aspects of the job, like blood, gore, and bodily fluids. As first responders and medical professionals, we're not supposed to talk in such detail. It makes people squirm, understandably so. But as I've come to learn, speaking the words out loud releases them from my head. Talking about it is therapeutic in a way, especially with someone who understands.

The only downer to Trevor's and my hot tub hangouts is that they do little to stop my illicit dreams. I've had at least two more since the car dream. And somehow, they've gotten steamier. One even involved the hot tub itself, which is proving to be more awkward than I'd anticipated it would be.

I sink into the warm water until the bubbles hit my chin. "His poor wife and kids. Cody wasn't the cheating type in high school. He was dedicated to me, basically a human golden retriever. He's changed so much . . . Then again, I guess that's *men* for you."

Trevor pokes my shin under the water with his toe. "Don't lump all of us in with him. Not every guy is a cheater."

"Enough of you are. And then us women are called crazy for being paranoid about it. Seth was like that," I note bitterly. "He and Ingrid were friends while he and I were together, actually. They were always texting in those last three months. When I'd look at their conversations, they were overtly flirty. When I called him out, he acted like a victim, like I was some monster for not trusting him. And then they were dating right after we broke up. This is why men deserve less," I grumble, glaring into the night.

"Think of it this way: you dodged yet another bullet," Trevor concludes. "And now you don't have to worry about sexting."

"True. But I won't lie, it was kind of exciting." I bite my lip, shifting away from the blast of the jet, which isn't helping the perma-tension between my legs. "Don't laugh at me, okay? But I haven't had sex in over a year." *And I'm having very inconvenient sex dreams about you.*

He clears his throat, resting his elbows back on the edge of the tub. "Really? An entire year?"

"Yup. Actually, more like a year and a half. Seth and I weren't having sex regularly in the last few months."

He winces in sympathy. "That's rough."

"We'd been together for three years," I say defensively. "At the one-year mark, things tend to just go downhill."

"How so?" he asks curiously.

I swallow, all too aware I'm discussing my pitiful sex life with my roommate, of all people. "Well, actually that's not accurate. It was never all that amazing to begin with. He just liked to dive right in there. No warm-up. Never really cared to ask what I liked."

He slaps his hand over the surface of the water, disturbing his pile of bubbles. "That's fucked-up. Making sure you were satisfied should have been his number one priority."

"I guess I can't really blame him," I say, shifting in my seat. "He was a busy guy, being a doctor and all." I withhold the fact that Seth also had a fiery grudge against sex toys for some reason, because the poor bugger thought I was supposed to get off on his skill set alone (lol).

He gives me a horrified look. "Um, no. Being busy isn't an excuse to be selfish in bed."

I toss my palm to the sky, growing increasingly frustrated. Not over this conversation, necessarily, but over the stark reality of what I put up with. What I thought was normal. "I don't know, Trevor. Maybe I just wasn't great in bed. Maybe he just wanted to get it over with."

Trevor's jaw tics as he stares moodily into the middle distance in the space behind my shoulder. "I sincerely doubt that, Tara." That statement rolls off his tongue with so much ease, a dull tension thrums between my thighs.

I shift in my seat, reminding myself he's just being nice. As usual. "Either way, my point still stands. After a while, passion fades."

He shakes his head in haughty disagreement. "No. Nope. Just because you're in a long-term relationship doesn't mean you stop having sex."

"It absolutely does. Ask any stable, long-term couple. Lack of regular sex is practically a rite of passage."

"Wow. You're making long-term relationships sound so appealing," he quips. "Sign me up."

"The cuddling makes the lack of sex worth it," I assure him. "Wouldn't you rather cuddle with . . . say . . . Kyla than bang some random?"

His eyes widen at the mention of his flight attendant ex-girlfriend. After keeping tabs on her Instagram on Trevor's behalf, which is full of all her extensive travels, I discovered she's returning to Boston in a few days. I brought this to his attention and spent the better part of last night convincing him to DM her. Finally, he caved and typed *Hi*. Lucky for him, I was there to peer-review his texts to ensure he didn't use too many periods so as to come across too harsh.

They agreed to meet up for drinks when she comes back to the city next week. It's hard to tell whether he's excited about it or not.

"It's not as bad as you're making it seem," I continue while he distracts himself with bubbles. "It's kind of like . . . If you eat Pop-Tarts for breakfast every day for years. You still like Pop-Tarts. You're still attracted to Pop-Tarts. But you don't feel this carnal urge to devour them every day."

He smirks. "This is why I switch it up. Smoothies, cereal, omelets. Maybe you should try it sometime. Break out of your comfort zone."

I'm about to scrunch my nose at the thought of a stranger's

naked body over mine, but I stop myself. Maybe Trevor has a point. Why the hell shouldn't I switch things up? Maybe a meaningless hookup with a total stranger is just what I need to distract me from my lack of success with my exes and this ridiculous crush on Trevor.

Crystal used to swear by casual sex, claiming Tinder hookups were therapeutic. I never believed her, but maybe I've been overly stubborn. Based on the sounds I've heard coming from Trevor's room, perhaps it's high time I find out what I'm missing.

"You know what? I'm gonna do it," I say, abruptly launching from the water.

Trevor blinks. "What? Have toast tomorrow instead of a Pop-Tart?"

"No. I'm gonna have a one-night stand!"

♥ chapter eighteen

TREVOR BALKS AT the mere suggestion, his laugh echoing into the cold night air in a plume of vapor. "I was just kidding about the breakfast metaphor."

"No. You make a good point." I retrieve my towel with the renewed energy of a bad bitch on a mission. "I don't switch it up enough. I've never had a one-night stand before. I've never even touched the penis of a dude whose middle name I don't know. But I hear it's liberating."

He follows me out of the hot tub. "It is . . . But you don't like new things. You said yourself you hate the idea of casual sex."

"I mean, I've never actually tried it. How can I proclaim to dislike something I've never tried?"

"But what about your exes? You still have Daniel. What if he's the One?"

"Daniel is a long-term play. I'm still trying to find a way to track him down," I say with a dismissive eye roll. As of yet, Daniel is entirely unsearchable online (not even a deceased grandparent's obituary to be found). I've actually contemplated draining my meager savings to hire a private investigator. "I need something more immediate."

"I guess—"

"We're going on the prowl tonight. You're my wingman." The badass, empowering beginning of "WAP" plays in my mind as I toss my towel over my shoulders like a cape.

He groans, shivering as he pats himself dry with his own towel. "As in going out? Why don't you just use a hookup app like a normal human?"

"Because. I tried it and it wasn't for me."

"Do I even get a say in this?" Trevor asks.

"No," I call over my shoulder as I head inside. "But it'll be worth your while. I'll do all the cleaning for the next two weeks."

"I've heard that before," he groans.

Turns out, plotting your wardrobe and makeup choices is ten times harder when you plan to end the night getting hot and heavy with a stranger instead of a pint of Ben & Jerry's. The half hour spent in the shower carefully shaving and exfoliating better be worth it.

By the time I finally emerge from my room, club-ready, Trevor is still lying on the couch where I left him, his eyes closed like he's dreading impending doom but is willing to give in. At the creak of the floor under my footsteps, he cracks a lid.

Mouth agape, he gives me a judgy once-over, taking in my trusty little black dress—the only college-era dress that still looks remotely flattering. It's short, many fingers above the knees, with a daringly low scoop back that prevents me from wearing a real bra. His eyes linger over my bare legs, to which I generously applied a vanilla shimmer cream.

"You look . . . uh, nice," he says, his tone obligatory as he fights to summon the words, like someone complimenting their granny's new living room lamp. This only serves to underscore the importance of this mission: to stop having errant sexual thoughts about Trevor. And, of course, sexual liberation and all that jazz.

"Thanks," I say dryly, chucking my duffel bag onto the floor. I get on hands and knees to search the bowels of the front closet for my black heels. Of course they're hiding in the very bottom.

"What's with the duffel bag?"

I stand, trusty heels in hand. "It's an overnight bag. Brought some makeup and a change of clothes."

"Why would you bring a change of clothes to the club?"

"Just in case. What if my hookup wants to hang out tomorrow?"

He runs both hands down his stubble in exasperation. "Tara, this is a bad idea. You do not, under any circumstances, hang out the next day. That defeats the entire purpose of a one-night stand."

I scrunch my face in silent protest.

"Are you sure you want to do this?"

"Yes. Completely sure," I say with more conviction than I actually have.

"Then put the overnight bag away."

• • •

THE ZOO CLUB reeks of eau de teenage boy after a hard gym class under the sweltering sun. The burning smell of the fog machine certainly doesn't help. I haven't been here since college, but I'm well acquainted with the glittery black rubber dance floor, having once face-planted while trying impress a dude wearing a beanie with a dance move I saw in a music video.

Tonight, the floor is barely visible with the sea of people bumping and grinding to the beat of an electronic Justin Bieber remix. Every square inch of this club is packed with desperadoes searching for someone to keep them warm on this frigid winter night. As I watch from the sidelines, I come to the startling realization that *I* am a desperado.

For me, dancing with strangers for free drinks in college was easy. I'd make casual small talk about the most random of topics before slinking away to my circle of girlfriends, long before the guy asked to take me home. But searching for a potential man to sleep with is a whole different ball game. The looming reality of swapping bodily fluids with a sweaty rando with shifty eyes and a bad haircut fills my gut with impending doom.

I'm inundated with flashbacks to middle school health class warnings of possible death via sexually transmitted infections. Even my gag reflex is triggered, although it may be the scent of hundreds of patrons' body odors combined. It's hard to say at this point.

Paranoia of STIs aside, I need this. My body needs this.

I clasp the thin yet soft fabric of Trevor's plain white tee as he leads me through the crowd like he's my bodyguard and I'm a celebrity VIP. Though I'm certainly not the one turning heads.

Women and men alike are eyeing him up and down like he's a *snack*. No—a full six-course meal. The appetizer, soup, main course, dessert, cheese, and coffee. And they would be right.

Trevor is objectively flawless. The best-looking man in this club, and the asshole isn't even trying. He didn't even style his hair after his shower, and yet it's impeccable.

Despite his thirsty onlookers, he remains cool as a cucumber as I buy our drinks (beer for him, vodka cran for me). The moment we shift into an open space adjacent to the bar, a woman in a tight python-print dress makes her move, introducing herself like a confident queen bee. Trevor doesn't seem to mind the attention, so I shove down my jealousy and give them some space, inching forward to eye up the dance floor for potential mates.

It's challenging to accurately assess the possibilities under seizure-inducing strobe lights. Just when I spot a cute guy in a ball cap bobbing his head on the perimeter of the dance floor, Trevor pulls me back by the elbow, shuffling me into a darkened corner.

I frown. "Where'd your friend go?"

"Are you sure you'll be able to handle it?" he asks over the music. I don't know if he's ignoring my question or if he simply didn't hear me.

I level him with a stubborn stare. "Metcalfe, stop treating me like some delicate flower. I'm an independent, progressive, sexually liberated being living my truth. And if we just so happen to connect on a deep level—"

"See, that's your problem. You can't expect to connect on any level with a one-night stand. That's the entire point. No cuddling. No emotional attachment."

"I won't get attached. Relax."

He's gearing up to argue with me when a heavily tattooed woman who looks like Kat Von D rocks up next to him and shoots her shot. Side by side, they just look like they belong. I picture them ripping around on their respective motorcycles. They'd spend their days doing hard-core things like tattooing each other's bodies or rocking out to Kurt Cobain. The moment I catch him staring at the thorny rose tattoo on her ample cleavage, I can't be bothered.

Taking it as my cue to leave, I pirouette onto the edge of the dance floor when an Ariana Grande jam comes on. Eyes closed, arms in the air, I solo dance, feeling the beat. Surely I look sexy and carefree, maybe a little mysterious. Just the type of chill woman all the guys want. The ideal type: with zero emotions and most definitely zero basic needs. Come at me, eligible bachelors.

By the time Ariana Grande abruptly transitions to a Drake song that doesn't inspire me, not a soul in the crowd has asked me to dance.

Trevor's warm honey eyes briefly meet mine from the side of the dance floor. He's still in casual conversation with Kat Von D, but he's now wearing his crooked, irresistibly sexy smile. The one he wears when he's trying not to laugh in my face.

His amusement at my expense sparks a flame inside me. I promptly motor to the other side of the bar. Half a song goes by before Trevor finds me. His new friend hasn't followed him.

"Why are you looking at me like that?" I demand, my hand on my hip.

"You were dancing like an injured daddy longlegs. Why did you take off on me?" he demands.

"You were laughing at me. And you were too distracted to be of any value as a wingman, so I'm going solo."

He leans in close to my ear when the beat drops on another EDM hit. "I'm sorry. Really. I didn't mean to hurt your feelings.

I'm ready to wingman for you now." He casts his hawk eyes around the club, surveying.

"What about that guy?" I point to a pleasant-looking dude standing near the bar, timidly waiting his turn to order as some drunk oaf pushes in front of him. "He looks like he has a kind heart."

Trevor shakes his head with far too much authority. "No. He looks like a youth pastor."

"What's wrong with a youth pastor? I don't want to hook up with an asshole."

His eyes cut to me. "You're looking for a good fuck, Tara. Not an angel. And let me tell you, that guy isn't going to satisfy you." His voice vibrates against my skin, sending an electric thrill rippling down my spine.

Before the buzz branches to other places, I shake it off. "Satisfy me? How would you know what would satisfy me?"

He sighs toward the ceiling, as if I've asked him a trick question. "I have a lot of experience."

I go up on my tiptoes, brutally failing to match his height. "Not with me." I'm not entirely sure what I'm trying to accomplish with that statement, but his eyes blaze for the briefest of moments.

"Obviously. But that guy is wrong for you. Try someone else."

I assess a hard-core duo near the bar. One wears a leather jacket while the other is in a literal denim vest, which accentuates his tattoos. Neither of them is remotely my type. But maybe that's the point of tonight. Maybe I need to venture outside my comfort zone. "What about them?"

His expression screams *Have you lost your marbles?* "They look like hit men."

This is the status quo for the next twenty minutes. Trevor is a bottomless pit of contradictory critique.

He looks like a douchebag.

He's wearing a velour tracksuit. Next.

Look at his shirt. Do you want to sleep with a man who pops his collar?

His head is weirdly shaped.

Way too short, even for you.

Definitely a murderer.

I groan when he rejects the last half-decent-looking guy in this joint. At this rate, finding a suitable hookup is about as likely as Seth suddenly turning into a good person. Or me giving up potato chips. "Look, I appreciate your help, but I think I should carry on alone. You're killing my vibe here. Besides, let's be real. I'm a dowdy, flat-chested nerd who still gets carded at the liquor store. Not some supermodel. Time is ticking. I can't afford to be picky."

He blinks, aggrieved. "I thought you said you were going to be picky because you have standards."

"Yes, but your standards are impossible to meet."

He tosses his hands in the air. "I'm not just gonna leave you here."

"Yes, you are. This isn't a *Dateline* episode. You're treating me like a child. I don't need your help. Go back to that woman with the tattoos. Or better yet, give Kyla a call." Truthfully, the pin prickles return at the thought of him bringing home someone else. But I can't dwell on it. I have to push the green monster back inside. We aren't going to be anything more than roommates, as he made very clear. This is Trevor Metcalfe, after all. Him hooking up with someone new is just a fact, as sure as the sun rising tomorrow.

His jaw is tense. "Okay. Fine. If you want me to leave, I'll leave."

"I want you to leave." It's the right call. If he stays, this entire night will be a wash, which is why I remain stone-faced when he lingers for a few moments before finally disappearing into the crowd.

His departure is like the chill of heavy clouds when you're desperate for sun at the beach. I've never been in a club alone before without my friends. It feels . . . vulnerable. Before I start panicking, the youth-pastor guy at the bar catches my eyes, inviting me over with a simple smile.

"Hey, gorgeous," he says with a slight Southern drawl as I advance. Innocent and neighborhood pastor–ish as he may look, he's definitely not ugly. Semi-square jaw. Soft hazel eyes. Slender build. Plaid flannel shirt. "What are you drinking tonight?"

"Vodka cran, you?" I yell over the music.

He holds up his glass and clinks it against mine. "Me too. Are we the same person?"

"Let's find out," I say, bravely closing the distance between us.

• • •

IT TAKES MITCH half an hour to ask if I want to "get out of here."

I can barely suppress my delight at the prospect of getting straight to business, especially after listening to him drone on about his master's degree in economics.

In the yellow hallway light of the apartment, Mitch isn't as angelic as I'd originally thought. In fact, he's not my type at all. I try to remind myself it doesn't matter, so long as he's going to rock my world. However, I begin to doubt his ability to do so when he drunkenly leans all his weight on me as I unlock the door.

Even though Trevor left the stove light on in the kitchen, I still manage to stub my toe on the overnight bag he forced me to leave behind. Mitch attempts to steady me but ends up nearly toppling over himself.

Trevor's bedroom door is closed, and his light is off. I expected to hear the ecstasy-filled cries of Kat Von D, but it's dead silent. There are no women's shoes at the door. He hasn't brought anyone home. While I know he doesn't have to work tomorrow, I feel a tinge of guilt for potentially ruining his sleep.

Mitch hangs out in the living room for a few minutes, checking out my succulents (Louisa is my newest addition) while I dart into the bathroom to swish some last-minute mouthwash and ensure my armpits are stubble-free. On my way out, I catch my reflection in the mirror. My makeup is flirting dangerously close to raccoon chic. I resemble that meme of D.W. from *Arthur*, ominous purple circles shadowing her tired-AF eyes.

Mitch's lips greet me the moment I exit the bathroom. He's like a rabid dumpster dweller, pouncing out of nowhere. His kiss is so hard and fast, his front tooth stabs against my top lip.

I try to ignore the sting as he slides his sopping-wet tongue into my mouth. All I can taste is the bitterness of the vodka cran as he backs me into the wall. I've always wanted to be backed into a wall like in all the hottest sex scenes. But what those scenes leave out is the impact of your shoulders and tailbone hitting the drywall.

"Sorry." He stifles a laugh as his tongue comes in for the kill.

I dart left, narrowly dodging it. "Everything good?"

"More than good. You?" His eyes are kind, concerned.

I nod away the doubt clouding my mind, kissing him back as we stumble into the darkness of my room.

We fall on the bed together in a strange mess of limbs. Instead of holding his weight up, he quite literally belly flops, knocking the wind out of me with his deadweight. I gasp for air like an awkward teenager losing my virginity all over again in my twin-size bed, my Beanie Baby collection bearing witness to the sweaty proceedings. Even an apologetic teenaged Cody Venner was ten times smoother than this guy.

"Do you have a condom?" Mitch whispers, tickling my neck with his moist breath.

My eyes snap open. As someone who doesn't typically sleep with guys who aren't my long-term boyfriend, I haven't purchased condoms in years. "Oh. Damn. No, I don't."

"Shit. Me either," he mutters, leaning back onto his knees. What guy doesn't have a ten-year-old expired condom folded in his wallet? Really, Mitch?

Clearly he's not exactly a pro at this random hookup thing, either. And that's when I remember. I know someone who is. I leap out of bed like a trapeze artist. "Hold on. My roommate will have one." I jog across the hall and knock.

Through the door, there's a heavy sigh, followed by footsteps. When Trevor pulls the door open, he's shirtless, his hair disheveled. "You okay?"

"Superb. Never better. Actually, I just need a condom," I tell him with the casual air of a frat bro who freeloads condoms on the regular.

His face hardens, evidently irked I woke him up for this.

I cross my arms, refusing to let him guilt me after the three times his sex-capades woke me out of my peaceful slumber. "Would you prefer I have unprotected sex with a stranger and contract an STI?"

He sighs and stomps to his side table to grab two condoms.

"Here." He thrusts them into my hand. Then, without another word, he slams the door in my face.

I peer at the condoms and work down the lump in my throat. I'm doing this. I'm going to have sex with Mitch.

This is fine. No. This is great. Marvelous. Perfectly splendid.

Or is it?

My current stance (palms to knees, hyperventilating) tells me otherwise.

I remind myself why I'm so hell-bent on a one-night stand to begin with. I'm sexually frustrated. And more than that, I want to lose all inhibition and have casual sex, like everyone else my age seems to do without a care in the world. There's nothing wrong with it morally. And yet, I can't ignore the overwhelming urge to slam the brakes. Stat. Will sleeping with sloppy Mitch be any better than taking care of business all by myself? At this rate, probably not.

"Did you get them?" Mitch asks from the end of the bed.

"Yeah." I hold them up like a sad carnival prize from the doorway, keeping my distance. "Mitch? I'm really sorry, but . . . I don't think I can do this."

His brows dip. "Oh, okay. Did I do anything to make you feel uncomfortable?"

"No. Definitely not. You've been great. I just don't know if I'm cut out for one-night stands."

He scratches the side of his head like he's in deep thought. "I'm kind of thinking the same thing, if I'm being honest. I mean, you're beautiful. I just . . ."

"It's just not right." My shoulders ease in relief.

We nod in mutual understanding, and I see him out. When I close the door and turn around, Trevor is sitting in the chair in the living room, one of my thriller books in hand.

I muffle a scream, clasping my palm to my chest. "Holy shit, Metcalfe. Why are you sitting out here in the cloak of darkness like a weirdo?"

He sets my book on his lap. "Couldn't sleep after you woke me up. Figured I'd try finishing my book."

"Oh." My hand is still pressed to my chest, feeling the thrum of my heart beating wildly from the events of this strange night.

He's looking at me, his expression unreadable. I don't know if he's going to chew me out for waking him up or say *I told you so*. He doesn't do either. He stands and comes toward me, making a *come here* motion. "You okay?" he asks, pulling me into a hug.

I sigh into the warmth of his bare, solid chest, which is more reassuring than I'll ever admit. My heart rate settles immediately at his touch. I wish I could close my eyes and stay here until the sun comes up and goes back down again. "I'm not cut out for that life. I don't know how you do it. I'm exhausted, and I didn't even get it in."

"Please don't say *get it in*."

"Do you prefer *going to bone town*?"

"No."

"Bumping uglies?"

"No."

"Boinking? Bruising the beef curtains?"

He closes his eyes, pained. "Never say any of those again."

"No promises."

The rumble of his low chuckle gives me an overwhelming sense of comfort. "You are just . . ."

I peek up at him. "I'm just what?"

A brief smile plays across his lips. "Nothing. Wanna go get a greasy twenty-four-hour-diner breakfast?"

"Yes, please."

♥ chapter nineteen

A RE YOU AND Uncle Trev an item?" Angie so bluntly wants to know. She casts a suspicious eye at the folded red construction paper in my hand. Arts and crafts with Angie during lunch break has become a regular routine. We're making Valentine's Day cards today.

I'm particularly thankful for the opportunity to pretend I'm a child for an hour. Prior to lunch, we had our bimonthly NICU all-staff meeting. Seth used the opportunity to launch a number of petty, non-job-related claims.

People have been stockpiling the good Keurig pods.

People have been clogging the kitchen sink with their lunch containers.

When the meeting was adjourned, I overheard him updating another doctor in the lounge about my ex-boyfriend search after my latest social media update, boisterously delighting in the fact that I only have one ex left. He went on to ramble about how embarrassing and unprofessional it is to post these things and how I must have "scared off the other nine."

I have a working theory that Seth suffers from youngest-child syndrome. His three older brothers are a bunch of bullies whose immediate instinct is to pretend to wrestle in any given social situation. As the smallest, he always got bulldozed. He was relegated to the scraps, the leftovers. He never got to choose what to watch on television. And because the poor lamb missed out on so many cartoons, he'll wield his power any way he can have it.

Crystal picked up on this straightaway. The first time I brought Seth home to meet the family, he debated her on a variety of fitness and nutrition topics, brushing off her credentials because he was a *doctor*. The entire family was outwardly disturbed when I proposed. When we broke things off, Crystal sat me down with a prepared list of every reason Seth was wrong for me.

For the longest time, I was convinced she was just trying to make me feel better. She didn't know the real Seth, the one who saved the lives of newborn babies on the regular and showered me with affection in those first few months of our relationship. But the more he shows off who he really is, the easier it gets.

I'm grateful to have Angie to occupy my mind and prevent me from spending my lunch hour in the stairwell, plotting revenge scenarios I'll never have the guts to carry out.

My lips part in a blend of shock and amusement at Angie's question about her uncle. "Me and him? An item? As in dating? No way." I stare down at my card for Trevor. It's totally nonromantic, or so I assumed. I've cut out a mini succulent in a flowerpot with a smiley face. For a dude who was vehemently opposed to my succulents, I think they've grown on him. In fact, he's been watering them for me, single-handedly keeping them alive.

I've written *My Life Would Totally Succ Without You* across the top of the card in faux calligraphy. This card screams friend-zone. At least, I thought it did. Technically, I've made the eyes tiny hearts. Under Angie's critical eye, I'm now paranoid Trevor will mistake it for a declaration of love, which is the last thing I need.

"But you live together," Angie reminds me, carefully cutting her next red heart along the pencil line.

As I draw over the heart eyes, transforming them into innocent, totally casual circles, I remind myself I'm attracted to Trevor purely on a physical level only. It's just a minuscule, microscopic, basically nonexistent crush. If I repeat that enough times, it must be so. Besides, Trevor Metcalfe doesn't do love.

"We live together as platonic friends." My tone is clipped as I press down a loose corner of one of the succulent leaves where the glue didn't hold.

When she scrunches her nose and asks what *platonic* means, I'm reminded I'm speaking to a nine-year-old, despite her disgruntled-adult vibes. Time for a crash course in the bleak reality of love.

"Platonic means strictly friends. No romantic feelings. At all," I explain, holding the booklet of construction paper to obstruct her view of my flaming cheeks. "Do you have any friends who are boys?"

She smothers a cutout heart with white school glue. "My best friend Dylan is a boy. He's not cute. And he only shares his snacks with Sally." She grimaces, apparently displeased with this Sally person.

"Aw, give him a break. He's probably in love with her." I let out a nostalgic sigh, abandoning Trevor's card to start on Crystal's. "My first crush, Daniel, gave me butterflies. Every year on Valentine's Day, I'd give Daniel the biggest, most extra card. He'd give me a full-size chocolate bar when everyone else got minis." If that's not true love, I don't know what is.

Daniel and I had an adorable meet-cute on the first day of kindergarten I'd be proud to tell my grandchildren about. He was wearing denim overalls and an oversize red ball cap, which I later learned covered the botched bowl cut his mother had given him. He was sitting in the sandbox, ugly crying and being an overall miserable little twat.

Daniel never grew to like other kids. I didn't mind his antisocial tendencies in the slightest, mostly because I did enough talking for the both of us. It also meant I had Daniel all to myself. We bonded over our shared love of boxed sugary snacks, reading all the books we could get our sticky hands on, and a morbid obsession with pretending to be ghosts in his attic. We were inseparable, so much so that Mom and Dad referred to Daniel as the son they never had.

Bypassing the cootie stage entirely, we graduated to awkward, prepubescent hand-holding and close-lipped pecks by age ten. According to my doodle-filled notebooks and diaries, I was the future Mrs. Nakamura. It was destiny, or so I thought, until Daniel's parents took a grand dump on my life plan and moved the family across the city partway through middle school. We sent emails back and forth for a year and a half, but their frequency fizzled the longer we were apart. We lost touch entirely by high school.

Angie isn't buying it. "Butterflies?"

"Imaginary butterflies. Inside." I point to my stomach. "Imagine a bunch of butterflies fluttering around in there."

Angie giggles and scrunches her tiny nose. "That would tickle."

"Exactly. That's how it feels when you like someone. Like all the butterflies are flapping their wings inside of you, ready to spread their wings and soar." I probably sound like an old kook, but Angie seems to understand.

"Why didn't you marry Daniel?" she asks.

I woefully explain how he moved away and how I've been unable to locate him since, which is unfortunate given he's the lone ex left on my list. Far too many hours have been logged searching all the variations of Daniel's name I can think of, with zero success. I'm beginning to wonder if he was the unfortunate bystander of a Mafia hit and had to go into witness protection.

"I get the butterflies around Matty. And Oliver," Angie admits shyly. She tells me all about Matty and Oliver, two boys in her class who are "cute" for different reasons (one is a bad boy who gets a lot of time-outs; the other is a dependable nerd). She reminds me of my young self, hopelessly rotating between crushing on literally every boy in class.

"Exactly my point. Attraction is key. I'm not attracted to your uncle Trevor," I point out. "I mean, he's handsome, but not my type." My eye twitches again. I've lied to a child. A hospitalized child waiting for a heart transplant, no less. I'm officially going to hell, and my permanent residency is well deserved. At the same time, coming clean about my crush would only result in a myriad of questions, all of which I can't answer. The last thing I want to do is explain to a nine-year-old that her uncle has deep-rooted commitment issues.

Angie gives me a sassy head tilt. She knows I'm full of shit, but she's allowing me to live in denial. Bless.

"Why? Has your uncle said anything about me?" I ask, pretending to be wholly focused on Crystal's card. I cut out a little container of protein powder and write *I'm WHEY into you* along the top.

A devious smile spreads across her tiny face. "He says you have the worst singing voice he's ever heard. He likes to talk about you."

I lurch forward in my chair, ready to demand a play-by-play of the entire conversation, start to finish. Context is key. But I manage to rein it in.

"My mom calls Uncle Trevor a spinny door." She twirls her finger around in a clockwise circle.

"A spinny door?" I repeat, rifling in Angie's pencil case for the glitter glue.

"Like the ones downstairs that spin around. Because of all his girlfriends," she says matter-of-factly. "He has lots. But he doesn't let me meet them."

I laugh, realizing she's referring to the revolving doors in the hospital lobby. Angie's mom isn't wrong about Trevor having a revolving door of women. Though in his defense, he hasn't brought anyone home since Gabby over two and a half months ago—back when my feelings toward him were simple and not a chaotic shitstorm. Now I'd rather undergo an unnecessary rectal exam before hearing him and a random rocking each other's respective worlds through the tissue-thin walls of our apartment. And still, emotionally unavailable men like Trevor are to be regarded as potentially lethal plagues, to be avoided at all costs.

"So, Angie," I say, clearing my throat, eager to change the subject from Trevor's sex life to my main objective—party planning. "Is Rapunzel still your favorite princess?"

Distracted by the glitter glue, she nods, slightly less enthusiastic than the last time she told me.

"Do you want to dress up like her for your birthday?" I ask, spreading glitter glue over Crystal's card.

Her brown eyes light up for a split second, before darkening in disappointment. "Marissa says I can't be Rapunzel because I'm not blond."

My heart aches at her admission. Whoever this Marissa is, I want to give her a piece of my mind.

"That's not true." I move from my chair to the end of the hospital bed. It creaks under my additional weight. "When I was growing up, there was only one Disney princess who looked like me. And Mulan was great, don't get me wrong. But just because I didn't have blond hair like the other princesses didn't mean I couldn't be who I wanted to be."

She stares at me for a moment, like she's not sure whether to believe me. "Do you think that's true?"

"Of course. Think about Rapunzel. She's funny, right? Brave?"

Angie nods, holding her completed card an arm's length away to examine it. "She's nice to animals too. She has a pet chameleon."

"Exactly. Pretend all the princesses looked the same. They'd still have their own unique personalities. Whoever's personality you like the most is the princess you get to be, no matter what you look like on the outside. Rapunzel is still the same princess even when she loses her magic hair."

Before she can respond, her eyes light up at the presence of a woman in a powder-blue bomber coat in the doorway. "Hi, Mom."

Upon first look, there doesn't appear to be much of a resemblance between Angie and her mom. Angie has soft, round features contrasting her mother's angular, sharp lines. But the moment she opens her mouth, it's evident the resemblance is in the mannerisms. The leftward curve of her lips. The slight indent that isn't quite a dimple but wants to be.

Her mom gives me a curious smile. "I'm Payton, Angie's mom. Are you one of the new nurses?" Her voice is low and a bit gritty, almost worn.

I stand and extend my hand in a friendly shake. "Oh, um, no, actually. I am a nurse, but not on this floor. I'm Trevor's friend . . . and roommate."

She lights up. "Oh! Taryn, right?" Before I can tell her my name is Tara, not Taryn, she pulls me into her bony embrace. "He told me you were helping with her party. And about the money you were raising on your social media. Seriously, I can't thank you enough. You have no idea how much we appreciate this. Really."

"I love planning parties. I have a lot of ideas," I say, smiling at Angie.

Payton looks solemn for a moment, waving me into the hallway. I follow her out. "Honestly, sometimes I feel like a shit mom. I mean, what kind of mom can't even plan her own kid's birthday party?" she whispers.

"A mom who has her priorities straight," I offer. I know from Trevor that she's working two jobs to pay for Angie's treatment. She probably doesn't even have time to sleep, let alone plan a birthday party.

She blows her overgrown bangs from her face. "Trevor told me you were going the extra mile. We really appreciate it, especially with her dad out of the picture." She says it so nonchalantly, like it's just a straight fact. Nothing to be weird about.

"Where is her dad?" I ask.

Her heavy eyes narrow, like she's confused. "Trevor didn't tell you about Logan?"

"No. He's not exactly an open book."

She nods in knowing agreement. "Logan left two years ago. Hasn't even come back since Angie got sick again. He's working out in Louisiana on the oil rigs."

I frown. "Oh, I'm so sorry."

She shrugs. "He wasn't all that involved when he was in Boston anyways. It's not much different. Though Trevor was raging mad when he left. Went all the way down South to try to get him to come back. They got in a pretty bad fight over it."

My heart aches. No wonder Trevor gets all tense when I ask about Logan.

Payton senses the drop in my mood and gives me a reassuring smile. "It's all good, though. We're just thankful Trevor's been there for us. Ever since the beginning. With all the medical appointments . . . God, he's even helped us financially. He's a good guy," she says, like she's trying to convince me for some reason.

As much as I would love to deny that fact for my own self-preservation, she's entirely right. Sure, Trevor isn't your standard cinnamon-roll nice guy. He's grumpy. Blunt. Rough around the edges. I've held on to those facts, trying to convince myself those qualities automatically count him out. That he's somehow *not* good, for me at least.

But continuing to deny it is becoming an impossibility, especially after everything he's done for me the past few months. All the dating advice. The company. Ensuring I've eaten on any given day. The most endearing part about it all is that he isn't one of those smug people who waltzes around being a do-gooder to make themselves feel better (*cough* Seth *cough*). He doesn't do things for glory or status. He's never once bragged about his job or how many lives he's saved.

He's pure, authentic, and good.

How maddeningly inconvenient.

• • •

"WHAT THE HELL is that supposed to be?" Scott points his tube of school glue in the vague direction of Trevor's oddly shaped cardboard structure.

"It's a horse, dick-wad." From his cross-legged position on the floor, Trevor casts an envious scowl at Scott's surprisingly well-executed outline of Cinderella. The three of us are at Crystal and Scott's, constructing life-size cardboard cutouts for Angie's Disney party. Crystal is on party store duty, picking up plates, cups, balloons, and goody bag items.

Ever since my lunch with Angie four days ago, where I confirmed the vision and direction for her party in less than two weeks, I've been in full Disney planning mode. I even booked the lounge in the hospital to host the festivities. The lounge's décor is a vague attempt at cheer with its canary-yellow walls, but a couple Disney-themed plates and hats won't change the fact that she's celebrating her birthday in a hospital. Life-size cutouts of her favorite Disney princesses may be *extra*, but I'm determined to give her an escape from reality, if only for an afternoon.

Scott squints at Trevor's creation, tilting his head as if a different perspective will help its cause. "Looks like a sad, mangled giraffe, man."

"It kind of does." I nod in agreement. "Maybe next time, thicken the neck a bit?"

"I still don't get why we got stuck with craft duty." Disgruntled, Trevor tosses the cardboard figure into the growing trash pile.

"Because grown men who wear Crocs can't be trusted to make good decisions at a party store," I retort, shooting daggers at their feet. Ever since I called him out for the army-green atrocity, Trevor has been wearing them around the apartment and at work like a second, terror-inducing skin.

Turns out, Scott recently purchased his own pair. Wearing Crocs is this bizarre joke that all the crew at the firehouse have adopted like a badge of honor during their off time. I'm currently developing a plot to steal them in the cloak of darkness (Grinch-style) and burn them at the stake. I'll drop them into the fire, one by one, using barbecue tongs to avoid direct contact. They'll emit witchy squeals and maybe even refuse to burn as I douse the flames with gasoline.

Scott stretches his bright-blue Crocs toward me, giving me a gentle kick. He's not even my official brother-in-law yet and he's already finding ways to antagonize me. "I'll never take them off. You'll have to bury me in them."

"Not in the Chen family plot." I snort, my gaze falling over Trevor, who apparently can't be bothered to take the task at hand seriously. He's too distracted admiring his hideous footwear. I launch a pencil at his chest. "Stop wasting cardboard. You need to outline it before you start cutting at random."

"Sorry. It's this music. How am I supposed to work under these conditions?" Trevor casts a troubled look at my phone, which is blasting a bomb Disney playlist.

"Oh, come on, you're practically itching to break out into song and dance," I tease, nodding at Scott, who's tapping his Croc merrily to *Hercules*'s "I Won't Say (I'm in Love)."

Trevor rewards me with a dead-eyed stare. "Don't compare me to *that*."

"You can't tell me you never watched these movies as a kid?" Scott chucks a balled-up wad of construction paper at his head.

Trevor catches the ball of paper before it hits him, like he's some genetically modified super soldier. He tosses it into his personal trash pile, neatly stacked next to him. "Not by choice. The real question is, why did *you*?"

"I grew up with two sisters, man."

I swing a warning glare at Trevor. "You better learn some of these tunes if you're gonna be a half-decent prince at the party. All the good princes sing and dance."

Trevor scoffs. "For the hundredth time, I'm not dressing up."

"You are."

"I'm not."

Scott snickers. "I would pay money to see this. Good money."

I scrutinize Scott up and down. "Oh, you'll be there too. You're going to be Prince Charming."

Scott ponders that for a moment. "Works for me."

"See? Scott's gonna do it," I goad.

Trevor glowers at him like he's just broken sacred bro-code. "Because he's a sucker. And he likes attention—"

"Hey, fuck off." Scott chucks another wad of paper at him. This one hits him clean on the forehead, bouncing onto the floor.

Trevor continues on valiantly, like he didn't just get smoked in the head. "And even if I were going to dress up, which I'm not—"

"You are—" I interject.

"Nope."

I level him with a poisonous stare. "Do you realize how happy Angie would be if you dressed up? Besides, I already promised her you would. You can't back out now. She'll be heartbroken." Truthfully, I never made such a promise to Angie. But he doesn't need to know that.

His eyes meet mine, softening instantly. Bingo. I've pierced him straight through the heart with my arrow of guilt. He slumps his shoulders in grumpy resignation. "Okay. Fine. But no pictures. And why does Scotty get to be Prince Charming?"

"Because he's *charming*," I explain, to Scott's delight. Normally, I have no interest in feeding my brother-in-law's already inflated ego, but I'm willing to take one for the team if it means grinding Trevor's gears.

Trevor places a hand over his chest, offended. "And I'm not?"

I try my best to keep a straight face while denying his natural charm. "You're certainly not a wholesome type of charming." I let my gaze flit over the intricate Celtic knot tattoo adorning his right arm.

Trevor mutters something unintelligible under his breath and starts slicing into the cardboard with his X-Acto knife as the soothing, instrumental melody from the lantern scene in *Tangled* fills the room.

Suddenly, I'm hit with a momentary stroke of genius. "You're going to be Flynn Rider."

"I don't even know who that is. Why do I have to be some off-brand prince?"

Before I can explain that Flynn Rider is anything but *off-brand*

and happens to be Angie's favorite, Crystal bursts through the door with a hefty load of plastic bags on each arm.

"What took you so long?" I demand, popping up to inspect the bags.

"The roads are bad. I had to drive slow," Crystal explains, kicking off her slushy leather booties in the entryway. She sets the bags on the floor and shuffles over to admire my Rapunzel tower, which will double as a photo shoot prop. "I was also busy with a little research."

"What research?" I ask, smirking when Scott not-so-subtly checks out her backside.

"Found out where Daniel works," she says nonchalantly, like it's no big deal. Like he isn't my very last hope.

I drop my Sharpie and lurch forward on my heels. "What? How did you find Daniel before me?" I ask, though it probably comes out more like *HOWDIDYOUFINDDANIELBEFOREME?* I wait with bated breath as the rush of adrenaline plunges my body into all-out chaos.

For dramatic effect, Crystal waits a few seconds before revealing her findings. "He works at that big tech company downtown. Flopify. That one that took over the old Macy's building."

"How did you find him? I've looked everywhere."

"I have my ways," she says, her eyes glinting, keeping the mystery alive. "Just kidding. I found him on LinkedIn. It really wasn't that hard. I texted you the link to his profile."

"I'm forever indebted. Seriously, though. I would lick your gym shoes if you asked me to." I throw my arms around my sister's shoulders, only narrowly avoiding stepping on the hot-glue gun.

She inches away from my smothering hug. "Really not necessary."

"Are you gonna DM him?" Trevor asks, not looking up from his latest attempt at a horse cutout.

I shudder at the thought. "Oh, no. I can't reunite with him via DM. I only have a week and a half before the gala. It's not enough time to reestablish our rapport. I need to run into him naturally."

Trevor sighs. "You're going to stake out the front of his workplace, aren't you?"

"Correction: *we* are."

♥ chapter twenty

EVERY STATION IS running ads. Posturepedic mattresses. Car dealerships.

Trevor emits a tortured sigh as I fiddle with the radio dial, finally landing on an old Wilson Phillips song.

"I will turn this car around if you change the station one more time," he warns, alarmed that I'm messing with his preset channels.

"Sheesh. You sound like my dad," I say wryly. "It's not my fault you don't have Bluetooth. I'm just trying to enhance our experience. Now smile and wave to your fans," I order, angling my phone to him.

When he sees it's on Live video, he grumbles, promptly covering my phone with his free hand. "No. You're distracting me while I'm driving."

"Oh, come on. Give the people what they want. Just a quick hello," I urge.

He rolls his eyes and gives a frosty hi before fixing his stare toward the slush-covered road. I take this as a sign to end the video.

Unsurprisingly, Trevor had to be bribed with Five Guys milkshakes to accompany me to Daniel's workplace during a snowstorm. The windshield wipers are working overtime to clear the flurry of snow streaming off the SUV ahead. Trevor is aggrieved, muttering softly about the legalities of wiping the snow off one's car. He's driving turtle slow, simply to make the point.

He's also taken to posing hypotheticals:

What if he works from home?

What if he's sick today?

What if he exits through another door?

What if he already left the building for a meeting?

What if he's on vacation?

What if he got facial reconstruction surgery, rendering him virtually unrecognizable?

While Trevor makes (some) valid points, at least I will be able to say I exhausted every avenue before desperately sliding into Daniel's LinkedIn DMs.

"You're kind of killing the mood here," I say, dropping my phone in the cupholder. "This is my very last and most promising ex. The only one on that list who knows the real me. I would regret it forever if I didn't pull out all the stops."

He peels his eyes from the road to meet my gaze. "I'm just . . . worried you'll be crushed if it doesn't work out with him."

Oof. I rest my head against the seat as the stifling wave of reality washes over me. In all the excitement of this ex-boyfriend goose chase, I haven't fully considered the possibility of none of them working out. My hands clench in my lap, envisioning Seth's smug face if I fail in my pursuit and show up at the gala alone. And worse, I think about the crushing pain of scratching Daniel's name—the very last name—off the list. I can't let that happen. After Seth, my heart simply can't withstand more carnage.

I avert my stare out the window, avoiding Trevor's worrywart expression. "I know it's dumb. I know the whole ex thing seems frivolous. But how pathetic would it be if I, the biggest romance novel fan ever, failed to find book-worthy love in real life?"

"Tara—"

"I never told you, but this time last year, after Seth broke off the engagement, I was at a real low point. I could barely get out of bed. I thought no one would ever want me. Even a year out . . . I still can't help but think that sometimes."

"If this is about going to the gala, I'll go with you." His offer is so casual, I'm unsure I've even heard him correctly.

"Really? You'd waste your Valentine's Day to come to a random gala with me?"

He lifts a shoulder in a shrug. "Yeah. Why not? It's for the heart center. And what else would I be doing on Valentine's Day?"

I fiddle with the heat vent, considering this proposition. "Maybe. If things don't work out with Daniel, I guess."

"Right," he says, distracted as he parallel parks in front of the building. "Here we are."

I expected Daniel's workplace to be an all-glass modern skyscraper. But upon arrival, it's a Romanesque medium-rise with ornately detailed windows and doorways. It's bougie, kind of old-school.

The prospect of coming face-to-face with Daniel after nearly twenty years is hot flash–inducing. I imagine him in a corner office, thumbing through urgent files, dressed in a perfectly tailored sharkskin suit. He channels some *Devil Wears Prada* energy, icing out his staff with just one glance. Everyone knows Daniel doesn't do small talk. His receptionist only bothers him with important stuff, although he will take calls from his beloved mother.

As I gawk up at the building, Trevor nudges my arm over the console. "Look, three o'clock. Pale, six-foot, brown hair. Is that him?"

I scrunch my nose, watching the pimply-faced teen with an oversize backpack as he shuffles past the passenger window. "Mr. Metcalfe, you need your eyes checked. That kid is like fourteen. At most."

"I don't have a lot to work with here. You didn't have a photo of him on your hit list," he retorts.

This is how it goes for the next fifteen minutes as we watch people filter in and out of the front doors. Trevor has, somehow, transformed from miserable twerp to James Bond. He's checking his mirrors, murmuring physical descriptions of passersby, none of whom are Daniel. He might as well be a Man in Black with one of those fancy earpieces, speaking into his watch.

Since this isn't my first rodeo being a certified creep, I'm well aware that surveillance in the movies is much more exhilarating than it is in real life. But it doesn't make it any less dull, especially for an impatient soul like me.

Out of nowhere, Trevor reaches over the console. I suck in a sharp breath at his hand's proximity to my legs. For some reason, the mere prospect of the splay of his palm spanning my thigh floods me with heat, like a wave of caffeine or straight-up sorcery, jolting me alive.

Something heavy drops over my knees. It isn't his hand. It's the glove compartment. Before I can even reconcile my dangerous thoughts, he extracts one of my paperback thrillers. Ignorant to the hammering of my heart and the crimson shade of my entire face, he casually flips to the middle of the book, silently picking up where he left off.

Did I really get that excited at the prospect of my womanizer roommate's hand inches from my leg? Am I that desperate for human affection? Maybe my followers' comments advocating for a room-ance with Trevor have somehow wormed their way into my subconscious.

I will those errant, nonsensical thoughts to a decrepit, condemned corner of my mind and padlock it for good measure. But now I'm far too aware of the heat blasting through the vent. In fact, I'm sweltering under my layers. Trevor's car, which was perfectly comfortable two seconds ago, is now a claustrophobic, shrinking closet.

"Wanna go sit in the lobby? I need to stretch my legs," I say, rolling the window down for some much-needed air.

Trevor is alarmed, like I've proposed a mass atrocity. When I unbuckle my seat belt, signaling I'm going with or without him, he relents with a heavy sigh, following me inside.

The lobby itself is your standard corporate space with shiny marble floors and gold elevators lining the back wall. An oak reception desk blocks our ability to reach the elevators, although there's currently no one occupying the desk. Next to it is a row of three turnstiles where a man in a dowdy suit scans a badge to enter.

Trevor parks himself on a leather tufted bench next to the turnstiles. It's the perfect view, directly across from the elevators.

I plop down next to him, kicking the snow off my boots. "By the way, I forgot to mention, guess who I met at the hospital the other day when I was visiting Angie?"

"My sister-in-law?"

"Yup."

"She look okay?" A hint of concern tinges his tone.

"She looked a little worn down. She kept calling me Taryn."

"Yeah. She's been working her normal job at the bank and waitressing at night to keep up with Angie's medical bills."

"I can't imagine. Sounds like she could use a break."

"Sometimes I think staying busy is the only way she can cope. Otherwise, she'd worry herself sick at the hospital. I'm pretty sure Angie would get sick of her too." A flicker of a smile is visible.

"Does Payton date?"

"She had a boyfriend last year, but when Angie got sick again, he bailed too." His brow furrows. "Guess a kid with heart disease was a deal breaker."

"For assholes," I point out. Selfishly, I use this as a springboard to pose my burning question. "What's this drama with your brother all about?"

I expect him to tense up and shirk my question, but he nods like he expected it. "It's complicated. Logan and Payton weren't together when they got pregnant. They moved in together right after. That went about as well as a *Jerry Springer* episode," he explains sarcastically.

"Does he know the extent of Angie's heart problems?"

"I keep him updated, even though he doesn't bother asking. I think he just expects I'll tell him if there's anything important. He's no Dad of the Year, that's for sure."

"What about your dad?"

"He and my brother are a lot alike," he admits. "He was barely around before my parents split. Moved down to Texas for some construction job when Logan and I were in grade school. We never saw him except for the odd holiday visit, even after my mom died."

"I can't believe he didn't step up after that."

He lets out a bitter sigh as a boisterous crowd of people make their way through the turnstiles in front of us. "It was probably for the best. He was kind of a dick when Logan and I didn't want much to do with him. Didn't understand why we were standoffish. He moved back here when I was sixteen and randomly started picking us up from school on Fridays. He'd take us to Burger King because it was all he could afford. It was weird. It was like he was trying to make up for lost time or something. Logan was always a bit indifferent. He was at that age where he didn't want to spend much time with anyone. So my dad and I had a lot of one-on-one time. We got pretty close, actually."

I stay silent, trying to avoid spooking him with any given reaction.

"I'd ask him for advice on girls and money. He was a cheap bastard too. That's where I learned it." He chuckles softly. "After a few months, I forgave him for being a shit dad. And then he moved for another job and it kind of felt like the first time he left, all over again. But it was almost worse, because I blamed myself. I didn't understand why I wasn't good enough for him to stick around."

Instinctively, I place my hand on his forearm. When his muscles clench under my touch, I remove it. "Him leaving had nothing to do with you."

His hard eyes search mine. "You either." Without explaining, I know he's referring to Seth.

I unzip my coat, my neck prickling with beads of sweat. "Do you still talk to your dad?" I ask, shifting the spotlight back to him.

He rakes a tired hand through his hair. "I hear from him every now and then. But haven't seen him in years. Logan is exactly like him. Not proactive. Doesn't really bother unless it's convenient." I'm silent for a few beats, just letting it all sink in when he nudges me. "Now do you see why I don't do relationships?"

"Is that why you broke up with Kyla?"

He picks at a tiny leather tear on the bench. "I guess so. We dated for over a year when I came back to Boston after dropping out of college. I broke things off when Angie's health got really bad. The thought of losing Angie was so fucking terrifying. I wasn't in any shape to be there for anyone else. You probably think that's ridiculous, huh?"

"No. It's not ridiculous at all," I assure him.

His grief makes my heart ache. I think I finally understand the glaring difference between us. The difference that renders us entirely unmatchable. While Trevor and I are both wounded by abandonment—him more severely—we handle it in opposite ways. He's locked his heart entirely. It's hidden behind an impenetrable fortress, surrounded by shark-infested waters. On the other hand, I've left my heart wide open, a gaping, only partially healed hole. And to be honest, I'm not sure which tactic is more advisable.

"I still think you should give Kyla another chance," I say. "Hey, didn't you two plan to have drinks soon?"

Before he can respond, the elevator dings, swinging open. Six people in various shades of black and gray wool winterwear filter out. I'm immediately drawn to a familiar face in the back.

Partially blocked by a Hulk-size man's massive shoulder is Daniel. My long-lost childhood love.

I haven't laid eyes on this face since he was a prepubescent teen, but I'd know those glass-cutting cheekbones anywhere. He still has that dark, silky hair and ever-so-serious expression. But he's gotten broader. His neck is thicker. His shoulders are wider underneath his black jacket and brown corduroys. Adult Daniel could surely handle himself in a boardroom of high-powered executives, return home at a reasonable hour, roll the sleeves of his dress shirt (exposing his veiny forearms), and dutifully assist his wife with the children's nighttime routine.

While I've missed him terribly, coming face-to-face doesn't give me any sense of comfort. Quite the opposite, in fact. My body goes into flight mode as he heads for the turnstile directly across from us.

Panicked, I let out a hacking, dry cough as he stops to pull his building pass from the front flap of his messenger bag. Before he goes to scan it, I whip my head toward Trevor's chest, shielding my face with my hands. "Shit balls. He's coming this way! He's gonna see me." For once, I'm not overexaggerating. This bench is diagonal from the turnstiles. There's absolutely no hiding.

"Isn't that the point?" Trevor whispers.

"I didn't *actually* think he'd be here! Hide me!" I'm about to curl into a ball or hide under my own coat like a coward when Trevor clasps a hand around the back of my neck. His grip is firm and demanding, but not aggressively so.

There's a fire in his eyes as they search mine. It's like he's asking for silent permission. I have no idea what for, and frankly, I don't care.

I'm in, my blazing eyes tell him.

He receives my silent cue and conceals me completely.

With his face.

♥ chapter twenty-one

WHEN TREVOR'S SOFT, pillowy lips settle against mine, my soul exits my body.

Nothing can resuscitate me. *Here lies Tara Li Chen.* At least I had a decent life.

Trevor Metcalfe is kissing me. He. Is. Kissing. Me. There is nothing else. There is no life, no reality outside the confines of this bench. Daniel who?

His hands are strong and urgent on either side of my head. He does something with his thumb, like a mini massage against my temple. It's such a small thing, but it feels like affection. It brings me to life.

My previously motionless lips traitorously follow his lead. His tongue sweeps across my bottom lip and melds against mine so expertly, I force my eyes open momentarily to confirm that this is real. This is happening. My hands slink up his muscled shoulders and through his soft, thick hair. With both hands, I pull his face closer to mine a little more aggressively than intended.

When his low groan vibrates into my mouth, my body descends into chaos. Blood courses through me like a riptide. My heart is thrashing so hard, I'm convinced someone has broadcasted the audio over the building's PA system.

His hand is still clasped around the back of my neck, his fingers moving in possessive circular strokes that do little to suppress the cavewoman inside me I didn't know existed.

Just as I contemplate a side-aerial onto his lap, he rips his lips from mine.

For a span of far too many prolonged seconds, our faces are inches apart. His chest rises and falls rapidly, in sync with mine, heavy and labored, as if we've just completed a Spartan race, not made out for a mere few seconds. Or was it minutes? An hour? Who knows?

His horrified eyes fuse with mine. Lips parted ever so slightly. Head tilted like a dog. Expression of pure anguish, as if that was the single worst moment of his entire life.

He breaks eye contact, peering out the lobby window behind us. I follow his gaze to Daniel, strolling down the snowy sidewalk outside, his nose buried in his phone, none the wiser.

"What are you waiting for?" Trevor urges. When he leans in, I hold my breath. I half expect him to kiss me again, but all he does is shove me off the bench. "Go."

My legs are no longer attached to my body. I'm like a shaky newborn deer. All limbs, no balance. No sense of direction.

By the time I actually reach the sidewalk, I can barely see ten feet in front of me. Trevor wasn't wrong about the snowstorm.

Everyone rushes by, heads down, hoods up, desperate for shelter from the harsh elements. A juicy snowflake pelts me straight in the eyeball.

Half-blind, I can only vaguely make out the back of Daniel's head approaching the intersection. I make a weak attempt to call his name, but all that comes out is a muffled retch marred by the howl of nature. I'm helpless, frozen, watching him disappear into the white, icy void.

I should be pursuing him with the gusto I had all of an hour ago, but I'm too stunned to go on, thanks to Trevor Metcalfe.

By the time I have the wherewithal to return to Trevor's vehicle, he's already inside, seemingly dazed, staring straight ahead out the windshield, into the void.

The click of my seat belt quells the dense silence. "I couldn't do it."

He gives me a sideways glance. "Really? We came all the way here and you're chickening out now?"

If I'm being honest, my mind is not in this conversation. It's stuck on loop. On the events of literally a few minutes prior. "You kissed me." My statement comes out harsher than I meant it to.

"I did," he says, as if he can't believe it himself.

It takes a lot to leave me speechless. And he's succeeded. "Why?" I finally dare to ask.

As if he can sense I'm descending into an internal spiral, he presses his fingers over the bridge of his nose. "I'm sorry. It was a shitty thing to do. I wasn't thinking. You asked me to hide you and I thought people would look away and . . ." His explanation is entirely logical. He's told me this before, how PDA makes him cringe and turn away. "Please don't read into this," he begs.

The kiss wasn't real. No feelings. Or rainbows. Or butterflies. Realistically, I should be grateful he had the wherewithal to try to conceal my stalking. He was being a good friend, helping me in dire straits, right? Why am I so disappointed?

"I'm not reading into it." *I might be.*

"Are you sure?" he asks slowly, like he's expecting me to confess my obsession with him right here, right now.

I hate that he sees me in such a pathetic light. "Relax. I'm not. I may be in the market for a soul mate, but even I'm not naive enough to think it would be you."

He watches me for a moment, his expression stony. "Good."

"And your kiss leaves a lot to be desired," I add for good measure. I fold my arms and glare out the passenger window. It's a lie, of course. It's the best kiss I've ever had. But he can't know that, lest his ego explode.

His stare burns through my profile, like he's waiting for me to crack and admit his exceptional talent. "Excuse you. I'm a great kisser."

"I've had better," I say, suddenly very focused on the lint from my cable-knit sticking to my jeans.

"You're lying. In fact, my skills have been corroborated by highly reliable sources."

I shrug. "Sorry, Metcalfe. It is what it is. Maybe you're just out of practice."

When I don't relent, he sighs and squints at the windshield like he's trying to solve a riddle. "Anyways. We can't do that. Ever again."

♥ chapter twenty-two

W E DON'T TALK about the Kiss.

We don't talk about it on the treacherously snowy drive home. We don't talk about it as we hoof it up the stairs. We don't talk about it while Trevor makes us a nutritious grilled chicken dinner. And we definitely don't talk about it while we watch *The Bachelor*, him seated safely in the armchair instead of his usual spot on the couch.

Even days later, Trevor still takes painstaking efforts to avoid looking me in the eyes, like I'm a human solar eclipse. He's also extra broody and grump-tastic, with his clipped one-syllable responses and general skulking about the apartment.

Meanwhile, I'm still struggling to understand what the hell happened in that lobby. Have I really had a lifetime of rusted Honda Civic–equivalent kisses? Because comparatively, Trevor's kiss was like being behind the buttery leather wheel of Mel's Tesla. Is it humanly possible to kiss someone like *that*—the fervent, suppressed passion of our breath colliding, him claiming me entirely—with zero authentic emotion spurring it on?

It's taken every morsel of self-restraint I have (which isn't much) not to crumble like a rainbow chip cookie and demand a detailed explanation. But I don't. What if the answer is simpler than I want it to be? Maybe it's exactly as he said: an unexpectedly effective way to avoid attention. And if that's the case, where the hell do I go from here?

It doesn't help that my followers have doubled down on the room-ance thing. Now that they've seen Trevor's annoyingly handsome, perfect face on video twice, it's game over. In fact, no one really cares about my exes at all. And I'm left to wonder (in a Carrie Bradshaw voice), do I really care about them, either?

Did I really go to Daniel's work with the intent to stage a run-in? If so, why did the reality of seeing him turn me into a fleeing gazelle at the sight of a lion at the watering hole? In fact, has this entire endeavor become so all-consuming because I truly want to find love with my exes, or am I merely basking in Trevor's assistance?

Luckily, I have Crystal's bridal shower to distract me from emotional ruin. We spent the morning pampering her and ourselves at the spa with manis, pedis, and facials. Now we're at our childhood home for the shower. Originally, Aunt Lisa, the eldest sister on Dad's side of the family, offered to host. But ever since she hosted a Lunar New Year celebration last week, which allegedly resulted in a permanent radish stain in her brand-new carpet, she refuses to entertain more than five adults in her home at a time.

Mom is a ball of anxiety when Mel, Crystal, and I arrive, clutching a trembling Hillary over her boob. Hillary is one fierce abomination of a creature today in her white cashmere sweater, snarling at every woman who dares get within a two-foot radius of Mom.

"Just put her upstairs," I tell her, reaching to grab her myself. Hillary practically foams at the mouth when my hand grazes her pointed left ear. Mom turns, shielding her like I'm the Wicked Witch of the West.

"We just have to make sure we keep her away from the women," Mom says casually, like it's totally normal for a dog to be a misogynist. She flashes Mel a fake smile over my shoulder before heading upstairs to administer Hillary's daily dose of joint inflammation medication.

The kitchen is at capacity with Dad's side of the family. Grandma Mei stands at the island, meticulously arranging the food, clad in both a leopard-print blouse and a leopard-print apron. She's always been extra. Vibrant prints, random pops of fluorescent, the brighter the better. With her turquoise eye shadow and mauve lip, she's straight off the *Crazy Rich Asians* movie set, sans rich.

My family always says I look like a younger, happier version of her, minus the weathered skin creased between her eyes, giving the illusion she's perma-scowling, even when she's not.

Everyone cheers when Crystal enters the kitchen. Before Mel and I follow her in, I direct her to the mudroom to remove our coats on account of the sweltering heat emanating from the steaming pots on the stove. It reminds me of chaotic summers working in the restaurant as a teen. The staff, even those who aren't literal family, feel like family. On any given day, no matter the time, everyone can be heard singing and tossing loving yet scorching burns back and forth in a mix of English and Mandarin, all while working diligently to prepare massive vats of delicious food.

"Explain the family dynamics to me," Mel requests on our way back to the kitchen.

"Okay, so Dad is the second eldest. He's the favorite, to the dismay of the aunties and Uncle Michael, who isn't here. See, they all work at the restaurant, except Dad, and he still gets preferential treatment." I point to Aunt Lisa and Aunt Rachel, who are hovering around Mei as she chops water chestnuts. "Those two have an unspoken rivalry going on. They like to one-up each other with material possessions. Like when Aunt Lisa got a Louis Vuitton tote, Aunt Rachel had to get two."

Mel gives her best attempt at a laugh, a far cry from her typical enthusiasm for juicy gossip. Now that I think of it, she's been uncharacteristically quiet all day.

"You okay?" I ask.

She fusses with the ruffled collar of her blouse. "Yeah. It's just . . . you're really lucky to have such a close extended family. On both sides." I don't know much about Mel's extended family, aside from the fact that she isn't close with them.

"You're always more than welcome at our family gatherings," I pledge.

"I'm fairly certain your family doesn't want some rando at their holidays."

"You would be wrong." I nod toward Dad, who's barreling around the corner to give Mel a high-five greeting.

He slaps her delicate hand far too hard, barely noticing her wince. "Mel! Good to see you. Maybe today I can finally teach you how to use chopsticks," he teases.

She cracks a smile. A couple of months ago, she dropped a massive fish ball on the floor at family hot pot night. Hillary lunged out of Mom's arms and gobbled it up before Mom could wrench it from her teeth. "I'm not that bad, am I?" While Mel is Chinese, she was adopted as an infant and raised by her white parents, whom she doesn't talk about much. She doesn't know a lot about her roots, aside from what she picks up from me and Crystal.

"Terrible." Dad shakes his head solemnly and gives her a fatherly arm pat. "But no fear. We'll get you in tip-top shape."

"See?" I side hug her, nuzzling my head against her shoulder even though I know she detests hugs. "You're stuck with us as your family. Sorry about your luck."

For once, she's not entirely disturbed by my lack of boundaries, accepting my hug without a fuss. "I love you guys."

In pure Chen fashion, Grandma Mei, Aunt Lisa, Aunt Rachel, and my tween cousins, Kendall and Maddie, descend on us the moment our butts touch the stools on the island.

Aunt Lisa, the most direct sibling, quickly becomes bored with Aunt Rachel soliciting Mel's advice on eyebrow microblading and angles herself to me, bracelets clinking against the granite counter. "I saw online you're dating your ex-boyfriends?"

I'm taken aback as Mei passes me a full plate of carefully selected appetizers she knows I'll eat. She's one of the only family members who doesn't snark on my picky eating habits. "I didn't know you knew about my book account."

"Your dad linked me." She regards me like I'm a sad lamb, as she has since my wedding was called off.

"I always liked the skinny little one with the bowl cut who

came to the restaurant with you," Aunt Rachel cuts in, stealing a fried wonton from my plate.

"Daniel Nakamura?"

Aunt Lisa nods vigorously. "Oh, I liked that boy too. Never spoke a word, the little thing," she says with an evil grin, turning to Aunt Rachel. "You know I like a man who can be easily controlled."

Aunt Rachel makes a whip motion with her hand, followed by a *swish* sound. "I think Tara needs an equal. A man who can match her personality and energy. Someone outgoing, extroverted, not afraid to take up space."

Aunt Lisa disagrees. "Oh, no. It never works when both parties are talkers. Only leads to frustration and resentment. Opposites are ideal."

I move my fried rice around my plate absentmindedly while they bicker about which ex is least likely to grow tired of me. My mind trails to Trevor again and how he explicitly stated he never gets sick of my stories. That was weeks ago. I wonder if that's still the case.

Aunt Rachel clasps both hands together, prayer-style. "Oh, I hope your true love is Cody. I always adored him. Such a little gentleman."

I sigh, dipping my sesame ball. "Turns out, Cody Venner is happily married with kids." I say *happily* sarcastically, though my meaning goes over Aunt Lisa's head.

"You're telling me he's married? Happily? Nonsense," she says, waving my words away.

As Mei pushes a basket of dumplings in front of Mel and me, my phone lights up with a text.

TREVOR: Hey. Hope you're having a good bachelorette day. Scott almost threw up at the Ninja Warrior gym. Too many pancakes this morning. 🤢

TARA: Lmao! Oh no. Hope he's okay! You would never catch me dead at the Ninja gym. Things are dandy over here. Crystal got pampered this morning. Now we're eating.

I send him a photo of the table spread.

TARA: Are you guys having a good time? Heading to the club tonight?

TREVOR: Ya.

TARA: Have fun!!

TREVOR: Thx.

TARA: I've been meaning to tell you . . . I think you still need some help with your texting game. You better not be texting Kyla like this

TREVOR: My texts are perfectly fine.

TARA: For the 39434th time, you simply cannot punctuate with a period. It's a mark of death! You're an emotional person's nightmare texter 🙀

TREVOR: THE HORROR!!!! From now on I'll make sure I end all my texts with exclamation marks okay?! Just for you!

TARA: I feel so special 😍

TREVOR: You should! I'm only doing this for you!

"Is that a heart-eye emoji? For Trev?" Crystal peeks at my screen as she reaches for a dumpling. Her *Bride to Be* sash nearly dips onto my plate.

I dispose of my phone in the back pocket of my jeans and lean against the island. "Yes. But don't read into it. There's nothing going on with us."

"Figured as much," she says casually. I don't know why her knowing tone irks me so much, but it does.

Mel analyzes me, her expression marginally less critical. "You're not telling us something."

I buckle immediately under the pressure of her callout. "Fine. He kissed me. When we did surveillance at Daniel's work. One minute, Daniel was coming out of the elevator, and the next, Trevor was kissing me. With tongue." I elegantly gnaw at a chicken wing, awaiting my crucifixion.

Crystal's eyes bulge, as if I've regaled them with a tall tale about running a 10K, or something equally unbelievable and outlandish.

I rehash our hot-and-heavy make-out, explaining his justification—how he was diverting attention away from us. When I say it out loud, it sounds weak. Surely, he could have taken less drastic measures, like tossing his coat over my face or pushing my head down.

Crystal scrutinizes me, shifting out of the way as Aunt Lisa inches behind us to the perimeter of the kitchen, eager to serve her lemon cake. "You're not overthinking this, are you?"

"No," I say quickly, my eyes turning to my chicken wing bone.

"You are. I can see the wheels turning," she says leerily.

"Okay, fine. I can't help but wonder sometimes. We have the best conversations. He's opened up to me a lot in the past month. There's actually a lot more to him than meets the eye. He's sensitive and he listens, like, really listens," I gush.

Crystal gives me a pitiful look, like she doesn't want to hurt my feelings. "Is he still . . . sleeping with other women?"

"I don't know." I hang my head. "The last girl he brought home was Gabby. From your gym. Though he is casually texting one girl he used to date. Kyla."

"Has he ever given you any hint he has real feelings for you?" Mel asks.

"He smiles at me a lot, mostly when he thinks I'm not looking. Oh, and he feeds me," I add, grasping at straws. "He even tries to make food I'll like." Just a few evenings ago, he made me a flatbread pizza. Half was loaded with veggies, while the other half was plain sauce, pepperoni, and cheese, just for me.

Crystal's doubtful expression tramples my theory to dust. "I mean, the smiling . . . he's a bit of a flirt in general."

I frown. "Maybe. But hypothetically, what if I'm not reading too much into things? What if he did catch feelings for me?"

"Expecting to be the exception to the rule is like eating Taco Bell and being shocked when you get mad diarrhea," Crystal says pointedly.

Mom huffs at us as she passes by with beady-eyed Hillary. "Crystal! People are eating."

Crystal mouths a lazy *Sorry* and looks to Mel for support. "I love you. But the last thing I want is for you to get hurt again." She watches me for a few more beats. "Do you mind if I consult Scott?"

I barely have time to agree before Scott's face takes up Crystal's phone screen. He tells her about the trauma of being kidnapped and nearly punching Trevor in the face. Crystal laughs, her face aglow at the sight of her soon-to-be husband, as if they've been apart for days and not mere hours. "Can you step away for a minute? I have a question for you."

"About what?" Scott asks, taking refuge away from the guys in the gym changing room.

I press my cheek against Crystal's so I'm visible on camera. "We need your advice. A behavioral analysis, if you will."

"We need your help with Trevor," Crystal clarifies, giving him a brief rundown of my situation. "Has he said anything about Tara to you?"

He raises a contemplative brow. "He talks about her sometimes at work."

"Why didn't you tell me before?" Crystal waves a hand. "This is important information, babe. Care to elaborate?"

"I didn't think it was a huge deal." Scott frowns. "He'll just laugh at texts she sends at work. Nothing too major."

"He's your friend. Could you ask him for us? Get the intel. Whatever it is that dudes do," Crystal requests.

Scott is mildly taken aback, like we've just asked him to commit a crime on our behalf. "You want me to flat-out ask him if he likes Tara?"

"Yes," we say in unison.

He leans against the hand dryer, accidentally turning it on. "Fine. But he's gonna know something is up. We never talk about feelings," he shouts over the fan.

My lips twist like I've just sucked a lemon. "Seriously? Never in your decade of friendship have you talked about feelings?"

"Unless you count our feelings toward hockey, Crocs, or fire calls, no." When we shake our heads in derision, he gets defensive. "Hey, it's not like I've never tried. He's just not a very open guy."

I sigh. "That's . . . pathetic."

Crystal scoffs in solidarity. "Gotta love toxic masculinity."

"Yeah, yeah, I know." Scott rolls his eyes and leans in close to the camera, suddenly channeling FBI agent vibes. "Okay, I'll ask him tonight when we go out once he's liquored up. How should I play it? Casual? Or like I'm an overprotective new brother who'll murder him if he breathes amorously in your direction?"

"I mean, I appreciate the brotherly support, but definitely not the latter," I warn. "Just be casual and report back."

"Deal."

TARA: Hello?? I haven't heard from you in like an hour. You promised a play-by-play.

SCOTT: Sorry. At club now . . . Trev ordered a beer. He's hanging out with a girl.

TARA: A girl? Who?

SCOTT: She met him here. I think they already know each other. Her name is Kayla or something.

TARA: Is she tall? Smiles with her mouth open?

SCOTT: Yeah.

Kyla. It's Kyla.
Trevor's ex-girlfriend.

LIVE WITH TARAROMANCEQUEEN—THE PLAYBOY TROPE AND WHY I HATE IT

[Tara's face is partially obscured by poor lighting. She is neck-deep in a hot tub, her hair crunchy and partially frozen, looking like a straight-up mess.]

EXCERPT FROM TRANSCRIPT

TARA: *Hello, romance book lovers, welcome back to my channel. If you've followed me for an ounce of time, you'll know I'm absolute trash for most tropes. I'll take anything: secret babies, love triangles. But for some reason, I can't handle playboys lately. Now, I'm not against people sleeping around. You do you, boo. But I have a problem with the double standards.*

The playboy hero is often rich and powerful, maybe a duke, a CEO, or the firstborn son of a crime family. As a commitment-phobic man-child, he sleeps around to cope with his overt emotional problems (due to a tragic backstory). He's cruising through life, an empty robot until a doe-eyed, virgin heroine unexpectedly piques his interest. She's only immune to his charm for a hot second before falling for his rakishly handsome looks and secret, true self that only she knows.

More often than not, these heroes are hyper-controlling, brooding, and possessive. They practically breathe fire if another man looks in her general direction, even though they've just slept with another woman an hour before.

Now, it's known that heroines are held to a much higher standard than heroes. But why do we let our heroines fall for scum for the sake of the hero's character arc? I'm all for a redemption story, but if I wouldn't choose this guy to date my best friend, I just can't root for him.

Thoughts?

COMMENTS:

Noooooo. Rakes are THE BEST. The payoff is always the most satisfying when they inevitably change their ways for THE ONE. ♡

I like my playboys fictional. I have no time for them in real life! 💀 ♡

chapter twenty-three

LIKE THE EMOTIONALLY balanced millennial I am, coping with my problems by being petty on social media is my go-to. Unfortunately, one of the most beloved romance tropes got the brunt of my passive-aggressive callout.

I make the wise decision to delete the video entirely as I stomp down the stairs from the rooftop in Trevor's hideous Crocs. Aside from being ten sizes too large for my feet, they're disgustingly comfortable and convenient for hot tub sessions. The tiniest sliver of me partially understands the hype, but I'd rather commit to an exclusive diet of raw vegetables for life before I admit that.

The lights are off in our apartment, which tells me Trevor is still out on the town. I imagine he's in his glory right now, surrounded by beautiful, large-breasted women, on track to bringing home another Instagram model of his choosing to ravage. Maybe five. Though he'll concentrate most of his efforts on Kyla.

I seethe with jealousy at the mere thought of him with Kyla. How does one properly prepare themselves to hear the guy they like having sex with another woman across the hall?

Perhaps this was inevitable all along. Aside from moving out and taking up residence in a cardboard box on the street, what else am I supposed to do but suck it up? Maybe it'll get easier with each successive woman.

The acoustics of my trusty Taylor Swift breakup playlist fill the apartment as I await my fate in the living room, engulfed in darkness (to match my mood). Like my Ex-Files box, this playlist has been with me since my breakup with Tommy in ninth grade. With each new album, I strategically add the gloomiest songs in advance of such a time as this.

I'm seven songs deep when Trevor returns, interrupting the emotional bridge of "All Too Well" (the ten-minute version, obviously). Bracing myself for Kyla's inevitable high-pitched giggle, I drag myself into a seated position, taking in Trevor's massive outline in the doorway. It appears he's returned alone. Kyla is nowhere to be seen. I do the mental running man, followed by a couple of air punches. I'm far more elated about his temporary lone-wolf status than I should be.

"Hey," I rasp through the darkness, hitting pause on Taylor Swift.

"Why are you lying in the dark alone?" His tone is lazy and slurred, a far contrast from his typical terse, rushed cadence. He wobbles a tad, groping at the wall for support. He is definitely not sober.

Drunk Trevor doesn't care that he's kicked his shoes into a messy pile. Or that his coat slipped off the hanger the moment he walked away. Drunk Trevor even props his feet on the coffee table the moment he slouches onto the couch.

A chunk of his usually tamed, ashy waves branches upward, Alfalfa-style. I stand to pat it down before my brain sounds the alarm, reminding me he's like a rescue dog wearing one of those *Do Not Touch, I Bite* vests because he can't be trusted yet. And neither can I.

"I've never seen you under the influence before. I hope you Uber'd," I say, forcing both hands at my sides where they belong.

"Course I did. What'd you do tonight?"

"Hot tub. Self-loathing. The usual."

His chuckle is light and easy, almost giddy. He runs his hand through his hair, inadvertently making his cowlick worse. He fishes the remote from the crack between the cushions. Without notice, he tosses it to me, thoroughly entertained when I dazedly fumble it like a slow loris. "Wanna watch *The Bachelor* with me?"

"You're going to watch it without me either way, aren't you?" I venture. "Who knew you'd become such a proud citizen of Bachelor Nation."

He swings me a lazy, resigned grin. "What can I say? I'm invested in Wyatt's life now. Come on, sit with me."

"Spoiler alert: he will choose a bride and they'll split up six months later," I inform him, not budging. If I know myself as well as I think, spending more quality time with a guy I have unrequited feelings for can only end in a tsunami of tears.

He pats the middle cushion next to him for emphasis. Like the weak-willed individual I am, I concede, settling on the far cushion. My entire body is engulfed in flames. I've basically just agreed to a TV date with Satan.

I'm profusely sweating in my flannels throughout Wyatt's group date. The girls are quite literally boxing and taking punches to win his affection. One girl is hard-core, nearly breaking another woman's veneers.

Trevor nudges me on the thigh with his knuckle. "I could see you breaking someone's nose. You're like a little scrappy hamster."

"I once bit another girl who tried to kiss Daniel at recess," I admit.

"You're a biter?" He pretends to recoil to his side of the couch.

I peel my eyes from the television to shoot him my best faux-evil look. "It's my secret weapon."

"That's officially my new favorite thing about you." When he beams at me, I have to avert my gaze back to much less desirable Wyatt on the TV. I couldn't look into Trevor's eyes and not feel a little something. One more second of eye contact and my poor little soul would shrivel, unable to cope with the beauty.

"You have other favorite things?" I pry.

"Oh yeah." He doesn't bother to elaborate. He's too distracted by sexy grade school teacher Mona, his favorite *Bachelor* contestant.

After many beats of cruel silence, Trevor shifts his attention back to me when the host moseys into the mansion to give Wyatt a pointless heart-to-heart. "You must have really liked Daniel to bite another girl."

"He was my best friend. Ever. In the whole world."

"Umm, ouch. I'm sitting right here." He folds a hand over his heart and pretends to wince in pain. "I thought *I* was your best friend."

"I didn't realize we'd advanced to that level. Am I *your* best friend?"

"Maybe. You know all my secrets now. Most of them, at least."

I don't respond. I'm plagued with far too many feelings over this statement. On the one hand, I'm mush. Being labeled as Trevor Metcalfe's best friend is the highest of compliments. On the other hand, the only thing more unromantic than friend status is *best friend* status.

He's still watching me. "If your *best friend* Daniel hadn't moved, do you think you'd have dated?"

"A hundred percent. I was in love with him . . . though to be fair, I was in love with all the boys in my class. But no one topped him."

Trevor smiles lazily. "Think you'll go back to try another run-in?"

"For sure." I have no specific plans to stage another run-in, but the gala is in a week. I need to figure something out. "I just hope he remembers me."

"He will."

Through the rose ceremony, Trevor sinks horizontally on the couch, unexpectedly resting his head in my lap. I'm frozen as he adjusts the weight of his head evenly over my thighs. My senses magnify. I'm all too aware of the rhythm of his breath, a few beats slower than my own. The poke of his hair through the fabric of my flannel pajama bottoms. The delectable yet not overpowering smell of his aftershave.

My fingers twitch, unsure what to do with my hands. Do I keep them like noodles at my sides? Rest one hand on his hard, impeccably honed pectorals? Give him a head massage? Cradle his head and sing him to sleep like any perfectly normal best friend would do?

I make the safe decision to keep my hands to myself.

He doesn't even bat an eye when I make the executive decision to put on *Tangled*.

Throughout the majority of the movie, Trevor is the only one paying attention. My mind is a rush-hour traffic jam during the winter's worst snowstorm. Hurried thoughts collide and cut each other off. Sitting on the opposite end of the couch was nerve-inducing enough, but this up close and personal view of his face is hazardous. Having feelings for Trevor Metcalfe is like driving in the opposite lane on a busy freeway as oncoming traffic barrels toward you.

When *Tangled* ends, he peers up at me through the dense forest of his lashes. I take in the perfect slope of his nose. The mixture of dark and light stubble along his defined jaw. The little half-inch scar over his left eyebrow, which I know he sustained falling face-first into a coffee table at age five. Even through the darkness, the TV light casts a reflection off his eyes, making them shine like crackling sparks in the wildfire raging through me.

"*Tangled* wasn't awful," he admits.

"Are you telling me you actually liked a Disney movie?"

"I didn't mind Flynn Rider. He was cool."

"See? I told you he wasn't off-brand. You should be happy I assigned you him and not . . . the Beast."

He chuckles softly. "This was fun."

"Yeah. Beats lying here alone in the dark, self-loathing."

He makes a *tsk* sound and frowns up at me. "I wish you wouldn't do that. There is absolutely nothing about you to loathe."

"It's actually healthier than it sounds—getting real with myself. Having cathartic cries every now and then. My therapist highly recommended it." I work down a swallow, nearly crossing into the spirit world when he runs his index finger over my knee, catching a piece of lint.

"You see a therapist?" he asks.

"I used to see one on and off since high school. Her name was Wendy. I called her my breakup therapist. My mom forced me to see her after Cody dumped me. I was inconsolable in my room for weeks, and no one knew what to do with me. I'd see her every time my life went off the rails. Went back recently after my split with Seth, but she retired last spring. I haven't tried anyone new since."

He presses his cheek against my thigh. "You should. Spilling your guts on the regular seems like it would be healthy for you."

"Probably. I'd recommend therapy for anyone, actually." I absentmindedly pat down the section of his hair that's sticking out. Working my fingers through his dense, silky mane shouldn't feel so comfortable, so ritualistic, like I've done it a million times before.

"I don't know about therapy for everyone," he decides after a few moments of silent enjoyment of his head massage. His eyes are closed now, which is probably safer for everyone involved—mainly me.

"You don't think it would be healthy to talk to someone about your . . . baggage?"

He cracks a lid and smiles up at me. "You think I have baggage?"

I level him a serious look. "Metcalfe, you have a full luggage cart of baggage. You've gone through a lot with your parents, your brother, and Angie. I know you don't love talking about them, or your feelings in general, but maybe it would help."

"I think it's the talking-to-strangers part I have an issue with."

He peers up at me again. "Maybe you can be my therapist. I like talking to you."

I meet his gaze, holding my breath. Somehow, that seemingly insignificant statement means everything. Regardless of whether he has feelings for me, he feels comfortable talking to me, of all people. "I like talking to you too."

"You like to talk to everyone, though." He pauses, letting out a one-syllable laugh. "You're gonna be the death of me, Chen."

I have no idea how to interpret this, nor do I have time to, because from the sound of his labored breathing, he's fallen asleep on my lap. As much as I'd love to be his pillow for the night, this does not bode well for either of us. He stirs as I gently shift his head.

"Where are you going?" he slurs.

"Bed. We both need to go to bed."

He opens his eyes and frowns. "Can't we stay here?"

"If I let you sleep on the couch, you'll just complain tomorrow about having a sore neck."

"Yeah . . . You're right." With a long sigh, he stands, stretching his arms toward the ceiling, allowing me the briefest flash of his delicious abs when his shirt lifts.

Head down, I follow him into the dark hallway. I expect him to head straight to his room and close the door, but he lingers in the middle of the hall outside my bedroom doorway. As I pass through the tight space toward my room, his fingers just barely graze mine.

"'Night," he says, ever so formally.

I smile. "Goodnight."

A beat of silence.

He doesn't go to his room, and neither do I. We're standing in our respective doorways in a weird, nonconfrontational face-off.

Why isn't he going to bed?

Why aren't I?

My heart thumps wildly against my chest wall like a steel drum. Just like that moment of intense telepathy in Daniel's lobby, right before he kissed me, I hold his stare, mentally daring him to approach.

And he does.

♥ chapter twenty-four

SWEET CHRIST. I am not equipped for this.

Panicked, I wet my bottom lip, readying for another earth-shaking kiss.

Is this really happening? Why am I wearing ugly flannel PJs, of all things? I ask myself as his hand cups my cheek with the lightest touch. His thumb does a gentle sweep over my bottom lip, sending a shiver hurtling down the back of my neck. In a startling whoosh, that same hand reaches downward, toward my waist.

"Goodnight," he whispers, reaching for the doorknob. He pulls it shut, cruelly separating us.

For an indeterminate amount of time, I blink in the darkness, in the confines of my own bedroom. I press my palm against the door, royally dumbfounded.

What the actual fuck was that?

IN THE LIGHT of day the next morning, Trevor's shoes are arranged in a straight line and his coat is now safely back on the hanger. When I emerge from my room in my scrubs to eat my morning Pop-Tart, he's already parked at the kitchen island eating an omelet. He greets me with a shy chin dip.

"You're looking suspiciously healthy after a night of heavy drinking," I say, waiting for my Pop-Tart to toast. Unlike the rest of us mere mortals, Trevor doesn't resemble a corpse after a night out. No. He looks like an angel with his bright eyes and perfect, hydrated complexion. He could probably hike the Dolomites right now if someone asked him to.

He shrugs. "I don't really get hangovers. You off to work?" he asks casually, as if everything is totally normal. As if that heated encounter in the hallway last night didn't happen.

I blink, wondering if I dreamed the entire scenario. Before I head to work, we talk about a myriad of topics, like final preparations for Angie's party, Trevor's disappointment that Scott didn't get drunk last night at his own bachelor party, and my unwavering position that he should be indicted on a federal offense for smothering his omelet in ketchup. We touch on literally everything except his bizarro behavior from last night.

There's little time to overanalyze today, because work is insanely busy. We get an influx of patients, including a week-old patient with a severe case of sepsis we're particularly worried about.

Seth catches me on a five-minute breather in the nurses' lounge and decides it's an opportune time to inquire about my personal life.

"Hey," he says, sidling up beside me in front of the Keurig. The fancy coffee machine in the doctors' lounge has long been repaired, but in an unfortunate turn of events, Seth has concluded he prefers the machine in here. "How's the search coming along?"

"You've been actively keeping up with my search online," I say, making it clear I know he's watched every single story. "I'm sure you're already aware."

He ignores this fact. "Think you'll bring one of these lucky guys to the gala?" he asks, even though he knows full well there's only one left—Daniel.

"Yeah. I think I might." I make a concerted effort to sound optimistic. The gala (Valentine's Day) is now only days away. It would be nice to have someone by my side, like Daniel.

"I'm proud of you, you know? I thought this was all a little ridiculous at first. But I'm glad you have something else to focus on." I don't miss the condescension in his tone.

I'm tempted to strike him in the forehead with a coffee pod as a distractive measure and run away, but alas, I'm a professional. Instead, I just force a smile, take my coffee, and GTFO.

While interactions with Seth are never pleasant and often require spiritual recuperation, maybe this was the kick in the pants I needed. Far too much energy has been expended over Trevor in the past week, and for what?

With all the confusion with my roommate, I've nearly lost sight of my original goal of securing my storybook second-chance romance. I can't let these strange little moments with Trevor knock me off course.

I think about all my followers and how invested they are in my relationship journey. It's like I'm a romance heroine they're rooting for. The last thing I want to do is report to them that it's all been a complete and utter failure.

I also made a vow to Crystal and Mel months ago that I'd focus on my exes, and I am not the kind of person to break a promise.

• • •

——————— WEDNESDAY, FEBRUARY 8 ———————

Tara Chen · 5:46 P.M.

Hi Daniel,

This is going to seem random, but we used to be best friends as kids. In case you forgot who I am (and I don't blame you if you did, I'm forgettable), I'm the girl who used to make you embarrassingly gushy Valentine's Day cards. The one who used to eat most of the Dunkaroo icing and leave you with the dry biscuits. You gave me a pink Furby for my sixth birthday party, and we named her Roxy.

We lost touch after middle school, which is probably for the best. I did not thrive in high school. Now we're 30. I've spent a lot of time mourning our youths and I miss you. It appears you are not online anywhere except here on LinkedIn. Of course, I've thought about emailing you at dragon_ball_z_is_kewl@xmail.com (LOL), but I assume you are no longer using that email address.

Anyway, no pressure, but I'd love to hear from you. It would make my day (no, my life!).

—Your Best Friend, Tara

• • •

"THIS IS PROBABLY a massive waste of time," I grumble to myself as I hit *Send* on my subway commute home. I make a pact with myself that if he ignores my LinkedIn DM, I'll take it as a sign to give up on love entirely and purchase a rescue dog who won't break my heart.

Luckily, I have a brand-new audiobook to distract me while I await a response. This one is another second-chance reunion romance, about Shelley, a New York City socialite who goes back to her down-home roots after a scandal. Upon return, she discovers her ex-boyfriend, Kent, a muscly cattle rancher, has been running her late father's farm.

When I return to the apartment, I hit *Play* while I prepare a sophisticated dinner of chicken nuggets and curly fries. The narrator's buttery smooth voice drowns out the noise of my excessive thoughts.

While I'm waiting for the oven to preheat, Trevor emerges from his bedroom and quietly begins rooting around the kitchen for his own food. The sultry, late-night-radio-show voice of my audiobook fills the dead air between us.

"Shelley gripped the base of his cock, feeling its pulse against her palm . . ."

He clears his throat behind me, chucking a head of broccoli onto his cutting board. "Whoa. What are you listening to?"

The bold voice plows forward with gusto, entirely shameless. *"Kent let out a low, hungry growl as his eyes feasted upon her glistening . . ."*

"My audiobook," I say, my tone clipped as I arrange my nuggets on the pan in the shape of a heart.

He snickers and mutters something I can't hear.

No fail, listening to sex scenes via audiobook is painfully awkward, even solo. Double the awkward when someone else is in the room. I go to hit *Pause* and shriek.

I have a LinkedIn notification. It's a DM response. From Daniel.

If this were a movie, an upbeat pop song would fade in. Something with a heavy piano. Maybe "A Thousand Miles" by Vanessa Carlton or "Brighter Than the Sun" by Colbie Caillat. Regardless, it's the sound of everything in my life finally coming together. The weight of my failed engagement with Seth, moving two times, my exes, and the emotional turmoil that is Trevor have seemingly dissolved now that I've finally made contact with Daniel.

Trevor's too busy chopping his broccoli to notice my reaction to my phone. Either that or he doesn't care.

I slink away to the privacy of my own room to read it.

─────────── WEDNESDAY, FEBRUARY 8 ───────────

Daniel Nakamura · 7:13 P.M.

Hi Tara,

Are you kidding me? Of course I remember you. In case you forgot, I don't like many people. You were one of the few. If you can believe it, I too was very uncool in high school. It might have been nice if we could have been uncool together, don't you think?

You're definitely right—I do not use my old email address anymore. Though Dragon Ball Z is still KEWL. I thought about writing you as well, but I figured you weren't still at exesandohs93@xmail.com.

I plucked my first gray hair the other day. How did we get so old? Let's catch up for dinner soon? Things are really busy with work, but I could make myself available this Friday or Saturday night, if you're free?

—Your Best Friend, Daniel

Ps. I am so glad to hear from you.

You and me both, Daniel.

chapter twenty-five

I LOOK RIDICULOUS." TREVOR pouts at his reflection in the full-body-length gilded mirror, tugging at the fabric of his costume like it's a monstrosity.

We're at a costume rental store trying on our respective Disney getups, one of the last remaining birthday party planning tasks. Despite his admitted enjoyment of *Tangled*, Trevor is not enthused.

I pull the vest to center on his chest with a hard tug, taking a mental picture for safekeeping on days I need an instant mood boost. "Shut up. It looks amazing. Instant panty-dropper."

Like the dashing and effortlessly charismatic Flynn Rider from *Tangled*, Trevor liberally fills out his impossibly tight pair of camel-colored pants. I'm tempted to bounce a coin off his ass. Like the monster he is, he somehow manages to pull off the ornate green vest better than cartoon Flynn.

He grunts, fussing with the front clasp. "*This* is a panty-dropper? Maybe in medieval times."

"Stop messing with it," I order, swatting his hand away. "And FYI, the vest is basically the historical version of a Henley. It's a staple in the romance hero wardrobe."

"What's a Henley?"

I glare at him. "You did not just ask me what a Henley is."

"Never heard of it."

"Further proof you are not romance hero material," I conclude, more for my own benefit, lest I slip up and continue to forget that glaring, indisputable fact.

Shockingly, he doesn't debate it. He goes quiet for a moment before conceding, "I still don't know what a Henley is."

"It's one of those cotton pullover shirts. Round collar with the little buttons? Scotty wears them all the time," I explain, softening my tone.

He checks himself out again in the mirror. "I could rock those."

"I wouldn't be so sure. They require a certain kind of swagger." Truthfully, I'm both startled and affronted by the mental visual of his tattooed biceps, corded forearms, and broad chest doing overtime under an unbuttoned Henley. He's going about his day, doing the normal things romance heroes do. Rolling up his sleeves. Leaning on various supportive structures, arms crossed to accentuate said biceps. Being an overall walking thirst trap. I'd follow him straight into a pyramid scheme in this getup.

"Swagger. *Pft.*" He waves my blatant lie away, unbothered, probably because he knows he looks flawless in just about anything (and nothing at all). He eyes his Disney costume in the mirror once more and whines like a small child. "Can I please lose the tights at least?"

Depriving the world of his ass in those pants would be an international war crime. "First, those are not tights. And you can't get any worse than me. I'm basically a gigantic bumblebee." I gesture to my ill-fitting yellow Belle gown. If I needed any proof that yellow does nothing for me, it's right here and now in the mirror.

He makes no attempt to spare my feelings. "Why would you choose *Beauty and the Beast* of all the princesses? She's pretty damn boring, from what I remember." He waves a dismissive hand at my excessively poofy dress like it's a steaming pile of shit.

"I thought you said you didn't watch Disney?"

"Not as an adult. I've seen all the old ones."

I glower at him, my hand on my hip. "Well, if you must know, Belle and I are the most alike. We're both bookworms, we try to see the good in people, we don't like being told what to do. If you call her boring, you're calling me boring."

He tilts his head like a dog, giving the dress another gander. "I just meant her outfit is a little . . . much. With the bows and all the fabric. Why didn't you go with *Little Mermaid*?"

"We have an Ariel costume," Glenda, the crotchety store owner, informs us from across the room, where she's steaming a Captain America suit I'm tempted to rent for Scott, given his uncanny Chris Evans resemblance.

"We're good with Belle, thanks," I say gratefully, and turn back to Trevor. "You just want to see me in a shell bikini top."

"Nobody would complain about that." Is this Trevor's way of admitting he wouldn't mind seeing me, his *best friend*, in a seashell bra?

I tug at the itchy sleeve of my ball gown, unable to discern whether he's being serious or sarcastic. "My boobs are not appropriate for your innocent niece's tenth birthday party."

"If you say so." He's distracted by his phone. I can't help but peek at the screen. My eyes zero in on an open text conversation with Kyla.

"So, how was your hangout the other night with Kyla?" I ask, trying to make my voice as casual, sweet, and Disney princess–like as possible. "Was she as amazing as you remember?"

He pauses, his brow raised, evidently perplexed. "How'd you know I met up with Kyla?"

"Scotty told me."

"I see." He tucks his phone back in his pocket. "It was good to catch up with her. We might do drinks or something in the future."

This news doesn't sit right with my spirit, so I take cover behind the heavy velvet dressing room curtain, where it's safe.

"What are you up to tonight?" he asks.

"Oh, uh, I have plans actually," I tell him, sweating as I stumble over the inner layer of this godforsaken gown.

It took a full day before Daniel responded to my enthusiastic, all-caps-lock DM about being free on Friday. Crystal and Mel had to talk me off the ledge multiple times. I thought for sure I'd scared him off.

Trevor clears his throat. "You have plans?"

I'm too distracted by my hair tangled in the clasp of my bra to enlighten him on my plans with Daniel. After a solid minute of bending and contorting my body like a pretzel, far beyond my natural flexibility, I let out a strained, cowlike groan. "Help," I plead.

Before I get the chance to hike the gown back up to cover myself, the curtain rips open. When I yelp, Trevor's eyes rivet directly to my cleavage bursting over my double-push-up bra and downward to the tiny triangle of lace fabric between my legs.

He swiftly clamps a hand over his eyes like his retinas have been scorched and backs out of the changing room. "Damnit, Tara. You could have told me you were half-naked."

"I didn't know you were right outside the stall. And don't act scandalized. You see me in a bikini almost every night in the hot tub. It's the same thing," I hiss, still struggling. "Get back here. I need your help."

"Seriously?"

"My hair is stuck in my bra clasp. I need you to untangle it."

He lets out a tortured sigh, like a teenager being forced to finish their calculus homework. When he finally peels back the curtain again, his hands are still snug over his eyes. It's not a large space by any means, but it feels infinitely more claustrophobic with a Thor-size man behind me, along with my massive, fifty-pound dress. Maybe Trevor has a point about the excessive fabric.

His proximity behind me instantly dries my throat. I'm desperate to chug a gigantic water bottle. His strained, minty breath soothes the sensitive flesh on the back of my neck, which is bent at an odd angle from the weight of the tangle. When his rough fingertips graze my back, a hum of electricity comes alive, circuiting to all my nerve endings from my fingertips to my toes.

He tugs my tangle free, little by little, careful not to rip my hair out. The odd, gentle graze of his knuckles brushing against my back is enough to send any straight woman into a bout of unconsciousness. After a couple of deep inhales of his scent, I'm a rag doll. Pliable, floppy, and an all-around hot mess. When he tugs one stubborn section of hair a little harder than expected, I tip into him, relying on his body for support. He splays his massive hand over my bare hipbone to steady me.

My breath hitches the moment the small of my back presses flush against something very unexpected. And hard. My mind splits into fragments. Trevor Metcalfe is insanely turned on.

"Why are you . . . ?" I don't dare move, backward, forward, sideways, or otherwise.

He instantly backs up half a step, which doesn't mean much in the tiny changing room stall. He lets out a frustrated huff. "Can you blame me? You're half-naked and pressed against me," he quips, evidently offended and entirely broken up about it. I whip around, about to descend into manic laughter when he wags his finger at me. "Do not laugh."

Holding my dress over my boobs in one hand, I slap the other over my mouth to suppress my reaction while trying not to look directly at *it*. "Okay, okay. It's forgotten." *No, it's not.*

Pained, he pointedly stares at the ceiling, probably wishing he could eject himself out of here, straight through the roof, Iron Man–style. He looks about as uncomfortable as Dad when Mom forced him to be part of our birds and the bees talk when I was thirteen.

"What exactly are your plans tonight? Girls' night?" he probes.

Is he really trying to have a ridiculously casual conversation after *that*? No wonder the man doesn't do small talk. I log this as a victory, no matter how scientific. Then again, I have heard of men popping boners over less.

"I'm going on a date, actually," I say through a cough, inadvertently ripping the remaining lock of hair free from my bra clasp. I have a bald spot now, I'm sure of it.

He perks up with renewed curiosity. "A date? With who?"

"Daniel."

"What? You didn't tell me you got in touch with him."

I lift my bare shoulder with a dismissive shrug. "Sorry. I meant to tell you." I describe our LinkedIn DM reunion in great detail.

He clears his throat, awkwardly resting his arm on the wall behind my head. "So . . . you're going to dinner? Tonight?"

"I'm taking him to that Italian place I told you about a few blocks from our place. Mamma Maria's. Grandma Flo had her engagement party there last year. Their fettuccini is on a whole different level," I say over the echo of my heartbeat. "Sorry if I'm rambling. I'm just nervous. It's been so long since I've seen him. What do you think the chances are that he'll also be down to be my gala date on Tuesday?"

His eyes search mine, but he doesn't respond. The silence is palpable as the walls of the changing room threaten to close in around us.

"You think I'm getting my hopes up, don't you? Being too intense about it?" I venture.

"I don't think that at all." He catches a loose strand of my hair through his fingers. His jaw is so tense, he's at risk of cracking his beautiful teeth. He's literally inches away from my face, and if I went on my tiptoes, I could probably close that gap. I think he might even want to, until he says, "You're gonna make some guy really happy one day. And I hope for your sake that it's Daniel."

I flinch. His words solidify the harsh truth. Regardless of

whether or not he was turned on by me in an enclosed space, he sure as sugar is not my hero.

The sooner I come to terms with that glaring, indisputable fact, the better.

There's a stretch of silence as he exits the stall, closing the curtain between us yet again.

♥ chapter twenty-six

"C AN I OFFER you a drink yet, ma'am?" Rogan, the waiter, asks for the third time in a faux Queen's style British accent. For the past twenty minutes, he's been silently judging the shit out of me from afar as I demo the house breadsticks.

"I'd still like to wait for my date, thanks." I give him my best breezy, unbothered smile, like I'm perfectly content alone at this table for two. Just me and my breadsticks.

Rogan gives me a tight-lipped nod and shuffles away to observe from afar with the other waitstaff. I'm convinced they're taking bets about me based on their not-so-subtle glances and whispers. After years of working in my grandparents' restaurant, I'm painfully aware that making dumb bets on customers is sometimes the only source of entertainment in an otherwise monotonous shift.

Ten bucks says her date won't show.

Let's wager a guess when the waterworks start.

Why is it that sitting alone in a fancy establishment is so much more humiliating than in your average chain restaurant? No one would judge me if I were eating these breadsticks solo at Olive Garden.

I drum the toes of my heels against the lush carpet, trying to block out the classical music, which probably wouldn't be so grating if I weren't languishing all by my lonesome. Daniel is late, and I'm starting to wonder when it's appropriate to phone it in and order a slice of the twelve-layer chocolate cake on the menu, to go. I curse myself for not confirming the date and time after my fitting at the costume shop.

When my phone lights up, a jolt of electricity rips through me. It has to be Daniel, telling me he's on his way posthaste, followed by a long-winded explanation of the harrowing incident that caused his tardiness.

But no such luck. The text is from Trevor.

TREVOR: How's dinner going?

I'm half-tempted to ignore his text, simply to avoid the pity.

TARA: 💀 I think I'm being stood up. Going to leave soon probably. Do we have chips at home? I'm gonna need them.

TARA: *GIF of Sad Pablo Escobar all by his lonesome on ugly patio swing*

At the half-hour mark, I shoot Daniel a DM, letting him know I'm waiting at the restaurant. He has yet to respond.

At the front of the room, Rogan whispers to the hostess, who has vacant eyes and fuchsia lipstick on her teeth. They simultaneously cast grim expressions toward me. If I had to guess, they're stressing about the lack of table space. I can't say I blame them. Mamma Maria's is a full house tonight. The lineup is out the door, spilling down the brown, slushy sidewalk. I'm the annoying customer needlessly wasting a table, throwing everything off.

I hold my breath as the hostess sashays over. "Do you know if the other member of your party will be here soon?" she asks, brandishing a frighteningly fake lopsided smile. Her name tag is only half-visible behind her blond curls, allowing me to make out the first few letters (*Mer*). "We have another reservation in half an hour."

"He'll be here. In ten minutes," I say reassuringly, though more to myself.

She gives me a pitiful expression and sighs dramatically, like she's doing me a massive favor. "Ten more minutes," she warns, like a weary parent granting their child extra playtime at the park.

I picture an ancient, hand-carved hourglass emptying with just two measly grains of sand stubbornly holding on. At the nine-minute mark, Rogan strides forth to officially kick me out. He clears his throat, cruelly forcing me to look him in the eyes while he does so. "Ma'am, I apologize, but I'm going to have to ask you to—"

"Hey, I'm so sorry, babe. I got held up in a meeting," a booming voice sounds over his shoulder.

It's not Daniel.

It's Trevor.

His eyes are warm, almost amber-colored from the glow of the candlelight. And he's dressed in a suit, no less, casually taking a good decade off my life-span.

A good suit can elevate any man at least two notches. Some men are just born to wear suits, like the Christian Grey or Chuck Bass types, the ones who command respect when their suave selves stride into a boardroom, their brows raised inquisitively. They smell like mahogany, radiating status and sex appeal with a dash of sociopathic tendencies. The mere fastening of a cuff link is enough to make the postmenopausal secretary shift in her chair. On rare occasions, they may be spotted in the wild in casual wear, and it's jarring, like seeing your first-grade teacher next to you in the condom and lube aisle of the local pharmacy.

Then there are men like Trevor Metcalfe. The rugged, emotionally damaged types who would rather wear literally anything else, preferably their ripped, distressed jeans and leather jacket that smells like danger. But in exceptional circumstances when they wear a suit, it's game over for humanity. Personally, I'm offended I've been deprived of such a magnificent sight until now.

A dark-charcoal jacket spans Trevor's broad shoulders like a glove, the fabric straining a little over his physique, accentuating his tapered waist. His wavy hair looks like shaved dark chocolate, slightly damp, fresh from a steamy shower straight out of my dreams.

Rogan frowns as Trevor settles into the seat across from mine, relaxed and self-assured.

I bumble out some garbled nonsense, unable to speak English through my shock.

Trevor gives me an easy wink over the menu that makes my heart dolphin-flip. In return, I flash him a half-terrified, half-thankful smile while stuffing a quarter of a breadstick in my mouth.

"What can I get for you tonight?" Rogan asks, callously reaching to swipe the bread basket.

To his shock and horror, Trevor snatches it with superhuman speed, setting it back on the table where it belongs. "Sorry, sir. We aren't done with the bread. And I'm good with whatever you have on tap, please."

He certainly did not request to keep the bread for himself. One does not simply get a hard body like that by mindlessly shoveling empty carbs down their throat. He saved that basket of bread for me, knowing damn well I'll go down in a blaze of wheaty glory in the name of carbs. Maybe I've been wrong about Trevor's romantic lead potential all along, because that was some real hero shit.

Rogan shoots eye lasers at the bread basket, mentally turning it to a pile of ashy crumbs. "And to eat?"

"I'll take the twelve-ounce steak, medium rare, veggies on the side." Trevor pauses, regarding me. "I assume you want my baked potato?"

"Um, hell to the yes. Twice baked, please. If you're not having it, I mean," I add.

Trevor smiles and folds up his menu. "What are you having, sweetheart?" For the second time tonight, a term of endearment rolls off his tongue so naturally, I'd assume we really were a real-life married couple with plans for a bright future with two kids, a yellow Lab, and maybe a beta fish I'll inevitably forget to feed.

Oh dear. I'm in too deep. I require a bright-orange life raft and a couple of flares, stat.

I snap my focus back to Rogan, who's bouncing on his toes,

probably itching to report back to his colleagues. "Uh, I'll take the fettuccini alfredo?"

"She'll take a glass of merlot too, please." Trevor gently collects my menu and hands it to Rogan. When he runs off to his minions, Trevor gives me a dazzling, mischievous grin over the glass candelabra, which is too large for a two-person table. "Hasn't anyone ever told you? Pasta is the worst date food."

I hold his stare. "Hasn't anyone ever told you? I don't play by bullshit rules."

He chuckles. "That's my girl. You look great tonight, by the way. That dress is just . . ." He waves a hand at my tight blue dress with a plunging neckline.

I didn't realize the extent of Trevor's acting abilities. He deserves an award for pretending to be a supportive, sweet boyfriend. I shoulder check, expecting one of the waitstaff to be standing behind me, observing his performance. There is no one there. "Can I ask what the heck you're doing here?"

Trevor shrugs, like giving up his night and busting out fancy attire from the depths of his closet didn't put him out in the slightest. "You told me you can't stand the thought of eating alone, right? That depressing story about the guy at your grandparents' restaurant. But I figured you'd need some moral support. I wanted to be here for you. Just in case. I know I'm no Dwight K. Schrute, but . . ."

A flame lights up my insides, filling me with a liquid warmth so comforting, I don't know what to do with my body. In fact, I don't realize I'm smiling until the moisture threatens to pool over my lash line. This is the single most thoughtful thing anyone has ever done for me.

"Hey, you okay?" Trevor asks, reading my expression. He even nudges the bread basket toward me. Why must he be so damn thoughtful?

I suck in a deep breath, willing back the floodgates as the blur of Rogan brings our drinks. "Yeah. I really am. Thank you for coming. I'm sure you had better things to do with your night."

"Like what?"

I give him a knowing look while shamelessly dipping a breadstick in the tiny tray of whipped butter. That is definitely not something I'd be doing in front of Daniel. "Like having some hot sex with an Insta model?"

He smirks. "I'm eating an expensive meal with an Insta model. That's gotta count for something."

I make a *pft* sound at his flattery, swirling my wine. "I'm no Insta model. I don't photograph well, remember?"

"Right. The Satan eyes," he says through a snort. "You really missed your opportunity. When your meme went viral in high school, you shoulda trademarked that shit. Started a Crazy Ex-Girlfriend mass following or something."

I drum my fingers together. "You make an excellent point. I could have been a charismatic cult leader of all crazy girls everywhere."

As Trevor and I contemplate all the ways I could have monetized that meme and reclaimed the term, our food arrives. To the waitstaff's horror, Trevor and I eat slowly, not out of spite, but because we can't stop talking about random things, like what we'd do in the event of an apocalypse (him: head for fresh water; me: curl up in a ball and succumb to inevitable death) or what we'd choose to eat for our last meal on death row (him: this steak; me: a bag of Cheetos).

A couple emitting some serious first-date vibes is seated at the table next to us as I devour my pasta before it gets cold. "This is exactly why I refuse to date online," I whisper as the man awkwardly remarks that the woman looks *totally different in person* than in her profile photo.

We eavesdrop as the woman asks the man whether that's a "good thing or a bad thing" and proceeds to grow visibly annoyed and understandably offended when he changes the subject.

Trevor gives me his Jim from *The Office* look, his chest rising and falling with silent laughter. "Yeah. That guy might as well just give up now."

"I think she's about to leave," I mouth.

"Sorry, I was just being honest. You don't look like your photos," the man says, his palms up.

Miffed, the woman tosses her cloth napkin on the table with a no-nonsense grumble. "Well, your voice doesn't match your face. Have a great night, Richard." Trevor and I (and probably the rest of the patrons) watch in stunned silence as she wrenches her coat from the back of her chair and leaves. I'm tempted to applaud her for having standards, but I've already peeved the waitstaff enough tonight.

"Ouch." Trevor winces from secondhand embarrassment, scrutinizing his napkin before he pats the corner of his mouth with it.

"Something wrong with your napkin?"

"I really don't like cloth napkins," he explains.

I lean forward, resting one elbow on the table. "Me either. I mean, I know they're more environmentally friendly and all."

He sets the napkin back on his lap. "Whenever I look at them,

I think about all the people who've used it. Blown their nose in it. They're always full of lint too. And weird scents. Like hotel towels."

"This is a wonderful date convo," I say, unable to stop grinning. "Very romantic."

He lifts his shoulders. "Hey, you always want to know more about me."

"Have you always been a germophobic neat freak?"

I expect him to grunt and ignore me, but he lowers his gaze to his empty plate. "My mom worked a lot and didn't have time to clean. Our place was always a shitshow. We had one of those houses you'd want to wear socks in. Logan and I were too embarrassed to have friends over because of the mess."

I almost reach to place my hand over his, but I stop myself, settling for a frown instead. "I don't blame you. Now I feel like a dick for not wiping my crumbs off the counters. Although my crumbs are nothing compared to naked women on the kitchen island," I tease.

He shakes his head, partially burying his face. "I thought you were gonna leave and never come back that day."

"Trust me, I contemplated it. But I was pretty desperate for a place to live," I admit, taking the last sip of my wine. "Was it weird to have a stranger living with you after rooming with Scott for so long?"

"No, actually. That first time we talked—"

"When you gave me Cheetos in the bathroom?"

"Yeah. I felt like I already knew you. It was like we'd been friends for years."

Womp, womp. There's that word again. *Friends.* I deflate a little. "Really? It still took you forever to open up to me." The fact is,

Trevor is a good friend. An amazing friend. While he may not see me romantically, I should be entirely grateful for his support.

He waves away my statement. "Oh, come on. I told you about Angie fairly quickly."

"You already knew all my emotional trauma by then," I remind him. "In all seriousness, though, I can't imagine living with anyone else."

"Yeah, you'd be hard-pressed to find someone who takes care of you like I do." He gives me that disarming wink again, accompanied by a light tap with his shoe under the table. "Actually, speaking of taking care of yourself, I got called out west to help with the wildfires for a few days. I'm leaving tomorrow."

I straighten my spine against the padded chair, caught off guard. "Really? Isn't it the rainy season in Cali right now?"

"It is. But this year is one of the driest in history. I should be gone a couple days. But it'll be good money. Lots of overtime." He pauses and lowers his head. "I'm trying to make sure I'll be back for Angie's party, though." There's an unmistakable somberness in his tone.

"Trev, it's okay. We could switch it to a date you're home for sure?"

"No. I already talked to Payton about it. We're gonna keep it as is. You've done too much work to switch it all."

I nod silently. "Angie will understand if you can't make it. She'll miss Flynn Rider, though."

He lets out a labored sigh, his expression pained. "I'm going to make it. What if it's her last birthday?"

"It won't be," I promise, immediately wishing I could take the words back. They're cruel to say out loud, because there's no way to know for sure. "I'll be there to make sure everything goes perfectly."

"Thank you." Pure gratitude is written all over his face. Unexpectedly, his hand brushes my kneecap under the table. It's the lightest touch, but the warmth of his fingers sends a flurry of sparks dancing through me.

"Everything will be okay."

His eyes catch mine again, and I'm lost in them until my phone has the nerve to vibrate on the table, rattling the silverware.

It's Daniel.

Hey, Tara. I am SO sorry. I'll probably be at the office all
    night. Huge project. Can we postpone?

Logically, I should feel angry. Betrayed. Sad. But Trevor's presence cushions the fall. If I know myself like I think I do, the pain will hit me later, once I'm at home. Alone. In my bed.

Trevor winces, plucking my phone from my fingers. He turns it facedown on the table. "You're not gonna reschedule, are you?"

"I mean, I can't fault him for working—"

"Forget about him," he urges. "Your soul mate isn't gonna stand you up."

My cheeks burn at his declaration. "He's my last ex."

Trevor's hard expression softens. "He doesn't deserve you."

I try to brush it off by smoothing my finger over the base of my wineglass. "I wouldn't go that far."

"I would."

I have enough self-awareness to acknowledge my tendency to overanalyze, obsess, and draw grand conclusions based on completely innocuous clues. But as I note his stiff-backed posture against the chair, his hand in a fist on the tabletop, the clench of his jaw, and our weird moment in the changing room, I'm certain there's something behind this.

I mimic his posture and his stare, holding it for a few frantic heartbeats. Bright-red fire truck warning sirens in my head be damned. I polish off the rest of my wine and go for it.

"Trev?"

"Mm-hmm?" he asks casually, oblivious to what's coming.

I rest both forearms on the table, my hands folded. "I'm about to ask you something, and you need to be two hundred percent honest with me, okay?"

He shifts farther against the chair, his Adam's apple dipping. "I take it it's not about what I ate today, is it?"

"No."

"Tara. Don't." His eyes plead with me, like he knows what I'm about to ask. And like a child who's been told not to touch the button, I have no choice but to do so.

"Is there something . . ." I gesture to the space between us. "Going on here?"

His gaze shifts to the guy whose date peaced out. He's most certainly eavesdropping on our conversation while he polishes off his spaghetti Bolognese. Trevor's jaw clenches, and he eyes me as if silently warning me.

"Please," I beg, lowering my quivering voice. "You've been acting weird lately and I'm confused. I know I'm probably just reading into things . . . but I just need a yes or no. And I swear I'll never ask again."

He watches me, silent, and I can see the gears turning in his head. On the plus side, he hasn't said no. That has to count for something.

As I wait with bated breath, my senses tunnel to him. I don't hear the classical music. The murmur of conversation around us. I don't even register Rogan's presence right away when he brings the bill, saving Trevor from my burning question.

I reach to snatch the debit machine, but Trevor gets it first, tapping his card before I can protest. Surely he's paying out of pity, to soften the blow.

We're stone silent the entire drive home in some unspoken face-off.

Who will crack first? Who dares to be the first to speak? Certainly not Trevor, who's gripping the steering wheel so hard, I'm afraid he might rip it right off the console. The entire climb up the stairwell to our unit is much the same, with only the echo of our footsteps to quell the silence.

It isn't until Trevor closes the door behind us that I lose it.

chapter twenty-seven

M Y FIRST ORDER of business when we return home: update
the ex-boyfriend board.

My lips quiver at the finality of striking Daniel's name out. The
very last name. Though if I'm being honest, I'm not convinced it's
the sole cause of my disappointment.

When I head back into the kitchen, Trevor is still in his winter
gear, his eyes wide. He's tracked slush onto the floor, which is hor-
rifically off-brand for him. When he sees the devastation in my
eyes, he folds me into a full-body embrace. I sink against his chest,
defeated.

He pulls back to study my face, which is twisted into an ugly
cry. His fingers tremble against my cheek as he brushes my tears
away. "Don't cry, please," he whispers as his lips lightly brush my
cheek like the harshest tease, as if kissing away my tears. Taking my
pain, built up over the past four months.

Trevor is a walking sign that reads *Do Not Enter*, wrapped twelve times over in cautionary tape. I know this, and yet I barge through, lifting my chin, brushing my lips to his. It's the lightest illicit touch.

A rush flows down my back when I feel his body stiffen against me, as if he's just realized that the carefully constructed fortress around his heart has been breached.

"Am I actually crazy? Am I imagining all of this?" I ask again.

"Tara . . . No."

"Why are you doing this to me? Why can't you just tell me how you feel?" I'm all too aware of the single juicy tear sliding down my cheek, about to splatter onto his jacket.

He wipes my tears again and laces his right hand through my hair, massaging the back of my head. "Because I can't be another asshole who breaks your heart. I can't do that to you, of all people. You deserve everything. Every. Thing."

I step back, out of his embrace. "No. I think the person you're really scared of hurting is yourself."

His pained, crumpled expression says it all.

"I know you're scared. You're terrified of losing the people you love. Especially Angie. And I get it. But you can't just bottle things up until they eat you alive to the point where you're not living and pursuing what you really want."

He scoffs. "And you think you know what I want?"

I toss my hands in the air. "No. I don't. I don't pretend to know. I don't know what you're thinking about at any given moment. I don't know if you want to kiss me or tell me to fuck off entirely. I don't know these things because you refuse to tell me. And it's driving me nuts."

"I refuse to tell you because—"

"Because you're the emotionally constipated playboy who can't overcome his baggage. The guy who screws the heroine over before she meets the real hero."

My words come out like bullets, and I immediately regret being so trigger-happy.

Based on his menacing stare, I've hit a nerve. "My life isn't some kind of trope. I'm not a stereotype for you to pick apart and mock."

"I'm sorry. I didn't mean that." I feel like the worst human being in the world. But I'm also thankful I've gotten an iota of emotion out of him at all.

"I'm not like you," he says. His eyes glisten with moisture, and for a split second, I think he might be on the verge of tears, until he sucks it all back. "I can't just go around getting my heart broken, putting myself back in the cross fire at every opportunity."

"You think getting my heart broken over and over is easy for me?"

He closes his eyes, like he's saying a silent prayer. "No. That's not what I meant."

"So that's just it, then? You're going to avoid your feelings forever and dodge the truth?" My breath hitches as I await the verdict.

He doesn't respond.

"Fine. You do that. But do me a favor and leave me out of it." I rip my gaze away, unable to look at him. Desperate for space, I stomp out of the kitchen, down the hall, and into my bedroom, slamming the door behind me.

My hands tremble at my sides as I lean back against the door. This man is single-handedly the most frustrating person I have ever met. I meant what I said to him, though I never should have verbalized it. Another apology is in order, though at this moment in time, I don't have the energy.

As I contemplate curling into bed to escape reality with a trusty book, there's a soft knock at the door. "What?" I grumble.

"Tara, please open the door."

Against my better judgment, I open it the tiniest crack. Trevor is still in his coat and boots, his chest heaving, his hair disheveled like he's run his fingers through it a thousand times.

"I'm not talking to you until you tell me the truth," I warn.

He tips his head back, as if to see me from a different perspective. "You want the truth?" he asks, his voice strained.

"That's all I want," I whisper, my hands on either side of my cheeks to cover the redness.

He sighs. "You were right. I—have feelings for you." The declaration knocks the wind out of my chest. I tamp down the urge to ask a million questions, letting him continue. "Big feelings. To the point where I don't even know what to do with myself half the time. I've tried to get you out of my head for months, but your stubborn ass just won't leave."

"Really?"

"I've wanted to tell you so badly. Every single day since I realized it."

"Why haven't you?"

"Because I'm scared that I can't give you what you need."

"What do you think I need?" I ask, my voice barely above a whisper.

"You want a full-on fairy tale. The perfect guy from your books. Marriage. Kids. Everything. And you deserve it all. But what if I'm not capable of giving that to you?"

I consider that. I think about all the exes who've made me similar promises in the past. How empty their words were. How it all meant nothing. Because in the end, they all left.

"But what if you are?" I counter. "I don't need another man who makes elaborate promises he can't commit to, Trevor. I need someone who's going to be open and honest with me. I want someone who is willing to try."

A sigh that sounds like relief escapes his lips. "If there's anyone in this world I want to try for, it's you," he whispers.

My chest caves, and my eyes mist. Somehow, those words mean more to me than any elaborate declaration of love from my exes. "We're really doing this?" I confirm.

"I'm going to give this everything I have. I just . . . I might need to take things slow. Slower than you're used to."

I nod. "I can do slow."

He regards me, his lip tilting in a smirk. "Can you, though?"

"Yup." I cover my face to hide my half lie, and he laughs.

"You've already come up with baby names, haven't you?"

My heart swells. We've been in a relationship all of a minute and already Trevor knows me better than any guy I've ever been with. "Maybe. But you're right. We'll go slow. Glacial slow. No marriage or baby talk. And just kissing. We'll keep it G-rated." I press my hand over my chest in a vow.

He's quiet for a few beats as his eyes search mine. For a split second, I'm certain he's about to walk it all back. "Maybe not G."

"No? Would you prefer PG? Just light pecks and hand-holding?" I tease.

"At least PG-13, smart-ass. Get over here." Before I have the chance to pounce, he pushes the door open, crosses the threshold, and pulls my wrists from my face. And then his lips collide with mine. Hard.

The intensity is overwhelming in all the best ways. Breath ragged, he cradles my head with both hands, anchoring me so close, a piece of paper couldn't slip between us. He's absorbing me with everything he has, and I don't ask questions.

His tongue skirts my bottom lip and slides against mine effortlessly, like two pieces of the same puzzle. My mind takes a few moments to catch up with my body, taking it all in. The flutter of his lashes against my brow bone. The way his fingers massage the back of my head while the other hand glides down my back, vertebra by vertebra.

I mimic his movement, slipping my hands under his coat and up his back, tracing each of his many muscles one by one as they flex against my touch. When I gently scrape my nails against his skin, he groans into my mouth, his enthusiasm for the situation evident against my stomach. He grinds hard against me, pressing me back into my dresser. The roughness seems to bring him back to the moment, because he pulls away ever so slightly.

I'd bet on my life that he's going to turn around and walk away. Instead, he moves a strand of hair behind my ear, more gently than I thought possible, breath coming down in pulsing waves against my neck.

"Are you okay?" he whispers.

"More than okay."

He smooths his thumb over my bottom lip, his eyes searching mine, as if silently asking whether I'm sure. I tighten my grip around him, and he swiftly kisses me again. It's tender, sweet, and laced with suppressed passion. It lasts for so long, I think I'm going to pass out from euphoria. It's overwhelming, how good it feels to be held and desired.

Our lips finally part, and I bury my face in the crook of his neck, taking in his intoxicating scent, trying to memorize how this feels. Apparently, my feet have an agenda, because it's me who walks us backward to my bed.

When my shins hit the mattress, I make it a mission to strip away his many layers—his winter coat, suit jacket, and dress shirt. I'm like an impatient Regency-era hero finally peeling away his lady's dress, only to find a slip and a corset underneath. I catch only a glimpse of the masterpiece that is his abs and the dusting of ashy hair disappearing into his dress pants before I go for his belt, hungry.

He places a trembling hand over mine, sucking in a labored breath.

I meet his heated gaze in a challenge, my breath quickening. "You sure you want to keep this PG-13?"

His expression is grave, like a mobster tormented over ordering an execution. "No. I want to do way more than that."

"I want you to. Please," I whisper.

"Are you sure?"

"Yes." I think I would sell my soul to have more of him, in any way I can.

♥ chapter twenty-eight

TREVOR IS A magician. It's an undisputable fact. By the time I've figured out that the tattoo on his ribs reads *Alice Metcalfe—1969–2006*, in memory of his mom, he's managed to strip his boots and my dress.

"That dress looked so fucking perfect on you," he tells me, tossing the blue fabric aside.

I shiver as he unhooks my bra, trailing kisses along the underside of my jaw. "My followers wanted this."

"None of your followers wanted it more than me." In one swift motion, he lifts me, pulling me over him on the bed in a seated position.

I wiggle closer, locking my legs around his thick torso. My hands roam down the plane between his muscled shoulder blades, over the swell of his biceps, everywhere I can manage. After months of pining, he's mine. I'd die before I'd let him out of my reach.

He's solid underneath me, like a brick house, as I clench around him again. I kiss him everywhere I can reach, savoring every inch of flesh I can find. Cheeks. Nose. Neck. Forehead. Chin. Shoulders. I take every location as a victory. A new discovery. A checkpoint.

"Holy shit." His voice comes out like a strained whisper, leaning me back to take me in with that incinerating stare I've grown to love. He sucks in a breath before letting his thumb brush the underside of my breast, followed up by the most intricate dance of his tongue. I suck in a long inhale, memorizing the scent of his bodywash, the same one I inhaled like a drug on move-in day.

I moan into his neck as he rocks me against him, straining against the zipper of his pants. I make an impatient motion to undo the button. He laughs, lifting me with little effort as he stands, stripping both his pants and briefs in one smooth movement.

I almost choke on my own saliva. He is genetically gifted. Blessed. Exactly zero flaws—to me, anyway. Not even a lazy eye. Or a slightly warped toe. How unfair.

He stands in front of me, and his smile makes me want to melt into nothingness. "Why are you looking at me like that? You've seen it before."

Because I want to grope every inch of you with heedless abandon.

With a featherlight touch, my fingers trace the artwork that adorns his chest. I curve over every detail of the striking gray phoenix that covers the left section of his chest, sweeping onto his shoulder and biceps.

"I love this one," I murmur. "When did you get it?"

"It was a celebratory one. Right after I got accepted to the fire department."

Still dancing my fingers over his chest, I catch the set of Roman numerals on his forearm that I've never been able to decipher. "What about this one?"

He swallows. "This one is Angie's birthday."

I inwardly groan. Must he be so unexpectedly sentimental and adorable? I squeeze my eyes shut, pressing firmly into his flesh. His muscles clench and flex at every touch, his breath coming out in hot, quick bursts, like he's about to lose all patience the lower my hand travels.

Evilly, I sweep a painfully slow circle dangerously close, around his inner thigh, before snapping my hand away.

"You okay?" he asks, lifting my chin.

"It's just . . . I have a question."

His throat bobs with a swallow as he kneels on the mattress in front of me. "Okay."

"What's your middle name?"

His muscles relax, and the corners of his eyes crinkle ever so slightly. The rumble of his laughter vibrates into my mouth when his lips touch mine again. "Why are you so random?" he mutters between kisses.

I giggle into him, kissing the tiny patch of skin behind his ear. "I need to know. I have a bit of a personal rule . . . with . . ."

"Right, you can't touch my dick unless you know my middle name."

"Hey, I don't have to touch it if you don't want me to," I tease.

"Oh, I want you to. So long as you don't bite me," he warns, pressing the softest bite into my neck. "I hear you have a history of biting."

"Deal. I promise," I pant, desperate to speed things along. "Now make with the middle name."

With one smooth move, he climbs over me, pressing my back flat against the mattress. His forearms cage me in on both sides, bracing his weight. "It's James," he whispers as he pulls my right thigh over his chiseled waist.

"Trevor James Metcalfe," I repeat, loving the way it rolls off my tongue.

"Say my name again," he orders, his voice low and gravelly.

I do as I'm told, three times over.

"There is no one like you, Tara Li Chen." The warmth of his breath tickles against my neck as his hand sweeps down the valley between my breasts.

Gently, he pushes my other thigh open. The coolness of the air sends a tingle through me, settling in my belly. Without hesitation, he tugs the lace of my thong aside, not bothering to remove it completely before smoothing his fingers over me with the precision of a heart surgeon. He lets out a garbled string of curses when he feels how much I want him.

"Yes," I say through a sharp intake of breath, fighting an embarrassingly dramatic quiver. All my thoughts burst into mist and nothingness. I'm gone. Down the rabbit hole. Already lost in wonderland as the friction builds with each swipe of his finger.

"Does that feel good?" he whispers, easing one finger in, followed by a second.

"Mm-hmm," I manage, clipped, as I clench around him, rocking against him in a slow rhythm. My nails grip into his back, probably leaving scratch marks on his perfect skin.

He's mumbling a bunch of things I can't fully hear down there, about how sensitive I am to his touch. How tight I am. How wet I am. How much he wants me. And when he says, "Tell me what you like," he nearly sends me over the edge.

I've had exes who've asked me for instructions during sex, almost to the point of ruining the mood. But it drives me wild when Trevor asks in that rough, primitive voice that grabs hold of my insides. There's an air of confidence that tells me he doesn't truly need instruction. He knows exactly what he's doing, moving at the perfect pace and angle, cherishing me, taking care of me like I've never been cared for before.

"I think you already know. Somehow you know. Maybe you're a psychic," I say through a half moan, half gasp.

"No," he mutters. "I've just had months to agonize over it. Over you. Walking around the apartment in those little sweater-dresses. Running from the bathroom to your room in your towel when you think I'm not looking. It's been a lot of long, cold showers."

"Really?"

His gaze incinerates me on the spot. "Did you not notice how long I have to wait before getting out of the hot tub after you? You've been driving me fucking wild."

At his words, I buck unexpectedly against his hand, clenching around him. "Trevor, that feels so good. So good."

"You have no idea what you do to me."

"I've had a couple dreams about it," I admit. *Or ten.*

He smiles. "Dreams like this? Care to elaborate?"

I nod. "In the first one, we were in your car. You had your mouth on me."

"Did it feel good?" He picks up the pace, meeting my eyes.

"The best," I pant. "Except you didn't make me come. Because the real you woke me up."

His soft laugh vibrates into my neck as he runs his finger over the band of my thong, finally tugging it down all the way. "Trust me, that won't be a problem this time." He gives me one more cocky smile before lowering himself between my legs.

Seamlessly, his mouth takes the place of his hand. Just like in my illicit dream, we're connected. He knows what I want before I can even tell him. Every languid swipe, turn, press, never lingering for too long before telling me how good I taste, how he can feel me pulsing on his tongue.

My legs tremble, and he holds them wide open, taking control entirely, winding me up until I'm convinced I'm facing impending death. Every nerve ending is a live wire, on fire, multiplying with every swipe.

Unexpectedly, I cry out as it all surges into one powerful, un-relenting release. I don't hear a thing as wave after wave sizzles through me. I'm still trembling when his gaze locks with mine, visibly taking pleasure in how he's made me feel. Right before his eyes, I'm unspooling like I never have before, like twine pulled tight to the point of snapping. The aftershock leaves me breathless, floored, motionless.

I'm only brought back to earth when he moves back over me, pressing a soft kiss to my temple.

I can't find the words to express my gratitude, so I slip out from underneath him, shifting my weight on top of him. For the first time, he relinquishes control. He lets me hold him down, a smile tugging at his lips as I retrace all the artwork adorning his chest with my lips. I'm taking my sweet time, savoring the moment, moving over each line of his abs, one by one, like he's a gourmet feast.

By the time I finally take his length in my hand, he shudders, letting out an unexpected groan that does something to my insides in the best way. It's oddly gratifying to have such an impact on him without really doing anything at all.

"You don't have to do this," he says, lifting my chin with a single finger.

"I want to." There's nothing I want more than to hear how he sounds when I take him in my mouth. I want to see what he looks like when he comes undone.

"I can't believe you're right in front of me like this." His words quiver with raw emotion, letting his hand roam down my back.

"How much have you thought about me doing this to you?"

"More than you want to know," he admits.

I squeeze him a little harder, feeling the pulse of his blood pumping. "Tell me exactly."

"Since the day you moved in, I wanted you," he manages. "I've never wanted someone so bad in my entire life. You've wrecked me."

When I give him a teasing lick, he lets out a string of breathy curses. "Holy fuck."

I release him for a split second. "Is that good?"

"I—I can't speak right now," he says, breathless, which tells me all I need to know. He lets his head fall to the pillow as I settle into what I can tell is the perfect speed. Even submitting, he's still dominating, threading his fingers through my hair, holding me in place, how he wants it.

I watch his hand twist the sheets for grip as my pace picks up. Given the earth-shattering orgasm he just gave me, I'm eager to pull out all the stops. Apparently, he's found the strength to speak again. And judging from all the filthy things coming out of his mouth—how much he loves my mouth, how wet he imagines I am, all things that could make even the most seasoned romance readers blush—I'm confident in my abilities.

When he's done, he pulls me upward by the biceps and folds me over him. We lay like that for a few moments, skin to skin, chests heaving in unison.

"Can I ask you something?" I blurt out.

"No," he chuckles, running his fingers up and down my spine.

I ask anyway. "Was it okay?"

"Was what okay?"

I give him a sideways glare. "You know."

I can tell by the devilish smirk on his face that he knows exactly what I'm talking about. "You're bad at a lot of things." He lets that statement linger in the air for a few beats too long. "But believe me, blow jobs aren't one of them."

I nuzzle into his chest and peek up at him.

"You never listen to me," he says, his lips curled into a boyish grin. "I thought I told you never to let me kiss you again."

A bubble of laughter escapes me as he traces the pad of his finger over my shoulder. "*That's* your idea of kissing?"

He squeezes me tighter against him. "Was it as bad as you claimed the first time?"

"Wow, I really bruised your ego, didn't I?" I swing him a side eye, contemplating letting him out of his misery.

"I mean, yeah. You said I was the worst kiss you'd ever had."

I run my hand over his cheek, curving at his jaw. "Metcalfe, you were a perfectly fine kisser. I couldn't let your head explode," I tell him. "Listen, I'm not a good judge, because for me, it's less about the mechanics. It's all about—"

"The emotion," he cuts in knowingly.

"Exactly. So, while your kiss that day was fine, I thought there wasn't anything behind it. No deeper feelings or anything."

"Well, now you know that wasn't true."

He's telling the truth. I know it in the way his soft lips mirror mine at just the right angle, feathering light kisses over the corner of my lips. Unlike the hungry collision of our lips in my bedroom doorway, this kiss is soft, unrushed, but no less purposeful. With each tiny inhale, each press of our lips closer, every slide of our tongues.

I melt like butter against him, thighs parting on either side of his torso as he moves under me. Every touch and taste of him drives me wild with need. My teeth graze his lip, giving the softest bite. I'm not sure what to concentrate on as his hands wander my backside, gripping my ass, grinding me to him.

He loses all control at one point, sitting upward, capturing my lips, my neck, my breasts with urgency. My skin erupts in gooseflesh everywhere he touches. I reach to feel him under me, pressing against me, teasing. He tenses as I move my hand over him, guiding him closer.

He presses his forehead to mine. "We don't have to do anything else if you don't want to."

"I do want to. I really want to," I whisper, meeting his eyes with urgency.

His gaze searches mine for any sign of doubt. When he fails to find any, he shifts me aside to retrieve a condom from his wallet in his pants pocket. I watch as he rolls it on with ease, quick to re-settle us exactly as we were.

He allows me to set the pace, taking his size in gradually, inch by inch. Halfway, I pause, shuddering at the overwhelming feeling of him stretching me, filling me. "I don't know if this is going to work," I manage.

He cups my cheek, pressing a soft kiss into my neck. "It's okay. Just go slow." A low groan escapes him as I lower myself, his voice driving me wild with need. "You can take it, baby. That's it."

"Fuck," I moan, tipping my head back as I fully sink onto him, feeling him hit me exactly where I want it. When we find the per-fect rhythm, chests melding together, I can't believe we've wasted so many months.

"God, you feel . . . I never knew it could be this good," he whis-pers against my lips, giving my bottom lip the softest bite as I rock against him, increasing my speed.

I'm surely a broken record of cries as he moves his hand be-tween my legs, thumb swiping exactly where I crave the pressure. I curl my nails into his neck, his hard back, his shoulders. Every-where I can reach.

We watch each other climb higher and higher, exchanging slow, shallow breaths. We're in our own strange bubble. We're floating above earth, away from all reality, intrinsically connected.

His rough free hand works its way over my waist, setting the pace in the final stretch, flexing and working against me. His eyes pin me in place when he finally detonates in me, sending me plunging into another dimension along with him.

When it's all over, I'm not even sure I have control over my own body. The aftershocks rip through me, rendering my limbs Jell-O. Our eyes snag in the dark, and he holds my gaze. All the seemingly insignificant strips of him I've banked slowly, one by one, in my memories make up the man right here, holding on to me like I'm about to disappear. The tiny arch of his brow when he looks at me. The way he looks to the ceiling, pretending to be hopelessly annoyed with me when I know he isn't. The way he'll go out of his way to help me in all my ridiculous situations. And the way he cares for Angie. The way he cares for her so much that he can't fathom losing anyone else in his life.

"You have to leave in a few hours," I whisper, collapsing over his chest. "I don't want you to."

He squeezes me tighter, melding us together, savoring the moment. "I don't want to leave you, either."

"Will you wake me up before you go?" I plead. "I don't want to wake up alone."

He responds by kissing the top of my head. I burrow into his neck, taking in his scent, fighting to stay awake in the darkness, wishing I could slow down time. Maybe stop it altogether.

Before I fall asleep, holding on to him for dear life, the realization pours over me like a bucket of cold water. There's no coming back from this.

♥ chapter twenty-nine

TREVOR RUNS TOWARD me through a lush, green, tranquil field. The sleeves of his white Flynn Rider dress shirt billow in the breeze with each strong yet graceful slow-motion stride. Sunlight bathes his skin in liquid gold.

He's half a football field length away and it might as well be a continent. The sun doesn't extend to my half of the field, which is cold, slate-gray, and shrouded in miserable decay. A cruel cloud hangs directly above me, ominous, inky, and full, threatening to burst at any moment to drench me in an icy sheet of rain.

Desperate to sprint into the warm safety of Trevor's arms, I ready myself for the first stride. But my limbs refuse to budge. I'm stuck. Immobile. I can barely even exhale a breath.

The more I struggle, the more pressure builds against my ribs. Something black, shiny, and thick has coiled itself around my entire body, squeezing tighter and tighter, intent on sucking the life out of me. Strangely, it smells like a mixture of sweet and soothing, like my White Strawberry Herbal Essences shampoo.

It's my own hair. I'm being strangled to death by my own Rapunzel-like hair.

A gray, frizzy-haired Mother Gothel–like figure with Seth's shark face transplanted over the top looms behind me, running its bony, shriveled hands over my shoulders. Her villainous eyes glint, delighting in my distress, jagged yellow fingernails scraping my skin.

"Let me go. I think he likes me," I rasp, my throat as dry as the Sahara, staring longingly at sunlit Trevor. He's still running, but somehow, he's not getting any closer.

Mother Gothel releases a witchy cackle into the shell of my ear. "Likes you? Please, Tara, that's demented!"

• • •

MY CHEERFUL, CHIRPING bird alarm snaps me to a welcome consciousness. Yellow strands of light poke through the slats in my blinds, confirming I am indeed safe in my bed, not in a sketchy field.

That enthralling cinnamon scent—Trevor's scent—grounds me with the comfort of home. Like a drug addict, I attempt to flop onto my side toward the source, craving more, but I'm still stuck.

Unlike in my dream, my limbs are not bound by my own hair, which is both relieving and disappointing. Having lusciously thick, long, glossy shampoo-commercial-worthy hair a la Mel's wouldn't be too shabby, so long as it doesn't try to strangle me to death.

In reality, it's my sheets that have cocooned me like an Egyptian mummy in an ancient tomb. They're pulled tight all around me, military-style. The other pillow is smoothed and plumped. For the first time in years, my bed is made . . . with me in it.

This is a surefire sign that Trevor Metcalfe was here. That last night wasn't another one of my elaborate, R-rated dreams.

My alarm is still going off. Bleary-eyed, I struggle to free myself from the tightly wound sheets to hit *Stop*.

It's eight thirty. Trevor's flight was at six forty-five.

I lug myself out of bed and tiptoe across the hall to check his bedroom. Just as I suspected, his bed is made. Everything is in its place. Except for him, of course.

He's gone. He left without saying goodbye.

I return to bed, smoothing my hand over the empty space where he fell asleep next to me, replaying everything he said to me yesterday about how he wanted to try. How he was going to give this relationship his all. How I agreed to take things slow with him, emotionally at least.

I wish I could magically summon him back to talk through it all again in more detail. To confirm it was all real. I wish I could summon the feeling of the pads of his fingers hypnotizing me with small circular strokes. The tingle of my skin as his lips danced over me in an intricate, private show. The feeling of being more in sync with another human being than I ever thought possible.

I fall back asleep, my heart filled with hope but also fear.

DANIEL: Please call me. I'm so sorry about Friday night.

This is Daniel's third apology.

I haven't responded yet.

As Mel leads us through the mall in search of a dress for the gala in two days, Crystal lectures me on the art of forgiveness. "I know you hold a mean grudge. But Daniel's only human. He's obviously really sorry."

"But he lit-ral-ly forgot about me. Who forgets about dinner with their long-lost childhood best friend?" I'm still feeling some type of way about being stood up at Mamma Maria's. And frankly, does it even matter anymore, now that I have Trevor?

"He's your very last ex, right?" Mel asks bluntly, reminding me of that sad fact as we veer to the side, avoiding a trio of adorable elderly women doing some gentle mall walking in matching velour tracksuits.

As expected, the Sunday pre–Valentine's Day at the mall is all-out anarchy, packed with bumbling fools last-minute gift hunting for their special someone. Today's crowds are even worse than the Boston subway at rush hour and the grannies at the grocery store combined. Mel even sustained a broken acrylic nail battling for the last baby-blue cashmere sweater. RIP nail.

"He is the last one," I say, barely masking my neutrality. Neither Crystal nor Mel knows what happened with Trevor, mostly because mic dropping this plot twist that we're suddenly together now via our iPhone group chat just didn't seem appropriate. I'm waiting for the opportune moment to spring it on them today.

As we enter a cute formalwear boutique, Mel gestures to a mannequin in the window posing broken doll–style in a seventies neon-yellow feather cocktail dress. "Is that too much for your gala?"

"Honestly, I don't know if I want to go. Maybe I'll just fake sick," I tell Crystal and Mel, rooting around a rack full of gorgeous yet out-of-budget dresses. Further confirmation I should sit this event out.

The existential dread of going to the gala alone without Trevor hits me like a wrecking ball. I miss him. Terribly. And it's only been a day since he left.

It doesn't help that we've barely texted, aside from a quick message when his plane landed. My entire being has been itching to ask him how he's doing, how the fires are, what he's been thinking about, and if he still feels the same way about me as he did on Friday night. I'm desperate to unpack our brief conversation from before we had sex. Sure, we agreed we were giving this a shot. But we never discussed the logistics of how our relationship would change, whether we were an "official" couple now.

Last night, I even woke up at the devil's hour, opened my Notes app, and started typing a half-baked declaration of love so at least he'd know where I stood. When I realized my text was nearly a full screen length long, I remembered what Trevor told me that night when I was texting Brandon.

He will run far, far away if you send this.

The last thing I need is to scare him off with my obsessive self, only days before Valentine's Day. There's also the fact that he specifically told me he needed to take things slow. I promised him we would, not just for him but for me too. I want to do things differently this time. I don't want to cannonball headfirst like in my past relationships, all of which crashed and burned. I want to be measured, sure of myself, not desperate like I usually am.

"But it's Valentine's Day. You shouldn't be alone with your thoughts. Do we really want a repeat of last year?" Crystal gives me a pointed stare. I spent last Valentine's Day crying on Crystal's couch while she petted my hair like a destitute stray in a Sarah McLachlan animal welfare commercial.

I press my hand over my heart. "I solemnly swear I won't require emotional support this year." I turn to Mel, who's examining a gold sequin number that costs one month's rent. "This is your first Valentine's Day alone in years. Want company? I can supply the wine, excellent company, and cuddles," I offer eagerly.

"Sorry, Tara," Mel says sympathetically, like she feels sorry for *me*. "It's tempting. Really. But I already committed to a Live makeup tutorial with one of my influencer friends." She points me toward the dressing room area. She's selected an armload of overpriced gowns for me to try on.

"You sure? I could even hang out in the background and watch. I won't get in the way," I suggest, desperate.

"Maybe you wouldn't have to be alone on Valentine's Day if you text Daniel back," Crystal reminds me.

Mel holds a black cocktail dress in front of me, one eye closed. She frowns, like I'm a disgraceful contestant on *America's Next Top Model*. "I don't think I like black on you. Too gothic," she mutters. "Anyway, I disagree. Don't call Daniel. He deserves to suffer a little after making you sit alone at the restaurant like a loser."

Yeah, until Trevor showed up and proceeded to change life as I know it.

Mel drops a heaping pile of gowns on the bench in the dressing room, oblivious to my internal freak-out over whether now is a good time to come clean. On second thought, the chaos of the dressing room hardly seems like a suitable place to drop this bomb. "I'll be back with more options. I don't know if I like square necklines on you. It shortens your torso."

Crystal comes in as Mel darts out of the dressing room on a

mission. She stuffs a ball of cherry-red fabric through the crack in the door. "Try this one. It's very you."

The next half hour consists of me sweating, changing in and out of various dresses, most of which are either too expensive or do nothing for my figure.

My mood lifts when I try on Crystal's pick, the red one-shoulder dress with the sexy thigh-high slit up the leg. Admittedly, it's kind of perfect, accentuating my waist and elongating my middle with the over-the-shoulder bejeweled strap. According to Mel, the harshest critic, the rich tone brings out the olive hue of my skin. She even threatens to shun me if I don't buy it. The best part? It's on sale for half price and won't require alterations.

I snap a few mirror selfies, examining the dress from every angle, my mouth open like the *Sisterhood of the Traveling Pants* girls in their magic jeans, astonished by the flawless fit. I can almost envision myself at the gala in full glam. This dress screams love. It screams Valentine's Day.

By the time we return to Mel's condo with take-out sushi, I'm jittery, my knee bouncing uncontrollably under the glass coffee table. My body is physically rejecting keeping my Trevor secret for so long.

Crystal notices straightaway. "Why aren't you eating your sushi?" she asks, dipping a spicy crab roll into her soy sauce.

I struggle to swallow a pitiful mouthful of seaweed salad, tossing my disposable wooden chopsticks on my plate. It's time to come clean.

I spare no detail about the entire evening, from nearly getting kicked out of Mamma Maria's to Trevor showing up, saving my ass and my breadsticks. I explain how, in a moment of weakness, I demanded to know Trevor's feelings, which directly led to an explosion of emotions, followed by a passionate hookup.

When I conclude my story, a thick silence falls over Mel's open living area. Crystal looks like she's about to choke on her roll. Across the coffee table, Mel's mouth is crooked and partially open—her trademark face when the logic doesn't add up because her Botox prevents severe forehead lines.

"No freakin' way. You slept with Trevor?" Mel finally clarifies, breaking the stretch of silence. She pretends to fan herself. "Was it life-changing? I bet it was. I need details."

I bury my face in my hands. "It was."

Through my splayed fingers, Crystal pins me with a hard, judgmental stare. "Wait, you mean you two are actually a thing? How is that even possible?"

"No wonder you've been so blasé about Daniel. You've fallen for Trevor. Hard. *Literally*," Mel declares, eyeing me with righteous suspicion.

"Yup," I admit.

"Have you talked since he left for California?" Mel asks, struggling to use her chopsticks despite Dad's fifteen-minute lesson at Crystal's bridal shower. She quickly gives up and eats her sticky rice with a fork.

I lift my phone from the coffee table to find nothing, as I predicted. "He texted once to tell me he arrived safely."

Crystal's expression is one of ultimate doubt. "Wait, that's it? You're together and he's barely even texting you?"

Her question is like a gut punch. I straighten my spine, suddenly feeling even more insecure than I already was. "Is that weird? Should we be texting?"

"I would think so. Scott texts me constantly when he's gone."

"Okay, but Scott and Trevor are two different people," Mel reminds us, although I barely register her words given the alarm bells going off in my head.

Heat prickles my body as I straighten my spine. "Shit. This is a bad sign, isn't it? Do you think he's freaking out and regretting everything?"

Mel makes a face as if to say, *Don't ask me.* "Why don't you ask him to FaceTime? Ask him straight up if you're still on the same page?" I don't know how Mel's question can be both so logical and so hive inducing. "Or send him the smokin'-hot mirror selfie in the red dress you took in the changing room. See how he reacts."

Crystal's eyes go wide like Frisbees. "Mel, I love you, but are you *okay*? That's the worst idea I've ever heard. A mirror selfie will send the wrong message for sure."

"Wrong message? Is she a nun? She's hot and wants to show off her bod to her man." Mel scoffs and gives her a kick under the table. "Personally, I think it's genius. If he sends some sort of sex-related response, we'll know he just wants your ass. If he says something lame, he's changed his mind and decided to friend-zone you. And if he offers a sincere compliment, we can probably guess things are still good."

"You do have a point." In my looming sushi coma, I'm easily suggestible. I grab my phone and impulsively open my text window with Trevor. My fingers flex, hovering over the option to attach the photo.

Before I can make a decision either way, Crystal shrieks, "No!"

In a blink, she's ripped my phone from my hands before I have the chance to firm my grip. She stuffs it down her sports bra for good measure.

I cock a brow. "Really, Crys? I'm not afraid to go in there." I make a pretend advance, and Crystal leans away from me, her hand clamped over her chest.

"Come on. Think about this. I'm not sure any of this is a good idea."

"Texting him?" I ask.

"No. Like, all of this. I mean, from what you said, he never gave you any specific commitment other than an *I'll try*. Are you really willing to accept that?" When my eyes start to well, she's quick to add, "I love you, Tara, and I want you to be happy. But I also want what's best for you. I just don't want you with another guy you have to fix. Someone who needs so much maintenance. Especially someone you're rooming with."

"But have you seen him? Let the girl live!" Mel makes a surprise attack from across the table and stuffs her hand down Crystal's shirt. She ends up dipping the elbow of her silk blouse in the tiny plastic container of soy sauce, which nearly dribbles on her plush cream area rug.

I reach across the table to assist Mel before she stains anything else. Crystal sees this as an attack and rolls away into the fetal position on the floor. It all goes downhill from there. Mel dives over her, and I launch myself on top of both of them with a blood-curdling battle cry.

The three of us are screaming like children fighting over the last slice of pizza at a birthday party. Someone has scraped my neck with their fingernail (probably Mel), and somehow Crystal's messy bun has come out and Mel's blouse is wrinkled and disheveled. We're seconds away from an all-out catfight.

Given Crystal's superhuman strength, it takes both Mel and me to pry my phone from her hands. I even resort to tickling her on the ribs to give Mel a window of opportunity to swipe it. By the time Crystal finally relents, we're flat on our backs laughing hysterically on Mel's floor, our chests heaving like we've just completed a gruesome spin class.

"Okay, on second thought, let's rethink this," Mel says breathily. "A random photo of yourself may be a little weird. I think your best bet is a straight-up conversation when he gets back to make sure you're still aligned. In person. It's too important a conversation to have through text."

"You're probably right." With what little strength I have left, I reach for my phone to exit the text window.

And that's when I see it.

Somehow, through our tussle, we have collectively managed to hit *Send* on the mirror selfie.

Not once.

Not twice.

But three times.

No. No. No.

Fuck my life.

Mouth agape, I show Crystal and Mel what we've done.

Mel looks identical to *The Scream*, the famous painting from the 1800s with the gaunt, skull-like man with both hands on either side of his head, his eyes wide like he's just seen death itself.

Crystal is so disturbed, she launches to her feet and starts speed walking around the living area, her hands to her temples, mumbling, "Oh my God, oh my God, oh my God," which does little to quell my nausea.

Near deceased, I collapse onto Mel's stylish yet uncomfortable couch, an arm over my eyes to block out my reality. It's time to defect to the fringes of society. I'll live out the rest of my days in rugged nature, using twigs, stones, and poisonous berries for currency.

Then again, my animal friends wouldn't be an adequate substitute for human company. No. I think I'll stay here in this very spot for all of eternity. It's only a matter of time before the buzzards descend to feast on my innards. "I don't suppose you can unsend a text?"

"I don't think so," Crystal says, cringing. "But I'll Google it to make sure."

"It's okay. It's fine. No big deal. You like him. He likes you. It's totally normal to send him photos of yourself," Mel assures.

"But that's the thing! I don't know anything that's going on in his head," I shriek. After all, what if Crystal has a point? Is everything he said to me on Friday at odds with his behavior since he's been gone? Actions do speak louder than words.

"Wait!" Mel rockets up to a kneeling position, her eyes glinting. "Tell him you meant to send it to me or Crystal."

As per Mel's sage advice, I craft a new text, which reads, *Sorry, I meant to send that to someone else.*

My stomach dips, roller-coaster style, when the little ellipses appear in our text screen. Just knowing he's seen the photos makes my body react in a way it shouldn't. The dots are there for a solid minute at least. I know because I've gone ghostly pale from hold-ing my breath. As soon as the dots appear, they disappear.

By the time Crystal drops me off at my empty apartment, Trevor still hasn't responded to my THREE selfies.

This can't be a good sign.

♥ chapter thirty

ADULT DANIEL ROCKING a bow tie is a level of devastatingly adorable my body was not ready for.

Despite the fitted navy suit that covers his long limbs, I still can't help but picture Daniel as that nerdy, unsociable kid with cowlicked hair and no fewer than two noticeable stains on his clothes.

I finally messaged him back this morning after his fifth message asking for forgiveness for standing me up. He was super apologetic and asked to call me while I was at work.

Inviting Daniel to the gala wasn't my intention, but it seemed like the natural thing to do when he wished me a happy Valentine's Day, recalling how it was my favorite holiday. And I'd be lying if I said Seth smugly inquiring only moments beforehand about whether I'd successfully scared off all my exes wasn't a secondary factor.

I made it clear to Daniel that I was inviting him as a friend, explaining I was seeing someone who was out of town. He seemed perfectly fine with that, reassuring me he wasn't expecting anything other than platonic friendship.

When we met in the lobby of the trendy boutique hotel hosting the gala, he goofily pretended to run toward me, nearly tripping over the loose laces of his dress shoes in the process.

"This reminds me of hiding behind the bleachers during dodgeball," Daniel says, peering around the drywall pillar for signs of human life. We've spent the better part of the cocktail hour in a darkened corner, hiding from my nosy, overtly curious coworkers, nibbling on fancy appetizers. It's just like middle school, when we'd both fake sick at the same time to get out of gym class.

I scrunch my nose, straining over his shoulder for a glimpse into the ballroom. From what I can see, there are red balloons everywhere (very on theme), ornate red charger plates, pink silk napkins. "Remember when Jason Yardley hit me in the face with the ball?"

He winces at the memory. "Oh God. The blood. I almost passed out. I remember your grandma Flo came to pick you up because your parents were working. How is she doing?"

"Grandma Flo is great, actually. She got remarried last summer to her childhood sweetheart. She's still super involved in the church and stuff. She has a more active social life than I do."

We've managed to catch up on the past two decades of our lives. Just like it used to be, Daniel asks a lot of questions and I respond with long-winded answers, all while managing to extract some key pieces of information.

Daniel is working as a software developer for Flopify. He's loving it, although he readily admits his job is practically his life. In fact, it doesn't seem like he does much else, aside from work and video games. Being a person without other hobbies aside from reading, I can relate. The most exciting development in his life as of late is his newly adopted cat, Grandma Whiskers.

"She's an orange tabby," he explains, showing me a photo of her lounging in a playboy pose, soaking up the sun in front of a window. "She's been a little cranky lately because she's on a diet. My vet said I had to cut her food intake because she was becoming obese, though I disagree. I mean, after being in the shelter for months, I think the poor girl deserved some extra food," he justifies with an adorable smile that reminds me so much of him as a kid.

He tells me how he's considering purchasing a cat stroller because Grandma Whiskers refuses to walk outdoors, and I nearly die laughing. My amusement makes him smile, and it reminds me of all the days after school when he'd come over and play house with me in Crystal's and my playhouse. We always pretended to be a married couple, mimicking our parents, pretending to scold our doll children. As a dutiful husband, he'd offer to make me fake coffee, which was usually paired with a bundle of dandelions freshly pulled from the lawn.

The memory reminds me of the bouquet of a dozen red roses that arrived at my door as I was on my way to the gala. I assumed they were apology flowers for missing our date on Friday. In my rush to catch my Uber, I barely had time to even look at them, let alone thank him.

"Hey, I meant to thank you for the flowers. You really didn't have to send—" I'm mid-sentence when Seth not so casually saunters by in a velvet maroon suit, champagne in hand.

He appraises Daniel, giving me a conspiratorial brow raise before extending a hand to him. "I don't believe we've met. I'm Dr. Reinhart."

Before shaking his hand, Daniel glances at me as if to say, *Who the hell is this d-bag, and why is he talking to me?*

I clear my throat. "Seth, this is my ex, Daniel. Daniel, this is my other . . . um, ex, Seth."

Seth smiles, displaying all his tiny teeth. Now that Trevor has pointed it out, it can't be unseen. He gives Daniel a condescending pat on the shoulder. "If you need any advice on this one, I'm here for you, man."

My hand stiffens around my vodka cran. If I grip it any tighter, I'll surely crack the glass.

Daniel rights his posture, his expression deliciously frosty. "And what kind of advice would that be?"

Seth's patchy brows nearly reach his prematurely receding hairline. "I'm just messing with you." He turns to me. "You good? You look a little tense."

"I'm good," I say, loosening my grip around my glass.

Luckily, Seth is easy distracted by shiny things. In this case, the shiny object is Dr. Patel, one of the most senior NICU doctors, who's just walked by. When Seth darts after him to suck up, Daniel leans in.

"Was he one of the exes on your list too?" Daniel asks. Earlier in the evening, I spilled the tea about my ex-boyfriend endeavors, and he admitted he already knew from watching my stories after I reached out on LinkedIn.

I chortle at the mere thought. "No. I never considered Seth. Only the good ones, like you."

Daniel's cheeks turn pink, tickled by this. "True. I was your followers' favorite. Only second to your roommate. The one you're seeing, right?" he asks.

"Yeah. Trevor." I lean against the wall, frowning at the mere mention of Trevor. He still hasn't responded to the selfies I sent him, which only confirms Crystal's doubt.

"You must really like him," he says, his mouth curving into a small smile. After this long, Daniel can still read me like a book.

"How'd you know?" I whisper.

"I remember all the boys you used to crush on in school. You'd always try to pretend like you didn't like them around me, but I could always tell," he says with a casual shrug as he sips his drink.

"Really? How?"

He studies me for a beat. "You'd do that thing where you talk a mile a minute, twirling the ends of your hair. You get a little flustered. And you get that glassy, starry-eyed look," he tells me, his eyes glinting with certainty like he's solved a riddle.

"You say that like you know exactly what I'm talking about," I venture.

He blushes. "Yeah. I've been battling a pathetic crush on my coworker Yua for years."

"Years? Tell me about her."

"She's another developer."

I bounce my brows suggestively. "Ohh, an office romance?"

He makes a pained expression and stares at his boots. "Not quite. We went on one date and she kind of freaked out. She's scared to ruin our friendship, especially since we'd be stuck working together. I completely get it, but it sucks."

"I'm sorry, Danny. Have you tried grand gesturing her?"

"Like declaring my love for her? Publicly?" he asks, aghast at the suggestion.

"Oh yeah. In front of tons of people, obviously," I tease.

"No, no, no. I wanted to respect her wishes too. It didn't feel right to push it. What about Trevor? Tell me about him."

And I do. I confide the entire story about Trevor, from day one to the events that followed Friday night. Telling Daniel the intimate details of my love life feels natural, because I'm talking to my former best friend. I'm also hopeful another dude's insight might shed some light.

He contemplates for a moment, tilting his head. "It's hard for me to say what this guy thinks regarding the texts. But I wouldn't rule him out. From what you've said, he's gone through some shit. Maybe he just needs some space. Or maybe he needs more reassurance from you. Like a grand gesture."

After sending Trevor *three* mirror photos with zero response, the last thing I'm about to do is humiliate myself further with a grand gesture. Besides, the last time I attempted a grand gesture, I ended up engaged to the likes of Seth. "No. He knows how I feel. I think that's precisely what scares him."

He dips his head back. "Remember that time you tried to kiss Spencer Hayfield at recess and he told everyone you were a witch?"

I fail to suppress a snort. "He told everyone I put a curse on him. The little shit. The patriarchy is so strong, even six-year-olds believe girls who go after what they want are witches."

Daniel bumps my shoulder with his. "My point is, you were always fearless. Don't lose that."

"Will you let me stay on your couch when it all inevitably backfires?"

He extends his slender hand, giving me a supportive shake. "Deal."

Before the dinner starts, I excuse myself for a bathroom break, leaving Daniel in the good hands of my nurse colleagues. On my way out, my nose is buried in my phone as notifications stream in for a photo of a red book cover I paired with my dress.

Out of nowhere, a shiver electrifies my spine. Goosebumps scatter down my arms, as if I'm standing directly under the chilly blast of a vent. A velvety, audiobook-worthy voice upends everything in my orbit, stopping me in my tracks.

❤ chapter thirty-one

M Y BODY MALFUNCTIONS like a laptop drowned by a spilled glass of water, screen flickering until it surrenders to the void.

For the briefest of moments, I convince myself Trevor's voice was simply an audio hallucination. Nothing but a vivid symptom of my general heartache. I'm sure of it, until my name slices the air for the second time.

"Tara."

I pivot as fast as possible in three-inch heels on carpet, confirming that for once, it isn't my overactive imagination propelled by emotional, golf-ball-size hailstones.

Trevor is here.

In the flesh.

My chest blazes with heat, trying to reconcile the vision before my eyes. Trevor is not fighting fires on the West Coast. He is five feet in front of me, dressed in the same perfectly tailored suit he wore at Mamma Maria's. He's single-handedly sucking all the oxygen out of the hallway, leaving nothing for the rest of us. "What . . . what are you doing here?"

He pins me with his heated gaze. "I came home early."

Everything but his perfect face blurs, like we're on a merry-go-round at double speed. "Why?" I ask simply.

He works down a swallow, hesitating, his eyes dipping to his feet, then back to me. "You look"—he gestures toward me, jaw slack—"absolutely beautiful."

Trevor isn't one to bullshit. He doesn't give a compliment he doesn't mean. The earnest expression on his face cements it. The corners of my lips threaten to curve into a shy smile, until I recall his blatant lack of communication over the past three days. I'm transported back to that sinking moment at Mel's. When I accidently sent him three photos in this very dress and he didn't even bother to respond.

"Why didn't you answer my text?"

He works down a swallow, hesitating.

I expect him to offer an excuse, like he was too busy doing hero shit, running into fiery blazes and saving lives. Or maybe he had bad reception and didn't even receive the photo. While I'm fairly certain that's not the case, given I specifically saw him typing, I've held on to the possibility, however remote.

Trevor doesn't offer either justification. "You didn't mean to send them to me, I thought."

As we take each other in, a hand touches the small of my back.

"Hey, I was looking for you." It's Daniel. By the way he's looking at me, blatantly confused, he's entirely oblivious to the rubber band between Trevor and me, ready to snap at any moment.

Trevor's lips flatten at the interruption, his steady gaze turning cold.

"Sorry, I was in the bathroom. Got distracted on my phone," I say, blinking away the white dots clouding my vision.

"Dinner is starting. The emcee is asking everyone to take their seats." Daniel nods toward the entrance to the banquet hall. Before turning us back, he double-takes, holding his hand out toward Trevor. "Apologies, I didn't introduce myself. I'm Daniel. You must be one of Tara's colleagues?"

Trevor's expression is unreadable. His jaw shifts, and I'm certain I'd be able to hear his molars grinding together if it weren't for the loud chatter filtering from the gala room.

"No, he's not my colleague," I cut in, nerves aflutter.

"Oh?" Daniel asks, still not picking up on the palpable tension.

The squealing feedback of a microphone pierces the air, followed by the soothing spa voice of tonight's emcee, one of the hospital switchboard operators, who definitely missed her calling as a stand-up comedian. "Testing . . . Please, for the love of all things holy, can everyone step away from the bar and take your seats—"

"Shit," I mutter, flustered as Daniel starts steering us back. When I look over my shoulder, Trevor is already walking away. His long strides have taken him three-quarters of the way across the cocktail room. Panicked, I raise my index finger to Daniel, signaling I'll just be a minute.

I'm a fresh baby deer, wobbling on my day-old, spindly legs. My gown is hiked like the class act I am, dashing after Trevor as he veers left, disappearing into the lobby. In hot pursuit, I take the corner too fast, too furious. My shoulder collides with that of a server's, nearly knocking over her tray of champagne flutes. I squeak out a muddled yet genuine apology, glancing back to confirm she's rebalanced her tray. By the time I zero in on Trevor's back again, he's nearing the doors.

"Metcalfe," I call, loud enough to turn the heads of bystanders who probably think I've lost my marbles.

His stubborn self doesn't stop until I'm right behind him, yanking his biceps. "I'm sorry, I've gotta go." He spares me a brief, heavy-hearted look, cautious about looking me directly in the eyes.

"Why are you running away from me?" I demand, louder than intended. The staff behind the lobby desk are giving me cross-eyed glares.

Trevor is desperate to bolt, based on his longing stare toward the door. He rakes a frustrated hand through his locks. "Because— Never mind."

"Tell me."

"Does it matter? You're here with Daniel." Trevor is jealous. He cares.

"He only came to make up for ditching me. I—I told him from the get-go we were just going as friends." I struggle over my words, unable to fully articulate my jumbled thoughts.

He levels me with a look. "Just friends? Really?"

My eye twitches. "How could you even think I'd do something like this to you?"

"Tara, I've listened to you talk about how much you miss that guy—ten different guys—for months. How was I supposed to know you weren't just settling for me as a last resort, until Daniel pulled through?"

I blink, stunned from the emotional whiplash of the past minute. "Is that really what you think? That I was only into you because no other exes worked out?"

"I don't know! You moved on from each of them just like that. It's like you just—you just convince yourself you're in love with everyone you meet."

"So you think I've just convinced myself I'm in love with you?"

"How can I not?" He gestures a hand back toward the direction of the cocktail area. "That guy is exactly everything you've been looking for. Why would you settle for me?"

I toss my palms toward the trendy beaded chandelier dangling above us. "I'm not settling. Why are you twisting this to make it about me, when you're clearly the one who has no idea what you want?"

"I do know what I want. I told you how much you meant to me on Friday night," he says, his expression pained.

"How was I supposed to know you meant it? I got nothing from you while you were gone."

A vein pulses in his forehead. "You're the one who barely texted me. I've seen the texts you sent to your exes. Compared to what you sent me, it seemed like you didn't want to talk at all. And when you actually did send me those pictures, you said you meant to send them to someone else."

It takes a couple of moments for the realization to settle. Trevor actually wanted me to text him more? "I tried not to bother you because you said you wanted to go slow. I didn't want you to think I was being clingy."

"I wouldn't have thought that. Slow or not, I still want you to be *you*, clingy and all."

"The entire ex search, all you did was edit my texts, telling me they were too much," I point out.

"But you weren't with those guys, Tara."

"It doesn't matter. You're still one to talk. You barely texted me yourself."

"I sent you Valentine's Day flowers, for Christ's sake."

I freeze. "What? You sent me flowers?"

"Roses," he says. "You didn't get them?"

Something pinches in my chest at the realization. The roses were from Trevor. Not Daniel. I didn't have time to check the accompanying note because I'd just assumed. I never even considered they could be from Trevor. "I—I did. I thought they were from . . ."

"You thought they were from Daniel. Exactly." He shakes his head.

"Trevor . . ." He doesn't respond. A silence hangs in the air, like an invisible fog between us. "Don't leave. We should talk about this," I plead.

He gives me one last tormented look, his powerful arms pushing through the door. "Please, just go back inside."

I watch helplessly as he leaves me behind without a second look. I'm tempted to pursue him, chase him into the cold air in my heels. I want to scream into the void until he comes back. I want to tell him how badly I missed him. That I'm desperately in love with him. No one else.

The other half of me is burning red, shaking with anger. Watching Trevor give up and walk away so easily catapults me to the night Seth officially ended things with me. Our relationship had deteriorated long before that night. And yet I held on to it like a life raft, regardless of the fact that it was punctured, dragging me down into the choppy sea. I begged for him to take me back for weeks, because I mistook wild emotional turmoil and dysfunction for love, yet again.

I wasted months trying to put the pieces back together, trying to pinpoint where things went wrong, and I don't think I ever fully bounced back. I've been on a relentless search for love again, trying to prove to myself that I'm worthy of the fairy tale I thought I had, that what's old can be new again. And what could avenge my damaged ego more than someone who once broke my heart coming back to me?

Maybe Trevor was right. There's something cheapening about chasing all these men who don't want me. Maybe I've felt more comfortable romanticizing my past, convincing myself all those toxic relationships were true love. Maybe that was more comfortable than moving forward.

But after Friday night, I'm now all too aware that I've spent my entire thirty years loving in the shallow end. It's different with Trevor. It's a hard-hitting gravitational pull in my very core, grounding me to the earth, filling in every last crater of my heart. The ones I never knew could be filled. The ones I never even knew were empty. It's confirmation that a different kind of love—love in the purest sense of the word—is real.

And I might have screwed it up already.

Someone clears their throat behind me.

It's Seth.

He steps forth, both hands in the pockets of his slacks. "You all right, T?" His brows knit together in convincing concern.

"I'm fine." I squeeze my eyes shut, praying he'll vamoose by the time I open them again. No such luck.

He advances to usher me to the small bench near the doors. "Hey, come sit down."

I follow him, too stunned by my interaction with Trevor to protest.

When Seth's shoulder brushes against mine, there's no comfort. Only confusion. Hurt. Anger. "What happened? Was that one of your exes?" he asks.

"No. He's the guy I'm seeing. Or at least . . . was. I don't know."

"Ah, I see." He leans forward slightly. "Things not working out?"

I blow the air out of my cheeks. "Ha. You could say that. But that's the story of my life, it seems. Every time I get close to finding someone—"

"If I could give you just one piece of advice—" His tone is pompous, and he plows forward before I can even protest. "It would be to lower your expectations."

"Lower my expectations, really, Seth?"

"I've always said your books and movies have filled your head with unrealistic expectations. Men aren't like that in real life. And I think it's time you finally accept the fact that life isn't a fairy tale." If I had a dollar for every time Seth whined that my books were tainting my expectations of real relationships, I'd be a baller.

I stand, refusing to look at him, my face stiff, masking the emotion overflowing on the inside. "I'm well aware of that, thanks to you. And I'm sorry you feel so threatened by depictions of fictional men doing more than the bare minimum." For a fraction of a second, the self-righteous look on his face is swapped for momentary disbelief. I relish my small victory, the rare opportunity to shake him to his core.

"Threatened?" Seth retorts in derision. "I'm just trying to bring you down to reality. I doubt there's a guy out there that could meet all your demands."

I back away. "I don't consider basic honesty, respect, and healthy communication to be demands. And it's really too bad they're so unachievable for you. I feel terrible for Ingrid."

Well aware the hotel staff are listening in, he lets out a barking laugh. Unable to handle feeling smaller than me, he stands, towering over me. "See, this is exactly why we broke up. You get all crazy, reading into every little thing, take everything to the next level."

The word *crazy* hits me like a spiked wrecking ball. I'm brought back to the moment Nicky Tannenbaum called me crazy in the second grade when I gave him my homemade Valentine's Day card. All the times I pretended to laugh it off when that Crazy Ex-Girlfriend meme went viral in high school. The many men who've told me I was too clingy. The thousands of times before now when Seth would call me crazy whenever I got the slightest bit emotional, holding his demeaning, gaslighting stoicism over me like a deadly weapon.

You're acting like a madwoman.

Don't be so emotional.

You're acting so irrational right now.

I've known since before our breakup that Seth is a master manipulator. I've always doubted myself in his presence, second-guessing every word, every action, wondering why I wasn't enough for him.

The pain of the memories gives me the strength to meet his hawk eyes, once and for all. And this time, I know it's not me who wasn't enough.

"You can invalidate me all you want, Seth, but when you close your eyes at night, you know the truth. You know how you treated me. You know how shady you were in the lead-up to the wedding, taking off without telling me where you were or who you were with. Making me think I was nuts for even daring to ask you who you were always texting. Making me out to be a psycho when you suddenly locked down your devices and refused to let me use your phone or laptop." I pause to catch my breath, noting his shock. "And sure, there were times I overreacted. But I will never apologize for loving fiercely, even though you didn't deserve it."

Seth's jaw hinges open, and I immediately snap a mental photo of this glorious moment. Multiple bystanders have stopped to take in the spectacle. I've never roasted someone on a spit in front of a crowd in my life, and damn, it feels fantastic.

I stomp past him, back to the ballroom, imagining I'm in Taylor Swift's "Bad Blood" music video, strutting out of the Seth hellfire that's marked too many years of my life. I'm like the phoenix tattooed on Trevor's chest, reborn, renewed, and ready for the next chapter, whatever may come.

For three years, Seth made me believe my emotions were my Achilles' heel. Now I know better. I remember what I loved most about love in the first place. Love has the power to strip you raw, to the bone. And that's the beauty of it. There's an immeasurable bravery in opening your heart and baring your soul when all hope is seemingly lost. Knowing, even in the face of heartbreak, that this is not the end. That you're still standing, after it all crumbles around you.

My heart has now officially broken for the eleventh time. And strangely, I'm stronger than I've ever been.

LIVE WITH TARAROMANCEQUEEN—THE EX-BOYFRIEND SEARCH CONCLUDES

[Tara is cloaked in darkness in the back seat of an Uber.]

EXCERPT FROM TRANSCRIPT

TARA: *Hello, romance book lovers, welcome back to my channel. I wanted to hop on and let everyone know that my ex-boyfriend endeavor is officially over.*

I wanted to be transparent and tell you all that as brave as many of you thought this journey was . . . it was actually quite the opposite. I didn't realize it at the time, but I was terrified to get hurt again after my big breakup. I couldn't handle the thought of someone having the power to do that to me again. And so I gravitated to this idea that I could try to win my exes back. The men I was already familiar with. The men who'd already hurt me. I think I assumed that it would be easier to mold myself to be what they want me to be if I knew them. And I thought getting my heart broken by someone who already broke it would be . . . somehow less painful. I don't know.

On the bright side, Daniel and I are still really good friends. And going forward, I think I'm ready to jump into the deep end as my authentic self and risk a little more.

In any case, thank you all for being so supportive and for following along.

♥ chapter thirty-two

WHAT WAS THAT, dear?" Grandma Flo asks for the fifty-third time. She cups her hand around her ear theatrically, pretending she's losing her hearing. (For the record, she is not, according to her audiologist.)

"I said you should get a ring light for your videos." This is not at all what I've just said, but frankly, Grandma Flo isn't all that interested in anything else today except Instagram.

"What's a ring light?" Grandma Flo asks, finally closing her iPad. She takes her sweet time moseying over to the entryway in her slippers. She's insisting on taking me to the hospital for Angie's party so she can drop off the hand-knit dolls and blankets from my book stack fundraiser in person.

The party doesn't begin for a few hours, but I'm already alight with nerves at the prospect of seeing Trevor. We haven't spoken since last night, when he left the gala. When I got home, he was in his room, door closed, lights off. And this morning, I left to gather things for the party before he woke up.

My chest physically hurts every time I think about that last conversation. I've agonized over all the things I could have said differently, wondering if anything would have changed the outcome.

Under normal circumstances, not talking for almost twenty-four hours would drive me to the brink of mental ruin. I drafted a multi-paragraph text on my lunch break that I haven't sent about how much I love him and how badly I want to work things out. But since texting hasn't been the best mode of communication for us, I'm remaining uncharacteristically calm until we get the chance to talk in person, after the party.

Today is about Angie, after all. I can't wait to see Angie's face when she sees the décor, opens her presents, and blows out the candles on her princess cake. The last thing I want to do is bring down the mood with awkwardness between her uncle and me.

As I shove my feet into my boots, I explain the general concept of a ring light to Grandma Flo and why it may be beneficial for her nighttime videos. She doesn't need any prompting. Under a minute later, she's purchased one from Amazon with a single click.

Martin happens to lumber by, a rolled-up *Globe* paper tucked under his arm. He flashes me a knowing look as if to say, *Look what you've created*.

He's not wrong.

A year ago, Grandma Flo was your average granny downloading viruses on her desktop computer and sharing Charlie Brown memes on Facebook. And now she's a social media influencer.

I'm lucky if I catch her when her nose isn't buried in her iPad. We wait at least ten minutes in the driveway as she finishes responding to the comments on her Instagram video tutorial for her @LoopsWithFlo account. Since she first started her account, she's gained hundreds of followers. I attribute the rapid growth of her following to her Live video sessions.

In her latest video, she's parked in her La-Z-Boy in a pale pink sweater with a faux white collar. For twenty consecutive minutes, she does nothing but knit a pair of socks while listening to Cardi B and Megan Thee Stallion, profanity and all. This is the woman who used to make a cross over her chest at the word *shit* and exclusively listened to Christian music (Amy Grant).

Ever since she and Martin got together, she's been living her best life. And despite Mom's concern, Crystal and I are loving Flo 2.0.

Besides, Grandma Flo is much the same in most ways. She's still a hoarder, made evident by the box of old *TV Guide* magazines busting out of the drawer in the entryway table (because you never know when you'll need a cable schedule from the nineties) and the pile of *Oprah* magazines on the cusp of toppling over under the living room coffee table. She still attends Sunday and Tuesday sermons and reads her Bible daily. And she's still an excellent host. When I arrived to pick up some party supplies from her basement, she'd already prepared a cheese and meat plate, a tray of blueberry muffins, and a bowl of hard candies.

I grab the Holy Shit handle when she floors it, reversing out of the driveway in Martin's massive Lincoln faster than greased lightning, while simultaneously cranking the volume on the Hot 96.9 radio station. No wonder the family has discouraged her as much as possible from driving.

"Did you see my latest ex video?" I ask once we're safely in our own lane on the road.

She gives me a grave look, nearly missing the stop sign. My head lobs forward when she slams the brake partway through the intersection. "I did. It's a shame none of them panned out."

I grit my teeth as we take a sharp corner. I'm half contemplating asking her to stop so I can Uber the rest of the way. "On the plus side, I did come away with a good friend. Remember Daniel?"

"The kid with the bowl cut?"

"Yup. He doesn't have a bowl cut anymore," I inform her. "We decided we're better as friends."

She eyes me for longer than comfortable before shifting her focus back to the road. "You aren't as distraught as I assumed you would be."

"I don't know. I really hyped myself up for some epic, novel-worthy second-chance romance. But I think I was just trying to play it safe, really. And even the ones who seemed perfect on paper weren't quite . . . right."

"Spoken like a woman who knows what *right* feels like," she says knowingly, cranking the wheel to take a last-minute left-hand turn.

Trevor's easy smile invades my mind. I tug on the collar of my knit sweater as the heat gathers to my neck.

We're silent the rest of the way there. The hospital parking lot is crowded as usual as she careens into a rare open spot. She's dangerously close to the van next to us, so much so I'll probably need to exit through the driver's side. But I don't complain. It's truly a miracle we've arrived without mowing anyone over.

AMY LEA

"I accidently fell for my roommate," I blurt, unfastening my seat belt. I lean my head against the headrest and close my eyes, desperate for a few minutes to regroup.

"I know. Your sister told me yesterday during yoga." Grandma Flo is unperturbed by this revelation.

"Of course she told you," I grumble, mildly bothered they went to yoga without inviting me (not that I'd go, but an invite would be nice), but mostly pissed that Crystal had the gall to talk to Grandma Flo about me. "Anyway, so Trevor . . ." I give her all the details of Trevor's and my relationship over the past four and a half months.

She turns down the radio and listens intently, smiling the entire time. "Isn't it obvious? He was trying to declare his love for you at the gala. And seeing you on Daniel's arm last night, on Valentine's Day of all days, spooked him."

"But I told him how I felt and he didn't believe me. I think this is the first time a guy has accused me of not having enough feelings."

"Maybe he's projecting because his own feelings scare him," Grandma Flo posits. "You mentioned he's experienced a lot of loss, with his parents and his brother. And now with his poor niece's health complications . . ."

I consider that. "Maybe."

"Some people struggle with communication. Especially if they're afraid to get hurt," Grandma Flo points out, drumming her thin fingers on the steering wheel.

"Still. We've only been dating a couple days, and so far it's just been misunderstanding after misunderstanding with him. And I hate pointless misunderstandings in romance. Why can't people just have conversations like adults? Lay it all out on the line and avoid the next three hundred pages of turmoil?"

"Then there wouldn't be a book, would there?" Grandma Flo snorts, tossing me a schooling brow raise. "My dear, you have a lot to learn about relationships if you think all problems can be solved with a single conversation. Give yourself a break. You're in the beginning of your relationship. You're two very different people ironing out the kinks."

"I solve things with conversations," I point out stubbornly.

"But you've never been one to hide your feelings, even as a young girl. Saying what's on your mind comes naturally to you. But we're talking about men here. Human beings." She chuckles, fluffing her curls in the rearview mirror. "Take Marty, for example. He's about as emotional as they come. But do you really think your grandfather ever told me how he felt at any given time?"

Unlikely. Grandpa Roger was cantankerous as the best of them, always complaining about something, whether it was the weather (too hot or too cold, no in between), the slow cashier at the pharmacy, Vanna White's choice of dress on any given episode of *Wheel of Fortune*. Mom used to say he was unhappy when he didn't have anything to complain about. He was old-school, upholding antiquated gender norms with his stern rigidity.

"Your grandpa showed his love not through words but through actions," Grandma Flo explains.

"I remember he always cooked for you and got you flowers from the market on his way home from work." I smile at the memory of visiting on weekends. There was always a bouquet of fresh flowers proudly displayed in the middle of the dining room table.

The note always said the same thing: *TO MY DEAREST FLO*, in his all-caps block handwriting.

"He did. And he didn't love me any less. That's part of what makes a long-term relationship work. Real life isn't a ninety-minute movie or a three-hundred-page novel. It takes time to truly understand what someone else needs and how the other person communicates their love." She gives my kneecap another reassuring squeeze.

I crack a smile. Why is she always right? "What would you say to him if you were me?"

She presses her finger to her lips, contemplating. "I'd tell him how much you care for him. Put it all out there."

"I will," I say. "I just hope he'll believe me when I tell him how much I love him."

"And if he doesn't?"

"I still know I'm going to be okay." It feels so good to say that out loud. I know in my heart it's true, because every time I'm heart-broken, convinced I'll never bounce back, I always do.

"Of course you will." She places her wrinkled hand over mine and squeezes before adding, "My darling granddaughter deserves the best. No exceptions."

"Thanks, Grandma." A tiny seed blooms in my stomach, because for the first time in forever, I truly believe it.

♥ chapter thirty-three

PEOPLE ARE SERVING me some serious looks.

Then again, I am a human bumblebee in my massive Belle dress in the hospital elevator. A woman grumbles under her breath when I inadvertently bop her in the face with an obnoxiously large bundle of pink gift shop balloons. Along with the balloons, I'm also juggling a Flynn Rider piñata and one of Mel's cast-iron frying pans to break it with—like in the movie when Rapunzel hits him in the face with a pan.

The party is scheduled to start in half an hour. It's no Disneyland, but all the brightly painted whimsical cardboard structures serve as fuel for the imagination. Pink and purple streamers drape across the entire room, doing their best to mask the ugly hospital ceiling and walls. A long rectangular table sits in the middle of the room, draped in a hot-pink tablecloth, accented by sparkly confetti and princess plates, napkins, party hats, and gaudy plastic crowns.

Staff members are already milling about, assisting with the last-minute setup of the goody bags. Even Crystal and Scott are here, dressed as Snow White and Prince Charming, respectively. They're the designated muscle, moving furniture and doing the miscellaneous heavy lifting. Trevor is nowhere to be seen, which is honestly making my anxiety even worse.

Angie spots me right away from the "window" of Rapunzel's tower, which was a bitch to construct out of cardboard given its height. "It's Belle!" She's full of energy today, wide-eyed and giggly at the sight of the piñata in my arms. "And you brought the pan."

Payton enthusiastically approves, dressed in a Princess Anna dress. "Oh my God. You look fantastic!" Something is different about her today. Usually, she looks weary, worn, and in need of a long nap. But today, she's bright and lively. She folds me into a hug, although my hoop skirt prevents close contact. "I didn't expect all of this. It's above and beyond, honestly."

"Believe it or not, Trevor helped with the cardboard construction. I did the painting," I respond, setting the bundle of balloons in the corner of the room. I do my best to mask the somber look on my face as I mention Trevor.

"Where is Uncle Trev?" Angie asks. She tilts her head to see how far her braided wig extends to the ground.

"He'll be here soon. He's always early," Payton guarantees, turning to me. "Thank you, by the way. For everything," she adds.

"Don't mention it. Honestly, I love parties. I told Trevor I'll plan her party every year . . . if this one is up to Angie's standards," I tease, my voice cracking at the possibility of not being in their lives a year from now. Surely it would be strange for me to continue visiting Angie if Trevor and I are no longer a thing.

"No. It's more than just the party," Payton assures me. "Thank you for all the visits. And for keeping Trevor sane. He's usually a nervous wreck whenever he visits her. More nervous than Angie, even. But you calm him somehow." She glances at her daughter, and then back to me. "I've never seen him like this. Ever."

I eye her sideways, hoisting the frying pan under my arm. "What do you mean?"

"He's been sick over you, truly," she responds.

"Who's been sick?" Angie asks, her dark eyes darting back and forth between us.

"Uncle Trevor. He's in love with Tara," Payton explains, far too casually.

I nearly choke on my own saliva. Apparently, I'm the only one caught off guard by this statement, because Angie just rolls her eyes like this is last week's news. "Oh. I already knew that."

I'm about to launch into an interrogation when Angie's stare moves past my face, over my shoulder. Her expression brightens instantly.

"Ange," a deep warning voice grumbles.

Behind me is Trevor. In his Flynn Rider costume, filling out the vest and beige pants like a fantasy come to life. Except better, somehow. The tattoos embellishing his sinewed forearms peek from underneath hastily rolled shirtsleeves. I note that the buttons on his vest are buttoned unevenly, as if he didn't bother checking his reflection in the mirror before leaving the apartment.

Similar to cartoon Flynn Rider, he's generally disheveled. His hair is messy, like he's raked his hand through it one too many times. His eyes are bloodshot, in desperate need of a good night's rest. I idly wonder if he got any sleep at all last night.

Despite his obvious fatigue, his eyes still manage to ensnare mine, and the overwhelming sight sends my body into a state of shock. I'm at risk of flatlining from his mere proximity.

I barely register when Angie scolds him, ordering him to refer to her as "Rapunzel."

Trevor gives her a cocksure smile. "Miss *Rapunzel*, are you gonna let down your hair for me or what?"

Angie giggles and points in my direction. "Nah. But Belle might."

He swallows, tentative when he spots the piñata and accompanying cast-iron skillet in my hands. "Erm, I'm not so sure. Belle may prefer to bash my face in with cookware."

I raise my free hand to proclaim innocence. "I'm not in a violent mood, lucky for you."

He laughs. "That's a relief."

I'm not sure where to go from here, but under Payton and Angie's watchful eyes, I'm feeling hella uncomfortable and paranoid they'll sense the rift between us. Maybe it's best to avoid him until the party is over. "Sorry, I've gotta set up the piñata," I say, gathering the sides of my dress to walk away.

Trevor's fingers clasp my wrist before I can make my escape. "Wait."

When I stop, he releases my wrist, running a hand over the back of his neck.

I study him, waiting.

"God, I'm really fucking bad at this." His honey eyes meet mine, sincere and earnest.

I can't help but laugh. "Which part?"

He lifts both palms to the ceiling as Payton shuffles Angie away to greet guests, granting us some privacy in front of the cardboard tower. "All of it. I'm trying to grand gesture you. For the second time. And I'm trying not to make an ass of myself."

I wait for him to continue.

"I'm so sorry for ruining your night last night. That was never my intention. I had this whole perfect surprise planned out and it just . . . went to shit."

"It's okay, Trevor. Really. I understand."

He clears his throat over the squeal of some of the kids who have just entered, in awe at the décor. "I never should have walked away from you. But after all the hours I listened to you talk about how amazing Daniel is . . . I thought I could never compete. Especially after seeing you two together. I know how special Valentine's Day is to you. I guess I just thought it must mean Daniel is really special to you too. If he was exactly the kind of guy you were looking for, I didn't want to be in the way of that."

"For the record, you have nothing to worry about with Daniel. I love him as a friend, but it doesn't even compare to what I feel for you. And I know it's hard to believe after all my exes—"

"No, I was a dick for using that against you."

"To be fair, I get it. You were kind of right. I bounced between them all so fast because the truth is, I didn't love any of them anymore. I just convinced myself I did, mostly because I was trying to avoid my feelings for you," I admit, moving out of the way as Angie runs past me to greet more guests.

"I know. I'm a tool for doubting that." He gives a helpless shrug. "It's just, I've seen the way you are with guys you like. Sending multi-paragraph texts. You sent me one-word answers while I was gone, and I thought you—"

"You thought I didn't care?" I'm tempted to laugh in his face when he nods. I think about the hours I spent clutching my phone, willing him to text me. "Don't forget, you're the one who told me to rein my text game in. I was trying not to freak you out and send you *running far away*, as you would say."

He winces. "My advice was dead wrong. I love your long-winded texts. I just never thought you'd actually take my advice."

My corset makes digesting this new information more challenging than it should be. How do historical romance heroines keep their cool? I fidget, managing to regulate my breathing, replaying his words. I interpreted his lack of communication to mean he didn't care. And he assumed the same.

Grandma Flo's words echo through my head. *You have a lot to learn about relationships if you think all problems can be solved with a single conversation.*

He continues. "Anyway, I wanted to apologize again for my part in all of this. I know I've messed with your head the past few months, and I take full responsibility. And I know asking you to move slow didn't help."

"I'm sorry too. And for the record, I have no problem with moving slow."

The corners of his lips tug upward, deepening into a brief smile. "I think we tossed out moving slow on Friday night, didn't we?"

"Technically."

His incendiary look locks me in place. "Tara, I've had it bad for you for months. You. Are. Everything. You're the best thing that's ever happened to me. I was scared because I couldn't stop second-guessing whether you were real and whether you were going to leave too. I've always had issues expressing how I feel, especially after my mom passed. After everything, with my family and Angie, the thought of losing someone else I care about was too much. Shutting people out was easier. I just got so comfortable with that reality. And when you moved in . . ."

I let him continue his train of thought.

"You wanted to get to know me. You wanted to know everything about me. And for the first time, I wanted to let someone in. And when I did, it scared the shit out of me. But the time away gave me some clarity."

"On what?"

"It made me realize I missed you so fucking much. I was so miserable without you, I got sent home early because I was basically useless out there. I needed to come home and tell you that I want all the things you want. That I'm capable of giving you everything. And I don't want to go slow, because I can barely breathe when I think about living my life without you. I want to complain while you watch Disney movies. I want to alphabetize your books. I want to read with you at night. I want to tolerate your mess. I want . . ." He lets out a weak half laugh. "I want a family. One day. I want to do literally anything as long as it means being with you, because I am so in love with you, I don't know what to do with myself."

The weight of his words sends an electric thrill rocketing through me. There's a hopeful yet vulnerable look in his eyes I've never seen before. For the first time, there's no iron gate, fortress, moat, or velvet rope keeping me from him. He's right here, in front of me, dressed like a literal prince, warm eyes beaconing me to him.

Because I'm me, my mind blanks entirely, homing in on the

only coherent statement echoing in my mind. "I'm really not that messy."

He does that face, the mock-disappointed face he always makes. "Tara, I just told you I loved you and that's what you take out of it?"

I cover my face with my hand. "I'm sorry. I'm not used to declarations of love like this."

"The fact that no one has realized how amazing you are is just . . . mind-blowing." He reaches to brush the crest of my cheek with his thumb. I want to capture this very moment. His gentle laugh, like music to my ears. The sound of Angie and her friends laughing, running around the room. Even the antiseptic hospital scent. The look in his eyes that fades everyone and everything around us to a mere blur. Like we're the only ones who exist in this moment. "I understand if you need to take time to think about it. I just needed you to know how I feel."

"I don't need any time to think about it. You know I love you." I inch forward, and finally, we're chest to chest, nose to nose. The warm, welcome contact stirs something inside both of us, because within a fraction of a second, he's cupping my jaw with one hand.

"What are you doing?" I ask in barely above a whisper.

"What every good romance hero does." When I nod, he lets out a sharp breath before his lips fuse to mine, pleading for entrance.

This time, it's not soft, sweet, or tentative. It's deliberate. He's silently telling me he's mine and I'm his.

Finally.

♥ chapter thirty-four

WHEN WE RETURN to our apartment, Trevor presents me with something unexpected. A shoe box.

"What is this?" I ask.

He stands next to me at the kitchen island, teetering on the balls of his feet, nervous. "Look inside."

When I open the lid, he's behind me, his strong hands steadying me around the waist as my knees buckle.

The gasp I emit is embarrassing. The first item I pull out is a crumpled McDonald's receipt for a Big Mac and Quarter Pounder combo. From the night he took me out for food after my disastrous date with Segway Jeff.

"You kept this?" I ask, misty eyes catching his gaze over my shoulder.

He presses a soft kiss on my temple. "Yup."

"Why?"

"You said your parents' first date was at McDonald's. I guess I thought you might like it one day."

A burning match strikes in my stomach as I examine the folded-up, empty bag of BBQ chips from the first night we watched *The Bachelor* together, as well as a handwritten note with the cupcake recipe we made.

"But . . . this means . . ." I start, breathless as the admission takes hold in my gut. I don't think I can even muster the words to explain what this means to me. It's not just words. It's physical proof. "You really did have feelings for me . . . even back then."

"From day one. From the moment I heard your voice behind that bathroom door. I told you," he says as I pull out a drink menu from the bottom of the box. It's the drink menu from Mamma Maria's.

"I can't believe you stole this." This isn't your average disposable paper menu. It's encased in leather. Wheezy laughter escapes me as I hold it up, assessing its weight. "You hate keeping junk."

"Yup. That box has been killing me," he admits. "I keep it under my bed where I can't see it. Out of sight, out of mind."

I run my finger along the rim of the box. "I'm keeping this forever. You know that, right? It must be displayed prominently behind protective glass."

"Wouldn't expect anything less." He spins me around to face him, pulling me flush to his hard chest. "Now can we finally dispose of that Ex-Files box?"

"Hell to the yes." I laugh, already spinning on my heel to grab it from my room, eager to put the past behind me.

• • •

THE VAPOR FROM my breath coils into the night air as I set my bare feet onto the snow-covered deck.

We toss our towels over the banister. I've selected my favorite pale-blue bikini with a little fabric bow tying the front together. Trevor dips in first, his gaze blazing a trail from my face all the way down to my toes. His throat ripples as I follow him into the scalding water without hesitation.

"I'm really going to miss that Flynn Rider vest." I faux-pout as he extends his hand, tugging me closer.

He smirks. "I mean, I'm not super into role-playing, but I'm willing to make an exception."

I mock shock. "Oh really?"

"Anything for my girlfriend." His eyes widen, as if he's caught himself in an embarrassing mistake. "Unless you don't want an official label, though I assume you do—"

"Oh, I want the label," I assure him. "But on two conditions." I hold him at arm's length, my palm flat against his chest, glistening with water. After everything, I decide to set some ground rules.

He indulges me, nodding respectfully. "All right. Hit me with them."

I hold up my index finger. "One, you won't wimp out when I'm being extra. If I do or say anything that freaks you out, you'll be mature. You'll talk to me like an adult before running scared and avoiding conversation."

He sets both hands on my waist, his mouth slanted in a smile. "Just so you know, I love you most when you're being extra. It's a massive turn-on." He pauses, absorbing my serious expression. "And you can say whatever is on your mind, at all times, without worrying about whether you're too much. Because you're not too much. Ever. Okay? And I swear I'll talk to you first about anything that's bothering me. Anything we can't resolve, we'll go to therapy. We'll work it out in a healthy way."

"Deal."

"What's the second one?" he asks, pulling me closer. He's mere inches from me, and I'm losing my resolve. He knows it too, based on his knowing brow raise.

I fight to maintain my stern look by staring at the condensation flecking his lashes. "As my official *boyfriend*, you'd have to promise to hold my hand every ten minutes." My straight face doesn't last long before both our chests are heaving in silent amusement. "And you have to make a regular habit of kissing me in public. I want all the PDA."

"I think I can manage that." His deep laugh echoes into the void of the night around us. He studies my face for a moment, tracing my cheek with the back of his knuckle.

"You better," I warn.

He smiles, pressing his free hand to my chest, over my wildly hammering heart, audible to me even over the rumble of the jets. "Your heart is beating so fast."

I panic for a split second, willing it into a steady drum—the heartbeat of a calm, sane person. And as usual, my emotion trumps my logic.

It's like the floodgates of happiness I've chased my entire life have unleashed and I'm ready and willing to drown in it.

He tugs me closer to him, pressing another trail of kisses

around the edge of my lips as he hoists me up, wrapping my legs around his waist. He backs us up through the water, lowering himself onto the seat. I'm clinging to him like a spider monkey, straddling his lap, one hand in his hair, the other around his neck, pressing and pulling.

He drags his teeth over my skin. His tongue does something magical to the smooth skin below my ear, all while he's running the tips of his fingers down my back at an agonizingly slow pace, stopping at the waist of my bikini bottoms. His right thumb slips under the band, inching along the seam toward the front, exploring the sensitive area where my upper thigh meets my hip.

When I arch myself against him, he lets out a string of garbled curse words, desire radiating in his eyes.

"What if someone catches us?" I whisper. "Like Gerald."

"Please don't remind me of Gerald when I'm hard." He squeezes his eyes shut for a second before lifting his chin toward the door. "And I put the broom in the door. It's locked."

The words have barely escaped his lips before he's unhooked my top, shamelessly tossing it over the side of the hot tub.

He bends down slightly, his tongue sliding against the undersides of my breasts. Both of them receive their fair share of attention and lavish compliments before his fingers travel back to my bikini bottoms.

He isn't gentle when he tugs, signaling he wants them off. And quick. We stand frantically to remove our bathing suit bottoms, only feeling whole again when I settle back over him, skin to skin. He sucks on my bottom lip as he circles me with his thumb, testing. When his swipe nearly ends me, he slows the pace.

The jet underneath us hits me with the perfect amount of pressure, pulsing exactly where I want it.

"Did you know every second we were in this hot tub together before was torture?" he whispers against my neck. "All I wanted to do was—"

"What did you want to do to me in here?"

His eyes darken as he smooths his thumb where I want it, keeping his touch light as he shifts my leg over. "This. I'd spread your legs apart."

At my shudder, he groans, sliding another finger in. "You'd be dripping all over my hand, just like this. And I'd fuck you harder and deeper until you were begging for me."

I shudder at his words in my ear, doubling the pleasure of his hand. "Oh God. That feels so good."

"Fuck, I'm never going to let you go." His voice is strained in my ear as his pace picks up.

I angle a brow at him. "Now who's the possessive one? I never would have guessed."

"Only when it comes to you." He looks pleased with himself as I buck against his hand, relishing the control he has over me.

"Well, good luck ever trying to leave me now that I've sunk my claws in," I manage.

"True. I'd be a fool to ever leave you. Who knows what kind of messed-up shit you'd do to my car."

I pretend to smack him in the shoulder.

"Seriously, though. I love that you're mine," he tells me, eliciting a single tear from beneath my lid. He presses a soft kiss over it, absorbing it. "What's going on in that head of yours?" he whispers.

Seconds away from losing all control, I nod, unable to stop my grin as the emotion rolls over me. "I'm just . . . happy."

"Even if you're not getting your second-chance romance?"

"Trevor, you are a million times better than any trope I could ever dream up."

He meets my smile, and I swear his entire face lights up brighter than Times Square. He presses his lips to mine, sealing my declaration. And when he tells me to come for him, his voice pushes me over the edge, free-falling into oblivion without fear or hesitation.

He holds one hand over my mouth as I cry out, inner walls pulsing. I unravel in his lap, blinded by a white sheet of stars.

"Still good?" he asks, kissing my temple.

I respond with a gentle scrape up his back and shoulders.

"Good. I need you so badly right now." He taps me on the bottom, gently lifting me off his lap. He leans over the side of the tub, fishing in the pockets of his sweatpants hanging over the railing. He locates his wallet, pulling out a condom. I watch as he unpackages it and slips it over himself.

All is right again when he lifts me back onto his lap and eases me onto him, stretching me completely, inch by inch. His gaze fills with the unspoken tenderness and affection I've wanted for so long. Now there's no barrier. No wall. Nothing stopping me from venturing forward. He's letting me in. Completely.

I move against him, taking more and more of him. My body tingles as I anchor myself to him with abandon, the part of him I've only seen glimpses of over the past four months. The part of him he's never wanted me to see. I'm struck by the realization that he's giving himself to me. His whole self.

His head drops back as I take all of him. A visible shudder rolls through his shoulders, his low groan vibrating across my throat. His breath hitches, and he holds me still for a few beats, eye contact unbreaking.

"Are you okay?"

"If you move an inch, this is going to be embarrassing for everyone involved. Mainly me."

I shift slightly, and he makes a pained face. "You look like you're about to perish."

"I might. But I'll die the happiest I've ever been."

Our foreheads touch as we laugh, managing to stay as still as possible. After a few long breaths, he loosens his grip around my lower hips. I ride him slowly at first, speeding up in pace with his enthusiasm, meeting his lips with frantic kisses. He switches his attention between my breasts and my mouth, unsure which way to go as he grips my ass, pressing hard into my flesh under the water.

With one swift movement, he lifts me and turns me outward, toward the city. "Do you want to go inside?" he whispers from behind.

"No. Why would I?"

"Thought you didn't like water sex."

I peek at him over my shoulder. "I've never actually tried it." When the admission rolls off my tongue, his eyes blaze.

"First time in the water, huh? Then I better make it good for you," he says, pulling my hips to grind me to him before placing my hand on the side of the tub. "Hold on tight."

He anchors his knee on the bench as he positions himself to enter me with a powerful thrust that takes me to a parallel universe of pure bliss. Each movement plunges me deeper and deeper into an alternate dimension where the city skyline glitters like a sea of gold and diamonds. Where the wintery smell of the outdoors is like a burst of new life. For the first time, I realize my real life is ten times better than any romance book.

He's slowed down now to focus on me and my every reaction. He's gripping me tight as he moves in and out of me, reviving me every single time. Our breath matches, and soon so do our moans. It's like we've melted into each other. Absorbing each other's every sensation.

And then the crash hits me unexpectedly, even more intense than the first. My cry urges him on as he rocks into me faster and harder. "Look at me," he demands, turning my face toward him. Our gazes lock as he shudders over me with a groan that vibrates to my core, holding me tighter than anyone ever has. "I'm yours. Okay?"

"I love you." He presses a lingering kiss to my neck, sealing everything I've ever wanted.

Someone who wants me exactly as I am.

LIVE WITH TARAROMANCEQUEEN—ROOM-ANCE

[Tara appears on camera in front of an overflowing bookshelf.]

EXCERPT FROM TRANSCRIPT

TARA: *Hello, romance book lovers, welcome back to my channel. I'm hopping on here really quick today to discuss a topic that has been requested relentlessly. And that is forced proximity and room-ances.*

Forced-proximity tropes are like catnip. They can take place on road trips, confined to small cars. Workplaces. And the delicious "only one bed" trope. But my personal favorite take on forced proximity is room-ances.

The thing with living with your love interest is that they'll see you at your weakest moments. Late at night when you have no more shits to give. When you take your makeup and bra off. When you're flat-out done with life. The most fun room-ances are those accidental nudity moments, where Person A decides it's a good idea to be naked in the common area and Person B just so happens to walk by at that very moment.

One of the reasons it's my absolute favorite is . . . well, it happened to me.

[Trevor appears in the frame, albeit begrudgingly. He plants a chaste yet loving kiss on Tara's temple and peaces out.]

❤ epilogue

One year later—Valentine's Day

ALMOST THERE. JUST three more steps."

The low vibration of Trevor's voice in the shell of my ear ricochets through me.

"Is this blindfold really necessary? I could have just closed my eyes," I say as he guides me forward, his palms splayed over my shoulders. There's an unfamiliar floral scent in the air, masking the usual lemon cleaner scent in our apartment. All of my senses are heightened in the absence of sight, which I am dying to rectify. "Can you at least tell me where we are? Are we in the living room? The kitchen?"

He senses my impatience and preemptively folds both hands over my blindfold to prevent me from peeking. "Ask one more question and see what happens."

"You know I like to live dangerously."

"I'll hide all your books as punishment," he warns, inching me forward a few more steps.

Something that feels like string feathers against my nose. I scrunch my face to relieve the tickle. "You're bluffing. You'd have to alphabetize them all over again."

"As if I don't already do that on a biweekly basis." The tips of his fingers graze my cheeks as he gently removes the blindfold. "Okay, you can open your eyes."

We're in my old room, which has become the spare bedroom by default since last year. I blink, unsure where to look first, because it's a literal Valentine's Day explosion in here. At least twenty helium-filled pink heart-shaped balloons of all sizes cover the ceiling entirely, curly ribbons raining down on us like a weightless curtain.

The life-size stuffed bear I fawned over in the window of a department store a couple months ago, which Trevor argued was an "obnoxious waste of space," rests on the bed, propped against the headboard. On the bedside table sits a stunning hand-tied floral arrangement, vase overflowing with bulbous pink and white peonies. Next to it is a gigantic Kinder Surprise egg and a fresh bag of Cheetos. And that's not even the highlight.

The wall to my right no longer houses my sad, overflowing IKEA bookshelf. In its place stands a gleaming white shelf spanning nearly the entire width of the room. Strangely, the books are artfully arranged by color, which Trevor is vehemently opposed to. Nonalphabetical order causes him anxiety.

Even more, this wall of wonder holds hope. After every one of my (many) broken hearts, I wanted to give up on love. And each time, these tender, unforgettable love stories healed me with their happy endings, one by one. Without these blueprints for epic love,

I probably would have settled long before now. And I'm so glad I didn't.

My entire life, I thought I needed to hold on to love with an iron fist. It was a feeling I needed to trap, to smother, so it wouldn't slip through my fingers. Little did I know, when you're with the right person, being in love never feels like the bottom is going to fall out. It's solid, stable, and indestructible.

Sure, Trevor may be a massive grump with an irrational hatred for singing in the car. But he does what no one else has ever done. He accepts all of me. The parts no one else has seen. He listens to my every word, never cutting me off or rushing me. He accommodates my picky eating and my hoarding tendencies. I've even bought my own pair of Crocs to match his, which he deems "Couples Crocs." And thanks to therapy, we've learned multiple strategies on how best to meld our different communicative styles.

He's even kept his word, embracing the PDA with hand-holding and movie-worthy kisses in random places, like the frozen-food aisle in Costco. Or in the stairwell of our apartment. Or even in front of Angie, who makes a dramatic show of covering her eyes, complaining until it's over.

I've been spending a lot of time with Angie lately, as her designated party planner. This year's birthday extravaganza is going to be something special. She deserves it after the success of her heart transplant, only a few months ago. She's insisting on a boy-band-themed party—her latest obsession, because she's "over Disney." I've been attempting to learn a TikTok dance for her, a painful endeavor I do not recommend to anyone over twenty years old.

"I can't believe you did this for me," I whisper, running my index finger over the book spines. "This is pure shelf porn."

"Figured it was necessary to get you to stop leaving your books in random piles around the apartment," he says through a low chuckle. He wraps his arms around my waist from behind and plants a soft kiss in the cove of my neck.

I zero in on a vibrant pink-and-red book I don't recognize. It sits, cover out, in the middle of the shelf.

I pluck it from its spot. It's light, slightly thinner than your average trade paperback. Like all my other rom-coms, the cover is illustrated. The hero and heroine are lounging on a stack of pillows. The heroine is stretched out, her head resting against the hero's lap as she reads a book. He holds her tight, his arm wrapped around her, cherishing the moment. Artfully hand-brushed hearts fill the empty space around the couple. In bold font, the title reads, *Can I Ask You a Question?*

It takes a moment to register the tiny little hearts dotting the woman's sweater. The man's dark, tousled hair and tattoos partially visible under the rolled sleeves of his shirt. And, most telling, the way he's looking at her, like she is everything he never knew he wanted.

The adorable cartoon couple is *us*.

"Open it," Trevor urges gently.

My hands shake as I flip to the first page of the "book." Through the tears blurring my vision, I make out another illustration. Of this very moment. Cartoon Trevor and me, standing in front of this bookshelf, heart balloons closing in around us, hugging us. As I let the successive pages fall, one after the other, the illustration changes like a flip-book. Cartoon Trevor bends the knee, my cartoon eyes enlarge like saucers, my hands slowly come up over my face in shock and awe.

Before I can even register what's happening, Real-Life Trevor is on his knee. "Read the last page," he instructs.

When I flip the page, the script font reads:

Tara Li Chen,

Please know I hate myself for this title. But damn, it was appropriate.

The day you barged into my life and talked my ear off, you rewrote everything I thought I knew. I've told you this before, but I felt like I already knew you. I fell in love, fast, with your warmth, passion, and kindness. Somehow, you go to great lengths to make everyone in your life feel special, and you don't even have to try.

Most of all, after everything you've been through, you never once gave up hope for love.

I don't think I can ever repay you for the joy you've given me over the past year. I know there will be challenges ahead, but I want to face them head-on with you by my side. I promise to spend the rest of my life making sure you get the happily ever after you deserve.

Will you marry me?

Tears spring into my eyes, and I fumble the book. It plummets to our feet, facedown. Through my blurred vision, I see that Trevor holds a red box. In the cushion sits a stunning oval diamond atop a thin yellow band. It's an exact replica of the one from all my Pinterest boards.

The weight of his eyes on me produces an instant smile. "This is . . . the grand gesture of all grand gestures."

"You deserve all of this and more," he says, his tone unwavering. "If I'm going to keep up with those heroes in your books, I need to up my game."

"I don't need gestures, honestly." I stare into the eyes that captivated me from day one. They're brimming with pure love, drowning out every last bit of doubt I've ever had. "You are more than enough. Just you."

"I love you." He stands, giving me a tender kiss on the temple that makes me see stars. "Now can you please answer my question? I'm gonna pass out if you don't say yes right now."

I raise one brow. "Metcalfe, did you really think there was a reality where I'd say no?"

A grin lights up his entire face like pure sunshine, just for me. "Nah. But I want to hear you say it anyway."

"Yes!" I shriek, yanking the ring out of the box.

Trevor's steady hand helps to guide it onto my finger.

When I hold my hand up, the diamond hits the ray of sunshine streaming in from the window. Aside from my new fiancé's smile, it's the single most beautiful thing I've ever seen. I will never take this off as long as I live.

I go on my tiptoes, wrapping my arms around his neck. "Are you sure you know what you signed up for? Me, all over you, talking in your ear, forever and ever? Swooning over the other fictional men in my life?"

"I can't imagine a future more perfect than that," he says without an ounce of hesitation. "As long as I'm your favorite hero in the end."

Without notice, I leap into Trevor's arms, wrapping my legs around his waist like a koala. He holds me there, tight to him, laughing softly into my mouth.

I tell him I love him, over and over, planting feverish kisses everywhere I can manage, one for each of the infinite reasons I am *crazy* in love with him.

He's not just the hero of my dreams. He's the hero beyond my wildest imagination.

The best part? He's nonfiction.

acknowledgments

The struggle to write the second book is all too real (ask me how I know). *Exes and O's* took me much longer to write than *Set on You*, but it is truly the book of my heart. First and foremost, thank you to John, who held my hand as I wrote, trashed, and rewrote parts of this book over and over. I also owe so much to my sweet goldendoodle, Albie, who is always by my side through every book.

As I write these acknowledgments, I am gearing up for the publication date of *Set on You* (yes, publishing timelines are strange). There are so many people to thank for their role in getting my books into the hands of readers:

Endless thank-yous to my team at Berkley, including Kristine Swartz, Mary Baker, Fareeda Bullert, Yazmine Hassan, Tina Joell, Lindsey Tulloch, Christine Legon, Andrea Monagle, Daniel Brount, Vikki Chu, Allison Prince, and Alex Castellanos. Thank you for making my publishing experience an absolute dream. I couldn't have imagined a better team to champion my work.

ACKNOWLEDGMENTS

A huge shout-out to my hardworking, upbeat, and fantastic team at BookSparks, including Keely Platte, Grace Fell, and Crystal Patriarche, for all your work in spreading the word about my debut. You guys are amazing.

Thank you to my incredible team at Viking/Penguin UK—Lydia Fried, Harriet Bourton, Ellie Hudson, Federica Trogu, Olivia Mead, Tineke Mollemans, Samantha Fanakan, Rachel Myers, and Linda Viberg—for all your work in getting my series across the pond. I'm blown away by your enthusiasm and am overjoyed to continue working together!

I am so grateful to Penguin Random House Grupo, Editions Arquerio, Brainfood Publishing, Nemesis Yayincilik Hizmetleri, Helion, and Verlagsgruppe Droemer Knaur for getting *Set on You* into the hands of readers around the world.

As always, thank you to my amazing agent, Kim Lionetti, and the whole BookEnds team for all your publishing expertise and support, and for shepherding me through this process.

Piles of gratitude to Jackie Lau, Sarah Echavarre Smith, Denise Williams, Lynn Painter, Rachel Lynn Solomon, Kerry Winfrey, Jesse Q. Sutanto, Ali Hazelwood, and Helen Hoang for taking the time out of your busy schedules to read and endorse *Set on You*. I'm very humbled and grateful for your support.

I wouldn't have been able to get through the lead-up to publication without the emotional support of the Berkletes, all of whom have become such close friends. Thank you endlessly for all the laughs, love, and inappropriate GIFs.

Thank you to Jordyn, who talked me through the day-to-day life of a nurse, and Kathleen for inspiring Tara's hots for Dwight Kurt Schrute—a highly underrated love interest. 😉

ACKNOWLEDGMENTS

My sincerest gratitude to all of the passionate and creative bookstagrammers, BookTokers, bloggers, influencers, journalists, booksellers, and librarians for spreading the word about my books. The steadfast support of readers and creators has meant the absolute world.

Last, but certainly not least, thank you to all the crappy exes (my own and friends') who inspired this book, and thank you to Taylor Swift for inspiring me to turn my bad experiences into something beautiful.

Keep reading for a sneak peek
at Amy Lea's next book

The Catch

A THICK PLAID FLANNEL button-down covers a barrel chest so broad, I doubt I could wrap both arms around him and touch my fingertips. Not that I would dare get within a five-foot radius of someone whose hostile blue stare is so poisonous, I think he could vanquish all his enemies with a single look.

His commanding presence freezes me in place. A foreboding sizzle zips through me as I take in the thick, unkempt ashy beard concealing his jawline, barely covering a surly, grim expression. Dirty blond, overgrown hair wings out the end of his faded and frayed Maple Leafs ball cap, which has seen better days.

"Who the hell are you?" His voice is gruff and terse, like uttering anything beyond a single syllable is a herculean effort he'd rather not be bothered with.

My body betrays me with a bark of laughter. The moment it spills out of me, I hike my tote over my shoulder, righting my posture in a sad attempt to match his height. From his position on the staircase, my eyeline hovers at his distressed, oil-stained jeans. "Sorry, I didn't mean to laugh. Your voice took me by surprise."

He raises a thick, dark brow. "My voice?"

I blink. "It's just so . . . deep." I wave a hand, trying to unearth the words. "Kind of like an action movie bad guy?"

No response. Just a scowl.

"Um, is this the Whaler Inn?" I ask, despite the Whaler Inn information pamphlet displayed on the desk. Though based on the ad offering a quaint B and B that isn't in the midst of being gutted, it's a fair question.

He widens his stance like the loyal bodyguard of a young pop star at the height of fame. "Who wants to know?" His narrowing gaze is so skeptical, I bite my lip to stop myself from laughing again.

"Um, me, obviously. I just made a reservation on Airbnb. You're not the owner, are you?" Frankly, I'd imagined a folksy, salt-and-pepper-haired couple in matching Roots sweaters. They'd be in their seventies, though they'd intend to keep running the inn until the day they died (the same day, of course), because it would have been in the family for millennia. Upon entry, I'd be offered fresh-baked banana bread and an assortment of senior citizen candies from a crystal bowl. I'd be charmed by their tendency to add an "Eh?" at the end of every sentence while delighting me with tales of merciless Northern winters past.

Conveniently, the Plaid Giant fails to confirm or deny ownership. "You didn't make a reservation," he says matter-of-factly. That flannel is really doing overtime under the swell of his arms. He strikes me as the type who got those Thor-like muscles by doing honest work in the wilderness, trapping animals and hauling logs for the cabin he's building miles from civilization because he clearly hates humanity.

"Actually, I did. For a week." Panicked, I bend over to pick up my phone, overturned on the floor at my feet. Crystal has long hung up, though she's tried to call back four times, along with multiple texts. I pull up the Airbnb email, brandishing the screen at him, as if he can read it from this distance with bionic sight.

A trace of a frown forms under that bushy beard. "Nope."

"I have my reso right here." I hold out my phone, extending my arm completely, which only results in a deeper scowl. It's not like I want to stand here and argue, but I've had enough reservation mix-ups for one day.

His frown doesn't budge as he lumbers down the stairs, wood creaking under each heavy step. As he rounds the desk, I catch a rich, earthy whiff of campfire and maybe a hint of leather.

"Is it possible you didn't see my reservation? It doesn't really look like technology is your strong suit." I wave a hand in the vague direction of the clunky laptop.

"Yeah, technology is real hard to come by for kidney-stealing *backroad Canadians*," he grumbles, tapping his calloused finger on the counter impatiently as he waits for the laptop to boot up.

Unease settles along my spine as I mentally replay my call with Crystal wherein I took my sarcasm too far and insulted this place. But what does he expect? And trust, my expectations were not high. But this is a construction zone. There are exposed wires in the parlor.

I consider an apology, but before the words come to me, he grumbles something unintelligible and hunches over the keyboard.

Whoever constructed this desk didn't take someone of his height into consideration. He stabs the keyboard with his index finger, squinting at the screen with effort. "You requested the reservation, but it wasn't confirmed."

Crap.

In all the stress, I was just so happy there was any availability at all that I forgot about awaiting confirmation from the host, aka this miserable man, who single-handedly disproves the theory that all Canadians are nice.

"Can't you just confirm it right now?" I ask, flashing my Instagram smile, hoping it'll brighten his mood.

His eyes flare with deep irritation. "No. We're not open."

"But you are, according to Airbnb." I point to the link on my phone screen, which he waves off like a pesky housefly.

"Must be a glitch. Sorry, Your Royal Highness. You'll have to find alternative accommodations. I hear the Ritz Carlton down the street has vacancy." He conjures up the briefest half-hearted, crooked smile, which makes him look more constipated than smug.

"Can you please just let me stay for one night? I'm desperate," I plead.

"No. We're under construction, as you can see. Not open." He gestures to the parlor. His explanation sounds legit, which makes me feel a little better. Until he swaps his baffled expression for wariness. "Wait—you're not some developer, are you?"

"Does it look like I'm in the market to purchase a decrepit"—I bite my tongue when his glare ensnares mine—"an inn in dire need of repairs?"

His jaw clenches, but he doesn't respond.

"I promise to find somewhere else to go in the morning," I plead.

"Best of luck with that," he says cryptically. "It's fishing season."

I drop my shoulders. "So I've been told."

"I don't suppose you're here for fishing?" His lips tilt disarmingly, and for a split second, I wonder if he's joking. Before I can make a judgment call, it disappears, replaced with another glower.

"Yeah, I'm a pro angler," I say, tone rife with sarcasm. "I'm supposed to be staying at the Seaside Resort outside of Halifax. It's a five-star luxury resort, actually. It was even featured on the *Real Housewives*."

He treats me to a bored stare.

"Can you please just make an exception? I have to pee. Badly. I'll pay double," I beg. I even toss in a pouty lip. There goes my last shred of dignity. "You can even have my kidney, struggle free. I won't fight it."

The joke doesn't land. He's about to wave a dismissive hand at me when a shrill voice bellows from the room off the parlor.

"Evan! Why are you being such a dick-wad? This is not how you treat guests." A woman barrels around the corner and gives Evan a smack on the biceps. She looks about my age, rail thin, with thick, fire-engine-red hair. She's dressed in an oversize sweater with multicolor patchwork that looks like something Crystal and Tara's Grandma Flo would crochet. She's paired it with yellow leggings that give me Big Bird flashbacks.

She must be his wife. Pity overcomes me on her behalf. Having to deal with this man's mood day in and day out would be a special kind of torture. Maybe I should pull her aside and subtly ask if she needs saving. I'd be prepared to smuggle her over the border in the name of sisterhood.

"She's not a guest." Evan crosses his arms, tormented as the woman saddles up next to him, greeting me with a wide, toothy smile that just radiates good intentions.

"I *am* a guest," I retort.

"You're not."

"I am." Jesus, I feel like a small child.

"Just because you say it over and over doesn't make it true," he says, gaze searing.

"Ignore him. He gets like this when he hasn't eaten," the redhead advises with an exaggerated eye roll.

I raise a brow. I get hangry too, and you don't see me lashing out at innocent strangers.

She goes on her tiptoes, extending her pale, bony hand over the desk. She hip checks Evan out of the way in the process, which gives me a pang of satisfaction. Realistically, her tiny size 2 frame is no match for him. He moves because she wants him to move, which makes me feel guilty for assuming she's a helpless house-wife. She strikes me as a woman who demands to be noticed and gives zero fucks. I like her already.

"I'm Lucy. What's your name and where ya from?" She has a countryish twang in her voice that's much different from southern accents in the States. It's a little slower, with a heavier emphasis on the vowels.

"Melanie Karlsen—Mel," I say, taking her hand, thankful to be saved from this caveman. "I'm from Boston."

Lucy lets out an impressive whistle. "An American. What brings you up here?"

I explain my reservation mix-up, determined to ignore Evan's scowl. "I'm an influencer, so I came to capture some lifestyle content, see the sights, maybe check out some lighthouses."

"Well, you've come to the right place, then. We have more lighthouses in our area than the entire province combined. Hook Lookout just got a makeover by Garth. Just in time for tourist season. Though Ruth Fraser's been lobbying to get it repainted. She claims the stripes are too thin and that it's damaging her retinas," she adds with a slow shake of the head. Before I can begin to ask, she elbows an unimpressed Evan out of the way again and starts typing furiously on the keyboard. Her nails are painted lilac, with the exception of her ring fingers, which are a glittery silver. "Don't mind him. I'm getting you the room with the good lighting, then, for photos. And it has the best view in the whole house."

Evan casts her a ferocious glare. "Seriously, Luce? Tonight, of all nights?"

"Six nights, you said?" she confirms, ignoring Evan like he's but a speck of dust.

"Yes, please." I spare Evan an indignant look before he disappears into the parlor in a blur of fury and flannel.

Lucy photocopies my ID and plucks a skeleton key from the corkboard behind the desk. She grabs both suitcases, hoisting them up the stairs with zero effort, high ponytail bobbing up and down with each step. This tiny woman is freakishly strong. What she lacks in height, she makes up for with boundless energy.

"Oh, um, I can take it," I offer weakly, wheeling my tote and carry-on at her heels.

She doesn't seem to hear me as she bounds up the staircase,

leading me through a long, narrow hallway of doors. To my left, the hallway juts into an entirely separate wing.

The outdated floral wallpaper from the ad photographs has been unpeeled in the hallway, with random bits and jagged sections still clinging to the wall. It's as if someone ripped it all off in one careless stroke and didn't bother to go back for the stubborn smaller chunks.

Lucy parks my luggage outside the farthest door on the left and unlocks it. "It's our best room," she whispers.

I try to hide my cringe when the door swings open with a toe-curling creak and the light flicks on. The heavy oak wainscoting is the only thing that breaks up the overwhelmingly blue walls. A hefty-looking four-poster bed with a grandma quilt sits in the middle of the room, flanked by turned spindles. There's a massive window to the right, draped in the heaviest of fabrics, clad with an Astoria valance that belongs to the 1930s and shouldn't have left. It reminds me of those heavy drapes in *The Sound of Music* that Fraulein Maria *Project Runway*s into clothing for the children. I'd have preferred something from this century, but beggars can't be choosers. And at least it isn't a construction zone like the rest of the house.

Lucy takes the liberty of flopping on the end of my bed like she's at a slumber party, eagerly spectating as I deposit my things on the upholstered antique ottoman at the foot of the bed. I plaster on a fake smile and give her an exaggerated nod as I kick my boots off.

"There's a pamphlet if you need ideas for things to do around the village," she informs me, pointing to the stack of colorful brochures in a dusty plastic holder atop the dresser. "And if you run into Ray Jackson at the waterfront—which you will, because he loves newbies—always have an out. The man likes to talk. He'll trap you, and the next thing you know, he'll have told you his whole life story, from his conception over at the old movie theater to his hemorrhoids." When she sees the concerned look on my face, she adds, "Don't worry, I'll give you the full rundown tomorrow at breakfast, but the next week will fly by. You'll see."

"Thanks, Lucy," I squeak, eager for silence and serenity after a long-ass day, a symptom of living alone since undergrad.

She lingers, running a finger over the edge of the quilt. I get the feeling she wants to stay and chat. As much as I love girl talk, making conversation with a peppy stranger is the last thing I want to do right now. When I yawn and stretch my arms theatrically over my head, she gets the hint, stands, and wishes me a good night.

The moment the door closes, I commence my skin-care routine, strip my travel clothes for my pajamas, and slide into bed. The mattress squeaks with the tiniest movement. It's so firm, it feels as though I've draped myself directly over a box spring and called it a day. Chance of sleep tonight: near zilch. Then again, it's preferable to the alternative—my rental car.

Upon checking my phone, I hardly have any Instagram notifications from the travel story I posted earlier. In fact, I'm at the point now where every time I post, I lose followers instead of gaining them. Great. I'm becoming more irrelevant by the minute.

With that cheerful thought, I promptly close the app with a heavy sigh and fire off a *How are you?* text to Julian, followed by a brief explanation that I'll be staying an extra week. I brace myself for upset, but he simply responds with a selfie of him, smiling, thumbs-up, in my kitchen making a frozen pizza. It comforts me knowing he's having an okay day, despite my leaving.

When I plug my phone into the charger and close my eyes, Lucy and Evan's conversation is semi-audible from downstairs.

"What kind of people would we be if we tossed her onto the street?" Lucy asks.

"That's beside the point and you know it." The rest of Evan's response is muffled. The stomp of his heavy footsteps is the last thing I hear before I drift off to sleep.

Photo courtesy of the author

Amy Lea is a Canadian bureaucrat by day and a contemporary romance author by night (and weekends). She writes laugh-out-loud romantic comedies featuring strong heroines, witty banter, mid-2000s pop culture references, and happily ever afters.

When Amy is not writing, she can be found fangirling over other romance books on Instagram (@AmyLeaBooks), eating potato chips with reckless abandon, and snuggling with her husband and goldendoodle.